W9-BXY-347
NEWTON FREE LIBRARY
NEWTON, MA
WI

Pemberley by the Sea

A modern love story, *Pride and Prejudice* style

ABIGAIL REYNOLDS

Sourcebooks Landmark™
An Imprint of Sourcebooks, Inc.®
Naperville, Illinois

Copyright © 2008 by Abigail Reynolds
Cover and internal design © 2008 by Sourcebooks, Inc.
Cover photo © Getty Images

Sourcebooks and the colophon are registered trademarks of Sourcebooks, Inc.

All rights reserved. No part of this book may be reproduced in any form or by any electronic or mechanical means including information storage and retrieval systems—except in the case of brief quotations embodied in critical articles or reviews—without permission in writing from its publisher, Sourcebooks, Inc.

The characters and events portrayed in this book are fictitious or are used fictitiously. Any similarity to real persons, living or dead, is purely coincidental and not intended by the author.

Published by Sourcebooks Landmark, an imprint of Sourcebooks, Inc.
P.O. Box 4410, Naperville, Illinois 60567-4410
(630) 961-3900
FAX: (630) 961-2168
www.sourcebooks.com

Library of Congress Cataloging-in-Publication Data

Reynolds, Abigail.
Pemberley by the Sea / Abigail Reynolds.
p. cm.
ISBN-13: 978-1-4022-1356-4
ISBN-10: 1-4022-1356-5
1. Women marine biologists—Fiction. 2. Woods Hole (Mass.)—Fiction. 3. Bennet, Elizabeth (Fictitious character)—Fiction. 4. Darcy, Fitzwilliam (Fictitious character)—Fiction. I. Title.
PS3618.E967P36 2008
813'.6—dc22

2008016386

Printed and bound in the United States of America.
VP 10 9 8 7 6 5 4 3 2 1

David, for his constant love, support, and encouragement
Rebecca, for not saying her mom was nuts, even when she thought it
Brian, for believing in miracles
and
Elaine, for believing in this book, keeping me going when I was stuck, and uncomplainingly reading more drafts than I care to remember

Chapter 1

THE SEA WALL MARKED the beginning. Cassie had first glimpsed the ocean there while her jaded college friends told stories about their past vacations on Cape Cod. They didn't know she came from a place with asphalt seas, so she pretended the ocean was just as familiar to her. But she was captivated that very first day, tasting the briny sea air blowing in off the Sound. It cleansed her of the grime of the past.

Now, ten years later, the ocean was her life's work. She'd earned the right to watch the waves lap against the pitted stones of the sea wall. Place names like Sippewisset and Chapoquoit, which once sounded so exotic, were commonplace and comfortable now. The sea still held power, though it couldn't wash away guilt as easily as the pangs of adolescent shame. Today the ocean was only itself, changeable and rich with unseen life. She was on her own to do the work of forgetting.

She felt a tug at her arm. "I'm coming," she said, her eyes straying back to the dark water. The cry of gulls echoed a horn blast as the ferry from Nantucket returned to the harbor.

Erin tapped her foot, her blonde hair streaming behind her

.n the salt breeze. "The music's started. You can come back here later."

That was the best thing about the ocean. It was always there when Cassie wanted it. A long summer in Woods Hole stretched ahead of her, filled with time she could devote to the research she loved. She shrugged off her wistful mood and stepped carefully down to the sidewalk. "You're in a hurry to get there."

Erin didn't meet her eyes. "I promised Scott I'd be there early to help him learn the dances."

"Scott?" Trust Erin to have already found a man, even though she'd only been there a few days. "Another summer romance? You haven't mentioned him."

"I barely know him. And maybe you'll meet somebody."

Cassie laughed. "With you there? Not likely. Besides, what would I do with a man? He'd just be in the way of work." Men were usually too dazzled by Erin's lithe beauty to pay attention to Cassie, which suited her perfectly.

They followed the rhythmic lure of fiddle music down Water Street, past the library of the Marine Biological Laboratory. Inside the brightly lit Community Hall, the swirl of dancers chased away any serious thoughts.

There were some familiar faces among the dancers—other researchers from the Marine Biological Laboratory and grad students returning for the summer. Cassie spotted one of her old lab partners across the hall and waved to her grant administrator as he danced past. Since the New England folk dances were taught on the spot, anyone could participate. The contra dances were a social center of Woods Hole, one of the few places where scientists, townspeople, and tourists crossed paths.

Cassie danced first with a gangly, young grad student from the neurophysiology lab, a newcomer to the MBL. The dance was a vigorous one, and she threw herself into it, enjoying the complex patterns and laughing at her partner's jokes about his inexperience. Erin, partnered with a good-looking man sporting a dazzled smile, moved past Cassie down the line of dancers.

Despite the crowded room, Cassie chanced upon Erin again when the music ended. The windows of the historic clapboard hall were wide open, and Cassie welcomed the cool sea breeze on her arms after the energetic dance.

"Looks like you made a conquest already," Cassie teased.

"Scott? I met him at the biotech lecture yesterday." Erin's faint blush gave her away. "But he invited me to have lunch with him tomorrow. Will you come, too? I told him I was going to bring a friend along."

Given some of Erin's bad experiences with men, Cassie could understand her caution. "I can come to make sure he meets my standards for your boyfriends, but I imagine I'll be a third wheel."

"Of course not. It'll be fine." Erin had a faraway look Cassie hadn't seen for some time. She hoped this time it was warranted. Erin deserved some good luck for once.

Then Erin's eyes widened. "Oh, God. Is that who I think it is?" She didn't sound happy about the new development.

Cassie craned her neck to see the entranceway where a broad-shouldered man with wavy brown hair was paying the entrance fee. She didn't need to see his face to recognize him, even after three years. Her stomach tied in a knot. What was Rob doing in Woods Hole? Did he know she was there? She clenched her hand until her fingernails bit into her palm. If he knew, he wouldn't care. He hadn't even bothered to say good-bye to her when she left Chapel Hill. "Yes, that's him," she said grimly.

"Do you want to leave?"

Erin's tentative voice provided the challenge Cassie needed. She wasn't going to let Rob Elliott's presence chase her away. "No. I'm going to find a partner for the next dance." Preferably one that would make Rob think she'd never given him a second thought in the last three years.

"Good for you."

Cassie looked around quickly. Most of the dancers were already partnered for the next dance, but she spotted a tall man standing alone in the shadows by the front of the hall. She set out purposefully toward him. He didn't look like a scientist, given that his clothes matched and had the air of being recently purchased. Even in chinos he gave off the air of being formally dressed. Not her type, but still, one dance with a tourist wouldn't kill her, and it was better than letting Rob see her being a wallflower.

As she came up to him, the man's classic good looks gave way to a certain ferocity of expression. Cassie hesitated for a moment, but Erin was watching, and she wasn't going to admit to losing her nerve. Although the man seemed oblivious to her presence, she asked, "Do you have a partner for the next dance?"

For a moment he said nothing, and had Cassie been more timid, she would have been cowed by the look he gave her. "I'm not planning to dance, thank you." His lips barely moved when he spoke.

She was suddenly conscious she was still wearing her lab clothes and no makeup. But she hadn't gotten where she was by giving in to her insecurities. "If you've never tried it before, it's easy to pick up. Everyone here was a beginner once."

"I don't think so." He scanned the hall as if looking for someone.

His refusal stung, leaving her with the unpleasantly familiar feeling of having been judged and found wanting, even if *he* was the one violating the unspoken rules of the contra dance by refusing her. She hadn't done anything wrong. She was tempted to make a response as curt and rude as his had been, but she had higher standards for her behavior. "Never mind, then."

He turned piercing dark eyes on her for a moment, and then looked away, apparently dismissing her existence.

Something about his eyes struck her, but she had no intention of exploring what it was. One rejection was enough, and she still needed a refuge from Rob. There was one place she'd be safe from any of his nasty comments. Rob wouldn't try anything in front of Jim Davidson, their old grad school advisor. He was sitting out the dance, looking a little winded. *He* would welcome her company.

"Hey, stranger." She slid into the folding chair next to his.

"Cassie!" Jim said warmly. "I was hoping you'd be here. I have something to show you." He rummaged around in his pockets and handed her a folded paper with a flourish. "It's the latest spawning data. We just got the numbers in."

"Finally!" Cassie unfolded the sheet and ran her finger down the columns of figures, glad to have a distraction. She whistled silently. "Are you sure of these?"

"We've double-checked everything. In case you've forgotten, the results you came up with four years ago are on the back."

"Forgotten? I still see those numbers in my sleep. But this is worse than you expected, isn't it?"

"Much. I'm not happy about it, but it's going to make a hell of a research paper. It may even show up on the mainstream news, for the five minutes most people can bring themselves to care about species we're fishing to extinction."

"It's impressive data." It had been years since she had worked on the project as one of his grad students, but the excitement of it still touched her. She did a quick calculation in her head. The ramifications would be far-reaching. But it wasn't her project anymore. Reluctantly, she handed the data sheet back.

Jim gave her a pointed look. "I'm looking for someone to write it up for publication."

The temptation was so strong she could almost taste it. "Me? Jim, that's sweet of you, but shouldn't this go to one of your students?"

"They have their own projects, and you *know* this study. You were there at the beginning. You want to; I know it." So Jim still knew how to play on her passion for her work.

"But you deserve the credit."

"I have plenty of publications." Jim glanced around the hall and lowered his voice. "It could help you, Cassie."

"I still have plenty of time to get my publications in. I can make it, even if I didn't get publishable results last summer."

Jim patted her arm. "I didn't mean it that way. I know you can do great research. You wrote the best dissertation I've seen in years. But anybody can run into a string of bad luck, like last year's floods, and the tenure clock doesn't stop ticking. An extra paper could give you some leeway."

It was charity, and she knew it. But so much depended on her getting tenure, and she'd love the chance to work with Jim again. "All right. Thanks."

"Don't thank me. I'm getting a top-notch author out of it."

"You old flatterer. I'm going to tell Rose you were flirting with me." She elbowed him in the side.

Jim's devotion to his wife was well known. "You do that."

But a familiar figure was approaching them. "Jim, I finished the initial set-up, if you . . ." Rob's voice trailed off when he saw Cassie.

Cassie plastered a pleasant smile on her face. "Hi, Rob. Welcome to Woods Hole." This was her turf, and she wasn't going to cede it to Rob.

He looked as if he didn't know what to say. "Uh, hi. Want to dance?"

How typically Rob—at least typical of him since their breakup. No pleasantries, no "Nice to see you. How have you been?" She couldn't imagine he really wanted to dance with her. She put on her best professorial look and said, "Not now, thanks. Jim's filling me in on his spawning project."

"Some things never change. See you in the morning, then, Jim." Rob ambled away toward a redheaded woman who was apparently more inclined to dance. Cassie watched as they took hands in the line of dancers.

"Sorry." Jim seemed suddenly interested in his shoes. "I was going to warn you about that."

Cassie was well practiced at looking assured when she felt nothing of the sort. "No need. I don't have any problems with Rob."

"He won't be here the whole summer, just a couple weeks, if that's any consolation. And he isn't involved with Lisa anymore."

"It doesn't matter." Cassie ignored the stab of pain. Like it or not, she would have to get used to seeing Rob, especially if she wrote the paper with Jim. It would hurt, but there wasn't anything new about that. But the spawning results were amazing. She was already thinking of how to present them.

***

Although the start of the season was a few weeks away, tourists already clogged Water Street, the sole thoroughfare through the town of Woods Hole. The low blast of a ferry horn announced the arrival of another crowd of visitors.

"Erin, this has to be quick. I have a lot of work to do." Years of friendship had taught Cassie that men came before work for Erin.

"Even you have to eat lunch, Cassie, and I want you to meet Scott." Erin placed her hand behind Cassie's elbow and urged her on.

There was nothing wrong with a sandwich at her lab bench, like every other day, but meeting Erin's latest crush was important, too. Cassie needed to check him out before Erin became too involved. "Is he from the MBL or the Oceanographic Institution?"

"Neither. He works at Cambridge Biotechnology."

An industry scientist, then, rather than a researcher. It could be worse. Cambridge Biotech was reputable, at least. "What does he do there?"

Erin scuffed her feet against the curb. "He's the president."

"He's what?" Cassie stopped dead in the middle of the sidewalk. "And you're dating him? You just applied for a job there!"

"He doesn't know about that. I don't want him to think I'm using him to get a job. And we're not really dating. Not yet, anyway."

Cassie forced herself to keep walking. Men had hurt Erin too many times, and this was asking for trouble. "What's he doing in Woods Hole if he's with Cambridge Biotech?"

"He has a summerhouse here, and he came to a lecture at the MBL. That's where I met him."

The town drawbridge, raised to allow passage of sea-faring boats to and from the inner harbor, blocked their way. Cassie was glad for the brief respite. They waited with the other pedestrians behind the safety barrier as the boats, a pleasure craft and an MBL tug, left the harbor for the dark waters of Vineyard Sound.

When the bridge finally creaked down, they made their way across to the rambling, grey-shingled restaurant on the opposite shore of the narrow channel. The Dock of the Bay Café, with its unpretentious atmosphere and view over the harbor entrance, was one of Cassie's favorites. She wondered if it would be up to the standards of the president of Cambridge Biotech.

Cassie opened the screen door and stepped onto the worn wooden floor of the restaurant. No men sitting alone. Scott must be late.

A fragment of conversation drifted past her from the nearest table. "It won't be so bad. You might even have a good time," one man said to the other.

"I doubt it," replied a deeper voice. It was the man from the dance, the one who had turned her down. "You don't know who they are or where they're from. They could be groupies. Or criminals." His tone suggested the two were equivalent.

Erin came in behind Cassie. With a bright smile, she addressed the first speaker. "Scott, it's so nice to see you again."

Cassie recognized the deeply tanned man with curly hair now. She stiffened as she realized what the subject of their conversation had been. So Scott's friend didn't like having lunch with two little nobodies from nowhere. Used to more elite society, no doubt.

"Hi, Scott." Erin drew out the chair opposite him. "This is Cassie."

He shook her hand. "Nice to meet you, Cassie. This is my friend Calder."

The tall man beside him rose to his feet. "A pleasure." He sounded like it was anything but.

Cassie watched with amusement as he shook Erin's hand without any evidence of pleasure. When he turned to her, she smiled sweetly up at him and said, "Oh, yes, we've already met."

"We have?" he asked, taken aback and clearly none too happy about the possibility.

"Oh, yes," she said mockingly. "You're the one who goes to dances even though you don't want to dance."

He continued to look puzzled for a moment, and then his brow cleared. "Oh, the dance last night, you mean. I wasn't there to dance; I was just looking for Scott. I needed to . . . ask him something," he said, his voice declaring the subject closed.

Cassie raised an eyebrow, finding no evidence of apology or regret in his tone. "Well, to each his own." Unable to resist temptation, she leaned forward and said conspiratorially, "And for the record, Erin would be the groupie, so I must be the criminal element."

For a fleeting moment, he looked uncomfortable. "What's your crime, then?"

She lowered her voice dramatically. "I murder microscopic organisms and steal their secrets." Little did he know. She walked around the table to the empty seat by the window. Maybe if the great and powerful Calder understood she wasn't looking for a boyfriend, it wouldn't be so bad. "I hadn't realized anyone was coming with Scott."

"I just arrived last night." He seemed more interested in the menu than anything she had to say.

Scott turned to Erin as a young waitress came to take their orders. "What do you recommend?"

"I'm having the Gorgonzola salad, but the best thing here is dessert. They make wonderful pies."

Calder was the last to order. "I'll take the white marlin."

He might as well have used a cattle prod on Cassie. "Did you know white marlin is a threatened species?"

"No, I didn't. In that case I'll have . . . what would you recommend?" Calder turned his dark eyes on her.

His piercing gaze made her oddly uncomfortable. It was a relief to look down at the menu. "The striped bass and the mahi-mahi are fine, though mahi-mahi won't be local. Any of the shellfish. Not the cod."

"*Cod* are endangered?"

"Threatened, not endangered. Overfishing is a major problem."

"I'll go with the bass, then." He handed the menu to the waitress.

Cassie felt guilty about the sharpness of her tone. Snob or not, it wasn't Calder's fault Erin had decided to arrange this ridiculous meeting. If she had thought twice before opening her mouth, she wouldn't have said anything. "Thanks. I realize it doesn't make a difference when the fish is already dead, but I hate seeing it."

"I'd rather not support that kind of thing." He checked his watch.

So much for a peace offering. If he wanted to be aloof, that was fine with her. She turned her attention to Erin, who was explaining the history of the restaurant to Scott.

There was a brief silence when the subject was exhausted. Calder seemed to have nothing to say for himself. Cassie wasn't fond of small talk herself, but she couldn't sit there silently through the whole meal. "Scott, Erin tells me you have a summerhouse here."

"Yes. I've always wanted one, and this year I finally gave in." Scott had a charming smile. For Erin's sake, Cassie hoped the charm was more than skin-deep.

"Is it here in town?"

"Just outside, on Penzance Point. Do you know where that is?"

Of course Scott's house would be in the most exclusive part of Woods Hole. No doubt the president of Cambridge Biotech could afford it easily. His summerhouse probably cost enough to fund half the research at the MBL. She wondered if she could plead a heavy workload and leave early.

"This is my tenth summer here, so I know my way around pretty well." Cassie paused as the waitress set a bowl of fisherman's stew in front of her.

"The views are stunning. Have you been out there?" Scott asked.

"No." Cassie shelled a mussel with the ease of long practice. Penzance Point was privately owned; there was a guard on the road to keep out riff-raff like her.

Calder carefully moved his French fries aside with his fork. "So you don't live here year-round?"

Cassie's smile had an edge to it. "No, I'm a college professor. I come to the MBL every summer to do my research. I've had my own lab here since I got my PhD. Before that I was working with one of the senior researchers, studying species of fish threatened by overfishing." To her satisfaction, she could see Calder taking stock of her again. What had he thought she did, waited tables for a living? It was a good thing he didn't know the rest of her background. He would probably run a mile if he knew the truth. She looked out the window to avoid his eyes, pretending interest in a sailboat coming up the channel.

"You're interested in fish populations?" Scott asked.

"That was my grad school research. Now I'm looking at the effects of fertilizer run-off on the ecology of the salt marsh."

"Salt marsh? Sounds messy." Scott sliced into his lobster tail.

Erin said, "Careful, Scott. The salt marsh is Cassie's one true love."

Cassie laughed. "That's right. It's calm, peaceful, and more reliable than a man. And it won't waste my time when I'm trying to get tenure."

Calder crossed his arms, but Cassie thought he looked more

amused than anything else. At least now he wouldn't expect anything from her. Maybe she could relax a little.

"You do research too, don't you, Erin?" Scott refilled his water glass from the pitcher on the table.

"Yes, I'm helping Cassie with her study."

Calder paused, his glass halfway to his mouth. "I thought Scott said you were in biotechnology."

Erin cast a distressed look at Cassie. "I am. I'm taking the summer off from my dissertation research. Cassie and I worked here as undergraduates, and I wanted to do it one last time before I started teaching full-time."

Two lies in one sentence, but Cassie could understand why Erin didn't want Scott to know her real reason for being in Woods Hole. And a year ago the part about teaching would have been true, before Erin decided she was better suited for a job in industry than academia.

"Well, that's Woods Hole for you." Cassie gestured toward the window with her fork. "Half the population has a doctorate. There are probably enough advanced degrees in town to sink a battleship. You'd better be careful about how you talk to any odd-looking old men muttering to themselves, because they just might be Nobel laureates. It's a world unto itself, like summer camp for grown-up scientists. One little town, and it has the MBL, the Woods Hole Oceanographic Institution, the National Marine Fisheries, and a half a dozen other research groups."

Erin, no doubt grateful for the change of subject, began to tell stories of amusing Woods Hole encounters. The moment of tension passed, and Erin and Scott chatted as they ate, with occasional additions from Cassie.

Cassie noticed Calder was watching her. She wondered how far he would take his silent withdrawal. Scott and Erin were managing fine on their own. "So, are you always this talkative, or is it just the company?"

This time his dark eyes didn't move from her. "When I have something to say, I'll say it."

Cassie opened her eyes wide in a mockery of being impressed. "Well, if I have to carry the conversation all by myself, I hope you don't mind hearing about the life cycle of *Pagurus longicarpus* and the impact of algal overgrowth on the population. In detail."

To her surprise, a faint smile curved his mouth. "I'm sure it will be fascinating."

So he did have a sense of humor. Unexpectedly, Cassie wanted to smile back. Just then she heard a burst of giggling from behind the counter. Several of the young women who worked in the restaurant had congregated there, looking at their table. One of them pointed at Calder, sitting with his back to them.

"You have a fan club." Cassie gestured with her head, grateful for the distraction from her awareness of him.

His smile disappeared as if it had never existed. "Damn it. Scott, I'm going back to the house before there's a scene."

"Come on, Calder, they're not doing anything. Just ignore them."

"That's easy for you to say," Calder snapped.

"If you get up and walk out of here by yourself, that *will* make a scene. Finish your lunch."

"I've had all I want." He tossed his napkin on the table.

Cassie, dismayed by his sudden shift of mood, noticed Erin's unhappy look. At least this could give her an excuse to leave. "I'm done, too, and I need to get back to the lab. Maybe Calder and I could go part of the way together, and you two could take your time."

Scott's face brightened. "That won't be so bad, now! Is that okay with you, Calder?"

Calder gave a grim nod and pushed back his chair. Surprised by the speed with which this was happening, Cassie fished out a ten-dollar bill from her pocket and tossed it on the table.

Scott tried to hand it back to her. "My treat."

Cassie shook her head. "Sorry. I pay my own way."

"No, please, this was my idea."

"Scott, it's been a pleasure to meet you. Let's not spoil a budding friendship with an argument." Cassie hoped her smile took any sting from her words.

This seemed to disarm him, and she followed Calder outside. He strode off down the street at a pace she had to work to keep up with. Apparently he didn't plan to offer an explanation for the scene in the restaurant. So much for wondering if she might have misjudged him. Her first impression of him had been correct. It was disappointing.

They walked most of the brief length of the town in silence before he finally said, without looking at her, "Thank you."

"Not a problem. This is where I turn off. My lab's down here."

"I'll walk you there." He didn't sound particularly pleased with the prospect.

"There's no need. It's out of your way."

He paid no attention. Rather than argue pointlessly with him, Cassie followed his lead, glad it was only a block away.

"This is it. Take care." It was hackneyed, but it was more polite than saying, "Goodbye and good riddance."

He stopped between her and the building. "I suppose you knew all along."

"Knew what?"

His lips thinned. "Who I am."

Cassie's temper began to simmer, but for Erin's sake she didn't let it show. It wouldn't do her friend any good to have Cassie argue with Calder. "Look, I have no idea what you're talking about, I have no idea what went on back there, and I suspect I'm just as happy that way."

When he didn't respond, she flashed him a quick, if somewhat less than genuine, smile. "This is it, my home away from home," she said. "Enjoy the rest of your day." She turned and walked into the building before he could make any reply.

As she ran up the stairs, she didn't see him standing and looking after her, contemplating the rarity of a woman who couldn't seem to get out of his company fast enough. Perversely, he found himself wishing she would look back, but she never did.

Chapter 2

"CALDER WESTING? YOU MUST be joking." Cassie halted halfway through sorting a set of microscope slides. "As in the political Westings, the ones with old money? They wouldn't be caught dead with the likes of us."

"Not this one." Erin perched on the edge of the lab bench. "He's Senator Westing's son, and his brother is in the House of Representatives now. Calder hates publicity, but he still gets stalked by paparazzi. Scott says that's why he gets angry when someone recognizes him. Poor guy."

Cassie assimilated this new information. "Still, a little good manners would take him a long way. Assuming those girls did recognize him, all he had to do was to smile at them and there wouldn't have been a problem. That's all they wanted, I imagine—a smile and a story to take home."

"That's a good point," said Erin slowly, "but I don't suppose I can imagine what it's like to have that happen all the time. Maybe it's harder than we think."

"You would find a way to sympathize with the devil himself." Cassie had no sympathy for Calder Westing. No doubt he had everything in life handed to him on a platter, and if he was anything like his father, he probably thought women belonged in the kitchen and Darwin was the root of all evil. "How was the rest of lunch?"

"Great. Scott invited us both out to his house on Saturday to swim and go sailing. You'll come, won't you?"

"Wouldn't you rather go by yourself?"

Erin hesitated. "I like him, but I don't think I'm ready to go to his house alone yet. I haven't forgotten how wonderful Jack looked at first."

Cassie was glad Erin wasn't letting herself believe in surface charm this time. She didn't want to face another relationship where Erin's boyfriend sent her home with bruises. But after that experience, Cassie could understand why Erin would be anxious about being alone with a man she hardly knew. "All right, I'll come."

***

With a certain sense of unreality, Cassie and Erin approached the heretofore forbidden guard booth at the entrance to Penzance Point. The guard, who had chased away many years' worth of exploring grad students, was perfectly polite when Erin explained they were invited by Mr. Dunstan. He called up to the house to confirm the information before waving them through.

Cassie could see why the residents wanted to keep it to themselves. The walk along the winding road provided stunning vistas of Vineyard Sound and Buzzard's Bay. They passed a few old estates, as well as some elaborate newer houses. Scott's house, a modern construction of glass and wood, wasn't the largest or most extravagant, but it was big enough that she rapidly revised her estimate of its cost upward. "I doubt if that costs less than five million dollars!" she whispered to Erin. What a contrast to the tiny, well-worn rental cottage she shared with Erin!

"Oh, hush, Cassie! I don't even want to think about it! Remember, we're only here to have a nice afternoon."

"And I thought you invited me to protect your reputation," Cassie teased.

Scott met them at the door with a wide smile. He offered them a tour of the house, which only confirmed Cassie's impression of his wealth. She wondered if Erin understood what she was getting herself into. They ended in the dining room, where a catered lunch was set out.

To Cassie's surprise, they were joined by a silent Calder Westing. She hadn't realized he was staying with his friend, or she would have thought twice about accepting the invitation. Maybe even three times. His presence made her uncomfortable. Every time she glanced in his direction, his eyes were on her. She had no idea what it was about her that bothered him so much. She was relieved when he disappeared again as soon as he was done eating.

Scott shrugged apologetically. "Sorry about that. Calder can get pretty involved in his work and tends to forget about anything else."

"I hadn't realized this was a working vacation for him." Erin took a sip of white wine.

Scott hesitated for a second. "Well, he has some things he needs to do for the foundation he works with. But I'm more interested in what you'd like to do than what he's doing. What will it be? Swimming? Sailing? Lazing about on the porch?"

Erin's face lit up. "I love to sail. Do you have a boat?"

"I certainly do. Want to see her?"

Cassie accompanied them as they went down to the water to look at the boat, but she doubted they noticed her presence. She was definitely a third wheel now. When the subject of going out on the water arose, she said she would be perfectly happy sitting on the porch reading but hoped they would go ahead. Scott, looking delighted at the prospect of being alone with Erin, seconded the proposal.

Cassie found a comfortable chair on the porch and pulled out the book she had brought with her. It was soothing to sit in the cool salt breeze, the view of the Sound stretched out in front of her. She'd never be able to live anywhere with a view like this. But she couldn't complain. Woods Hole, surrounded by water on three sides, was a mecca for marine biologists, and she was lucky to get lab space there so early in her career. That was more important than a beautiful view.

She had read only a couple of chapters before Calder emerged from the house and asked abruptly where the others were.

She pointed out into the Sound. "They took the boat out. I decided to be a landlubber."

"You don't sail?"

"Actually, I do, though I haven't done it much. Not like Erin. She's from this area originally, and she practically grew up on sailboats." Looking out over the bay, she saw a few dark clouds beginning to roll in. She hoped Scott and Erin wouldn't stay out on the water long.

"Why didn't you go with them, then?"

Certainly not in hopes of having his company. "Because they're both good sailors, and they clearly wanted to be alone together. I knew I'd be in the way. That's why I brought a book." She held it up for his inspection, hoping he would take the hint and leave.

He barely glanced at the book, preferring to keep his eyes on her. "Why did you come, then?"

She wondered if all visitors to the house were subjected to this kind of inquisition or whether she was just lucky. "Because smart women don't go alone to the house of a man they barely know."

"You don't trust Scott?"

"Erin doesn't know Scott well enough to know whether she can trust him."

He frowned. "Don't you think you're being a little over-suspicious?"

Cassie couldn't suppress a smile at the protected world he clearly lived in. "Well, I don't suppose you've ever been in the position of being afraid of a woman forcing herself on you." She looked over his tall form appraisingly from head to toe.

His eyes showed a flash of amusement. "You might be surprised," he said with a certain self-deprecating humor. "But you don't have to worry about Scott."

"I'm glad to hear that." Not that she was willing to take his word on it. "Erin's last boyfriend put her in the hospital. That's why she's here for the summer. He kept violating the restraining order."

"I'm sorry." It could have been perfunctory, but it sounded like he meant it. "Have you known Erin long?"

"Since freshman year of college."

"An old friend, then."

"Yes." She looked out at the water again. She couldn't pick out Scott's sailboat anymore from the others crossing the Sound. "She's pretty fragile right now."

"Scott isn't going to hurt her." His quiet words surprised her. She hadn't expected him to understand her concern.

"I hope not. Erin trusts people too easily." But that was starting to change.

He didn't seem to feel the need to respond, making Cassie remember who she was talking to. This wasn't another scientist; this was Calder Westing, whom she couldn't begin to understand. Once again she had decided he was cold and haughty, only to have a thoughtful man with quiet wit emerge. Of course, she knew from last time that the aloof Calder was only a heartbeat away, ready to put her back in her place. She wasn't going to be drawn in this time.

Besides, she was crazy if she thought Calder Westing was someone she could ever be friends with. She shouldn't be talking to him this way. "It looks like it might rain soon. If you'll excuse me, I think I'm going to take a swim while the sun's still out."

He gave her a quick look but said nothing, so she walked down to the pier. When she reached the end, she stripped off her clothes, revealing a modest one-piece bathing suit.

Calder watched from the shadows of the porch, taking in the curves of her body as she neatly folded her clothes and set them on the dock. There was something about Cassie Boulton that made him want to know what was underneath her no-nonsense exterior and quick wit—not to mention what was underneath her swimsuit. His eyes remained fixed on her as she dove efficiently into the water.

No, all in all he was finding her far too interesting, and that wouldn't do. Deliberately, he forced himself to look away from where she was frolicking in the water and went back to his tidy study.

***

"Mind if I join you?" Rob stood across the cafeteria table from Cassie, tray in hand.

Cassie's relaxed mood evaporated. She had managed to avoid conversations with Rob so far by staying out of Jim's lab, but it looked like her luck had run out. "If you want to."

"Thanks." Rob sat down and placed his tray on the table. "I hear you're collaborating with Jim on a paper."

"That's right." Cassie took a bite of her sandwich. The faster she finished it, the sooner she could escape.

"Just like old times." He opened the ketchup bottle and shook it, but nothing came out. He reached for a new one on the next table. "It's good to see you, Cassie."

"That's Saint Cassie to you." Did he think she would forget the past that quickly?

He winced. "You weren't meant to hear that."

"Then you shouldn't have said it so often." The dry sandwich seemed to stick in her throat. She took a swallow of water.

"You're right. I was blaming you for something that was my own fault. If it's any consolation, nobody believed me."

"Some of them did. It doesn't matter anymore." It had mattered a lot then. It made her finish her PhD as quickly as possible, so she could get away.

"What I'm trying to say is I'm sorry. About everything."

There was a time when she would have given anything to hear those words from him, but that was long ago. "What do you want from me? Forgiveness? Okay, you're forgiven. You can go home with a clear conscience."

He had the gall to look wounded. "You and I were friends once. I'd like to be friends again."

He had told her he loved her once, too, not long before dumping her. He had no idea what she had sacrificed for his sake. "Why? I haven't changed. I'm still driven about my work and still as boring as I was then."

"It wasn't like that. I didn't like coming second to work, but I was proud you were my girlfriend. You were the golden girl. I just wanted more."

"More time? I spent every free minute I had with you." She regretted letting him draw her into the discussion. It only brought back the pain she had worked hard to put behind her.

"Not more time—more of you. We were together for a year and a half, and you never told me a thing about your family. I don't even know where you grew up. I took you home for Christmas. You met all my family, all my friends. You knew everything about me."

His pleading look was so familiar, even after all these years. Cassie turned her face away. It hadn't been completely his fault. She had been living a lie, and because of that, he never understood her. But she'd been right to keep it a secret. If he'd known the truth, people would have been calling her worse things than Saint Cassie.

Softening toward Rob was dangerous. "My parents ran away with the circus, and I was raised by gypsies in deepest, darkest Africa. Happy now?"

He looked down at his half-eaten hamburger as if it held some answer for him. Finally, he raised his eyes again. "I guess the answer on being friends is no."

"I guess it is."

He drained his soda and placed the empty cup on his tray. "I never realized our break-up affected you like this. It didn't seem to bother you much then."

"You knew how I felt, even if I put a good face on it."

He shook his head. "You were always so strong, so confident. Everybody liked you. I thought you bounced right back."

"I'm so strong. Right." She pushed her tray away. Loving him had only made her vulnerable. "I'm leaving now. Don't follow me."

Cassie dumped the remains of her lunch into the trashcan. Hurrying out of the building, she set off at a swift pace, heading the long way into town, around Eel Pond. She would be less likely to run into anyone she knew that way. She had dreamed for so long of Rob begging her to come back to him, and it turned out he never even knew how much he hurt her.

Rob's words were still with her when she reached the far end of Woods Hole.

She couldn't face the lab yet, especially with the possibility of seeing him there. She decided to stop at Harbor Books, a small bookstore near the ferry dock. It was one of her favorite destinations. The proprietor greeted her by name when she walked in.

"Any recommendations today, Ed?" She tilted her head toward the bookshelves. This was a good idea. It reminded her she had a full and complete life without Rob.

"There are a couple of new arrivals that might interest you." Leading her to a table in the middle of the store, he handed her an attractively designed trade paperback. "This is a strong first novel. Excellent characterizations, beautiful settings. But you might not like the ending. It's pretty painful."

The chain of bells at the front door tinkled. Ed turned to greet the new customer.

Cassie, perusing the cover of the book, recognized Calder's deep voice. Looking up, she acknowledged him with a nod of her head. He made no move to greet her, and she turned back to Ed as she set the book on table. "You know me too well, Ed. I like my coffee with cream and my literature with optimism." There were enough unhappy endings in real life.

"Fair enough. Have you read this one?"

"No, although I've heard of the author. She's supposed to be very good. Have you read it yourself?"

"Not yet, but it's had excellent reviews."

She could sense Calder moving behind her, inspecting the books on the shelves. Annoyed with herself for being aware of him when he didn't have the common courtesy to say hello, she forced her attention back to the conversation. "I'll give it a try."

"Tell me what you think of it when you're done. Oh, and here's one other you might like." He pointed to a hardcover book. "I read this one as soon as it came in. It's quite compelling."

Seeing the name of one of her favorite authors, Cassie picked it up, though the price of hardcovers went beyond her reading budget. "Oh, yes, I loved *Embedded in Amber*. I didn't know he had another one out."

"Yes, and this one's at least as good. I think you'd enjoy it."

Suddenly uncomfortable, she looked up to see Calder's eyes fixed on her in an unreadable look. She stared back at him challengingly, refusing to let him unnerve her. He didn't seem to be interested in the books. Was he bored with life in Woods Hole and killing time? Returning her gaze to the book, she ran her finger along the cover. Blazoned in dark blue letters across a picture of open sky was *The Edge of Tomorrow* by Stephen R. West.

Regretfully, she returned it to its place. "I'm going to have to wait for that one to come out in paperback. With a book habit like mine, I can't afford to indulge in hardcovers. I'll just take the other one today."

As Ed rang up the sale on the old-fashioned cash register, Cassie wondered what Calder was thinking. No doubt he had never thought twice about the price of anything in his life. Well, she was just one of the little people, and she had nothing to prove to him or anyone else.

She paid for her purchase, said good-bye to Ed, and then turned back to Calder. He held a book in his hand now but was still looking at her with disturbing intensity. She smiled with apparent sweetness at him and said cheekily, "Lovely chatting with you, Calder. We'll have to do this again some time." She made a quick exit, leaving the bells on the door jingling behind her.

Why did she let Calder disconcert her so much? He might be a fine-looking specimen, but he was a first-class snob with the social skills of a gnat. Why should she care what he thought of her? Perhaps it was because of Rob. Their conversation hadn't predisposed her to want male company, especially the great Calder Westing.

She stopped at her usual spot on the bridge to look over the harbor and the fleet of small boats anchored there. The view never failed to bring her a sense of peace, something she needed today. She looked to see if the MBL boats were in the harbor, but they were still at sea for the day. Unexpectedly, the intensity of dark eyes staring at her came to her mind, and she shivered. What was wrong with her? She knew better than to look twice at a man like Calder. Attractive men were off-limits. She never wanted to go through what she had with Rob again.

She shook her head, dismissing Calder from her mind. Chances were she'd never see him again anyway.

Chapter 3

CASSIE HAD DREAMED ABOUT Ryan again, about the day they went into Philadelphia to buy new, safer clothes for him to wear. In reality it had been a wonderful day, spent getting to know him again after all those years apart, but in the dream, the street outside the store was filled with men with knives. She tried to stop Ryan from leaving, but he said, *You know I have to, Cass.* She awoke in terror as the first knives struck.

The edgy feeling of it stayed with her all day, making her jump at unexpected noises. It was starting to fade by late afternoon, when Scott knocked tentatively on the lab door. Cassie managed a warm greeting, even when she noticed Calder following him.

Scott went straight to the microscope bench where Erin was working. "I tried calling you at home to see if you'd like to have dinner with me, but nobody answered. So I decided to walk over to see if you were here."

"I'd love to, Scott, but we're running some gels tonight. And I need to be here to watch them." Erin's disappointment was obvious.

Cassie wasn't going to pressure Erin into anything. "Nonsense. Run along and have fun. I can keep an eye on the gels, and counting bacteria can wait until tomorrow."

"Are you sure?"

"Absolutely. There isn't much to do here until the gels are done." Cassie wondered how much of a date it was going to be with Calder tagging along. Perhaps that was his intention. He had never given any indication of approving of the romance between Erin and Scott.

"Well, if you're sure . . . then I'd be delighted to join you, Scott, thank you." Erin dropped a clear cover over the microscope.

Scott looked pleased. Cassie could practically feel the electricity between the two of them. Well, no one deserved happiness more than Erin, and it looked like Scott's interest in her was genuine. She hoped Calder's presence didn't put too much of a damper on the occasion.

To her surprise, he remained behind when Scott and Erin made their exit. She looked at him questioningly.

He held out a book. "I wondered if you might want to borrow this. I heard what you said about it in the bookshop."

She glanced down to see a copy of the hardcover she had admired. Did it make him uncomfortable when she said she couldn't afford it? She doubted people in his social sphere made a habit of loaning out their possessions, but his intention seemed genuine. "Have you read it already?"

"Yes." One corner of his mouth quirked up, giving a slightly rakish look to his handsome features.

So he was back to monosyllables. "Well, thank you, then." She sounded a bit dubious even to herself. "I'd love to borrow it.

I'll get it back to you as soon as I've finished it." She set the book down on the counter, expecting him to say an abrupt good-bye now that the transaction was complete.

Instead he stood there looking at her in an indecipherable manner. Was he so bored as to consider her company a distraction? Sighing inwardly, Cassie invited him to sit down for a few minutes. After all, he had been kind about the book, and she could stand a little distraction herself.

"Perhaps I could help you with something, since Scott stole your assistant. If there's anything you can do with untrained labor, that is," he said, with more humor than she would have given him credit for.

She revised her estimate of his situation to one of truly *desperate* boredom. Did he know anyone at all on the Cape apart from Scott? She forced herself to laugh. "That's a very generous offer, but you have no idea how dull it is to watch gels. Apart from that, I'll just be doing some preliminary work to set up for the next batch. But thank you."

He didn't reply right away, but continued to look at her with his piercing gaze. Uncomfortably aware of him, Cassie picked up the book. She opened it to the flyleaf and saw a printed bookplate beneath the cover. She'd never seen a real bookplate belonging to a live person before. She traced the words "Ex Libris S. Calder Westing III" with her eyes. "What does the 'S' stand for?"

His face shuttered slightly. "Stephen."

She smiled at him. "Stephen—I like that. It's a little less . . . stuffy, or patrician, somehow. Does anyone call you that?"

"Nobody I know. If you like it better, you're welcome to use it."

"Stephen." She rolled the name around in her mouth for a moment, wondering why he had made the offer. He was being unusually enigmatic tonight. "All right." She would have to be careful. He could be much more approachable as Stephen than as Calder, and she didn't intend to let him close. She was already curious about what lay behind his facade, and that way lay danger. He was a Westing, and she was nobody. He would never have nightmares about knives in the street.

"My grandfather was Stephen. They called me Calder to avoid confusion."

"The name skipped a generation, then?" She realized she was being an idiot. Like everyone else, she knew his father's name perfectly well.

"No. His eldest son, my uncle, was Stephen Calder as well. You've probably never heard of him. The story is that he died in Korea during the war."

She looked at him sharply. "I'm not sure what you mean by 'the story.' I probably know less about your family than you think. Nothing personal, but it's just not the kind of thing I follow. I care more about a politician's positions than his relations. The lives of the rich and famous don't interest me."

He ran his finger along the edge of the lab bench. "You wouldn't know this bit even if you read every word ever written about my family."

Cassie was growing more and more puzzled by his behavior. "Well, I suppose every family has its secrets." Not that the Westings could ever have the kind of secrets her family did.

"He was in the Korean War and was badly shell-shocked—what we'd call severe post-traumatic stress disorder now. He was shipped home pretty much non-functional." Calder's voice became darkly sardonic. "That wasn't acceptable in the heir to the Westing fortune, especially as my other uncle was just beginning to succeed in politics. So he was secretly put into 'retirement.' When it became clear that he wasn't going to get better, they announced he had been killed in the war, quietly disinherited him, and made sure he was taken care of by people who would never breathe a word of it. It was much more acceptable to have a brother who died a heroic death than one who panicked any time he was in a room with more than two people in it."

He had her full attention now. She didn't know how to respond to a story like that. "Sort of like Mrs. Rochester in the attic?"

He grimaced. "Well, he was kept in a bit more comfort than that, but yes. He died about ten years ago, and his last few years were fairly good ones as better medications became available. I wasn't told the truth until after he died."

"I'm sorry." She felt a surprising urge to reach out and touch him. She wondered what his arm would feel like under her hand.

"As I said, I never knew him." He looked suddenly stiff. "You could sell that story to a tabloid for a great deal of money if you wanted to. I hope you won't."

Cassie could practically see him withdraw behind his eyes. He had seemed human for a few minutes there, but now the other Calder was back. Insinuating she'd violate a confidence for money, indeed! Of course, if that little story was any indication of what his family was like, she could hardly blame him for being unpredictable.

"Don't worry; no one will ever hear about it from me." It was good to have the reminder of how cold he was most of the time. For a moment there he had almost drawn her in. No, she found him altogether too attractive to risk allowing herself close to him. A man like Calder Westing was walking trouble.

"Thank you. And thank you for listening." His voice was an empty, polite formality.

"Any time." There was a brief, uncomfortable silence, during which he signaled an end to the conversation by looking around the lab.

She stood, more to get away from him than out of any necessity. "Hang on a sec. I need to check something." She walked over to the bench where the gels were and peered at them closely. To her dismay, he followed her, and she could feel him standing behind her. "No, not ready yet!" she said with a forced cheerfulness. "It'll be a late night, I'm afraid."

"What are they?" He was standing so close to her she could practically feel the heat of his body.

Cassie retreated into teaching mode. "Gel electrophoresis. It separates macromolecules—DNA in this case—on the basis of size and charge. Then, by comparing it with known standards, we can identify the DNA. It's the same method they're using in the Human Genome Project, if you've heard of that."

"Of course." His warm breath coursed along her cheek. "Do you use the entire DNA, or do you have to break it up?"

She straightened and looked at him in surprise. Was he actually showing interest in something outside his little world? She doubted he really cared, but the teacher in her could never ignore a question. "We break it up, using restriction enzymes."

"What DNA are you trying to identify?"

"Actually, we aren't trying to identify it at all. We know perfectly well what it is, but we need to see if there are any differences in the DNA in specimens from the different locations we study. We don't expect to find anything, but we have to prove the differing habits aren't the results of differences in the species."

"I don't think I know precisely what you're researching. Something about waste nitrogen."

She glanced at him, wondering why he was interested, wishing she weren't quite so aware of how close he stood to her, and that they were alone in the lab. "The effects of excess nitrogen in waste water on the salt marsh habitat. There's a lot of fertilizer use here. The Cape is an oversized sand bar, and it isn't suited to grow lawn grass. But people want their picture-perfect lawns, so they pour on the fertilizers, and then the fertilizers end up in the wastewater and then the rivers. It's like a free feast when it reaches the salt marsh, and it disturbs the natural checks and balances of the ecosystem." She almost bit her tongue when she remembered the swath of manicured grass that surrounded Scott's house.

But he didn't seem bothered by it and continued to ask questions about the different equipment in the lab. She showed him the specimen tanks, usually the most interesting part of the lab for visitors. Most would dip a finger in the seawater piped in from the harbor or ask to touch one of the crabs. Calder just looked from a distance as she identified the specimens. As she discovered he could grasp most of the concepts involved in her research, her explanations became more technical, until he inquired about the contents of a large metal container over the Bunsen burner at the end of the bench.

She laughed. "I'd love to tell you it's a new experiment we're trying, but in fact that's marinara sauce. Lab dinner, you know. I should be putting in the spaghetti as well. The water must be boiling by now. It takes forever." She lifted the lid of a lobster pot sitting on a hot plate, releasing a small cloud of steam. "Yes, it's ready. People who are working late will generally drop by for some. It's a specialty of our lab."

He didn't look pleased at the idea of people stopping by. "It smells good."

She smiled, wondering if he would say the same thing if he knew the history of the dish. She wasn't afraid to challenge him. "Well, you're welcome to stay for some, but I don't think you'd find it up to your usual standards."

"As long as there aren't any scientific specimens in there, I'd be delighted."

She let out a peal of laughter. "Oh, but there are!"

"There are?" His voice was guarded.

"Yes. It's a tradition here. We make it with squid from the neurology labs. Squid have a giant axon—that's part of a nerve cell—that's used in neurological research, so they catch hundreds of squid for the lab, take out the one long cell, freeze the rest and give it to anyone who wants it. So, yes, there are experimental animals in it."

"I can see that lab cooking is a science all its own." He peered into the pot of marinara.

"Oh, you've never lived until you've eaten autoclaved lobster and mussels. Autoclaves aren't just good to sterilize supplies."

He smiled. "Lab *cuisine*, then."

She couldn't recall seeing him with a full smile before, and it softened the lines of his face and added a certain charm. No doubt he could be a lady-killer when he wanted. She felt an odd tug inside her. The question was why he was wasting his time touring her lab.

She wished she knew the answer, especially as she was running out of things to show him. Well, perhaps he would leave then, and she could read the book while she waited.

Calder inspected a shelf of journals. "Do you do this research year-round or just in the summer?"

"I only have access to the materials I need while I'm here during the summer, but in the winter I do data analysis, writing, and planning for the next summer. It works well because I don't have the resources—or the time, for that matter—to do serious research while I'm teaching." She wondered where this sudden curiosity about her work had come from. He had reverted to staring at her, and she had no idea what to make of it.

"You must be very busy. Where do you teach?"

"You've probably never heard of it. It's a small liberal arts college near Philadelphia." She was oddly reluctant to tell him, for once wishing she could name a prestigious research institution.

"Near Philadelphia? Would that be Swarthmore? Haverford? Bryn Mawr?" He surprised her by being able to name some of the possibilities.

"Haverford, actually. So you *have* heard of it."

He crossed his arms and leaned back against the bench. "Yes, for some reason my parents decided to educate me, even if we did have more money than we knew what to do with."

She gave him a sidelong glance as she poured a box of spaghetti into the boiling water, aware of the challenge in his voice. She realized with embarrassment that he was right, and she had been talking down to him, treating him like nothing more than a rich dilettante, despite the evidence before her. "A good education is never wasted. That's why I do what I do."

"Do you plan to stay at Haverford, or are you looking to move on to a university where you can do more research?"

She wondered if he was deliberately trying to prove he knew his way around higher education. "No, I like Haverford. My primary interest is undergraduate education. I wouldn't be able to have any real contact with students at a big university—just anonymous lecture halls and regurgitation of material on tests. I saw enough of that while I was a grad student to last me a lifetime."

"You don't think much of big universities, do you?"

"For undergraduate work? No. I think the job of a college is to teach students how to think, and I don't think that happens to undergrads at a big university. Universities are wonderful places to do graduate work, but for a real undergraduate education, there's nothing like a college where you interact directly with the professors." She was a little defensive, having had this argument many times with her university colleagues.

"Where did *you* go to college?"

She looked at him challengingly. "Wellesley—on a scholarship. How about you?"

He smiled slightly. "Harvard."

"A university man! I should have known. Well, I stand by what I said." She watched to see how he would take this teasing.

"I don't disagree with you. I think I managed to get a good education there, but no doubt some things are taught better in a small college, although without the same range of courses available."

So he wanted a debate. "As an undergraduate, it's not so much *what* you learn as *how* you learn it."

"I guess some people must teach themselves *how* to learn on their own, then, since the universities have turned out a few successful graduates over the years."

She looked at him closely, sizing up his ability as an adversary, when one of the researchers from a lab down the hall appeared at the door. "Hey, beautiful! Is that marinara I smell?"

"It is indeed." The distraction was a relief from the growing tension between her and Calder. "Do you want to see who's around and hungry?"

"Will do!" He disappeared once more.

"Perhaps I should go."

She glanced at him, sensing discomfort. No doubt he wanted to avoid being recognized, especially in company like hers. For that matter, she wasn't eager to have to explain his presence. She would never hear the end of having spent an evening alone with Calder Westing in her lab. "Whatever you like." The urge to tease got the better of her, however. "You're welcome to stay, assuming you can stand watching people eat laboratory specimens off paper plates."

His eyes traveled down her face. "How can I refuse such a unique opportunity?"

Her lips tingled. If he were another man, she would have sworn he was thinking about kissing her, but that was ridiculous.

She crossed her arms and looked at him in amused challenge. "Have you ever eaten squid?"

He startled her again with an unexpected smile. "Only when it's called calamari. I spent a semester of the time I was *wasting* at a university studying in Italy."

She didn't understand her response when he turned that mocking look on her. Uncomfortable, she busied herself pouring out the spaghetti and digging out paper plates from a cabinet underneath the lab bench.

Over the next few minutes, several men drifted in, most carrying some addition to dinner—a bag of cookies, a six-pack of dark beer, and some pints of ice cream the bearer stowed away in Cassie's lab freezer. Cassie greeted them each warmly, trying to decide how to handle Calder's presence.

"This is . . . Stephen." Her eyes glinted with amusement as she looked at him. "He's a friend of a friend, visiting the Cape. Stephen, this is John and Simon, who do research in neurophysiology, using some of those squid axons I mentioned; Arlen, who's with us from the University of Stuttgart, looking into the effects of invasive species on the local ecosystem; and Jim, who studies the ecology of Georges Bank and the effects of overfishing there. Jim was my thesis advisor in grad school, and I spent a couple of summers working in his lab here when I was a grad student."

"And survived the experience, amazingly enough." Jim was clearly assessing Calder.

No one stood on ceremony, helping themselves to spaghetti. Cassie realized Calder was holding back and wondered if he had lost his nerve. She made no attempt to hide her amusement when she turned to him. "It's devil take the hindmost around here, Cal . . . Stephen. Dig in."

He sauntered over to the food and served himself a healthy helping of spaghetti. He turned to look at her before ladling on an extra portion of marinara sauce, the rings of squid easily visible within it.

They ate quickly, perched on lab stools, the conversation revolving primarily around the research they were doing. Calder was silent, but not inattentive. Every time she glanced over at him, his dark eyes were on her.

He made a point of taking a bite of squid when he caught her eye. "Tasty."

With a mischievous look, she said sweetly, "I'm so glad you like it."

Simon finished and tossed his paper plate into the trash. "I'm going to be here all night, but I don't have to check on my experiments for a while. Anyone up for a game?"

"I'm on Cassie's team!" John said immediately.

"Me too," Arlen chimed in.

"You're very popular," Calder said to Cassie a bit brusquely. She wondered if the situation made him uncomfortable.

"Cassie's team always wins." Arlen brought out a well-worn box of Trivial Pursuit. Calder eyed it as if it were a snake poised to bite him.

"It's yet another benefit of a liberal arts education," Cassie said with barely hidden amusement. "Everyone around here can answer most of the science questions, and some of them can manage the sports, but when it comes to history or arts and entertainment, I have a monopoly."

"And the rest of us are hopeless!" Jim turned to Calder. "Say, I don't suppose *you* know about anything besides science?"

Calder paused as if hesitant to commit himself. Cassie cocked her head at him and said, "Yes, what *was* that fancy university degree of yours in?"

He met her eyes with a level look. "Philosophy, actually. With a minor in history."

"That does it; he's ours," said Jim decisively. "We'll give you a run for your money yet, Cassie!"

"I hardly think . . ." Calder demurred. "I've never played the game; I have no idea of the rules."

Cassie was deriving distinct enjoyment from seeing the great Calder Westing at a loss in a setting so obviously foreign to him. It wouldn't do him any harm to discover he wasn't the master of every circumstance. "Oh, do give it a try." She dared him with her eyes. "You'll pick it up in no time. All you have to do is to answer the questions. Jim and Arlen can do the rest."

She couldn't read his look, but he nodded. They set up the board, and the first few rounds passed without any successful answers. Finally Jim drew a card and looked straight at Cassie. "In what futuristic novel does the character 'Winston Smith' appear?"

"*1984*." She cast a triumphant look at Calder.

"Damn, you got it!" exclaimed Jim.

The pattern emerged quickly. Calder demonstrated a wider range of knowledge than Cassie expected, though he was usually stumped by questions about popular culture. It didn't take long for the game to become a silent but intense contest between the two of them. Calder was no longer holding back; Cassie was very entertained by the sight of how actively her formerly quiet and reluctant opponent was participating in the game.

Her team landed on another Arts & Entertainment square, and Calder practically snatched up the card and then rolled his eyes, evidently finding the question too easy. He read, "What nineteenth century novel begins with the sentence 'It is a truth universally acknowledged, that a single man in possession of a good fortune must be in want of a wife?' That's hardly a challenge."

"*Pride and Prejudice*, by Jane Austen," answered Cassie promptly, rolling the dice again with a triumphant look at him. "One of my very favorite books, too."

He looked at her with calculation. "I'm hardly surprised, somehow. You have a few things in common with Elizabeth Bennet."

"Why, do you suppose I have little tolerance for rich men who stand around silently without a pleasant word for anyone?" inquired Cassie with deceptive sweetness. She didn't mind in the slightest being compared to the spirited heroine of the book, but she regretted her words as she continued the train of thought. If he saw her as Elizabeth Bennet, she didn't want to suggest she thought of him as Darcy.

"History," announced Jim before Calder could make a reply. "What was the date of the Great October Revolution in Russia?"

"November 7, 1917." Cassie eyed Calder thoughtfully.

"No, Cass, it's the Great *October* revolution," John said. "Not November."

"It falls in November because Russia changed over to the Julian calendar after the revolution," she explained.

John looked dubiously at Arlen. "It *has* to be October." Arlen nodded.

"I'm telling you, it was in *November!*" Cassie said with irritation.

Calder had a slight smile on his face. "What's the team answer?"

Cassie repeated her answer, but John stepped in. "No, I want to go with October 7, 1917," he said, looking apologetically at Cassie. "Arlen, what's your vote?"

"October," said the other man briefly.

"Is that your final answer?" Jim had his poker face on.

At John's nod, Cassie struck her forehead with her hand and said, "Idiots!" She looked expectantly at Jim.

"The correct answer is ... November 7, 1917." Jim smirked.

Cassie glared at her teammates. "I told you so."

Calder looked smug. "I guess there's a reason you're named Cassandra."

"Yes, my parents chose it so I could be teased for the rest of my life," Cassie muttered in annoyance. "Now you'll have to explain what you mean to the rest of these single-minded scientists."

He laughed. "In Greek mythology, Cassandra was a princess of Troy with the gift of prophecy, but after she refused to become Apollo's lover, he placed a curse on her that her prophecies would never be believed."

"Some men just can't take no for an answer," Cassie retorted.

He smiled slowly but said nothing, his dark eyes speaking for him.

Something about his look made Cassie embarrassed, and she turned to John and Arlen. "I hope you're ashamed of yourselves!" she said with mock severity. "Don't blame me if they win!"

"We'll never doubt you again," said John in a mournful voice.

Cassie laughed. "I'm going to walk off in a snit anyway and go play with my gels. I'll just be a few minutes, and you can always come crawling to me for the answers if you get desperate."

"The things we put up with!" Arlen said. "It's abuse, I tell you."

Cassie crossed the lab to the gels. They were indeed done, and she readied the camera to take pictures of them. As she arranged the lighting and focused in on each one in turn, she listened to the men's laughter and joking. She glanced over at the game between shots and saw Calder rolling the dice. Now that was a story she wouldn't mind selling to a tabloid. Calder Westing enjoying a game like a normal human being.

By the time she finished with the gels, the game was ending, with Calder's team well in the lead. "That's what you get for not believing me!" Cassie said good-naturedly to her teammates.

"You'll never let us live it down, will you?" John stacked the cards neatly and put them back in the box.

"Not a chance. Now shoo, all of you. I'm ready to close down here for tonight."

The men packed up the game with some good-natured grumbling. Calder lingered behind after the other researchers left. "Thanks for dinner."

"I'd say you were welcome if you hadn't broken my winning streak," she teased.

"I'm sorry." A worry line appeared between his eyebrows.

Cassie gave him an amused look of disbelief. "You don't need to apologize for winning!" she exclaimed. "It's part of the game. Now go home, so I can get out of here."

"Good night, then." He paused in the doorway and turned back with a look that made her skin tingle. For a moment she thought he might say something, but then he left. Cassie rubbed her arms.

She hoped it was just a trick of the light that made her see desire in his eyes. If Calder ever decided he wanted her, she was in trouble. The kind of trouble she couldn't afford.

Chapter 4

BY MORNING CASSIE HAD talked herself out of her suspicions. It was nothing more than the late hour and her own loneliness that led her to see something that wasn't there. Why would Calder Westing look at her when he could have any woman?

There was still no sign of Erin. She must have spent the night with Scott. Cassie hoped Erin wouldn't regret becoming involved with him so quickly. Cassie had done a little homework on him. It was easy enough to find him on the internet. To look at the news articles, one would think his first name was "Whiz Kid." He had earned an undergrad degree from MIT in biological engineering and an MBA from Harvard, and then he bought the failing Cambridge Biotech and turned it around in five years. She had found two pictures of him with women, both tall and blonde. Did he know there was more to Erin than her looks?

Erin, when she finally appeared, looked happy and seemed to take it for granted she would be spending that evening with Scott as well. Cassie was glad to see her looking so content.

***

Jim looked up from his computer. "Working late again?"

Cassie stood in the doorway. Now that Rob had left Woods Hole, it was safe for her to visit Jim's lab again. "Are you going to be around much longer tonight? I was hoping to catch a ride home with you when you go." She didn't like to bike back to the empty cottage alone when it was this late. Erin hadn't slept at the cottage for over a week.

"Sure. I don't think I'll be long, maybe half an hour. Pull up a stool, if you like." Jim paused to click the mouse a few times. "You've been working late a lot this summer."

She leaned back against the lab bench. "Is this the pot calling the kettle black?"

"I'm a hopeless case. I do my best work at night. You never used to stay this long, though. It's almost midnight."

"No. But I have a lot to do this summer, and not much time to do it. And I don't have any particular reason not to work late."

"That's what worries me, Cassie. And I don't see Erin around very much."

Cassie walked along the lab bench, picking up scattered pens and placing them in the pencil holder. "She's here during the day, and she works hard. She'd stay longer if I asked her to."

"Have you asked her to? It sure looks like you could use the help. You've got a lot riding on getting good results this summer."

Cassie hesitated. She had worked all weekend as well. "Erin's had a really tough year, and she has a man here she's madly in love with. I want her to be able to enjoy this summer. She deserves it."

"So, you're doing your lab assistant's job as well as your own."

She straightened a stack of notepads. "I don't begrudge it. I knew she was burnt out when I offered her the job. And she has a reason to want to be out of the lab, and I'd just go home and read."

"Wreaks havoc on your social life, though."

Cassie laughed. "My social life? What's that?"

"That's my point exactly. And stop cleaning my lab. You're not one of my grad students anymore."

"The ones you have must be slobs, then." She crossed to the sink and dampened some paper towels and then wiped down the bench. "Somehow I sense Rose's hand in this sudden interest in my hours. Did she put you up to this?"

"We've discussed it. We want you to be happy, and we worry about the chances you may be missing."

"What chances am I missing? Woods Hole is a grand place for a summer romance, but they don't last. All the men here have academic jobs that can't move, just like me, and a long-distance relationship doesn't interest me."

"Some summer romances last. Look at Rose and me."

"You're the exception that proves the rule."

He frowned and shut down the computer. "Seeing Rob upset you, didn't it?"

"Rob is ancient history. He and I talked, and it was fine."

"That's not how he told it, and he didn't decide to leave early because it was fine. He was looking forward to seeing you."

Cassie didn't want to hear about Rob. "Jim, I appreciate your concern, but I can manage my own love life."

Jim held up his hands. "Okay, okay, I get the message. I'll tell Rose I did my best."

"Thank you."

Later that night, when Cassie was alone at the cottage, the conversation came back to haunt her. It didn't matter how good a face she put on it during the day when she still felt lonely at night. Seeing Erin and Scott together was a constant reminder of what she didn't have. But Erin was free to pursue a relationship because she'd decided to jettison her academic career.

Cassie could never do that, not when she was so close to meeting her goals—a secure future and the companionship of stimulating and interesting people. She wouldn't risk it for any man, and she hadn't met one yet who didn't expect her career to come second. Men couldn't be depended on the way tenure could. Rob had taught her that.

But intellectual companionship didn't fill all her needs. She spent over an hour staring bleakly at the ceiling before she fell asleep.

***

Cassie rubbed her temples. No matter how many times she performed the analysis, her results weren't turning out to be statistically significant. No significant results meant no paper to be published. No paper meant no tenure. She tried to block the refrain in her head. It was a well-planned study, and she was getting new data every day. Panicking wouldn't help.

Maybe she needed to get out of the lab and remember why she loved this work. She closed her data notebook and turned to Erin. At least Cassie hoped she was working, rather than just emailing Scott. Maybe tonight she and Erin could finally do something together, just the two of them.

When Erin looked up from the screen, Cassie said, "It's a new moon tonight, and Jim says the dinoflagellate counts are high. I'm going to check it out. Want to come?"

"Can I bring Scott?"

So much for just the two of them doing something. "By all means, bring Scott. Though he could probably see the same thing swimming off his own pier, without trekking all the way to the marsh."

"Oh, but I'd like to take him. He's only here for two more weeks. I want to be with him as much as I can. I'll check if he wants to go." Erin sat down again and began to type.

"Careful, girl, that keyboard hasn't had a chance to cool down since your last email!" Cassie was glad to see Erin so happy again, even if the subject of Scott became tiresome on occasion.

Erin arranged that she and Cassie would walk out to Scott's house that night, thus avoiding the perpetual problem of parking in Woods Hole. They were waved past the gate to Penzance Point this time. Erin was a known visitor now.

Scott was already outside waiting when they reached the house. Cassie turned away, ostensibly to admire the view of the Sound, as the two lovers greeted one another tenderly. Finally she turned back after hearing conversation once again.

"Ready to go?" she asked brightly.

"All ready." Scott dangled his car keys. "I'll see if Calder's ready. He wants to check this out, too."

Cassie wondered if Calder understood this was playtime, not a scientific expedition. He had tagged along on a specimen-gathering trip they made to the salt marsh earlier in the week, and she had the time to explain everything to him then, but she wasn't interested in being a teacher tonight. He would just have to cope. She had no intention of babysitting him.

When he emerged from the house, Calder announced he would be driving as well. With a regretful glance at Erin and Scott, Cassie offered to ride with him, more from a desire to give the other two some time alone than out of any wish for Calder's company. She tried not to notice the luxuriousness of the car's interior as she buckled her seatbelt. "Very thoughtful of you to make sure the lovebirds get a little privacy."

He glanced at her as he turned the key and the engine came smoothly to life. "Or something like that. I hope you'll be able to give me directions."

She gave him an amused look. "I should hope so, after doing research there for eight years!"

"We're going to the marsh?" He seemed taken aback.

Cassie wondered if he was afraid of getting his feet muddy. "Yes, as it happens, there's a beautiful beach at the edge of the marsh; it's completely deserted, because there's no good land to build on. It's ideal for seeing the biolumes because there are fewer artificial lights there."

"Makes sense."

He said nothing further, only watched the road. It was starting to look as if it would be a long, silent ride. Cassie cast about for a topic of conversation. "Did Erin give you your book back? Thanks again for lending it to me. I really enjoyed it."

"Did you?"

She gave him a puzzled look. "Yes, I did." What game were they playing? "The characterization was very good, and the part where Elanora learned she had cancer was just heartbreaking. It was hard to imagine how Teddy was going to live without her."

"He did, though. He went on."

"Yes, though there was a point where I wondered if it could have any kind of happy resolution." She had almost stopped reading it at that point, something she rarely did, but the intriguing main character pulled her along.

"Loss and redemption."

"And the dangers of allowing yourself to care about people. I liked the imagery of the seasons changing. That helped balance out the loss."

"That's one way of looking at it."

Tired of his noncommittal comments, Cassie decided to let the subject drop.

After a period of silence, he asked, "How's your research going?"

He certainly had a knack for saying the wrong thing to her, even when he managed to be polite. "It's a little frustrating at the moment." She stared out the window into the darkness, hoping he wouldn't follow up on it.

"I'm sorry to hear that." He was quiet for a moment, guiding the car past a series of blind curves. "The work itself, or what you're finding?"

"The results aren't what I'd hoped for." Why was she telling him this, rather than a polite lie? Calder Westing would be the last person of her acquaintance to understand her dilemma. He never had to worry where the next dollar was coming from.

"That must be disappointing."

"Yes." She risked a glance over at him. His eyes were on the road, and his profile showed nothing. Perhaps *that* was why she was telling him. He was a long way from academia, and he wouldn't understand the implications for her.

"Will it be a problem for you?"

"It could be. I need good results. There aren't a lot of jobs out there for marine biologists who don't get tenure. At least not jobs I could take. I couldn't work for the fishing industry."

"No, I suppose not. There's still time, though, isn't there?"

"Yes." She was silent for a moment. It was too easy to feel close to him, too easy to forget who he was when they talked like this. She forced cheerfulness into her voice. "Anyway, that's why I wanted distraction tonight. The bioluminescence is something special, you'll see."

"I'm looking forward to it."

"This is where you turn in, right up here." She indicated where he should park and made her escape from the car as soon as she could. She was embarrassed to have confided her troubles to him. What did he care whether she got results or even whether she got tenure? It was a million miles from his world.

She took her towel from the back seat. Scott's car was already there. "It looks like they've gone ahead without us. We have to walk from here."

She unclipped a small flashlight from her belt and led the way to the path through the woods. The silence of the nighttime descended on her, bringing its own peace, and she relaxed, letting go of her worries for a few minutes. At least Calder knew when to be quiet. A few minutes' walk brought them into the marsh. Cassie stopped by a stand of bushes, plucking a leaf and crushing it between her fingers, then raising it to her face to breathe in the fragrant scent.

She could sense Calder's questioning look. "Bayberry," she said in a hushed voice, as if too much noise might chase away the magic of the moment. "The leaves have a beautiful scent when you rub them." She held out the leaf to him.

Instead of taking the leaf from her, he took her hand in his and brought it to his face, inhaling deeply. A shock of awareness ran down Cassie's arm, and the sensation of his warm breath against her hand almost made her shiver. Her hand was intimately poised no more than an inch from his lips.

"Beautiful." He released her hand.

Discomposed by her reaction to him, she turned back to the path and began walking a little faster than was prudent in the darkness. She chastised herself for responding to a meaningless touch, reminding herself that women were a dime a dozen for Calder Westing. Besides, half the time she didn't even like the man.

They finally emerged from the rustling marsh grass onto the beach. It was deserted, as she expected. At the far north end of the marsh, several houses stood along the water, but they were across the river. To the south there was nothing but more marsh and sand. Cassie could barely make out two figures far down the beach. It was fine for Erin to want to be alone with Scott, but she wished her friend would consider the position it left her in with Calder. Still, she wouldn't let his presence interfere with her enjoyment. She put down her towel and kicked off her shoes.

"Where do we change?" asked Calder.

Cassie smiled to herself. Culture shock again. Well, he was the one who invited himself along on this adventure. "You're welcome to change anywhere you like, and I promise not to look. However, personally I think it's a waste of a moonless night to bother with a swimsuit, and I wasn't expecting company, so I didn't bring one." Before she lost her nerve, she stripped off her t-shirt with what she hoped was a casual air. Her shorts and underclothes quickly followed, and she walked to the water's edge before casting an impish glance over her shoulder at the still fully clad man behind her.

Calder made no effort to disguise that he was watching her. No, if Cassie Boulton was going to voluntarily take off her clothing in front of him, he was damned if he wasn't going to enjoy the view. After all, she hadn't said anything about not looking at her.

If she were any other woman, he would have interpreted her playful smile as an invitation, but he had the strong suspicion that if Cassie wanted something from him, she wouldn't bother with subtlety. That look was a dare. He watched her gently swaying body as she walked out into the water, his eyes lingering on her graceful curves, appreciating even her pronounced shiver when the water level reached her breasts. She didn't look back at him again, but instead seemed to become fascinated with the movements of her hands, running them through the dark water surrounding her.

Regardless of what his intellect said, his body insisted on responding to a situation it clearly felt should be acted upon. He fiercely damned the fact that she was precisely the sort of woman he shouldn't become involved with. He hated the thought that in two weeks he would leave and never again see that look of challenge flashing in her eyes. Why did the one woman he wanted in his life and in his bed have to be one his family would never accept?

If he couldn't have her, at least he could go out to her and look his fill. Stripping off his clothes with no more caution than she, he waded out into the water, grateful it would hide his arousal by the time he reached her.

Once the water was deep enough, he could see the bioluminescence. It wasn't the bright glow he'd expected, but rather sparks of light that appeared where the water contacted his body. Normally he would have watched it with interest, but now his thoughts were fixed on Cassie, who wore a look of enchanting happiness. She twirled around in front of him, her arms outstretched, tiny sparkles of light outlining her limbs as she moved. "It's magical, isn't it?"

He smiled slightly. "I thought it was science."

She laughed and deliberately splashed water at him. It flickered as it left her fingers and again as it ran down his chest, and he began to understand her delight in it. "It's dinoflagellates. I can explain it step by step, but it's more fun if you think it's magic."

"Ah, so it's science *and* magic," he replied loftily, just to see her smile.

"Here." She took his wrist in her hand. "Move your arm back and forth like this, and wiggle your fingers, and you'll get a light show. It's nice in long hair, too." She dunked her head underwater and swirled it around, creating a glittering net of tiny diamonds in her hair. She reemerged, smiling and looking like a naiad as the glittering water drained off her.

He was entranced by the visual spectacle of the lights outlining the curves of her body as she spun around once more. Stopping, she looked up at him and splashed him again. "Didn't anyone ever teach you how to play?" she asked with amused exasperation.

No, he thought, *no one ever did.* "I like watching you play."

His deep voice made Cassie suddenly aware of his physical presence. She looked out to sea, newly conscious of the sensuousness of the water moving along her bare skin and the mildly arousing sensation of it caressing her breasts, so different from when she wore a swimsuit. She hoped he couldn't tell what she was feeling. "Well, you're going to have to amuse yourself somehow because I'm going to swim out to deeper water."

She began to swim, glad to be putting a little distance between them, but had only gone a few strokes when a hand on her arm brought her to an abrupt halt. Startled, she stopped and looked up into Calder's face. "Don't, Cassie." He held her arm tightly. "It's not safe."

She was about to tell him she could do whatever she pleased when she saw the genuine anxiety in his face. More gently, she said, "I'm a very good swimmer. You don't need to worry about me. Honestly." With his greater height he was still able to stand, but she now needed to tread water to stay afloat. Fortunately, that wasn't hard in Buzzard Bay's buoyant water.

"It's dark, and you could get disoriented." He didn't loosen his grip on her.

Perplexed by his uncharacteristic doggedness, she paused. Her awareness that their unclothed bodies were only inches apart was increasing by the second, and she found herself admiring the breadth of his shoulders. To her chagrin, her body was beginning to ache to be touched. No doubt just a normal reaction to the proximity of an attractive male body. It didn't mean anything, except perhaps that she'd been celibate too long.

"Please, Cassie," he said, his voice surprisingly entreating.

She recalled suddenly that his uncle, the family patriarch, had died in a well-publicized boating accident. Had it been at night, too? Perhaps it had. She didn't remember the story well, since it happened when she was a girl. Although reluctant to give in, she understood his feelings. "All right, I won't."

"Thank you." His fingers tucked a stray lock of her wet hair behind her ear.

His gentle touch sent a surge of electricity through her. He paused as if deliberating, his hand in her hair, and drew his fingers along her cheek until they reached her mouth. As he lightly caressed her lips, a rush of desire filled her. Her entire body was awakening to his, her breasts tingling, and an insistent need began to grow deep inside her.

Their eyes met and held. Her breathing was growing irregular, and she suspected he could tell, just as his excitement was becoming clear to her. The sensuous feeling of the water flowing between her legs only made her long for a more intimate touch.

His expression was silently questioning her, his eyes intent even in the darkness. She couldn't fight herself any longer. The process of desire had already gone so far within her that she couldn't walk away and pretend she didn't want him to make love to her, that it wasn't the natural consequence of the intimacy of their setting and the history between them. She nodded almost imperceptibly.

His eyes flared. Unhurriedly he let his hand trail downward against her, past her cheek, down her neck, and finally submerging in the water, exploring down her arm and then catching her waist. The tiny sparkles of light in the water followed his movement, echoing the excitement he was creating in her. His look of desire was unmistakable.

His touch was almost meditative, though far from calming. His focused concentration on her, combined with the deliberation with which he was touching her, lent an excitement that went far past the stimulation he was giving her. Wanting to feel him as well, she slid her hands up to his neck.

She could see his body stiffen in response to her light touch, but it was as if they were both waiting for something. It came when his hand finally contacted the aching need of her breast. She gasped with pleasure as Calder, with a look of satisfaction, began to toy with it, watching her face intently.

It was impossible to keep her body still as his touch shot pleasure through her. She wanted desperately to kiss him, but if she did, it would bring their entire bodies into contact, and she had some sense of the conflagration that could set off. She could only gaze helplessly into his eyes as he read the increasing desire in her expression. His enjoyment of her low moans was obvious as his fingers sent currents of pleasure running through her.

She could hardly bear it when his hand abandoned her breast and moved downward to her hips, causing a new shock of sensation to race through her. How could she already be craving him deep within her, when he had barely begun to touch her? Her tension spiraled as he drew her closer, moving painfully slowly to prolong the moment until finally, at last, their bodies met. Then Calder drew in a sharp breath and crushed her to him, his leisurely pace abandoned, his mouth seeking hers with a desperate hunger.

Their lips met and his tongue teased her lips apart and thrust inside her mouth on a voyage of discovery. She slipped her hand into his hair as her tongue danced with his, each contact sending a wave of heat through her. There was nothing unhurried about his approach any longer. He moved with the urgency of a man who needed to claim every inch of her body.

His lips traveled down to taste her neck as his hand returned to her breast, this time eagerly seeking out her nipple for stimulation. As Cassie succumbed to the sensation he was creating in her, it became difficult to focus on remaining afloat, and she found herself limited by the need to hang on to his neck. "The water's too deep. I can't stand up here," she whispered.

He reached down and grasped her thighs, parting them and lifting her legs until she had little choice but to cling to him with her legs as well as her arms. In sudden intimacy, her center pressed firmly against him, creating an overwhelming pulse of deep pleasure. She pulled his head down to hers once again to demand her satisfaction of his lips.

She moved her body against him, making him groan with desire, until his arousal lay directly beneath her. Intense bursts of pleasure raced through her as she made her hips undulate, using his hardness to excite them both. Sensation built within her until she could hardly bear it, and she felt him insinuate his fingers between them so he could control more directly the surges of pleasure he gave her. He caressed her there, the pressure of need inside her growing and growing until finally she was overtaken by deep waves of satisfaction.

Her climax had barely ceased to rock her when he slid himself deep within her. She met him eagerly, riding the currents of pleasure he created in her until his body stiffened as he found his own release. He remained immobile for a minute and then reached down to touch her intimately until he brought her over the edge once more.

Overcome by the pleasure he had given her and the lassitude that followed it, she laid her head against his as their breathing began to return to normal, their bodies still connected. Still wrapped in a world of sensation, she luxuriated in his closeness and the comforting feeling of being held. It had been so long since she had felt a man's body against hers, and the sense of release and relief persisted for some minutes as neither spoke.

As a greater consciousness returned to her, a realization of the awkwardness of the situation began to permeate her. She had never been inclined toward casual sexual encounters. How, then, could she explain finding herself in the arms of a man she couldn't even say she liked? She could hardly claim he had seduced her; she had been as active a participant as he. She had always found him attractive, but she hadn't ever considered the possibility of anything happening between them. He belonged to a different world than she did.

Yet was there anything wrong with accepting this comfort for a little longer, given how far she had gone already? Perhaps it was an excuse, but would it not be simpler, less awkward, to let it follow its course, at least until she was safely at home? He was no doubt used to women who were far more sophisticated about these matters than she, and she didn't want to appear gauche. There was no need to worry, after all, about word spreading of what had happened. He had more to lose than she did in that regard. And in truth, she didn't want to let go of him so quickly, completely apart from the embarrassment that would be involved in trying to establish that this had been a mistake. She let herself relax in his arms, accepting the pleasantly soothing movements of his hands upon her back.

"It's getting a little cold," he said at last. "Perhaps we should get out of the water."

Despite his words, he seemed reluctant to let her go when she tried to disentangle herself from him. Determined not to let her discomfort with the situation show, she smiled at him mischievously. "Race you," she challenged.

Catching her hand, he pulled her back to him and kissed her. "Trying to get away already?" He put an arm under her legs, holding her to him as if he planned to carry her off.

She linked her arms around his neck, amused at being caught in a position she associated with cheap romances. "You may like this now, but you'll find I'm not so easy to carry once I'm out of the water."

"I'll just have to enjoy it while I can," he said, his pleasure enhanced significantly by the sight of her naked body so close to him. He gave in to temptation and leaned over to pull her nipple into his mouth, tasting the saltiness of the water on her as he stimulated her gently.

He had meant it only as a quick tease, but as he felt the rapid increase in tension in her body, he couldn't resist continuing his actions until she moaned with pleasure. Taking advantage of the ease of supporting her in the buoyant water, he shifted his arm until he could slide his fingers deep inside her. She arched hard against his hand, encouraging him to thrust his fingers into her again and again.

"I thought you said you were getting cold," she teased, her voice trembling from the pleasure he was giving her.

He released her breast just long enough to say, "I changed my mind." He was deriving great satisfaction from the discovery of how free Cassie was with him, her apparently unabashed enjoyment of his body and what he did to her a refreshing change from the more jaded women to whom he was accustomed. That she could carry her playfulness into a situation like this was a challenge he couldn't resist. He waited until he brought her close to her peak before he said, "Not quite so much to say for yourself now?" As if in response, her body shuddered and then with a soft cry of fulfilled pleasure, she went limp in his arms.

He could definitely grow used to this. He took advantage of her slow recovery to prove himself perfectly capable of carrying her into shore. She laughed when he set her on her feet on the beach.

"This is a little clichéd, don't you think?" she asked him.

"Clichés are about the last thing on my mind at the moment." He reached down and handed her towel to her before walking off to find his own. Next time, he'd make sure the towels were together. He didn't like being even this far away from her. When he came back, she was toweling her hair dry unselfconsciously, her body completely exposed to his appreciative eyes.

Cassie looked up to see Calder's eyes moving up and down her form. Her blush was hidden in the darkness, but she couldn't help but wonder what he was thinking. He was no doubt accustomed to women with bodies toned and shaped by sessions with personal trainers, and while she had no great complaints about her body, she doubted it could be held to the same standards. She wondered why she even cared what he thought. After all, he obviously found her attractive enough for a temporary amusement, which was all there could ever be between them.

She threw her clothes on quickly, uncomfortable with the situation. She could no longer make out the other two, and she didn't want to spend any more time standing around with Calder than she had to.

"Do you think we should wait for Scott and Erin?" she asked.

He shook his head. "They can take care of themselves, and I doubt they want company at the moment."

They walked back through the marsh without speaking. Cassie grew more anxious as they went, wondering what kind of expectations he would have of her now. Obviously a real relationship wasn't a consideration under the circumstances. Would he expect her to be willing to sleep with him again? Would he expect her to make demands? Or was this never to be mentioned again? She wasn't looking forward to sorting it out. By the time they reached the car, Cassie was intensely nervous about what would happen next and almost wishing she had a little more experience with the etiquette for casual sex.

She wrung her hair out again with her towel before entering the car. He was already in the driver's seat when she got in. "Sorry," she said with as much cheerfulness as she could muster. "I don't want to get salt water all over your nice car."

"Don't worry about it." He paused with his hand on the key. "Would you like to come back to the house?"

He wasn't going to just let it go, so it was up to her to extricate herself. "I have to be at the lab early, so I really should go home."

He busied himself with starting the car and finding the way out to the road. "You'll have to show me the way," he said with a sidelong look at her.

"Of course." She directed him quietly to the cluster of cottages reserved for MBL researchers, reminding herself the whole time of all the reasons why any kind of continuing connection with Calder Westing was asking for trouble.

He pulled up in front of her cottage, but before she could say anything, he leaned over and kissed her slowly and lingeringly. As soon as she felt his lips on hers, her resolve began to weaken. Her mind might have been made up to have nothing further to do with him, but her body was still frighteningly ready to respond to his touch. She damned herself for being so susceptible to this brand of persuasion, even as desire began to flow through her once again. His hand came up to cup her breast.

Without planning it, she found herself saying, "Would you like to come in?"

He gave her a slow, devastating smile. "I thought you'd never ask."

Chapter 5

CASSIE AWOKE EARLY THE next morning to the pleasant sensation of a warm male body against hers, his leg pinning hers to the bed and his hand curled around her breast. Memories of the previous night flooded back—showering off the salt water with Calder's hands slowly and seductively washing her from head to foot, cramped together in the small shower stall; how she returned the favor, deliberately arousing him with intimate stroking; how they dried each other off afterwards and went to the bedroom where he pleasured her thoroughly with his mouth before taking his own pleasure in her.

She must have been out of her mind. Casual sex didn't work for her. Once she'd gone to bed with a man, she couldn't separate her emotions from her physical reactions. Now she was already experiencing that dangerous tenderness toward Calder, who had never done anything that impressed her beyond providing some of the most spectacular sexual pleasure of her life.

She closed her eyes. She couldn't afford to fall for Calder Westing. He would eat her alive, using her as an amusing sexual partner, and no doubt completely clueless to the impact on her. She had never learned how to be cautious with her affection. She could find herself in too deep with him without ever intending it.

She needed to get away from him. Her physical response to him was too strong. As soon as he woke up and touched her, she would be unable to resist. The prickings of desire were already starting to eat at her. No, there was only one way to stay safe, and that was to stay away.

Trying not to wake him, she extricated herself from his body and the bed sheets. It was hard to leave his warmth behind, knowing she would never feel it again. She took the first clothes she found from her dresser and went into the small living area to put them on, without even a thought of showering first. She looked back in on him. He was sound asleep still, one hand hanging over the edge of the bed. She could take the time to write him a note.

Calder,

Had to be at the lab early this morning and didn't want to disturb you. Help yourself to bagels in the fridge and cereal in the cupboard if you want something to eat, and I've left the coffeemaker out on the counter.

She chewed her pen for a moment. Should she say anything else? Even a generic "Have a nice day" might suggest she expected to see him that night, and she wanted to be completely businesslike. It seemed abrupt to leave it at that, but she didn't want it to sound too affectionate. He might take that the wrong way. Finally she just signed her name to it and left it on the kitchen table. She wondered if he even knew how to make coffee.

He would no doubt be embarrassed enough seeing the cottage by daylight. It served its purpose for Cassie but consisted of little more than a living room, kitchen, and two small bedrooms. The furnishings showed the signs of wear from many summers' use by renters. It couldn't be more different from Scott's shiny and pristine mansion on the waterfront. The gulf between their lives was beyond bridging, no matter how appealing he looked with his tousled dark head on her pillow.

She let herself out of the cottage quietly and unlocked her bicycle. In the shade of the scrub pines, she rode down the bike path to Woods Hole. Soreness from the night's activities made it difficult to forget what had occurred even for a minute. When she finally arrived at the lab, she took the unusual step of closing the door behind her.

Setting up the day's work didn't provide enough distraction to keep her mind off Calder. Would he try to call her? Would he come by the lab or worse yet, to the cottage some night? Or would he make no particular effort to be in touch at all and decide he just got lucky?

Why had she responded to him the way she did? Though she generally enjoyed lovemaking, she had never responded as quickly or as easily as last night. Why Calder? Why was he the man who could bring her pleasure so effortlessly?

She closed her eyes in pain. The answer was obvious. He was from a different world, and he was far more experienced than any lover she had before. None of them had his opportunities to learn on as many women's bodies as he chose. How could she have let herself be one more? Why did she have to care?

She took the heavy biology textbook off the shelf and let it bang on the lab bench. She knew better than to think this was real. It was nothing more than a physiological reaction. Orgasm in the female caused a release of oxytocin, the same hormone that made mothers feel bonded to their babies. She felt attached to him because of a biological imperative, not because of anything between them.

She wouldn't allow herself to be led around by her body's urges. No, she had a good deal of experience at spotting dangerous connections and cutting them off, even when her heart was involved, and this wasn't that bad yet. She had to remember her goals. Emotional ties could keep her from achieving them after all the years she had poured into her work. In a disciplined manner, she reminded herself of the cost of failure, and by the time she was done, she knew she could manage Calder Westing.

Erin didn't arrive at the lab until almost ten o'clock. Cassie, already exhausted, was hard put not to feel annoyed when she floated in, her mind clearly still on Penzance Point. But it wasn't Erin's fault Cassie had made an embarrassing mistake. Cassie returned to adding a chemical reagent to row of beakers, watching each drop carefully.

She noticed Erin looking at her strangely as she finished. "Is something the matter?" It came out sounding too abrupt.

"It didn't pass my notice that Calder wasn't home until this morning."

Cassie's thumb slipped from the top of the pipette and the liquid ran into the beaker. She swore and poured the mixture down the sink. "And your point is?"

"The two of you weren't exactly quiet last night at the beach, and I have to admit I was sort of surprised."

"Why, don't you think I deserve a one-night stand with a rich man?" Cassie set down the empty pipette, jotted a note, and prepared a new beaker.

Erin's face fell. "Oh, Cass, I'm sorry. Was he nasty about it?"

"Oh, he didn't ditch me, more the other way around if anything. I just wish I hadn't done it. It's not my kind of thing."

"No, I know it isn't. I'm sorry. I didn't realize it was a painful subject. But if you ever want to talk about it, I'm here."

Talking about it was the last thing Cassie wanted. She was growing more anxious as the day wore on and had almost come to the conclusion that it would be better to have it out with Calder than live with the uncertainty of whether he would contact her. When the phone finally rang late in the afternoon, she jumped. Erin answered it before she could, a look of disappointment coming over her features as she realized it wasn't Scott.

Erin held out the telephone to Cassie. "It's Calder."

Cassie took a deep breath before putting it to her ear. "Hello," she said in a businesslike manner.

"Cassie, it's Calder." Even the sound of his deep voice affected her somehow. "I was wondering if you'd like to have dinner this evening."

"Thanks, but I'm afraid I can't. I have a lot of work to do here today and then there's a lecture I want to hear."

"All work and no play makes Jack a dull boy. And you need to eat anyway. Maybe I could bring something over to the lab, and we could eat there."

"All play and no work gets Jill turned down for tenure. Thanks all the same."

"Tomorrow, then?"

He wasn't going to take the hint. "Look, Calder, I appreciate the effort, but you don't owe me anything for last night. It was a special moment, and it went places neither of us expected, but let's not try to make it something it's not."

There was silence on the other end. Finally he said, "I'd still enjoy the chance to spend some time with you—no expectations."

"I appreciate that you're trying to do the right thing here, but it simply isn't necessary. Look, I really need to get back to my work, okay?"

"If that's what you want." His voice sounded very formal to her ears.

"Thanks, Calder, nice talking to you."

"Take care, then." She heard his reply just before she hung up the phone.

She rested her hands on the lab bench in front of her for a moment as she took some deep, calming breaths. At least that was over with.

"That was quite the brush-off." Erin's look was an accusation.

Cassie rounded on her, ready to snap, but caught herself just in time. "Let's face it, Erin. Calder Westing would be nothing but trouble for me. Scott may be a different story, and I'm glad you're happy together, but it would never work for Calder and me. Okay?"

"If you say so."

***

Cassie broke her own record for long hours in the lab over the next two days, but at least there was one good thing to say for it as her experiment finally began to show positive results. Late at night, as she lay in bed willing sleep to come, she remembered being in Calder's arms, feeling wanted and desirable, but she could ignore it during the day. She had results, and that was all that mattered.

She arrived at the lab early on the third day after sleeping poorly. A few hours of quiet before Erin arrived would be useful. But when the door to the lab finally opened, it wasn't Erin, but Calder.

"Cassie—may I come in?"

"Of course." Her response was automatic. "You're up early."

He looked at her seriously. "I wanted to get here before Erin." He pulled up a lab stool and sat near her. "How are you?"

Cassie steeled herself against feeling any vulnerability. "I'm fine. I've been getting some results here. I think I'll be able to get a paper out of it."

"So that's good news?"

"Oh, yes. I need a couple more papers if I want tenure, so this helps."

"You work pretty long hours."

"Yes, I do. I have a lot I want to accomplish."

He was silent for a moment. "Are you angry with me about what happened the other night?"

"Angry? No, not at all." At least he had asked a question she could answer honestly. "Why should I be angry? You didn't push me into anything. It was my idea as much as yours."

His eyes were fixed on her. "I just wondered. It seems like you don't want anything to do with me all of a sudden."

There was no point in hiding it. "I don't know why you should believe this, but I don't usually do one-night stands or casual sex. I'm uncomfortable with the whole thing. I don't know how to deal with a man I've had sex with but don't have a relationship with. You're leaving soon, so it's easier all around this way. And I have a lot of work to do; I don't have time for a man in my life."

"I suppose I can accept that," he said slowly. "There is one thing I wanted to say, though."

She looked up at him sharply. "What's that?"

"It isn't the kind of thing I do on impulse either, so I wasn't prepared for it happening on the spur of the moment. I'm usually a little more . . . careful than I was that night." He reached into his pocket and pulled out a business card. "This has my direct phone number and my private email. If there are any . . . untoward consequences, I'd like to know about it."

Why did he have to sound so much like a lawyer? She blushed fiercely when she finally understood his meaning. Did he know how insulting he was? "I don't think you need to worry. Even if there were any *untoward consequences*, which there won't be, you wouldn't need to worry about me making any demands. I would be perfectly capable of dealing with the situation *on my own*."

"That's just what I'm worried about, that you *would* try to deal with it on your own. I'd want to know. It was pretty obvious it had been a while for you, and I didn't want to assume you were on the pill."

"I *am* a biologist, and I have a very good understanding of when I might be fertile and when I'm not, and you may be certain it isn't something I would ignore, no matter how tempted I was." She wouldn't look at him.

"Will you tell me, though, if anything should happen?"

"Fine," she snapped, looking at his card as if it were a snake. "And I'll tell you if the tides don't turn, too. Now, if you don't mind, I have a lot to get done today."

He was baffled by her anger. "I didn't mean to upset you," he said. "I just . . ." All he wanted was a chance to have her tease him and smile at him again, and to show her he did take his responsibilities seriously, but he couldn't say that. "I'm sorry."

She forced herself to breathe deeply. "It's okay; I'm fine. But very busy."

He rose and pushed the stool back under the bench. "I won't bother you then. Good luck with your paper."

"Thank you."

Despite her tone of dismissal, he didn't move, and finally she looked up at him and met his eyes. It wasn't his fault she had made a mistake, or that he was from a different world. The least she could do was to be pleasant. "Good-bye, Calder."

His dark eyes remained fixed on hers unreadably for a moment. Then he nodded and was gone.

***

Jim stopped by her lab that night. "Working late again? I'm about to leave and thought I'd see if you wanted a ride."

"Thanks, Jim, but I'm going to be here for a while yet." Cassie turned back to the journal article she was reading. She didn't want to sit at home alone with her thoughts any longer than she had to.

Instead of leaving, he leaned back against the lab bench and crossed his arms. She looked up at him questioningly.

"All right, Cassie, what's up?"

"What do you mean?" she asked irritably.

"Something's bothering you. What is it?"

"I'm fine, Jim. Now stop being a mother hen and go home."

"I've known you a long time, and I know when something is wrong. You haven't been yourself for a few days. You've been quiet, you don't smile, and you're working even harder than usual."

She closed the journal with a snap and dropped it on her desk. "Have you decided to give up biology for psychology?"

"How did you guess? It's my mid-life crisis. And you're trying to change the subject."

"Jim, really," she said, exasperated.

"Have you talked to Erin about whatever it is?"

Cassie sighed and rubbed her forehead with her hand. It was hard to resist his gentle insistence. "No, not really."

"So tell Uncle Jim all about it, or Rose will have my head. Take pity on an old man."

She couldn't help smiling. "When did you get old? You were having a mid-life crisis a minute ago."

"You're changing the subject again."

She closed her eyes. "All right, all right. I made a stupid mistake."

"We've all been known to do that. What was yours?"

"I slept with a man."

"And the mistake was . . . ?"

"He was the wrong man."

He looked at her sympathetically. "Who was it? It's a small world here at the MBL."

She shook her head silently.

"You know I won't tell anyone, Cassie."

She was quiet for a moment. Maybe if she talked about it, she could get it out of her head. It certainly couldn't make it worse. "It was Calder. The one who played Trivial Pursuit with us one night."

"Calder? I thought his name was Stephen."

She realized her slip. "Right, that's the one—Stephen."

"He seemed nice enough, if kind of quiet."

"He's the wrong sort of man. He'd never be seriously interested in someone like me. It was an impulsive thing on both our parts. I don't even like him most of the time. My problem is I can't let it go."

"And what about him?"

"Calder? He won't have any problem letting go of it."

"Wait a minute. I'm getting confused. Is it Calder or Stephen?"

"Calder," she said, feeling defeated. "I introduced him as Stephen as a joke because I didn't want you to know who he was."

"And who is he?" Jim sounded mildly scandalized.

"Stephen Calder Westing. As in the senator's son. As in high society, old money, and never had to work a day in his life. As in his only concern is that I might get pregnant and try to take him for everything he's got."

Jim whistled silently. "You're right. He's not your type."

"To say the least." A hint of her usual humor came back to her. "I don't think he even has a graduate degree."

"Your standards are slipping. I thought you liked your men educated. He *is* pretty good at Trivial Pursuit, though."

"True on both counts."

"I'm not too surprised. He certainly seemed interested in you."

"That night? No, I don't think so. He was just bored and had nothing better to do."

"Beg to differ. He was watching you every minute. I was surprised not to see him around again. Though I guess you must have seen him again after all."

She shrugged, not wanting to go into details.

"So he said he didn't want to see you again?"

"No, not exactly. But it couldn't have gone anywhere, and a quick fling isn't my style. So I told him I didn't think it was a good idea for us to see each other again."

Jim eyed her suspiciously. "Cassie, did you ever give the poor man a chance to say what *he* wanted from you?"

The very last thing she needed was to start worrying about whether Calder might have wanted something more. "Jim, believe me, I have nothing Calder Westing wants beyond a warm body. I know you want to see me happily married off, but he isn't the one."

"I'm not asking you to marry him, just to think about whether you're sure what he wants from you because I have my doubts."

"You're an old romantic, Jim, and you should go home to your wife."

"Always trying to get rid of me. All right, I can take a hint."

"Since when?"

He laughed. "I know better than to try to get the last word in. Goodnight, Cassie."

"Goodnight," she said affectionately. She hoped his words wouldn't haunt her.

***

Cassie's fingers tapped the steering wheel impatiently as she slowly drove up the Penzance Point road. The last thing she wanted was to risk seeing Calder again, but here she was. Another one of Erin's messes.

Why did Erin want to leave Scott's house at this hour of the night, anyway? And why all the secrecy? When she'd called, she hadn't explained why she wanted Cassie to say she was needed for a problem at the lab. If Scott had turned nasty, she was going to give him a piece of her mind.

The house looked even more imposing at night. Cassie took a deep breath before ringing the bell. She hoped Scott or Erin would answer the door. Anyone but Calder. She stepped back into the shadows, away from the front light.

Luck wasn't with her. The door opened to reveal Calder's height, Calder's shoulders, Calder's dark hair, and all the things about Calder she hadn't been able to put out of her mind. Including the same look of surprise he wore that night in the water when he touched her.

He couldn't think she was there to see him, could he? The possibility was mortifying, that he might think she'd come crawling to him for more. "I'm here to pick up Erin," she announced crisply. "Is she ready?"

His lips tightened. "I don't know. I'll go see." He disappeared down the hallway and into the living room.

He hadn't even invited her in. She stepped inside anyway, refusing to be left on the doorstep like a beggar. Men's voices drifted toward her. Apparently they had company. Maybe that was why Erin wanted to leave.

Scott appeared by the living room. "Hi, Cassie. I'll tell Erin you're here. Come on in and have some wine or something."

So Scott didn't know Calder wanted nothing to do with her. Well, Scott had invited her, and it would be rude to refuse. Besides, she was curious to see how Calder behaved around other people.

She realized her mistake as soon as she stepped into the living room. Two older men sat in the overstuffed armchairs. She recognized one of them from the evening news. So that was why Calder hadn't wanted her to come in. He hadn't wanted his father to meet her. He wouldn't want his family to know the kind of riff-raff he associated with.

Senator Westing set his brandy snifter on an end table. Rising to his feet with an old-fashioned courtesy, he looked questioningly at his son.

Calder had his stone face on. "One of Erin's friends." He turned and looked out the window.

So she didn't even have a name anymore. Cassie wouldn't let Calder see her mortification. She stepped forward with all the confidence she could muster and held out her hand to Calder's father. "Cassie Boulton," she said.

"I'm Joe Westing," he said in an elegant southern accent. As if she wouldn't know who he was.

"A pleasure, Senator." Polite lies. Under normal circumstances, she'd want nothing to do with him, not after he'd had a hand in cutting federal support for scientific research.

"Hiram Stettson," the other man said. He shook her hand as well.

Senator Westing said, "I take it you know Calder."

"We've met," she said. She wished she had never laid eyes on him. He was ignoring her so pointedly it must be obvious to the others.

"Aren't you going to offer the lady a drink, Calder?" The senator sounded disapproving, almost disparaging.

Calder turned to face them again. "Would you like a drink, Dr. Boulton?"

Oh, yes, he was denying they were anything but the most casual acquaintances. She was half-tempted to tell his father what his son did behind his back. "No, thanks. I need to get back to the lab. We've got a problem there. That's why I need Erin."

"Working at ten o'clock on a Friday night?" Senator Westing sounded dubious.

Cassie smiled tightly. And this was one of the men responsible for setting the budget for the National Science Foundation. "You don't know many researchers, I take it. Science doesn't keep nine-to-five hours."

"What sort of research do you do?"

"I'm a marine biologist."

"I see." The senator's tone suggested he didn't like what he saw. Hardly a surprise. Some of his beliefs put him distinctly at odds with the biology community.

Calder came forward into the light. "Do you need some help? I know your time is tight."

Was he really offering to help with her non-existent problem? He looked serious, but a few minutes earlier, he hadn't known her name.

Before she could say anything, his father cut in. "Calder, you've caused enough trouble without spending time in a *biology* lab. I don't need the media getting hold of that." This time the scorn was out in the open.

It was more than Cassie's barely contained temper could manage. "Oh, we couldn't have that," she said, her voice dripping sweetness. "People might start thinking he was smart enough to understand science. Or even that he has a mind of his own. Fortunately, Erin and I can manage on our own. But thank you for the offer, Calder." She might not like how his father talked to him, but it still stuck in her throat to thank him for anything.

The senator's scornful look was directed at her now. She didn't care. All she wanted was to get out of there as soon as possible.

Erin, with exquisite timing, chose that moment to appear in the hallway. "Are you ready, Cassie?"

Erin couldn't possibly imagine how ready she was to leave. "Sure." Cassie looked back at the men. "Sorry I couldn't stay for more of this lovely chat. I hope you enjoy your visit to the Cape."

***

The light on the answering machine was blinking when they arrived back at the cottage. Cassie paused to push the button. Calder's voice, sounding subdued, or as if he was trying to keep from being overheard, floated from it. "Cassie, I wanted to apologize for my father. I wish I could say he isn't usually like that, but it wouldn't be true. But I'm sorry he talked that way in front of you." There was a pause, as if he had considered saying more, and then a click.

Cassie stared at the machine in dismay. Just when she finally accepted that she meant nothing to Calder, he turned around and did something like this. What was she supposed to do? Maybe he was like his father, warmly polite one moment, nasty the next. She followed Erin into the kitchen.

Erin filled the dented teapot and placed it on the burner. "Thanks for rescuing me. I didn't feel comfortable staying with Scott's father there."

"Scott's father? You mean Calder's father." Cassie tossed her sweater over the straight-backed chair. The cottage felt particularly small and shabby after Penzance Point.

"The other one. Hiram."

He had barely registered with Cassie. "But his last name was different from Scott's."

Erin developed an intense interest in looking through their stash of herbal teas. "Scott's illegitimate. He has his mother's name."

Cassie pulled up a chair to the wobbly kitchen table. She'd always thought Scott came from the same sort of background as Calder. "Surely his father knows Scott sleeps with his girlfriends."

Erin peered inside one of the mugs and rinsed off a microscopic piece of dust. "Oh, he knows, all right. It was how he made me feel about it. Like I was a possession, along with the fancy house on the ocean and the sailboat, another sign of Scott's success. The pretty blonde in his bed. It was creepy."

"Eww. What did Scott do?"

"I don't know if he noticed. He doesn't know his father very well."

"How can he not know his father?"

Erin finally selected a box of tea. "He only met his father a couple of times when he was growing up. Hiram didn't acknowledge him until he was in college and becoming a credit to the family."

"Ouch."

"Really. Scott's never met his half-brothers and sister, though they know all about him. Daddy's proud of him but doesn't let him mix with the real family. When he gave Scott the money to buy Cambridge Biotech, he told him it was an early inheritance, because Scott won't be mentioned in his will." Erin poured the hot water into the mugs and handed one to Cassie.

"Because his mother was the other woman?"

"Worse. It's because his mother is a quarter African-American, and his father is a Southern so-called gentleman. Tainted blood, and all that."

Cassie wrinkled her nose. "What does Scott think about all this?"

"He's never talked about it. I found this out from Calder. Their fathers are buddies. Calder knows his legitimate kids. I don't think he likes them."

"Why?" And why would Calder have told Erin any of this?

"I don't know. I asked him what they were like, and he said, 'Well, you won't see me spending the summer with one of them.'"

"How long is Scott's father staying?"

"He's leaving tomorrow, thank God." Yawning, Erin put her mug in the sink. "I'm going to bed. I can't keep your hours."

"Good night." Cassie remained at the table, her hands wrapped around her tea. Maybe Erin would have a little more time for her now. It felt good to talk to Erin, to really talk about something important, not just work. She'd hoped they would have lots of times like this over the summer, but that was before Scott. Cassie had probably told Calder more of her problems than she had told Erin. But she couldn't blame Erin for her choice. Erin had fun with Scott, and all Cassie had to offer her was more work.

When had she given up having a life of her own? There was a time Cassie had socialized more, joining other researchers for an evening out or a day trip to Boston. At Haverford she had friends she spent time with. But this summer was different. Maybe it was the tenure pressure.

She wished Calder were there, the quiet Calder who listened to her. He never expected her to be strong for him, and when she let her guard down and admitted something bothered her, it didn't make him uncomfortable. But that was only a small part of Calder Westing, and she could never survive an affair with the cold, silent man he was most of the time. Discouraged, she rested her head in her hands. It wasn't going to be easy to forget him.

Chapter 6

ERIN TRUDGED INTO LAB at ten in the morning. Cassie, with one look at her friend's stricken expression, limited herself to a quiet hello.

"He's going to stop by on his way out of town to say goodbye." Erin didn't have to say who. Scott was leaving that day.

Cassie had been looking forward to this day almost as much as Erin had been dreading it. She was tired of worrying about whether she would run into Calder somewhere in town. The stress of it only made her turn even more into her work. Then, the previous night, as she lay in bed, she had horrified herself by bursting into tears when she realized she would never see him again. But it was better this way. Now it was over, and perhaps she could get on with her life.

She had planned to ask Erin to enter data today, but her friend was in no condition to concentrate on anything important. She'd have to do it herself. Casting about for a task where Erin could do no harm, Cassie suggested cleaning out the specimen tanks.

The physical effort seemed to calm Erin. When Scott finally arrived an hour later, she was able to greet him with a shaky smile.

Cassie didn't bother to get up from her desk. Scott wasn't there to see her. She turned back to the computer to give them some privacy. The data spreadsheet was almost done.

It was hard to ignore the whispered conversation in the background. Cassie wished they would leave and let her work. Maybe she should go down to the coffee shop for a few minutes. Scott would probably be gone by the time she returned.

She saved and closed the spreadsheet. Pushing her chair back, she caught sight of a figure in the doorway. Calder was watching her silently, as he had so often in the past. She could feel the heat rising in her cheeks. Why was he there? He had his own car. He wouldn't be riding with Scott.

She looked back at him, remembering all the conflicting sides of him she had seen. She tried to summon her righteous indignation from their last meeting, but it had fled. And she could only think of his dark eyes, still fixed on her.

Erin and Scott were in each other's arms off to the side, oblivious to everything around them. At least Cassie hoped they were oblivious. If Erin spotted the tension flowing between her and Calder, she'd never hear the end of it.

She wondered why Calder didn't come in. Had he decided not to set foot in her lab unless invited? Perhaps she should take him to the coffee shop. It might give her some sense of closure if they managed to have a normal conversation. She crossed the floor until she stood near him. "You're leaving today, too?"

"Tomorrow."

His curt response reminded her of his proud and remote side, the Calder Westing who could barely spare a word for anyone else. It broke the tension she felt inside, that sense of connection. She didn't let any sign slip that it disturbed her, even though it hurt. No lover of hers had ever deemed her unworthy to speak to before. "I hope you have a good trip."

There was a moment's silence before he responded. "Thanks."

Why had he come, if he wasn't willing to talk to her? "Are you hoping to avoid the traffic?"

"No." He shifted from one foot to the other. "I'm just . . . not ready."

Somehow she knew he wasn't talking about packing. "It's hard to leave here at the end of the summer."

"Yes." His eyes locked with hers again.

It wasn't just her. Cassie recognized the look in his eyes. She had seen it that night on the beach.

Calder took her by the elbow and propelled her into the hall. She opened her mouth to ask what he thought he was doing, but before any words could come out, he was kissing her hungrily, tangling his hands in her hair. And she was responding, as if there had been no quarrel between them, as if she had no choice once he touched her, as if she had to steal every possible second with him.

They were in full view of anyone who might step out into the hall or come up the stairs. The thought was enough to shock Cassie out of her state of confused desire. She stepped back, but not far enough for safety. His hands were still on her face, her cheeks, her neck, and she didn't want him to stop. The way he was looking at her made her entire body hungry for his touch.

"Not here." She glanced around nervously.

His hands dropped to his sides. "Come back to the house with me."

She wanted to say yes, to forget everything she had decided, to live in the moment and pretend this wasn't going to hurt later on. "I can't. Erin's going to need me."

He must have been able to hear the conflict in her voice. "Later, then."

How could she have a PhD and still feel as if she had forgotten how to speak English? "I . . . don't know."

There was a sound from inside the lab. Cassie looked in and saw Erin in tears, as she had expected. She glanced at Calder. "She's going to fall apart if he drags this out any longer."

Calder nodded silently and moved past her into the lab. "Scott, it's time to hit the road."

"What?" Scott said. "Oh, right." He kissed Erin lightly one more time. "I'll be back next weekend, and I'm only two hours away."

Erin tried to sniff back her tears. "Drive carefully."

"I'll email you as soon as I'm home." At the door Scott gave Cassie a friendly kiss on the cheek.

"Bye, Scott." Cassie was far more aware of the man standing behind him.

With one last glance at Erin, Scott left the lab. Calder, following him, paused only a moment to touch the back of Cassie's hand.

Erin's hands were over her face. Cassie seized the distraction and put her arm around her.

"It's okay, sweetie. He'll be back in just a few days."

"It won't be the same. It won't ever be the same again."

Cassie hugged her. "You don't know that. Give him a chance. He's not some young grad student getting his first whiff of freedom."

"He doesn't love me." Erin started to cry harder.

"Did he say that?"

"He didn't need to. It's who he is. He's wonderful, warm, thoughtful, and fun, but his feelings are off-limits. He doesn't go there."

"That doesn't mean he doesn't care about you." Cassie half-led Erin to a lab stool. She knew from experience Erin's reaction could go on for some time.

By the time Erin was finally calm and back at work, if half-heartedly, Cassie felt exhausted. Too many emotional ups and downs. What had happened to the nice, calm life she had planned for herself? Calder Westing had happened to it, for one thing.

What had she been thinking, letting him kiss her like that, not to mention kissing him back? Or perhaps that was the entire problem. She *hadn't* been thinking. She had been feeling. He could make her forget herself with just a look. He had only said a dozen or so words to her, no more than twenty, she was sure.

Was he waiting for her at Scott's house, wondering if she would come? It was crazy. Why had he suddenly decided he wanted her again? It wasn't just amusement value this time, she was sure of that, but she was equally certain all he wanted was her body. Still, she remembered what he had said about not being ready to leave yet. She knew what it felt like, the sense of grasping at the last days of summer. Perhaps that was why. She somehow represented the summer to him.

She would be out of her mind to go. It would be asking to be hurt. She might as well stick her hand over a lit Bunsen burner. It wasn't as if *she* wanted to hold on to this long, lonely summer. She wanted to forget.

Cassie snatched her keys from the desk. "Erin, I have an errand to do. I'll be back in a while."

"Sure. Whatever." Erin, sounding dispirited, didn't even look up from the specimen tanks.

Cassie found her car in the crowded lot and tossed her lab coat on the passenger seat. There hadn't been a problem parking at six this morning, but she would have a hard time finding a space for her car when she came back. She drove carefully around the blind corner at the Marine Fisheries Aquarium, watching for children who often ran out heedlessly into the street in front of the seal pen. When she saw the guard booth at Penzance Point, she almost lost her nerve and turned around. But apparently she looked familiar enough to the guard, and he waved her through.

She stopped the car in the circular driveway of Scott's house. Her hand rested on the keys in the ignition. Did she really want to do this? It was completely unlike her. She looked uncertainly at the house. Calder was standing in the doorway. He must have heard her drive up.

She had come too far to back down now. Opening the car door, she made her way up the steps to the deck where he was waiting for her. He was watching her unsmilingly again, leaving her dizzy, her skin charged with electricity. She stopped directly in front of him.

It was like the morning all over again. There was no discussion, no slow, subtle approach, no flirtation, just his hands on her waist and sliding down to her hips. Her body had no uncertainties.

Without releasing her, Calder closed the door behind them. His hands went directly for the zipper of her casual sundress, then inside it, caressing her skin as if it were fine porcelain. She shivered with desire, wanting him to touch her in all the intimate ways he had before, to take her to the point where she didn't have to think anymore or ask herself why she was doing this.

Within minutes their clothes were scattered on the floor. Cassie held her hand out to him and then sank down on the plush carpet in front of the fireplace. He kissed her fiercely, pressing her shoulders back until she lay flat, where he could explore her body at will. His mouth at her breast and his hand between her legs, he built the tension in her to the breaking point as she arched and moaned and then he murmured something incomprehensible in her ear as he brought her back with powerful surges of pleasure. This time he had a condom, and she helped him roll it on before they made love with a fierce passion, right there on the floor, then again later in his bed, in the impersonally modern room whose only sign of his presence was a scattered pile of books on the bedside table. He seemed determined to give her no chance to reconsider; he would lie spent in her arms for only a few minutes before putting his fingers and mouth to work again on destroying her rationality.

When finally she stopped him, his muscles grew lax, and then he touched her lips. "Wait," he said, standing and padding over to the bathroom.

She watched after him and then heard running water. Calder was outdoing himself at taciturnity; he had said hardly a word since her arrival, but it didn't bother her. She didn't want to talk either. Now that it was over and she was out of his arms, she was embarrassed to face him. She pulled the expensive sheet over her, wondering how she could end this gracefully.

He returned and held out his hand to her. It was easier to take it and follow him to the ornate bathroom than to think. Steaming water poured into the sunken whirlpool that dominated one corner. She turned a questioning look on him, almost immediately distracted by the sight of his body, his shoulders tapering into the length of his torso, the quiet solidity that made her want to hold him again.

He stepped down into the tub, frothy bubbles swirling around him, and reached out for her. She followed him into the shockingly warm water, her legs tingling as she stepped into his arms. She could feel his chest moving with slow, deep breaths as he held her with an intimacy more sensual than seductive.

He sat on the molded side, bringing her with him so she rested on his lap. The tub was deep enough that the swirling water came almost to her shoulders, and Cassie relaxed into the soothing tranquility of it, resting her head on his shoulder. "This is the life," she said.

He caressed her forehead and her cheeks with his lips. "I've wanted to do this."

She wondered vaguely if he meant he had wanted to do it with her or with any woman. Probably the latter, but she didn't want to think about that. She wanted to savor the rare luxury of being held, of the warmth of another human body close to her own.

But time was passing. She must have been there more than an hour by now. She stirred in his arms. "I should get back."

“Not yet.” He nuzzled her hair.

She didn’t know how to read his tone; it wasn’t a command yet somehow not a request either. “A few minutes, then.”

He didn’t move, seeming content to remain where they were indefinitely. She might have been, too, except for her concern about Erin. “Is Scott going to break up with Erin once she goes back to Duke?”

His hand slid down to her thigh as he considered the question. “I don’t know. He’s attached to her, but he doesn’t like long-distance relationships.”

Poor Erin. “Nobody does, I suppose.”

“He doesn’t usually have to wait for what he wants.”

She imagined the same applied to Calder. Perhaps he was trying to warn her not to expect anything from him, which she supposed was thoughtful in a way, even if completely unnecessary. She had no illusions that he would even remember her name in a year or two.

The embrace that had felt so comforting a few minutes earlier suddenly became claustrophobic. She rose to her feet, the cool air raising goosebumps on her wet skin. “I really should go. She’s probably upset.”

He said nothing, only followed her out of the tub and draped an oversized, fluffy spa towel over her shoulders before donning a white terrycloth bathrobe.

She wondered what he was thinking of her. Feeling uncomfortably exposed, she wrapped the towel around herself and went downstairs with him to find their clothes. She stepped into her sundress and reached around to raise the zipper, but Calder forestalled her by doing it for her. It made it easier, whatever the strange feeling was that came over her whenever he touched her. But the moment his hands left her back, reality returned again and the embarrassing moment before her.

She smoothed her hair with her fingers and noticed his eyes were fixed on her again. "Why do you always watch me like that?"

He looked puzzled at the question. "Because I like to."

She wondered if that was the explanation for this encounter as well, but she wasn't about to ask. Instead, she tried to pretend a confidence she didn't feel and sauntered over to him to kiss him. "Bye."

He put his arms around her. She rested her head on the thick terrycloth of his bathrobe, feeling lassitude slip over her again. If someone ever discovered a way to bottle essence of Calder Westing, she would be an addict. Carefully, she stepped away.

"Bye," he echoed.

She knew better than to expect more than one word. Somehow she found the reserve to smile impudently before she opened the door and walked out of his life.

She didn't look back, not when she reached the car, and not when she pulled out of the driveway and left Penzance Point for the final time. Next year there would be a new guard who wouldn't wave her through. But that was all right. She didn't belong on Penzance Point anyway. Million-dollar houses and sunken bathtubs for two had nothing to do with her.

The MBL lot was full, so she took the excuse to drive back to the cabin. She could bike to the lab from there, and Erin could live without her that long. It would give her a few more minutes to get used to the idea that she had deliberately had casual sex with a man she barely knew and would never see again.

She parked beside the cabin and went in through the weathered doorway to the knotty pine interior. It was only a few steps into the bathroom, where she took the brush from the small vanity and ran it through her hair. But something was different when she looked in the mirror. She could smooth out her hair and pull it back, but there was nothing to be done about the pain in her eyes.

No. It hadn't been casual sex. It wasn't about love or even friendship, but it had meant something to him. Pleasure hadn't been his sole object, she was certain of that. She wondered if he also needed to forget something, but she couldn't imagine what a man like Calder Westing would ever need to forget.

Chapter 7

CASSIE WAS ALL BUSINESS when she returned to Haverford, settling into her apartment and getting ready for a new semester to begin. The campus, a pastoral expanse of trees and lawns in the Philadelphia suburbs, seemed unchanged from when she left in May. In some ways it was as if summer had never happened, as if her Woods Hole life was somehow separate from her Haverford life.

The routine of the new semester was comforting—getting to know a new group of students, training lab assistants, and preparing lectures. She was glad to return to her friends among the faculty as well, friends whose lives had nothing to do with any of the events of the summer.

Sometimes late at night her thoughts would return to Calder Westing. Now that she no longer needed to struggle to keep her distance from him, she could replay in her memory the astonishing night they had spent together, that last afternoon, and the remarkable ease and comfort she found in his arms. She could still see the way he looked at her when he touched her, and how he made her need him deep inside. Without any particular intention, he became a regular inhabitant of her fantasies.

She kept her thoughts very private. She never mentioned him to Erin in her daily emails. But at the end of September, Cassie noticed nearly a week had gone by since she had heard from her friend.

Concerned, she decided to call her. After several rings, Erin answered with an almost disturbing eagerness. When she realized it was Cassie, her voice fell a little.

"Hey, how are you?" Cassie asked.

"I'm okay."

Cassie knew immediately from her tone she was nothing of the sort. "No, you're not. I can tell." There was a long silence on the other end. "Erin? Are you still there?"

"Yes." Erin's voice was choked, and Cassie realized she was crying silently.

"What's the matter, sweetie? What happened?" Cassie had a sinking feeling she knew the answer.

"He broke up with me."

Slowly Cassie managed to piece together the story from the bits Erin told her. Scott had come to visit her at Duke about two weeks earlier, and everything seemed fine, but after he went back to Boston, his emails started to come more and more irregularly. Finally, Erin asked him straight out in an email if something was wrong, and after several days she received his response. He had decided that it wasn't going to work out for them; he didn't believe in long-distance relationships, he was too busy at work to have time for a social life, and their lives were too different. Erin, devastated, hadn't responded and had heard nothing since.

"I would have moved to Boston in a minute if he'd asked me to. I could have found some sort of job."

"I can't believe that was really the issue. He knew all along you weren't from Boston."

"I was an easy summer romance, the pretty blonde in his bed, just like his father thought. I wish he'd been honest about it. I was always at his house in Woods Hole. He never saw the reality of my life—that I live in an ordinary apartment I clean myself, eating ordinary food I cook myself. It's not as romantic as a beautiful mansion on the ocean. I was a fool to think it was anything more."

"I'm so sorry." So Scott had only been interested in Erin for as long as the relationship didn't require any work. "Maybe I should come down this weekend, and we can have some time together."

Erin didn't answer immediately. "Thanks, Cass, but no. I love you, but having you here would just remind me even more of him."

"Are you sure?" she asked anxiously, but finally allowed herself to be convinced.

She called Erin frequently after that, hoping to hear an improvement in her voice. Usually Erin bounced back relatively quickly after her romantic disappointments, but this was different. Still, a month later, when she told Cassie she had withdrawn her applications to biotech companies and was instead concentrating her job search on secondary education, Cassie was horrified.

"You can't do that!" she exclaimed. "You've worked too hard to settle for that!"

"It's what I have to do." Erin's grim resolution was new to her. "I'm sorry you're disappointed in me, but it's the right thing for me."

"I'm not disappointed. I'm worried you're making a decision in haste that could hurt you in the long term. You'll find something in biotech. Just give yourself time."

There was a pause. "I don't need time. Cambridge Biotech made me an offer last week, for the position I interviewed for in August. I turned it down."

***

Cassie had already lost Tim in the Crowley mansion. It was decorated with swags of Christmas greenery and hundreds of candles, just as it was every year, the candlelight lending a romantic air to the elegantly clad guests circulating through the rooms.

He had been right beside her a few minutes earlier, chatting with a tall blond man. Cassie had turned to take a glass of wine from a tray proffered by a uniformed servant, and when she looked back, he was gone. She hoped his mother wouldn't notice, since she was determined to think Cassie visited Tim every Christmas because of a romantic involvement, despite all the evidence to the contrary. Otherwise she might have to believe her son when he told her his interests lay in a distinctly different direction.

Still, it wouldn't hurt if Cassie moved on to another room. There would be plenty of congenial company elsewhere, and she might finally find Dave and Ann Crowley. She always enjoyed the convivial company of the older couple, even if they were Tim's friends rather than hers.

As she moved into the next room, she caught sight of a familiar form. She felt a lurch within her at the memory of Calder Westing, but it was just her overactive imagination at work. He couldn't possibly be there. Still, she found herself glancing over in the direction of the unknown man until he turned enough that she could see his face. Her breath caught. It *was* him. A sudden memory of that night at the beach came to her, and she felt herself blushing.

Fortunately, he hadn't seen her, and she began to edge away. She wasn't precisely sure why she wanted to avoid him, beyond a vague thought he would question her presence there, or that somehow he might know just how often he had crossed her mind since their last meeting in August.

She made her escape successfully to the living room but didn't find Tim there—only a group of older women sitting close together and gossiping. Feeling out of place, she continued into the dining room, and then the hallway, where she found herself face to face with the very man she was trying to avoid.

The look on his face bespoke his astonishment at finding her there. Astonishment and no particular pleasure, at least as far as she could see.

"Cassie Boulton," he said slowly.

His deep voice stirred memories in her, but she wouldn't be intimidated by his presence. Raising an eyebrow mockingly, she said, "Calder Westing. We both get full points for excellent memory for names."

"What are you doing here?"

As if it was against the law for her to show up at a fancy party! "As it happens, I was invited. But you needn't worry. I know how to mind my manners in polite company, and I even washed my hands before I came. You can always pretend not to know me if I commit some terrible faux pas. And what are *you* doing here?"

His eyes moved down her body, making her feel hot inside. "The Crowleys are old friends of mine. I'm spending Christmas here. Running away from home, if you like. Is your family from this area?"

"No, I'm just visiting. I don't get done with work until just before Christmas, with grades being due. It's too complicated to travel a long way on Christmas Eve, so I usually spend it with friends here." She felt like she was babbling. She tried to ignore the part of her brain that wanted to find out if he still smelled like evergreens and dark spice, to feel his skin under her fingertips.

A well-dressed older man came past and nudged Calder in the arm. "Westing, you lucky devil, you managed to catch a pretty one! All I found under the mistletoe this year was Mildred Samuelson." He pointed above them.

Cassie's eyes traveled upward to discover the sprig of mistletoe in the arch above them. She brought her hand up as if to hold Calder at bay and said quickly, "There's no need. It's just an accident of timing."

"Can't break with tradition, can you, Westing?" the older man said with a broad wink.

Calder smiled slowly and said in a tone of discovery, "You're right. I *am* a lucky devil."

She felt mesmerized as his fingers touched her cheek gently. Slowly, he leaned toward her until his lips caressed hers gently, and in a rush of sensation, she was transported back to the last time she had felt his kiss. He took advantage of her moment of weakness to tease her lips apart with his tongue.

Desire raced through her as he gently explored her mouth, drawing an undeniable response from her. Nothing had changed. Despite everything, he still had that unique power to arouse her.

She was so caught up in the pleasure of his lips on hers that she hardly noticed his arms going around her. Nothing could be more natural than for her to slip her arms around his neck. He groaned softly against her mouth as their bodies finally met, and she understood perfectly. The feeling of his body against hers sent an electric current of desire through her, fueling the ache deep within her where she had felt empty for months. With a sigh of pleasure, she arched against him, luxuriating in the feeling of his body pressing against her breasts.

Their tongues danced in an age-old manner, familiar from memories she had replayed so often, but with a new life. Finally, he released her lips, leaving her looking at him breathlessly. His hand lightly caressed her lower back, each movement creating a greater need in her.

It took an effort to remember where they were and how inappropriate this was. At least the older man had disappeared, probably embarrassed by their display. With a sense of shock, she realized how very close she was to giving him whatever he wanted, all for a kiss under the mistletoe she had tried to avoid.

It must be temporary insanity. With a touch of panic, she disentangled herself from Calder. How humiliating to discover she could still fall into his arms like that! Determined to hide how profoundly he had affected her, she said pointedly, "My, that's potent mistletoe."

He smiled that slow, satisfied smile that made her insides melt and reached for her again. Quickly, she stepped back and crossed her arms. "So, how is Scott these days?" she asked.

"The last I heard, he was working hard, but otherwise I believe he's fine." He paused, looking at her, and said as if as an afterthought, "How's Erin?"

Cassie lifted her chin a little. "She's as well as one can expect under the circumstances." Getting angry was preferable to feeling her attraction to him.

"Under what circumstances?"

How could he pretend not to know? She thought of the sadness in Erin's voice when they talked. In a deceptively calm tone, she said, "You know, I wouldn't have thought it of Scott. He seemed so genuine. I never guessed he was just amusing himself with her. Appearances are misleading, though. Not a lesson I'll forget quickly. Nor will Erin."

He looked taken aback at her words. Perhaps no one had ever told him before that discarded toys have feelings. And she had no intention of becoming one.

"Scott wasn't just amusing himself. He fell for Erin as hard as I've ever seen him fall, but with a little distance, he realized it couldn't work and decided it would be better to end it sooner rather than later."

"And why couldn't it work?" she asked evenly.

"They were following different paths. Don't get me wrong; I like Erin, but it wouldn't work for Scott to be involved with a woman in academia. He wants a wife who will be at home with him, not working all hours trying to get tenure. They would both have been unhappy."

Cassie forced herself to keep her breath even. "Let me guess. Being the loyal friend you are, you pointed this out to him."

"Well, we talked about it," he admitted, sounding puzzled.

Cassie had rarely been so furious, nor struggled so hard to hide it. "Well, bully for you. It's been lovely running into you, Calder, but I need to find my friends. Excuse me." She turned on her heel, not waiting to hear his response.

She hunted through the house until she finally found Tim. "Having a good time?" she asked.

One look was enough to tell him something was wrong. "Is everything all right, Cassie?"

"I . . . I'm just feeling a little headachy. Would it be all right with you if I took the car, then came back for you later?"

"Maybe I should take you."

"No, please don't bother. I just need to be out of the crowd."

"If you're sure." He cast his eyes meaningfully toward the attractive man standing beside him.

Cassie managed a strained smile. "I'm sure."

Tim gave her the keys, assuring her he could find a ride home. Cassie, glancing at the blond man, suspected she might not see him until morning.

She considered finding the Crowleys to thank them for the evening but decided in favor of bad manners in case Calder might be with them. She wasn't sure if she could remain civil to him. To kiss her like that, and then show no shame whatsoever about what he had done to poor Erin!

On the other hand, he had no reason not to think she would jump into bed with him the moment he touched her. After all, she'd done it twice already. Easy. That was the word for women like her. He was probably used to women who would do anything he wanted.

She asked a servant for her coat and was just putting it on when she heard an all-too-familiar voice at her side.

"You're not going already?" Calder asked.

"I have a headache." And he had caused it.

"I'm sorry to hear that. Can I get you anything for it?"

"No, thanks. I just need some peace and quiet." She didn't like it when he was thoughtful. It made it harder to stay angry with him.

"I won't hold you up, then. But I'd like to see you again sometime."

She gave him a disbelieving look. Surely he couldn't think that, after what he had said about Erin, she would be willing to have a fling with him? Trying to sound composed, she said, "Given our propensity for running into each other unexpectedly, it's just possible you will. Goodnight, Calder."

He caught at her arm. "Please, Cassie. I mean it. I want to see you again."

"But Calder, I'm an academic, and you know what *that* would do to a relationship. I'm sorry, but you'll have to find someone else to amuse you on *this* vacation." She wrapped her scarf around her neck.

"Cassie, I can understand why you're angry, but please listen. I know it won't be easy, but we can work things out somehow. God knows I've tried to forget you, and I can't."

She was too angry even to feel the shock of his declaration. "It's too bad Scott and Erin won't ever have that chance. And guess what? Erin isn't even in academia anymore. She has a nine-to-five job developing a science curriculum for a school system out in California. She decided to stop looking for a teaching position even before she came to Woods Hole this summer. She never had the drive to try for a tenure-track position, and she knew it."

His face registered disbelief. "That's not what she told Scott."

"What was she supposed to tell him? She'd already applied for a job at Cambridge Biotech. What would that have looked like? She wanted to get the job on her own merits, not because of knowing the boss. Unfortunately, they didn't offer her the job until October, and by then it was already too late. She withdrew every single one of her applications to biotech companies, just so she would never run into him at a conference."

"I'm sorry. I had no idea."

"No, you certainly didn't! And you didn't bother to ask!"

"Cassie," he began and then paused. "Cassie, could we try starting this conversation over again? I didn't mean to make you angry."

"That's nice." She shoved her hand into a fleece glove. "But you're wasting your time. I'm not a plaything to be picked up and discarded whenever you like. Scott had what he wanted from Erin and didn't give a damn how much it hurt her. And you think I'll let you do that to me? Sorry, it's not going to work. I am *not* a rich man's toy."

He looked at her as if she had slapped him. He dropped his hand from her arm. "I'm sorry. I didn't mean . . . Never mind. There isn't any point, is there? I'm sorry to have bothered you."

His pained, withdrawn expression was almost enough to engage her sympathies; almost, but not quite, and her temper, once lost, was near unmanageable. Torn by conflicting impulses, she wrenched the door open and walked out into the night. The cold air stinging against her cheeks was a relief from the blazing heat of anger within her.

It took her a few minutes to find Tim's car among all the others. She fired up the ignition and headed down the long, winding driveway. Her eyes were burning, but it wasn't until she reached the main road and found a safe place to pull over that she leaned her head against the leather steering wheel and gave way to the luxury of tears.

Calder stood alone in the cold on the steps of the Crowley mansion, hoping against hope she would turn back. So much for second chances. As the tail lights of her car disappeared from view, he said quietly, "Merry Christmas, Cassie."

Chapter 8

CASSIE'S INITIAL FORTHRIGHT FURY with Calder gave way over the next few days to a more complex mixture of grief, anger, and self-loathing. She grieved for Erin and the derailment of her career, but she couldn't blame Calder, or even Scott, for that. Erin had done that herself with her own fears. Calder's assumption that she was his for the asking still rankled, but she turned the same bitter anger on herself when she thought of how close he was to being right; how her body and her needs had betrayed her and come close to invalidating, if not destroying, the independence she had worked so hard to build ever since she was ten years old.

As the days turned to weeks and the new semester began, she taught herself once again to put the episode from her mind. She debated whether to tell Erin about what she'd learned, but she feared the knowledge would hurt her friend even more by reminding her of what she had lost. Then she opened her email one cold February morning to a surprise.

To: cboulton@haverford.edu
From: Scott Dunstan
Subject: Erin's email address

Hi Cassie,

I hope you don't mind me bothering you like this out of the blue. I've been trying to reach Erin, but the email addy I have for her at Duke doesn't work anymore. I tried calling the biology department, but all they say is that she's no longer there. I was about to give up when I realized I could get your address from the Haverford staff directory.

So anyway, could you send me Erin's new email addy and maybe her phone number? I would appreciate it more than I can tell you.

I hope you're having a great year. Maybe I'll see you this summer in Woods Hole!

Scott

Cassie debated what to do. It would be easy enough to forward it on to Erin and let the choice be hers, but she didn't want to take Erin by surprise, not when she herself was still hurting from the shock of seeing Calder at the Christmas party.

Had Calder told Scott about Erin's new job? She wanted to pretend it would be beneath him, but she couldn't forget his look of bewilderment when she lost her temper with him and the times in their acquaintance when he seemed to possess human feelings and failings—the night in the lab when he told her about his uncle, his fear for her safety in the water, and the sex. She wouldn't dignify it with the name of making love—no, it had been little more than physical gratification—but she couldn't deny that he was a considerate and tender lover, as interested in her pleasure as his own. He might well have talked to Scott after the party. It shouldn't matter to her whether he had or not, but it did.

Erin sounded tired and subdued when Cassie finally reached her that evening. Cassie took a deep breath. "Erin, sweetie, I have something to tell you, and I don't know if it's going to upset you or please you, so I hope you're sitting down."

Erin said, "You're not getting married, are you?"

"Far from it. The only offer I've had in ages was for a hot holiday fling—marriage wasn't in the picture, believe me. No, this is about you."

"Okay. Maybe you'd better tell me then."

"I got an email from Scott today. He's been trying to reach you and wanted me to send him your new email address."

There was silence on the line. Finally Erin said faintly, "Did you?"

"No; I thought I should ask you first."

There was a pause. "What did he say, exactly?"

"Do you want me to read it to you, or send it?"

"Read it. I don't want it sitting in my inbox."

Cassie read it to her as neutrally as possible and then said, "There's something else I need to tell you, too. At Christmastime I ran into Calder Westing at a party, and he said Scott broke up with you because you were too dedicated to an academic career to have time for him. I told Calder you weren't in academia anymore, and why you had said that you were. So maybe Scott has had a change of heart, if Calder told him that."

"So now that I have a job he likes, he wants me back?" Erin said, her voice shaky. "Cass . . . look, I need to think about this. I'll get back to you, okay?"

"Whatever you want. And I'm here any time you want to talk."

Last year at this time, Erin would have asked her advice and told all her feelings. Now she kept her own counsel more.

It was several days before she heard from Erin.

To: C. Boulton
From: Erin
Subject: Scott

Please tell him I said no.

To: Scott Dunstan
From: C. Boulton
Subject: Re: Erin's email address

Sorry, Scott. I talked to Erin, and she asked me not to give you her address or phone number. Wish I could help.

To: C. Boulton
From: Scott Dunstan

Please, Cassie. I feel terrible about what happened last fall. I really need to talk to her about it. Tell her I'm begging.

To: Scott Dunstan
From: C. Boulton

Scott, I'm truly sorry, but she still says no.

To: C. Boulton
From: Scott Dunstan
Isn't there anything I can do? Could I send you a letter to forward on to her? Help me, please.

To: Scott Dunstan
From: C. Boulton
Scott, all this is accomplishing is upsetting Erin even more. I'm sorry, but I'm not going to ask her any more questions on your behalf. I wish I could give you a different answer, but I don't have one.

To: C. Boulton
From: Scott Dunstan
Can I ask you just one more question, and then I promise to stop bothering you. Is she seeing someone else?

To: Scott Dunstan
From: C. Boulton
No, she isn't seeing anyone. She's still hurt about what happened between you, and I think it'll be a while before she's ready for a new relationship. I've never seen her take a breakup so hard. You were very important to her.

Give her time. She knows you want to talk to her, and how to reach you if she wants to contact you. It may just be a matter of time if you're willing to be patient.

Cassie looked at this last email for a few minutes before clicking *Send*. If Erin knew about it, she'd be upset with her for encouraging Scott. Cassie hoped he would take it in the spirit it was meant. She remembered how happy Erin had been when she was with Scott, and she hated to see her give up if there was still a chance. On the other hand, she wasn't sure patience was a virtue Scott possessed.

She didn't raise the matter to Erin again, and Erin didn't ask. Scott became a taboo subject between them, just as Calder had been. Cassie worried about her and hated feeling helpless over Erin's pain. But there was nothing she could do about it except to stay in close contact and hope that someday Erin would be willing to talk to her about her feelings again.

In March, right in the middle of midterms, Cassie received an unexpected phone call.

"Dr. Boulton, this is Ella Connors. I don't think we've met. I'm the director of finances at the MBL. I wonder if I could have a few moments of your time."

Cassie settled back in her chair. "Of course. What can I do for you?"

"I'm afraid there's a problem about your grant."

In the end, she had to cancel her classes for Monday and spent all day Sunday driving up to Woods Hole. She stayed the night in a small motel at the edge of town, nearly empty at this time of year. Woods Hole was like a ghost town. Although there were townspeople about, it was nothing compared to the crowds of summer.

The meeting in the morning with Ella Connors and the director of the MBL was short and painful. They listened sympathetically to her presentation, but facts were facts. It was little consolation to know they were impressed with her research when it didn't change the outcome.

She still had the long drive ahead to get home but couldn't quite bring herself to leave yet. On impulse she walked down to the drawbridge in town. Leaning her arms against the rails, she looked out over the harbor as she had so many times before. The water reflected the grey of the sky. It looked different without the forest of masts that usually filled it in warmer weather. She shivered a little in the raw March wind but didn't move. It would be full of boats again this summer, but she wouldn't be there to see it. Tears pricked at her eyes and began to run down her face.

"Cassie?" An unexpected voice spoke her name almost disbelievingly.

She dabbed quickly at her cheeks before turning to face him. "Calder—this is a surprise." She couldn't even bring herself to care that he was seeing her in this state.

"For a minute I thought you were a figment of my imagination." He was torn between an odd pleasure in seeing her and concern over what could possibly cause Cassie Boulton to be crying in the middle of the street. "Is something wrong?"

"No, I just . . . the view is very different than it is in the summer." She looked over the water again, tears pooling in her eyes.

He frowned. "It's too cold to talk out here. Let's get a cup of coffee and warm up."

Calder was the last person she expected sympathy from. Her voice was shaky as she said, "Thank you, but I can't. I was just about to leave, and I need to be back in Philadelphia tonight."

"Are you driving?" At her nod, he said, "I don't know what the trouble is, but I really don't think you should be driving right now. Better to leave a half hour late than have an accident on the way." She hesitated, and he added, "Please. I'll worry."

"All right," she said, her voice subdued.

"Good." He put a hand on her back to steer her across the street and into the Dock of the Bay Café, where they had been introduced so long ago. Given the season, it was empty, and they had their pick of tables. Cassie stared out the window as the waitress came over to them.

Calder waved away the menu. "I'd like a cup of coffee, please. Cassie, what would you like? Coffee, tea?"

"Coffee, please." Her voice was flat.

"Do you have pie today?" asked Calder.

The waitress nodded. "Apple, blueberry, or peach."

"One slice of apple and one of blueberry, then," he said.

Cassie looked at him questioningly.

"The first time we came here, you said you liked the pies," he said, a little defensively. "And I like both of those, so you can have whichever you prefer."

"I never knew you had such mother hen instincts." She sounded a little more like herself. "But what if I said I wanted peach?"

He smiled. "Then I'd get that, too."

Their coffee arrived. "So, what are you doing here?" She wrapped her hands around the cup. Her fingers were pale from the cold.

He hesitated. "I was doing a little writing when I was here last summer, and I came back for a while to see if I could get re-inspired," he said self-deprecatingly. "And what about you? More research?"

She stared at the table. "No, there were some problems about my funding for the summer. I came to see if we could clear them up."

"And were you able to?"

She paused to add a generous amount of cream to her coffee. "No," she said. She hoped he wouldn't ask questions.

"What happened?"

"Politics. The National Science Foundation had its funding slashed by the president. He'd rather fund his little wars than basic research. So NSF had to cut *their* funding to MBL. I'm one of the most junior researchers there, so my project was axed." She took a sip of her coffee. Seeing the closed expression on his face, she realized how tactless she had been. The president wouldn't have been elected without the backing of the Westing family prestige and money. "Sorry, I shouldn't have said that about the president."

He grimaced slightly. "Don't worry about it. I don't agree with my father on everything, and you're entitled to your opinions. Especially right now." He paused. "Are there other funding options?"

"It's too late for this year. I can apply for a new fellowship for next year, but I won't be as likely to get it if I'm not here this summer." She took a deep breath. "It'll be fine. I'll stay at Haverford for the summer and work on writing up the results I have, I suppose." She wanted to sound as if it didn't bother her, but her voice was quavering a little. "I'll just miss being here."

"You've been coming here for a long time, haven't you?"

"Since I was in college. It's been the big constant in my life. Some people have a home and family; I have Woods Hole and the MBL."

"You don't have a family to go home to?"

Her lips twisted into a wry smile. "Oh, I have a family; the question is whether I want to go home to them. You'd probably call them poor white trash, except they're from the South Side of Chicago. I'm the first one in the family to graduate from high school. My mother isn't really sure what a PhD is, or that marine biology has anything to do with the ocean, or why I'd waste time and money going to college when I could have found some nice boy and been married with two children before I was twenty. Needless to say, we don't have a great deal to talk about. I don't go home often."

"It's a little difficult to picture you in a setting like that."

She was surprised as well; she had expected a more negative reaction from him. What had inspired her to tell him? Even Erin didn't know that much. She supposed Calder was a safe enough choice to confide in. They had few acquaintances in common, and one of the few things about him she was certain of was that nobody would ever accuse him of talking too much. She glanced down for a moment and then looked up at him mischievously. "They've probably never even heard of your family."

"They may be fortunate in that."

She was unsure if he was serious or not until he smiled at her, and then she couldn't help laughing. "Perhaps so."

The waitress came over with their pies. "Who gets which?" she asked brightly. Calder glanced at Cassie.

"I'll have the apple," said Cassie with rueful amusement.

The waitress set the pies in front of them but lingered at the table as if expecting something else. After a moment, she said, "Excuse me, but we were talking back in the kitchen. Are you Calder Westing?"

"Guilty as charged," he responded with a polite smile.

"Oh, wow!" she said. "I heard you were here last summer, but I didn't know you were back. Can I have your autograph?"

Cassie expected Calder to go into his abrupt, monosyllabic mode, but instead he agreed pleasantly. "What's your name?"

The girl blushed. "Jessica."

He scribbled on the piece of paper she handed him. Cassie could read the words: "To Jessica, with best wishes from Calder Westing." The waitress thanked him profusely and hurried back to the kitchen with her prize.

Calder glanced at Cassie, then looked away. "Sorry." He seemed to be speaking to the view out the window. "I find that kind of thing pretty embarrassing. It's not as if I've done anything to deserve it, except for being my father's son."

Cassie sipped her coffee, puzzled by the difference from the man who had a tantrum the previous summer over being recognized in the same restaurant. "You were very nice to her."

He looked back at her. "That's Scott's doing. He finally managed to convince me that it's better to give in gracefully than to fight it, even if I hate it."

Cassie tried not to think of her embarrassing loss of temper the last time Scott's name had come up between them. "You made her very happy. Surely that's worth something."

"That's what Scott keeps saying," he said. Cassie noticed his cheeks were flushed. "How are things at Haverford?"

"Busy. My three-year review comes up in May, so I'm working on my file for that, on top of the usual work."

"Is this review important?"

"Oh, yes. It's when they decide whether to renew my contract or let me go, and they'll give me the first feedback on how I'm doing on the road to tenure. It's anxiety provoking, to say the least."

"I can't imagine you'd have any troubles."

"I hope not, but you never know." She took a last bite of her pie. "But now I really do need to be going." She wasn't looking forward to the hours in the car with no company but her own.

"Where are you parked?"

"Over in the MBL lot, not far. Right by my old lab." She smiled sadly.

"Let me settle up here, and I'll walk you back."

"You don't have to do that," objected Cassie automatically, reaching for her bag. "You must have been on your way somewhere."

"No place important." He leveled a stare at her as she opened her wallet. "You're not going to embarrass me in front of my legions of fans, are you?"

She looked at him for a moment and smiled impishly. "All right, but only for the sake of your fans." She watched as he dropped several bills on the table, probably twice what they owed. She hoped his fans appreciated it.

There was a moment of awkwardness when they arrived at her car, as if neither was sure how they should part. Finally Calder said, "Thanks for putting up with me delaying you. Can I ask you to send me an email when you get home, just so I know you got there safely?" He fished a card out of his pocket and gave it to her.

"What, no autograph?" she teased.

With an amused look, he took the card back from her and wrote a few words on the back and then tucked it in her shirt pocket. "Have a good trip," he said.

"Thanks. And thanks for the tea and sympathy."

"Any time." He watched her get into her car. She turned once to wave as she drove off.

Cassie took the back roads to Route 28. Watching the familiar scenery go by, she was once again saddened by the prospect of not returning this summer. If she thought about it too long, she would start to cry again, so she deliberately diverted her mind to consideration of Calder Westing. It was surprising enough they had managed to have a completely civil conversation, but the change in his manner when he talked to the waitress was remarkable.

Thinking of it reminded her of the card he had given her. She hadn't wanted to admit that she still had his card from the previous summer as a sort of memento. She had meant several times to throw it away, but something stopped her each time, so it continued to reside in her wallet. Shaking her head at her own foolishness, she pulled the new card out of her pocket and glanced down to see what he had written on the back.

To Cassie, with fond memories
of my very favorite trip to the beach.
Calder Westing

She felt a rush of heat run through her, embarrassed to discover he was thinking about it when they were together. Her embarrassment was quickly replaced by other feelings, though, as her body remembered his and the pleasure he had given her. She had a sudden mad impulse to turn back to Woods Hole and find him. The very image of throwing herself at him was enough to make her laugh, and she managed to make herself put the card back in her pocket and focus on her driving. But she could feel its presence against her body, lying over her breast like the touch of his hand.

It was after midnight when she finally arrived back at her apartment. She went to the refrigerator for a cold drink and then remembered Calder's request. She booted up her computer, thinking carefully about what to say. She took out his card again to read off his email address.

To: scw3@scwf.org
From: C. Boulton
Subject: home safe
Dear Calder,

As you can see, I managed to arrive home without alarming an undue number of state troopers. Thanks again for the pie.

Cassie

The next day Cassie grimly began to revise her plans for the summer, going through her data from the last three years to see where there might be more room for analysis. She spoke to one of her colleagues about using space in the main lab during the summer months and began to investigate what it would cost to transport some specimens down from the Cape. She could do some of the simpler work at Haverford. It would be slower without access to the more advanced equipment at the MBL, but it would be progress of a sort.

By the end of the week, she had her preliminary plans made. She refused to look back at what could have been, a skill which had always served her well. Even Erin, who understood better than anyone else how much this loss would hurt her, refrained from offering sympathy; she recognized Cassie was ignoring her own pain.

To: C. Boulton
From: C. Westing
Subject: Re: home safe

Glad you managed to avoid causing too much trouble on your way home. I would feel sorry for any poor state trooper who tried to stop you!

Calder

Cassie smiled a little as she read the message and marked it to save.

Chapter 9

TWO WEEKS AFTER HER return to Haverford, Cassie received a voicemail from Ella Connors at the MBL. She was tempted to put off making the call until later, knowing it was likely the expected denial of her appeal, but forced herself to do it right away.

"Cassie!" came Ella's energetic voice when she identified herself. "I've got some good news for you."

"Good news?" she asked cautiously, afraid to raise her hopes.

"It looks like we're going to have funding for you after all. We've been shifting some money around, and we should be able to offer you an unrestricted one-time grant."

"Really?" Cassie could hardly believe her ears.

"Looks pretty definite at this point. Hopefully we'll be able to get paperwork off to you next week, but in the meantime, we're holding your lab space unless you tell us otherwise."

Cassie couldn't stop smiling. "No, please hold it. I'll be there, you can count on that."

To: C. Westing
From: C. Boulton
Subject: good news

Just wanted to let you know I had some good news from the MBL today. I don't know how they did it, but they've managed to find some funding for me this year, so it looks like I'll be wading through the muck in the marshes again this summer after all. Sorry to have cried on your shoulder over what turned out to be nothing, but you know me. I'll do almost anything for a good slice of apple pie.

To: Cassie Boulton
From: C. Westing
Subject: Re: good news

Glad to hear you'll be going back. Hope you'll eat plenty of squid for me. And you're welcome to cry on my shoulder any time. By the way, I really do like blueberry best.

***

Cassie felt a particular poignancy in her arrival at Woods Hole for the summer. Instead of rushing straight to the lab to get started, she spent her first day walking up and down Water Street, stopping in the bookstore, enjoying the scent of the beach roses in the town garden, and sitting at Stony Beach looking out over the water.

She had hired one of her students from Haverford to be her lab assistant, and he was as excited and starry-eyed at having a taste of real science at the MBL as she had been her first summer.

Chris was a tireless worker, leaving Cassie more time for analysis and writing up her paper, and he also had an entertaining, quick wit. Watching him, she remembered how much more there was to experience at the MBL than she had taken advantage of in the last few years. She began to take time to learn about other people's research and attend more of the lectures and seminars offered by the MBL.

She made a point of taking a walk each day, sometimes around Eel Pond, sometimes through town, and sometimes along the edge of Buzzard's Bay. When she walked along the bay, she would see Penzance Point, once again forbidden territory, and wonder what had happened to Scott. Was he again spending the summer there, or had he made other plans? She was curious enough to go onto the internet once to check if he had sold the house but found nothing.

One benefit had come from her brief association with Calder Westing. Rob was spending the entire summer at the MBL, and to Cassie's surprise, the news didn't particularly trouble her. A year of being haunted by Calder had allowed her to put that pain behind her.

One day in July, Scott appeared unexpectedly at her lab. It took her a moment to work out what was different about him. He was dressed in a t-shirt and jeans that looked like they were off the rack, unlike the casual but expensive clothes he had worn the summer before. He seemed uncomfortable with Chris in the room. Saying he could only stay a minute, he asked whether she'd like to have lunch sometime. She agreed, with a bit of trepidation, and arranged to meet him the next day.

"Where do you want to go?" he asked.

She hesitated a moment. She almost always went to the Dock of the Bay Café when she ate out, but that might be too full of ghosts for both of them. "How about Shuckers, at noon?"

"Noon it is."

This left her a day to wonder why he wanted to see her. She hoped he wasn't going to ask questions she couldn't answer about Erin. But once they met, he seemed only interested in hearing about her year and her research, at least until the waiter took their orders.

Finally, he looked at her rather sheepishly. "I suppose you think I asked you to lunch so I could pump you for information about Erin."

"The thought did cross my mind."

"You're right, then." He played with his drink for a minute. "I've tried being patient, but it's been five months, and not a word from her. I'm not good at patience. It's been hard."

"I'm sorry. I wish I knew what to say."

"Can you just tell me about her, how she is, what she's thinking, that kind of thing?" His voice was pained. Cassie could see how much he hated having to ask.

"I can't tell you where she is, or how to reach her."

"I already know. She's working for the Sacramento Metropolitan School District as a consultant."

Cassie looked at him in surprise. "You said she hadn't been in touch with you."

His mouth twisted wryly. "She hasn't. After you wouldn't tell me, I had someone find her." In response to her suspicious look, he added quickly, "Don't worry; I'm not stalking her or anything. I couldn't stand not knowing where she was. It was making me crazy. There wasn't any snooping into her personal life, I promise you. And I've respected her desire not to hear from me."

"That was wise of you." She suspected Erin would be furious if she knew he'd done that much.

"If so, it's the only thing I did that was wise. Last summer I thought I was happy because I was finally taking some time off. I didn't realize it was her. I've dated a lot of women, but frankly, I wasn't all that interested in their minds, and they weren't interested in much besides my money. I picked out Erin because she was pretty. It was just dumb luck that she was also someone I could talk to, who understood about my job, the problems in the biotech industry, research issues. I liked that. When I figured out she didn't care about my money, I liked that, too. But even then I didn't understand. I hated it when she went back to Duke, and I decided it was because I didn't like long-distance relationships. When I finally came to my senses, I realized it was . . . other things, and that Erin was what I wanted."

"At least now that she's not in academia anymore." Cassie hoped she didn't sound as bitter as she felt.

His mouth twisted. "I hated Duke, no doubt about that. Everyone there treated me like I was a dunce because I was in business, not pure research. They wouldn't even let me in the labs to see Erin because they thought I would mess something up. I go into biotech labs every day, for God's sake."

So he hadn't liked being a second-class citizen. He looked so put out she almost laughed. "That's not why they wouldn't let you in, you know. They were probably working on projects they hoped would have commercial applications and didn't want somebody to beat them to it. None of them would be above selling you a finished product."

He leaned back in his chair. "Did Erin tell you that?"

"She didn't need to. I know academics. It was a big deal when Erin applied for the job at Cambridge Biotech. Duke would have made her sign all kinds of waivers before she left."

"She applied for a job at Cambridge Biotech?"

"It was before she met you. They finally offered it to her in October."

"Did Calder know? He never said anything about that."

That answered one question. "He talked to you, then."

"Read me the riot act is more like it. He said I should stop trying to convince everyone I was more successful and more white than my father and start thinking about what I wanted for myself." He took a long swig of his beer and looked over Cassie's shoulder for a moment as if fascinated by the view of the water.

Cassie made a decision. "She's going to be here in three weeks."

"Erin?" He sounded like a man just granted a reprieve. "Here in Woods Hole?"

The waiter appeared with their food, placing a salad in front of Cassie. "She's coming to visit."

She could see the change in the set of his shoulders as a look of determination crossed his face. He was silent, clearly considering the possibilities, and Cassie could see him as the successful businessman he was. Erin might be surprised by what she would face when she came.

"And how is Calder?" She tried to sound casual.

Scott sliced off a piece of steak. "He's insane."

She couldn't imagine anyone ever describing Calder Westing as insane. "Because he read you the riot act?"

"Not that. His new book is finally in press, and that always makes him crazy. He was driving his agent nuts, staying up all night doing rewrites when it was supposed to be in final editing, and then demanding that they hold to the same printing date. He's always frantic before one of his books comes out, but this is worse than usual. Now he's just hiding out. Personally, I can't wait for the damned thing to be published so he gets back to normal."

Cassie said slowly, "I didn't know he wrote books. I think he said something once about writing, but I thought it was just for his own pleasure or something." She had believed she knew Calder, at least a little. Discovering he had an entire side she knew nothing about was more distressing than she would have expected.

Scott stopped with his fork halfway to his mouth. "You didn't? You'd better forget I said anything. He's very private about his writing. Not many people know about it, but I was *sure* he must have told you. There was something, I can't remember what . . ." He paused for a moment. "No, I remember. He said you liked his books."

"He did?" Cassie was completely bewildered. "But I've never read them. I didn't even know he wrote until you told me just now. I still don't know *what* he writes."

"Novels. He writes under a pseudonym—Stephen West. He's reasonably well known for them in certain circles."

Cassie stared at him. "You're joking," she said flatly.

"No, not at all. You can find his books at any bookstore."

"I know that. I've read them. Oh, God, and he's right. I did talk to him about them, but I never knew he wrote them. Now I feel like an idiot." She had lost all interest in her food.

"Oh, please don't! How were you supposed to know? He keeps it such a secret. He says he wants to be seen as a writer, not 'the Westing who writes.' And his family isn't precisely happy about him writing, so it works out for them, too."

"Why would his family be unhappy about it? The books get excellent reviews," she argued, still trying to grasp the idea of Calder as one of her favorite authors. She remembered how he had loaned her the latest book—*his* latest book—without a hint of having a connection to it.

"It's not the kind of thing Westings are supposed to do. His father gets livid if you even mention Calder's books. Calder never puts dedications in his books because he'd be damned before he'd dedicate one to his family, and if he mentioned anyone else, he'd get even more grief from his father than he already does. Calder was supposed to be president, not a writer."

"President of what?" Cassie realized with embarrassment what he meant. "I guess that was a silly question. It's just so hard to imagine."

"Yes, Calder wasn't meant to be a politician."

A dry smile touched her lips. "I don't think he'd be very happy in that arena."

"Oh, God, no. I can't even imagine it. Calder getting up in front of hundreds of people and asking them to vote for him? I've never met anyone who works as hard to duck publicity as he does."

"No." Cassie pushed her food around her plate with her fork for a minute. "So he won't be visiting you this summer, then?"

"Already been and gone," he said cheerfully. "He was here for a couple of weeks in June, but he was so restless he left again. Sometimes I wonder why he puts himself through this. It's not as if he needs the money from book sales."

That was hardly the answer she had been expecting. Calder had been there and had made no effort to see her. She felt vaguely sick. Why would he have come to see her? All she had ever done was to throw him out, except for the one time she cried on his shoulder and told him all her problems. But she had imagined more from their brief emails and had hoped he thought of her with fondness. But it appeared he didn't think about her at all.

"He wasn't much company. He was always either stuck to his computer or sitting on the porch staring out at the Sound for hours at a time."

"I guess his writing process must be pretty intense," said Cassie quietly. "I take it he's not involved with anyone then?" She hadn't meant to ask, but it came out anyway.

"Not now. He's been off women for a while, though for a while there last fall he went through them faster than I could learn their names. Fast even for Calder."

Cassie took a much-needed sip of beer. "He goes through women pretty fast?" She wasn't sure she wanted to know the answer, but it was like a sore spot she couldn't resist poking at.

"Pretty much. Of course he usually isn't terribly serious about them in the first place. He never has to look for a girlfriend. There are always plenty of admiring women around him, between his name and his money. He just waits for one to come along who seems interesting and attractive, and he takes up with her. Then things go well for a few weeks, or even a few months, and then suddenly he starts getting quieter and quieter. That's how I know when the end is coming. He's very nice about it; he tells them very kindly that he's sorry, but it just isn't working out for him, and that's that." Scott took a bite of steak. "You know, there was a time last summer when I thought he was pretty interested in you."

Cassie flushed. She had forgotten Scott knew about the night they had spent together, just as Erin had. "I don't think so. I'm not exactly his type."

"No, you aren't." He gave her a sharp look.

She didn't think she could bear to talk about Calder any more. "But you wanted to hear about Erin. What more can I tell you?"

She still couldn't believe it. Stephen West's prose—no, *Calder's* prose—was marked by an unusual sensitivity and fine nuances. It was so out of keeping with the man who barely spoke and seemed so thoughtless of his impact on others. She couldn't begin to understand it. But she could make sense of one thing: she had made something out of nothing, had assumed that an odd friendship of a sort existed between them, and she couldn't have been more wrong. It was all in her head the entire time.

Chapter 10

CASSIE WAS STILL SHAKEN by Scott's revelations when she arrived back at the lab. She almost snapped at Chris when he asked about her lunch and couldn't focus when she returned to her statistical analysis. Finally, when Chris went to dinner, leaving her alone in the lab, she went to the computer and ran a search on Stephen R. West.

She found bookstores offering his books, several critical analyses of his work, and absolutely no biographical information or photographs. One review referred to him as "reclusive" and commented that he never gave interviews or did book signings. She typed in Calder Westing and immediately had dozens of sites, ones about his family in which he was mentioned as a side note, information about the Stephen C. Westing Foundation where he was a board member, society notes about what charity balls he had attended in the company of which beautiful young women, and pictures of his elegant home in Virginia.

Then there were the amateur sites, filled with photographs of him, many clearly taken without his knowledge, offering details about his life garnered from various sources. She read in shocked fascination a variety of rumors about his personal habits, his love life, the size of his fortune, and more. One site listed dates and places he had been spotted, and she was disturbed to see Woods Hole on the list, both for the summer and in March. She smiled grimly at an assertion that his family kept him out of politics to hide the fact that he was gay. None mentioned anything about writing.

How little of this she had understood before! Now she could see why he reacted badly to being recognized. She clicked back and looked again at his pictures, seeing expressions she recognized and remembering the set of his body. Not to mention his touch. But she couldn't afford to think about that now.

Cassie scrolled back to read the two emails he had sent her. Needlessly, as it turned out, since she remembered them practically word for word. With careful precision, she moved the mouse and clicked on Delete.

If only she could delete him from her mind as easily and destroy any ideas she had about whether she meant anything to him. Her first impression had been right. He had wanted sex. It was just a line when he had said at the Christmas party he couldn't forget her. He had been kind in March, but even then, what he wrote on his card had told her what he was thinking about. Sex.

Or perhaps he had meant it at Christmas when he said he wanted to see her again. But in March she had told him about her family, and in June he made no effort to see her. It wasn't hard to guess the reason. Why had she said anything to him about her past? Why, of everyone she knew, had she decided to confide in Calder Westing?

She shook her head. Instead of helping her reject Calder, this was making her feel cheap and dirty. It wasn't going to improve if she kept looking at pictures of him on the computer, so she closed the window and cleared the history for good measure. There would be no sign she had looked for him.

A distraction was what she needed. Perhaps Jim would still be around. They could talk about his project, and if he noticed anything amiss and pressed her to talk, at least he already knew about Calder. She slipped out into the corridor.

The door to Jim's lab was open, light spilling out into the hall. Cassie went in without hesitation. Not seeing Jim, she peered into his empty office and then noticed she wasn't alone. Rob was in the back of the lab, his eyes bent to a microscope. Cassie backed away, hoping to escape before he noticed her, but she was too late.

"Hi, Cassie."

"Sorry, I was looking for Jim. I'll try again later." She tried to put finality in her tone.

He swung to his feet and strolled over to her. "Anything I can help you with?"

Rob was the last person who could help her with this. Or the second to last, anyway. "Thanks, but no."

Rob cocked his head, watching her. "Something's wrong, isn't it?"

Bad luck, to run into the one person in Woods Hole apart from Jim who had some idea how to read her moods. She had been pleased her contact with Rob this summer had been civil, if distant. They even managed to converse over dinner one night at Jim and Rose's house. "No, I'm fine. Just need to get back to work."

With a mirthless half-smile, Rob said, "Whatever. Hope your evening is productive."

Cassie trudged back to her own lab. She would have to conquer this on her own. She couldn't focus enough to do serious work, so she started clearing out old samples from the refrigerator. She watched the solutions she had worked long hours on swirl down the drain and then cleaned and sterilized the containers. It was work Chris could have done, but it was all she could manage.

She didn't look up when she heard laughing voices in the hall. No one she knew was still here except Rob. But the voices stopped outside her door, and she heard Rob's voice saying, "Let's check."

There were four of them, Rob and three of the neurophysiology post-docs. Cassie straightened slowly as they came in. Rob had never set foot in her lab before. "Cassie, we're going out to the Kidd for a beer, and some of us may go to the movie afterwards. Want to come?"

"That's nice of you, but . . ."

"Or are you too busy being *faculty* to hang out with mere post-docs?"

Cassie had forgotten Rob's ability for light-hearted teasing. It had been a long time since she had gone out with a group of researchers, though she had done it often as a grad student, and even in her first year of teaching. She hadn't stopped until the summer of Ryan and Calder. Even dealing with Rob was better than thinking about Calder, and there were plenty of other people to talk to. "Why not?"

The warm wooden walls and floor of the Captain Kidd brought back years of memories for Cassie. Their group settled around a large round table in the alcove overlooking the harbor. Cassie made sure to take a seat well away from Rob. A salt breeze through the open windows teased strands of her hair loose from its practical ponytail.

Cassie had forgotten how much she enjoyed this, the talk and the laughter. The conversation shifted between individuals and the entire group, ranging from university politics to tourist bashing to the food in the cafeteria, and always coming back to science. It wasn't difficult to avoid speaking to Rob. The neurophysiologists were a sociable bunch, and several other friends of theirs joined them as the evening went on. Periodically she would remember what Rob had done to her, but it was easier to think of this as a trip back to her first years of grad school when they had been casual friends.

The pitchers of beer went around several times, with lively arguments over the merits of light and dark beer. "Real scientists drink dark beer," one of the post-docs said, eyeing Cassie's lager.

She fluttered her lashes at him. "I'm just a southern belle, after all," she said with a convincing drawl.

He laughed. "Great accent. Are you really from the south?"

Cassie shook her head. "I spent four years in North Carolina, and I'm good at accents."

"Where are you from, then?"

To Cassie's surprise, Rob stepped in. "Cassie's an incredible mimic. Come on, Cass, show them your imitation of Jim."

The others laughed as she did one imitation after another at their request. It had been years since she had done this party trick, but it came back easily. After all, the voice she used every day was nothing more than an accent she had put on in college to disguise her origins and was now habit.

She let herself be talked into going to the movie in the MBL auditorium, an old Marx Brothers film she had never seen before. It felt good to be part of a group in the dark auditorium, laughing at the slapstick on the screen, to remember there was a community at the MBL, not just researchers alone in their labs.

Cassie was still flushed with laughter as they straggled out of the auditorium after the film. It was starting to drizzle, the light pattering rain with a stiff breeze that often presaged a summer storm. One of the neurophysiologists complained he would get soaked on the walk home.

Cassie was in no hurry to leave her new friends and return to her cottage. "I can give you a ride. Anybody else need one?"

"Do you really have a car here?"

Cassie looked over her shoulder at Rob. "Yes, it's one of those *faculty* perks. Now that I'm in my third year as an investigator, I finally warrant a parking permit."

"Golden girl. Always rubbing it in." Rob's ribbing was good-natured. "I'll take a ride if you're offering."

In the end she had four passengers squeezed into her car, and she joked about providing taxi service as she dropped them at their shared houses on the fringes of Woods Hole. By chance Rob was the furthest afield of them, which didn't register with her until the last of the other post-docs stepped out of the car.

She had become more comfortable with him over the course of the evening, but it was one thing to be in a group together and another to be alone in a car in the dark.

They both kept an uncharacteristic silence, apart from the directions Rob gave her. When she pulled up in front of his apartment, he lingered before opening his door. "Thanks for coming tonight, Cassie. It was nice."

She kept her eyes straight ahead, watching the windshield wipers swish back and forth among the raindrops. "Thanks for asking me." The ease she had felt in his company was gone, replaced by the familiar sense of awkwardness and inadequacy. It had been nice while it lasted.

"I hope it helped take your mind off whatever was bothering you."

Cassie had managed to keep it at the fringes of her mind, but now it came rushing back. Calder, deceiving her about his book, listening to her praise without acknowledging it, and now what little use he had for her had passed. It wasn't worth his while to take a stroll into town to say hello, even when he had nothing else to do. Nothing else, nothing else. The refrain beat in her mind in time with the wiper blades. When had Calder gained this power to hurt her?

"Cassie? Are you okay?" Rob touched her hand as it lay on the steering wheel.

She took a deep breath and then forced a smile to her face as she turned to the other man who had once wanted her and then lost interest. "I'm fine."

He cupped his hand on her cheek and then kissed her. She froze in surprise, but then responded to the familiarity of the sensation as he traced his tongue along her lips. It was natural to kiss Rob back.

He drew back slowly, pausing just a few inches from her face. "Yeah," he said.

His voice stirred her self-protective instincts. "Rob, we shouldn't be doing this." It came out sounding more hesitant than she meant it to.

"Why not?"

"I don't do this kind of thing for old time's sake."

He kissed her again, more briefly this time, but enough to leave her wondering why she was saying one thing and doing another. "What about for the sake of starting over?"

Starting over? He couldn't mean it. Jim had hinted at a continuing interest on Rob's part, but Cassie had taken it as wishful thinking. "It was a long time ago."

Rob took her hand and squeezed it. "Can we go inside and talk about this? There are some things I'd like to tell you."

What if he had more than talking on his mind? She didn't want to have to fend him off. "Can we talk out here instead?"

"How about if I promise not to try anything? At least not much."

"If I go in, I'm only agreeing to talking." She should tell him not to kiss her again.

His mouth twisted in a self-deprecating manner. "Understood."

She opened the car door and stepped out into the pouring rain. Ducking her head, she half-ran to the apartment door, standing in the shelter of the eaves while Rob hunted for his key. He unlocked the door and held it open for her.

It was cool inside the dark apartment. As Rob flicked on the light, Cassie brushed a few drops of rain from her arms.

Rob cleared his throat. "Can I get you something to drink?"

"No, thanks." She wanted to be free to leave quickly if she needed to. Looking around the anonymously modern room, she chose the armchair over the couch. "You said you had something to tell me."

He sat across from her on the sofa, his arm resting along the back of it. For a moment he was quiet, a look of thought Cassie remembered well. "Breaking up with you was a mistake. A huge one. It wasn't what I wanted at all."

That was ridiculous. He'd engineered the whole breakup. Cassie crossed her arms, still damp from the rain. "Then why did you do it?"

"You were obsessed with that damn spawning project of Jim's. I was feeling neglected. So I thought if I threatened to end it, you'd pay attention. But you didn't even look surprised, just said you were leaving, and you'd collect your things when you found a place to live."

Cassie remembered the agonized wrenching she had felt that day, the sense that her world had suddenly lost any value. "You were trying to get a reaction out of me? Why didn't you just ask me how I felt?"

He met her eyes levelly. "I was afraid of what you'd say."

"Why? I told you often enough that . . ." Cassie couldn't bear to say the word love to him. "I find this hard to believe."

"I wouldn't lie about it. If I wanted to play games with someone, you'd be the last person I'd pick. I still need a good recommendation from Jim."

It was hard to argue with such a blatantly practical point. "Why now? Why didn't you tell me this years ago?"

"I've been thinking about it since that day in the cafeteria last summer, when I realized you did care about our relationship. Before that . . . well, I was angry. I felt like I'd never mattered to you, or you wouldn't have just walked away."

Could he really have misread her so badly for so long? Hadn't it been obvious how much she was suffering at the time, how much it hurt her every time she had to talk to him in lab as if nothing had happened? She carefully steadied her voice. "I'm sorry you had the wrong impression. I cared a lot."

"So did I."

This was moving out of control. She rose to her feet. "I think I'd better go."

"Wait." He crossed to stand in front of her and set his hands on her waist. "Is there somebody else? Is that it?"

She wasn't used to this much physical contact. "No. There's nobody else." The words were hard to say.

His lips brushed the corner of her jaw and then traveled across her face until he found her mouth. "Then why not give it a try?"

It was hard to resist his persuasion when her other choice was to remember the pain. "I don't want to get hurt again."

"Neither do I."

She let him kiss her, trying to remember the reasons this had seemed like a bad idea. "North Carolina is a long way from Philadelphia."

"University of Delaware has a good marine biology program. I could do a post-doc there and commute." He slid his arms around her, urging her closer to him.

"What about my past? I'm still not willing to talk about any of that."

His lips stopped moving along her skin. "I'm not thrilled, but I can accept it. I talked to Jim about it, and he reminded me you don't do irrational things. So if you don't want to tell me something, I'll assume you have a rational reason for it."

A rational reason. Cassie only wished she was always rational. If she were, she would never have slept with Calder, much less let herself care about him. It was certainly irrational to consider letting Rob back into her life after what had happened last time.

Or was it so irrational? Tonight was more fun than she had in a long time, and whatever their other differences, Rob understood her work in a way few other men could. And she knew him. She would never go to lunch with one of his friends and discover he had an entire life she hadn't known about.

"You don't have to say anything now. We can take it one day at a time. Commitment or no commitment, whatever you want."

"No commitment? You know I don't do that." Except with Calder, and it hadn't served her well. Perhaps it was time for her to remember Calder Westing wasn't the only man in the world.

Rob smiled. "I remember."

She leaned against him, feeling his comforting solidity. "This is very sudden."

"For you, yes. I've been thinking about it for a long time." His mouth sought out hers. "So, am I released from my promise not to try anything?"

Cassie wavered. Going home alone had no appeal, and unlike Calder, Rob wanted her. Closing her eyes, she said, "Yes."

***

Rob leaned over Chris's shoulder. "What if you limited the variable to anaerobic bacteria? Try running some quick numbers and see what you get."

"Okay." Chris erased a column of numbers and pulled out his calculator.

It was a good thing Rob's advice on Chris's research project was sound, since Cassie suspected Chris would follow his instructions if Rob told him to use the signs of the zodiac as a variable. Chris had developed a serious case of hero worship when Rob started dividing his time between Cassie's lab and Jim's. It didn't hurt that Chris's research interests dovetailed so neatly with Rob's.

She was distracted by the ringing phone. It was Scott, making sure Erin was still due to arrive on schedule.

"Now, don't go telling me your plans," Cassie told him. "I'd rather be able to plead total ignorance, thank you."

"Are you going to tell her I know she's coming?" Scott sounded anxious.

"I expect so. I'd rather be honest with her."

She had reckoned without Erin's stubbornness. She tried to raise the subject on the day Erin arrived, mentioning she had seen Scott a few weeks earlier.

"Please, Cassie, I don't want to hear this." Erin's face was frozen.

"There's just one thing I'd like to tell you, though."

"I don't want to hear about Scott," said Erin firmly, though her voice shook a little. "I don't want to talk to Scott, and I don't want to hear from Scott."

Cassie held her hands up in front of her in surrender. "Okay, not another word, then." She wondered whether she should call

Scott and warn him to stay away. She didn't know his phone number, and it would certainly not be listed. She could always email Calder for it. He had sent her another brief email, despite her lack of response to his previous one, and she had forced herself to move it to the trash file. She fought down the part of her that would welcome an excuse to be in contact with Calder again. It was simply too dangerous, and there was Rob to consider now. Scott would have to take care of himself.

Cassie returned her attention to Erin. "While we're on the subject of men you don't want to hear about, I should tell you I'm seeing Rob Elliott again."

"You're what?" Erin's horrified disbelief didn't surprise Cassie. Erin had borne the brunt of Cassie's misery after Rob broke up with her.

"He's here for the summer, and we've decided to give it another chance."

"*Why?* Didn't he hurt you enough last time?"

"It's not too serious at the moment. He can be good company."

Erin nodded, as if it made sense to her. She hugged Cassie. "It's hard to be alone, isn't it?"

Cassie swallowed hard. Her relationship with Rob wasn't about not wanting to be alone. They had a lot in common. "Yes, it is."

***

To Cassie's relief, Erin didn't show any of her doubts the next morning when Rob strolled into the lab for a quick hello. She was grateful they could be civil; Rob had worried that Erin might scare her off him. He stayed only a few minutes and then pleaded his own work and left.

Erin watched him depart. "Are you sure you know what you're doing, Cassie?"

"With Rob? We've talked about what happened last time, and I think he's grown up a lot. I'm willing to give him the benefit of the doubt." Cassie laid out microscope slides in a neat row.

"I can't forget what he did to you before. How do you know it won't happen again?"

Using an eyedropper, Cassie carefully put a drop of water on each slide. "Isn't that supposed to be my line? I thought I was the one who was always suspicious of men's motives."

Erin shook her head. "I'm done with trusting men."

Scott's voice came from the doorway behind them. "Is that for my benefit?"

Startled, Cassie squeezed the eyedropper too hard, squirting the water across a slide. By the time she had cleaned up the mess with a paper towel, Scott was standing next to them. Erin looked stunned.

"Erin, I need to talk to you."

Erin turned her face away. "I don't have anything to say to you. As you said last fall, what's over is over."

"One of the many stupid things I've said in my life. I was confused about what I wanted."

"And what I wanted didn't matter."

"Of course it mattered. I felt terrible about hurting you."

Erin looked straight at him and raised her chin. "Not terrible enough to be willing to talk about it then. You made up your mind. I was out, and that was that."

"Erin, please. I want to tell you how I've changed, not rehash the past."

"I'm not any more willing to talk about it now than you were then."

Scott's expression changed. "Is this turnabout, then?"

"No. It's that I don't trust you, and nothing you do can change that. I want you to leave."

"Erin . . ."

Cassie looked up from the microscope slides she had been examining as if a Nobel Prize depended on them. "Scott, she asked you to leave. I'm sorry."

He continued to study Erin, and for a moment Cassie was afraid he was going to be difficult. But then, without a word, he turned abruptly and left.

Chapter 11

THE END OF THE summer was rapidly approaching. Cassie began to wrap up the season's work. Chris moped around the lab for a few days until Cassie took pity on him and told him she'd be happy to have him back next summer, assuming her new grant came through. She could understand his feelings, remembering her own student days and how she had schemed to get back to Woods Hole each year.

Jim stopped by her lab one morning, a pile of papers under his arm. "Rob seems happy these days."

Cassie carefully measured the marsh water remaining in the beaker and marked down the amount. "That's good, but don't let him apply to University of Delaware yet."

"You're not as happy with him?"

She was happy enough, but Rob wanted to move too fast. "How do you find any time to do science with all this matchmaking? Everything's fine. I'm just not sure about it yet."

"Ever hear from your friend Calder again?"

"Jim!" Why did he have to mention that name to her? "Not recently."

"Just wondered." He dropped the stapled papers on the lab bench in front of her.

"What's this?" She picked it up.

"First draft of the MBL annual report."

"What about it?"

"Have a look under Major Gifts."

Suddenly nervous, she paged through to the fundraising section. There it was, among the short list of foundations and individuals donating $100,000 or more, *S. Calder Westing, III—Summer Research Fellowship Fund.* She had a sudden image of Calder's concerned face that day in March as she told him about her funding problems. And two weeks later she had received the call that the problems had been miraculously resolved. She had been so relieved she had never given any thought to how they found the money.

"Oh, God," she said. Why had he done it? Sympathy? No, sympathy was buying her a piece of pie. Guilt? At the moment, *she* was the one who felt guilty, as if she had somehow taken advantage of him without knowing it. Did he think she expected it of him? She didn't want to consider that possibility. And to think she hadn't bothered to answer his last email. What was she supposed to do now? Write him a thank you note? How could she even say thank you for a gift of that size?

"Guess he really likes Trivial Pursuit," Jim said. "Or something."

"Or something." She wondered what Jim would say if she told him Calder had been there this summer and made no attempt to contact her.

Cassie tried to focus on her work again once Jim left, but it was hopeless. She couldn't stop thinking about Calder and what he had done. It couldn't have been pure whim on his part, not given the problems it could cause him. If his father objected to him spending an evening in a biology lab, he'd have fits over Calder giving the MBL a small fortune. Finally she gave up any attempt to concentrate and told Chris she was leaving.

She started home, but on impulse stopped by the Woods Hole Public Library. Her copies of Calder's books were in Haverford, and she had avoided thinking about them ever since learning they were his. Now she felt a need to read them again.

Both books were on the shelves, as if they were waiting for her. She clutched them tightly once she had checked them out. As soon as she was home, she curled up in the worn armchair and began to read *The Edge of Tomorrow*.

It was a disconcerting experience, reading the familiar words with the unfamiliar sense of Calder associated with them. She could hardly imagine him writing some of the tender and insightful moments. She wished she could remember what Calder had said about the book that night in the car. Something about loss and redemption. She could understand now why he had been so oddly noncommittal. Another opportunity missed.

Rob called as darkness was falling. "Are you okay?" he asked.

"I'm fine." The lie came readily to her lips.

"Why did you leave without saying anything to me?"

Because she had completely forgotten his existence. She couldn't keep going like this. "I'm sorry. I don't think this is going to work for us."

"What?"

"Having a relationship. I was wrong to let it start." She had ended up in Rob's bed because she was so hurt by Calder's desertion. And now she was hurting Rob when it had been her mistake all along.

"What? Cassie, if you don't like checking in with me when you leave, that's fine. We certainly don't need to break up over it."

"It's not that. I've been thinking about it. I'm sorry." How had she ended up in this position? She, who prided herself on concern for other people's feelings, and now she was trampling all over Rob's. He'd done nothing to deserve it.

There was a silence on the other end. "Look, I'm coming over. We can talk about this then."

"It won't change anything." Cassie held the book close to her.

"I'll see you in a few minutes."

He arrived with a grim expression she had never seen before. "Now what's all this about wanting to break up? And I want some answers this time. None of your evasions."

No evasions. She supposed she owed him that much. "I said there wasn't anyone else, but that was only partly true. There was someone. He was already out of the picture, but I wasn't over him." Her hand caressed the cover of the book.

Rob didn't say anything. After a moment, he went to the refrigerator and took out a beer. He twisted off the cap. "Why is this coming up now?"

It had been almost a year to the day since Calder came to her lab, kissed her, and made her forget everything the second he touched her. "I found out today that I misjudged him. Like you misjudged me once."

He took a long swig of beer. "What are you planning to do about it?"

The blue sky on the book cover promised a deceptive calm. *The Edge of Tomorrow*, by Stephen R. West. She remembered the first time she had seen it, in the bookstore, with Calder watching her. "I don't know. Nothing, probably."

"Are you still in contact with him?" Rob dropped the beer cap in the trash can. Cassie could see the ridges it left on his palm where he had clenched it.

"No. He emailed me a few weeks ago, but I didn't answer."

"What did he say?"

"Nothing much."

The bottle clanged as he slammed it down on the counter. "*What did he say?*"

She tore her eyes away from the book and looked at Rob. "He saw squid on the menu at a restaurant, and it reminded him of me. He hoped I was getting plenty of it here."

"You don't work on squid."

"It was a joke. He's not a scientist."

"What does he do?"

A long minute passed as she considered how to answer. "He's a writer."

"You're still in love with him, I take it?"

Love. The word she had always tried to avoid using in the same thought as Calder Westing. It was so much easier to call it a fixation. "Yes. I'm sorry."

"Are you getting back together with him?"

"No. That isn't a possibility." She set the book carefully on the table beside her.

"Why?"

She shrugged. "He's rich. Famous family. High society." The corner of her mouth twitched. "Republican."

"Jesus, Cassie." He sounded disgusted. "I thought you were the one person I knew who wouldn't be impressed by money. So much for that theory."

"I don't care about his money. I don't expect I'll ever see him again."

He stared at her as if he wanted to keep fighting, and then he slapped his hand against the counter. "So what the hell does he have, then?"

Cassie expelled a long breath of air. Poor Rob. He had a right to be bitter. She had used him to forget her pain, and now she was discarding him just as Calder had discarded her. He deserved better, and instead he was paying for her mistakes.

He turned his face away when she stepped toward him. She put her hand on his shoulder. "I don't know. And I'm not evading the question. We didn't even get along particularly well."

"So you have a fantasy about this unattainable guy who sends you an occasional email about squid. Why does this have to get in the way of your real life? Why are you dumping me for someone you'll never see again?"

She let her hand drop. "I can't be involved with you when I feel this way about another man."

He paced across the room and then looked out the window. "What if . . ." He stopped, then turned back to her. "What if I'm willing to accept that you have a thing for him? Since you won't see him again, it shouldn't matter."

This time Cassie was the one to look away. "That wouldn't be fair to you. You deserve better than that, and you'd end up resenting me for it."

"*Don't* tell me what's fair for me. This sure as hell isn't."

"I'm sorry. I can't tell you how much I wish I'd understood this before you became involved."

Rob dropped heavily into a chair and rubbed his hand across his forehead. "I should have known it was too good to be true. You didn't need me. You already had everything you wanted. You wouldn't have looked at me twice if you hadn't been upset that day. Was it him then, too?"

Exhausted, Cassie wanted to tell him it was none of his business. "I'd found out he was in town for two weeks and hadn't tried to contact me."

Rob studied her, a peculiar expression on his face. "He really got to you, didn't he?"

What did Rob want? To humiliate her for her schoolgirl fantasies? "Yes."

"I never thought I'd see the day when you'd let any man be that important to you."

She had never expected it either. What kind of crazy, self-destructive game was she playing? Why Calder, whom she hardly knew? Suddenly it was too much for her. Without a word or even a look, she turned down the narrow hall into her bedroom and closed the door behind her. Rob would have to let himself out.

Embedded in Amber, Calder's first book, lay on her bedside table under the ceramic lamp with a crack down the side. Cassie placed her hand on it as if it offered some essence of Calder himself. But that was illusory. All she had of him was a three-sentence email, no doubt written off the cuff at some moment when he had nothing to do beyond remembering an old flame of sorts. She sat down on the bed and pulled her knees up, finally letting the tears leak out of her eyes. Tomorrow she would have to pull herself together and act as if nothing had happened, but tonight for once she would let herself feel.

The bedroom door opened quietly. Rob stood silhouetted in the light from the living room for a moment and then made his way over to the bed and sat down beside her in the half-darkness. "There's a reason why you're faculty and I'm still a post-doc." His voice was rueful. "I'm not as smart as you are. But sitting out there I worked out that I'd rather comfort you while you cry over another man than walk away. I know it won't change anything, but at least I can be here as your friend." He put his arm around her shoulder.

She knew she should tell him to leave, but instead she turned her face into his shoulder and cried.

***

Rob finally left when she cried herself into exhaustion. After a night of fitful sleep, Cassie woke alone to a gray morning. She would have to get used to waking up alone again. There would be no more chances to start over with Rob, and there never had been a chance with Calder.

There was no reason to rush to the lab on a Saturday morning. Chris had the day off, and Cassie had the rest of her life to sit in her lab. But her computer was at the lab, and it drew her like a magnet.

Sitting down in front of it, she drew a deep breath before opening her email program and clicking on Deleted Items. She didn't remember when she had emptied it last. Quickly, she scrolled through it.

The email from Calder was still there. She dragged it back to her inbox and read it. It was just as she had remembered it.

Calder was beyond her reach. She would never see him again, as his lover or even as his friend. That was reality. But it helped to know she still crossed his mind occasionally. Was there anything wrong with staying in occasional contact, as long as she understood the limitations?

Chewing her lip, she clicked on *Reply*.

To: C. Westing

From: C. Boulton

Subject: Re: squid

While the squid here are as tasty as ever, it's getting hard to rustle up a good game of Trivial Pursuit. It's no fun when there isn't any challenge.

So, what Mesoamerican civilization conquered an area of over 2,500 square miles on the Pacific Coast of South America?

She felt an odd relief as she pressed *Send*.

***

Cassie could tell Rob was avoiding her. She hadn't spoken to him since that night. Through the lab door she had seen him walking down the hall a few times over the last several days, but he had studiously avoided looking in. She had tried to respect his wishes by staying away from his end of the floor. Chris had maintained such a complete silence on the subject that she was sure Rob must have talked to him.

Today he didn't walk past but came into the lab carrying a plastic bag. He looked tired.

She swiveled her chair to face her assistant. "Chris, I'm going to be on this for a while. Would you mind running into town to get me a sandwich?"

"Sure." Chris stood up and stretched and then noticed Rob. "Your usual, I assume?"

"That'll be great." Cassie handed Chris a ten-dollar bill, and he loped out of the lab with a last glance over his shoulder. He probably hoped they would make up while he was gone.

Rob deposited the bag on her desk. "Some odds and ends of yours I found lying around my place when I packed up. I'm heading back to Chapel Hill tomorrow."

"I thought you were here for another week." Cassie felt guilty at his atypically sober countenance.

"Jim asked me to go back early to take care of some things for him."

She had no doubt Jim had manufactured whatever business he had for Rob, but it relieved her to hear it. Knowing Rob was just down the hall hadn't been easy. "I hope you have a good trip back." It was a little lame, but she had to say something.

"Right. See you." He turned to go.

"Rob?" There was a hesitation before he turned back to her. "What happened the other night was as much of a surprise to me as it was to you. It wasn't something lurking in the back of my mind the whole time."

He raised one shoulder in a brief shrug. "Thanks for saying that, but it doesn't really matter. I realized afterwards it really had nothing to do with another man."

"It didn't?"

"That night was the first time I'd ever seen your real feelings. The first time. That told me more about what I meant to you than anything you said."

Cassie rested her chin on her elbow. "That's not about you, or what you mean to me. That's who I am. It's always going to be an issue for me." How could she share her feelings about a life she had to hide?

"Something to work on in your *next* relationship."

"What next relationship? Do you think I'm going to find someone who's better suited to me than you? We share interests, I enjoy your company and your sense of humor, you understand about my job. Nobody's going to beat that."

"There's no need for melodrama. I didn't mean you needed to give up on men."

"No, I know you didn't. I was just telling you what I think, but it's probably best if we drop it there."

He hesitated. "Maybe it would help if you talked to someone about this. Someone professional, that is."

It would be nice to think all problems could be fixed somehow. "It's okay, Rob. If there's one thing in life I'm good at, it's facing facts and learning to deal with them. I'll be fine."

His face closed down. "Of course. Well, I'll see you around."

"Right. Take care." Cassie watched him leave and then pulled out her data notebook. There was no point in thinking about things she would never have. At least there was still her work and the salt marsh.

Chapter 12

CASSIE FELT A SUDDEN burst of gladness when an email from Calder popped up on her computer. She had told herself again and again not to expect a reply.

To: C. Boulton
From: C. Westing

The Incas. Was that just random, or did you know I lived in Ecuador for a while?

All right ... who was the author of Summa *Theologica?* No fair looking up the answer!

To: C. Westing
From: C. Boulton

I'm too embarrassed to send you my answer, having looked it up and discovered it was wrong. Now, for a little revenge: What capital city is located at the confluence of the rivers Gombak and Klang?

As for Ecuador, I read minds. It's part of my Trivial Pursuit strategy.

To: C. Boulton
From: C. Westing

Ouch. Kuala Lumpur, but I had to cheat. I'd never even heard of those rivers. Where did you dig that one up?

To: C. Westing
From: C. Boulton

Oh, good, I got one! I was afraid you were going to tell me you'd lived in Malaysia, too.

To: C. Boulton
From: C. Westing

Just Italy and Ecuador, I'm afraid. It's that limited university education, you know.

***

Cassie knocked on the door of the English Department conference room at Haverford. The email she'd received from Professor Amy Gottschalk had asked her to stop by the English House for a meeting at three o'clock. Cassie couldn't imagine why the English department would suddenly be interested in a biologist, and a junior faculty member at that, but Amy was a good friend. Maybe they wanted to do some sort of interdepartmental course. She'd be the logical choice for that, since the other Biology faculty members' interests didn't extend to literature.

The door was opened by Dr. Yang, the notoriously intimidating chairman of the English department. "Thank you for stopping by, Dr. Boulton. Won't you have a seat?" He gestured to the conference table where a half dozen English professors sat.

Amy Gottschalk flashed her a reassuring smile. "Thanks for coming. We're hoping to pick your brain about a writer."

The English department wanted to ask a biologist about a writer? Maybe they wanted a science writer, someone like Stephen Jay Gould. "I can't imagine what I'd know about a writer that all of you don't."

Dr. Yang shuffled the pile of papers in front of him, his eyes narrowed like a judge reading the charges against a defendant. "Stephen West, Dr. Boulton."

Cassie's cheeks grew warm. It was the last thing she expected to hear. Had she mentioned his writing to Amy, long before she knew who he was? "I've read his books, but I don't know how much else I can tell you."

"I understand you've met him." Dr. Yang made it sound like a crime.

Her breath froze in her throat. How on earth had he found out? "Yes, we've met. How did you know?"

Amy said, "You're mentioned in the acknowledgments for his latest book."

"I am?" An odd thrill went through her. "I didn't know his new book was out."

Amy handed her a hardcover. The title was emblazoned across the cover in elegant gold lettering: *Pride & Presumption*. Above the title was a stylized drawing of a couple in attire of the early nineteenth century. Below it, a photograph of a modern young woman on a deserted beach, looking out to sea, with a man standing beside her, his eyes fixed upon her. Amy said, "This is a pre-publication copy. He's applied for the writer-in-residence position for next semester. We're interviewing him on Thursday. That's why we're looking for information."

Her heart started racing. Calder would be there on Thursday? She flipped the book open to the acknowledgments page and her name jumped out at her.

Special thanks to Dr. Cassandra Boulton and Erin McKinley for first introducing me to the Marine Biological Laboratory and its traditions.

Dr. Yang cleared his throat, as if annoyed at her distraction. "There are a number of things about his candidacy that puzzle me. First, he's overqualified. This position is designed for writers who are just breaking into the field, and the salary is commensurate with that. Stephen West has two critically acclaimed novels, and a third coming out. Second, he has no teaching credentials at all, but even so, he could get a better-paying job just on the basis of name recognition. It's hard to take his interest in the job seriously, given the salary. Perhaps most curiously, we can't find any information about him. None at all, beyond the résumé he sent us. Hence our interest in what you might have to say."

How much should she tell them? They couldn't possibly know about her feelings for him. Nobody knew that except Rob, and he wasn't very likely to write a book. Her lips twitched at the idea of Rob writing anything without footnotes and citations. It was almost as funny as the idea of Calder applying for a job. "He's a very private person. The name is a pseudonym, which is why you can't find anything about him. Umm, I don't really know him well, but the salary wouldn't be an issue. He has an independent income." Enough to give away a hundred thousand dollars as if it were small change.

Dr. Yang looked at her over his glasses. "This is starting to make more sense. Did you tell him about the position, then?"

"No, not at all," she said, taken off guard by the question. "I didn't find out he was a writer until later."

"Hmm. Do you have any other insights about him you'd like to share?"

Cassie's palms were damp where she clutched the book. At least Dr. Yang hadn't asked what his real name was. "Not really. We talked once about the merits of liberal arts education and the advantages of a small college, but I can't think of anything else." That, and a few dinoflagellates. But the committee didn't know about that part, so she was safe. There was nothing wrong with having met a writer or giving him information for a book.

The faculty member seated to her right, a young man named Hal Bailey, swiveled to look at her. "I have a question." He looked distinctly amused. "*Do* you understand why?"

"Why what?" Cassie felt like she was missing something obvious.

He took the book from her, turned it to the next page, and then handed it back. There were two lines on an otherwise blank page.

To Cassie,
who will understand why

A flush of heat rose in her, but then good sense reasserted itself. Why would he dedicate a book to her? Scott had said Calder never put dedications in books. "I expect he's talking about somebody else named Cassie. He barely knows me."

Dr. Yang glared at the young man. "That is quite enough, Dr. Bailey!"

"Sorry." Dr. Bailey's apology was perfunctory and directed more at Dr. Yang than Cassie.

Calder was going to be at Haverford on Thursday, and he hadn't mentioned a word of it in his emails to her. Surely he couldn't have forgotten she worked there. She looked down at the book again and flipped open the front cover to read the flyleaf. Maybe there would be a clue there.

In this modern-day retelling of the classic tale of Pride & Prejudice, *author Stephen West turns his keen insight to the story of two people from different worlds. Sparks fly when Elizabeth Bennet, a dedicated marine biologist whose life is based on facts and rationality, meets wealthy Fitzwilliam Darcy, born to a family where power and prestige mean everything. Darcy's early attraction to Elizabeth grows into a compelling passion, consummated one magical night by the sea, but in the morning light, Elizabeth rejects him. In despair, Darcy realizes he will never win her friendship, much less her love, because of his failure to be honest with either himself or her. But modern life can prove even more restrictive than the social strictures of the nineteenth century, and West's tale takes a turn of its own as its hero fails to achieve the fairytale ending of the original Darcy and Elizabeth.*

In Pride & Presumption, *Stephen West brings his recognized eloquence and perception to a story of deep emotion, exploring the high cost of misunderstanding and miscommunication and the barriers we erect between one other.*

She stared at it in shock. A marine biologist? A magical night by the sea? Wealthy Fitzwilliam Darcy? No. He wouldn't have told their story. He valued his privacy too much. And a compelling passion? Men didn't conceive a compelling passion for women like her. No, he had taken a seed of truth and developed it into a completely different work of fiction.

"May I borrow this?" she asked, her mouth dry.

"Sure," Amy said. "You'll like it. It's a good read, though the ending's a bit weak."

"Thanks." Cassie turned to Dr. Yang. "Is there anything else?"

He shook his head. "Thank you for your time, Dr. Boulton."

She hurried out of the building, not even taking time to put on her coat, and started down the path across campus to the science building. The book dug into her hand where she clutched it tightly. This must be what Calder was working on when he ran into her in Woods Hole that day in March. And it was the book Scott had said was driving Calder insane. So that was why he never contacted her in June. He couldn't have come to see her and pretended nothing was happening while he was writing this.

She stopped beneath a gnarled oak tree and opened the cover to read the flyleaf again. A compelling passion. Heat rose in her cheeks.

"Hi, Dr. Boulton!" The voice made her jump.

She looked up guiltily to see one of the students from her seminar on marine biology, a worn backpack dangling from his shoulder. "Hi, Tony." She must look strange, standing there in the middle of campus, reading a book in the cold. "How's your lab report coming?" she asked, trying to at least sound professorial, rather than like a teenager in the throes of a mad crush.

"Not bad. I'll see you tomorrow!" Tony waved as he walked off in the opposite direction.

She had to pull herself together. Tucking the book under her arm, she made her way toward her office, trying not to be curt when the department secretary stopped her to ask a question and then wanted to chat. Finally she was safe in her office, the door closed behind her.

She sat down at her desk, pushing aside a pile of lab notebooks that needed to be graded, and set the book down in front of her. What if it said too much about her? And she was far from certain she was ready to hear Calder's feelings about her, even at one remove.

Reluctantly, she began to turn the first pages.

Chapter 13

Pride & Presumption

Chapter One

Fitzwilliam Darcy sped down the highway to Woods Hole. The changing scenery made no impression on him. He was in a foul mood after being caught in a two-hour traffic jam at the bridge over the Cape Cod Canal. It did not help that his uncle had insisted he should fly to the Cape rather than drive for that very reason. The habit of resisting his uncle's demands was deeply ingrained in him, so flying had been out of the question. Nor was his mood improved by the memory of the charity ball he attended the night before, where in order to placate his aunt he danced with several impeccably groomed young women who were only interested in his last name. Had it not been for that, he would have been at his destination a week ago, isolated from the crowds, publicity seekers, and hangers-on, rather than fighting his way through a swarm of minivans filled with noisy tourists.

Bingley's directions were accurate for once, though they did not mention having to dodge pedestrians constantly along the main street of Woods Hole. Not that he could have driven more than ten miles an hour anyway, given the narrowness of the street and all the cars blocking the road as their owners waited for parking spaces. By the time he made it through the town, his fingers were tapping impatiently on the steering wheel and his mouth was tight.

Fortunately, Bingley's new house was just beyond the edge of town, on a narrow peninsula whose one road was blocked by a guard, his sole purpose to protect the privacy of the inhabitants. Darcy was waved through with one glance at his note from Bingley, and his shoulders finally began to relax now that he was safe.

The house itself was less than a quarter mile farther. Darcy pulled into the driveway and examined it. It wasn't bad, as these things went; much larger than Bingley needed, but it did not scream "new money" the way some of his friend's impulse purchases did. The view over the water, though fading now into the twilight, was stunning. Even more important, the neighboring houses were far enough away to give the illusion of privacy.

He went up to the front door, pausing when he noticed an envelope taped to it with his name on it. He ripped it open impatiently and read Bingley's near illegible scrawl:

You're late! I've gone into town for a folk dance thing—good chance to meet some of the locals. Make yourself at home, or better yet, come on down to the dance. It's at the Community Hall, just as you get to the drawbridge.

You can't miss it!

Darcy gritted his teeth. He would rather have a root canal than go to some local dance. God! He'd had plenty of that last night, and at least the people at the ball had decent manners and didn't stare, at least not much. He reached to open the door, only to discover it was locked.

Cursing, he tried again, but without success. Damn Bingley and his thoughtlessness. He walked around the house in search of a back door, but that proved to be locked as well. He tried ringing the bell in case there was a housekeeper or someone inside, but to no avail.

There was no point even thinking about the windows. There was no doubt a burglar alarm, though chances were good Bingley would have forgotten to set it. He could not take the risk. The tabloids would have a field day with it. He could see it now: Fitzwilliam Darcy caught breaking and entering! The reporters wouldn't care that he had permission to be there; they would write it in the most damning way, just to attract their so-called readers. Parasites, more like.

He debated waiting until Bingley returned, but the wind off the ocean was cold, and he had no desire to sit in his car for what could be hours, especially if Bingley found some blonde he liked. No, the sensible thing would be to go get the key from him. Damn Bingley. Why couldn't he think for once?

Darcy decided to walk. It was not far, and he did not want to draw any extra attention to himself. Besides, he had been in the car all day, and the exercise would be good. Maybe it would help him sleep.

The walk calmed him. The evening was quiet, and for the first time he paid attention to his surroundings. Bingley was right; the privately owned peninsula was lovely, and it was isolated. Just what he wanted. No one to disturb him.

He found the Community Hall easily enough. He heard it long before he reached it, the quick and lively music spilling out into the street. His tension returned as he entered and his senses were assaulted by movement and sound. The mass of dancers resolved itself into two lines of couples, but it was hardly the kind of dancing he was accustomed to. Voices echoed around the large hall, competing with the music of a piano and several string instruments. There were too many people in too little space. He could hardly think straight, which was why he always avoided places like this. He scanned the crowd for Bingley, and finally spotted him dancing with a beautiful blonde. Predictable to the last, that was Bingley.

He waited impatiently for the dance to end, but as soon as it did, the dancers dissolved into an amorphous crowd, and Bingley was once again lost to view. Damn him! Darcy took a deep breath and was preparing with distaste to plunge into the crowd in search of him when he was accosted by a young woman. He had a vague impression of a cloud of dark brown hair and flushed cheeks.

"Want a partner for the next dance?" She smiled at him all too brightly.

He expelled his breath between his teeth. As if he'd ever want to go into that chaos, especially with some idiotic local girl who had no doubt noted the expense of his clothes and thought she could catch a rich tourist. "I'm not planning to dance," he said in a tone designed to send her on her way.

Unfortunately, she did not seem to get the message. "I'll be happy to show you how, if you've never done it before. It's easy to pick up."

"I don't think so." He needed to find Bingley and get out of there, and she was in his way.

She shrugged and turned away, searching out some other victim. With a sigh of relief, he scanned the crowd again, finally catching sight of Bingley. Darcy caught up with him just as he was lining up for another dance. "Charles!" he snapped.

Bingley smiled, completely oblivious to Darcy's distress. "Oh, glad you made it! Grab a partner and join in!"

"Charles, I just came for the key. You left the doors locked." His patience was running out.

Just then the music started up again, and Bingley took his partner's hand. "I'll catch you at the end of this dance, Will!"

"Charles!" But it was too late; the dancers were already off.

Having no choice, Darcy retreated to a dark corner of the room to wait out the dance. If he did not manage to get the key then, he vowed, he would go back and sit in the car all night if need be.

Cassie smoothed the page in front of her. This didn't sound like the Calder she knew. He hadn't looked uncomfortable at the dance. Perhaps he had learned to cover it well.

Or maybe Will Darcy was nothing like Calder Westing. Maybe this was all a fantasy, starting with a grain of truth. She paged ahead through the next chapter. The Dock of the Bay Café for their first lunch with Scott and Erin. The visit to Scott's house. It was their story, all right. Had Calder been frankly lusting after her already, like Will Darcy? If so, she'd been completely oblivious to it, but it wouldn't be the first time for that.

Then came the night at her lab. A shiver went up her arms at his description of how he was drawn by her warmth and animation. In one of the few departures from actual events, the story of his uncle was replaced by one of his parents' adultery and near divorce. Had he really imagined it to be a sign of growing intimacy between them?

Little did she know that he was only playing devil's advocate when he defended the university system. He was actually in agreement with much of what she said; going to Harvard had been the last decision he had allowed his family to make for him. Darcys always went to Harvard. But he was supposed to major in economics and then go to business school, preparing to take over his role in the family business. There had been bitter fights that had lasted for years when his parents discovered he was majoring in philosophy and had no intention of going into business. He had little doubt that he would have been happier at the kind of liberal arts college Elizabeth was describing.

But it gave him such pleasure to watch her animated debate, to see her eyes sparkling as she countered his points, to listen to her quick wit and lively responses, that he kept the discussion going by debating points he actually agreed with. God, she was beautiful when she was like that.

Beautiful? He must be joking. Erin was beautiful, not her. But she had misjudged him so badly, if this version was the truth. She turned the page to see what came next.

He had asked himself at least six times that morning why he agreed to do this. The simple answer—because Bingley asked him to—was deceptive at best. He could easily have pleaded a need to work or for some quiet time, or even an errand elsewhere. But he had not; he had agreed, saying it might be interesting to help gather specimens in the salt marsh. *Interesting* indeed—the only thing that truly *interested* him at the moment was the sight of Elizabeth Bennet's lively features and animatedly moving body, and the chance to gather more fodder for his fantasies. There had been a time, after that evening in her lab, when he tried to convince himself it could be more than fantasies, but he could not fool himself for long. He knew, no one better, that she did not belong in his world. If he was an outsider and a disappointment to his family and their society, she would be a disaster.

She was too independent, too determined, too disinterested in the importance of appearance. Her mocking wit would win her enemies in a world where saving face was paramount. No, they would try to eat her alive, and they would fail. He knew enough of Elizabeth's strength to know that, but they would destroy any affection that lay between the two of them. Their poison was insidious.

Yet he could not convince himself to stay away from her. It was as if she mesmerized him. Merely watching her gave him such pleasure—her energy, her contagious enthusiasm for life, and the native kindness that could not be completely disguised by her teasing and occasionally sharp-tongued manner. It had been a revelation that night in her lab when he realized that she was enjoying watching *him* enjoy the game. He could not recall anyone taking pleasure in his enjoyment of anything before. It was a novel experience, and it was hard to resist wanting more of it. Then there was that awful moment at the end, when he realized that he had won and she had lost. Losing was unacceptable in his family. Losing was failure, and failure was not to be tolerated. Losing meant facing harsh criticism on his performance, and winning meant losers taking out their anger on him. He expected her hostility, and it did not come. Instead, she seemed only amused. It made him want to sit at her feet and bask in her presence.

And so he found himself squeezed in a van loaded with sampling equipment and three vivacious people. It was relaxing to listen to them talk and laugh together; they seemed to expect nothing from him, which was just as he liked it. Elizabeth, as always, talked with her hands as well as her voice, even when limited by driving the van, providing a visual delight for him. His mind drifted into wondering how she would use her hands while making love, and whether her entire body would express her mood the way it did when she was excited by something. It was all too easy to imagine her hands exploring him, that striking intensity of hers focused on nothing but him. He let his imagination run free as they traveled along. It was the only part of himself he intended to make free with.

Soon they pulled into a small parking lot. Elizabeth and Jane hopped out of the van and began unloading boxes of equipment from the back. Bingley hurried to help them, while Darcy held back, willing to assist but not wanting to intrude.

Elizabeth gave him an amused look as she shouldered a backpack and picked up a box. "I hope you don't think we invited you along for your good looks. Make yourself useful." Her teasing manner took any sting of demand from her words.

"And here I thought it was for my charming personality." He wanted to keep her interest for a moment longer.

"No, just your strong back and your scintillating conversation." She started along a narrow trail through a bank of trees. "Watch out for the poison ivy. It's thick here."

As he watched Elizabeth's lithe body sway ahead of him, he reflected that poison ivy was not the only hidden danger for him there. Elizabeth was not conventionally pretty the way Jane was, but there was something about her air that enchanted him. He was so caught up in his admiration of her that it came as a shock when they emerged from the trees into a totally different world.

At first glance it was completely flat, a sea of deep grass unbroken by trees or bushes. Looking more closely, he could see variegation in the height and color of grasses in different parts and dark areas which appeared to be streams cut through the marsh. Underfoot, it was not what he expected at all; it was dry and solid as they walked along a path of darkened dirt leading into the grass. Twice they came to winding channels of water cut straight down into the peat of the marsh, too narrow to be called a river yet too wide to jump across, with simply constructed wood plank bridges allowing them to cross. Eventually they reached a side path, leading to a small, roped-off area marked with a grid.

"Here we are." Elizabeth set down her box and backpack. Instead of beginning to unpack as he expected, she stood and stretched and then gazed at their surroundings, a slight smile on her face. In all too short a time, she recalled his presence. "Sorry, I'm a salt marsh fan. Some people find it monotonous, but I think it's extraordinarily beautiful. I chose my field of research so I could spend more time here."

He enjoyed watching her pleasure in her surroundings. She seemed more relaxed and free here, in a very appealing way. "You must like grass then."

"The *Spartina?* That's what most of the grass here is, different *Spartina* species. Yes, I like it. And I admire it."

"You admire the grass?" He was sure he had misunderstood her.

"Yes, I do. It's incredibly tough, and it survives conditions that would kill any other plant." She squatted next to the boxes and began opening them. "This is an unbelievably harsh environment for plants, where the freshwater river meets the saltwater bay. As the tide comes in, the salinity of the water increases, then decreases again as it goes out and the river water moves in. Most normal plants would be killed by salt water. Only a few species have undergone the enormous adaptation they need to survive and thrive in the presence of salt. And salt marsh plants have to go one step further. They have to be able to tolerate fresh water from the river as well. These grasses you see—they're survivors in a harsh world."

She paused as she lifted out the coring equipment. "There are less than a dozen plants that can survive in this kind of environment, but do you know what the strange thing is? These grasses, as they decay and die, create the foundation for one of the richest ecosystems we know. On the surface, we only see a few types of grass, but below, where we can't see, there are all kinds of bacteria, fungi, and algae, then the insects, worms, crabs, snails, and fish. And it's all interconnected in one big web." She was silent for a moment. "That's part of what I love about salt marshes. They look so plain and simple on the surface, but underneath there is more going on than you can imagine. Even the simplicity is deceptive. It doesn't let you see the incredible feats of adaptation the grass has performed."

She glanced up at him. "Sorry, I didn't mean to lecture you. It's an occupational hazard, I'm afraid."

"No, it's interesting." He wished he could express himself more articulately. If only he could somehow capture her vibrancy and open contentment to savor and enjoy later.

Bingley and Jane arrived with more boxes, as well as chatter that disrupted the peace of the moment. It was probably just as well. It kept him from doing something stupid, which was definitely a risk when Elizabeth was as full of life and as open as she was at the moment. Her enthusiasm for her work was contagious, and he liked listening to her all too much.

For safety's sake, he reverted to quietly following instructions, trying to smother his impulse to watch Elizabeth constantly. Her teasing manner when she spoke to him kept undermining him. It made him want to smile back at her.

"I'm sorry," she said at one point when he was particularly quiet. "I'm forgetting that you're volunteer labor here, not a grad student I can order around."

"I've always wondered what it would be like to go to grad school."

"Oh, it's a little better than being tortured and a little worse than indentured servitude. But don't listen to me.

I actually liked grad school, which shows you how disturbed I am. Tell you what, though. When we're done with the sampling, I can show you around the marsh. Of course, not everyone appreciates the marsh the way I do, so that might not be a privilege."

She was irresistible when she was in this kind of irrepressible mood. He probably would have agreed to a tour of hell if she suggested it.

Bingley and Jane declined to join them, preferring to sit and enjoy the sunshine, but Darcy followed Elizabeth deeper into the marsh. "The part we've been in, the dry peat, isn't really all that interesting to the casual observer," she explained as she led him to one of the stream banks near the ocean. "Now here there's quite a lot to see. Look over there." She pointed to the opposite bank where he could see an amazing number of small crabs scurrying sideways between little dark holes in the peat. "Those are fiddler crabs—if you look at them, you'll see that one front claw is much bigger than the other. That's how they get their name. It's like a fiddler whose bow arm is stronger than his fingering arm."

"Quite a lot of them," he said.

"They're an important part of the ecosystem. They aerate the peat, as well as a number of other functions. Sorry, I'm lecturing again," she added with an apologetic smile.

"Don't worry, I like it," he said impulsively.

She looked surprised at his words. "Well, let me show you some of the other critters that call the salt marsh home," she said. She rolled up the legs of her shorts and began to clamber down the nearly vertical bank of peat. She slipped halfway down, landing on her feet in the water, laughing. "Always happens," she said cheerfully. "I don't know why I don't just give up and jump in."

The water was just above her knees, and she looked down at it as she walked through it. She dipped her hand in and pulled out a larger crab. "Green crab," she said, holding it out toward him. He watched the creature's claws flailing with apprehension. "This is the kind you can eat for dinner, though this one's too small." She tossed it casually back in the water and dredged out a handful of small snails. "*Littorina littorea*, or the common periwinkle—an invasive species that has pretty much overrun the coast here. It came here from Europe, probably in the ballast water of a ship. Oh, and here we go—this one's my favorite. *Pagurus longicarpus*, the hermit crab. I did my first salt marsh research on these, looking at their diet in differing habitats." She waded over to him, holding what appeared to be an empty shell. "Here, take it," she said.

A little nervously, he did as she asked and could just barely see tiny legs folded up inside the shell. "Now hold it in your palm," she directed. "Just watch for a minute."

As he did, the legs suddenly emerged, along with a tiny head and antennae, and the tiny creature began to scuttle around in his hand, tickling slightly. He smiled; it was an appealing little thing in an odd sort of way.

"They don't grow their own shells; they have to take another animal's discarded shell," she explained. "Here in the marsh, you'll see a lot of them in periwinkle shells, like that one. They're creatures of the intertidal zone, so they can survive for quite a while out of the water."

He sidestepped to a lower part of the bank to return the hermit crab to the water.

"Not there!" exclaimed Elizabeth as he moved, but it was too late. His shoe was already several inches deep in black mud. She tried unsuccessfully to hide a smile. "I'm sorry; I should have warned you. That's why I went straight down the bank instead of that way—the black stuff is mud a foot deep."

Darcy was off-balance in more ways than one. He did not like feeling embarrassed in front of the woman who had been inhabiting his fantasies. With an effort, he pulled his foot free, looking with some distaste at the dark mud clinging to it.

"Here, take that off and give it to me," said Elizabeth matter-of-factly. "I'll rinse it off. You'll want to clean it again with fresh water again when you get home, but salt water's still better than mud." She reached out her hand for it.

"That's all right," he said, a little stiffly. "I don't want you to have to get muddy."

With a look of amused exasperation, Elizabeth reached over and stuck her hand directly into the mud. "Look, it won't hurt me. It's nothing but rich soil packed with some extra anaerobic bacteria and no grass roots to hold it together."

He tried to imagine any other woman of his acquaintance voluntarily touching that muck, but it was impossible. She was different from them in so many ways, and she looked so alive in the afternoon sun sparkling off the water.

"Your shoe," she reminded him pointedly.

Feeling it more discourteous to refuse her offer of assistance, he removed it and handed it to her. "Thank you," he said, watching as she carefully rinsed the sides of it while keeping the inside dry. He said ruefully, "Why do I suppose you would have expected me to do that myself if I were one of your grad students?"

Her eyes glinted with mischief. "Not at all—I'd just have pulled you in and let it rinse off naturally," she said. "Somehow I don't think you'd appreciate that, though."

He had a vivid image of himself standing in the water next to her, taking her into his arms and feeling her soft body pressed against his own. The surge of desire that rushed through him was almost overpowering. No, he would appreciate it all too much if she pulled him in. Far better to avoid her playfulness. It was the only way to keep them both safe. The question, then, was why he felt so disappointed when she merely handed the shoe back to him.

It was a faithful rendering of a day that hadn't struck her as important at the time, but it was so different from how she had seen it. How could she have missed all this? And what else had she missed? Cassie's stomach churned as his narrative approached their encounter at the beach. This was hard enough without revealing their most private moments to the entire world.

The scene started much as it had in reality. It diverged while they were in the water watching the bioluminescence.

He was just out of arm's reach when she gave a sharp cry of pain. She went under the water for a moment and then came up and swam a few feet away. "Damn, damn, damn," she muttered with deep feeling.

"What's the matter?" he asked anxiously.

"Sea urchin. I stepped on one, and some of the spines broke off in my foot. I'll live; I just have to get to shore and get them out."

He knew instinctively she was minimizing her pain. "How can I help?"

"I'm fine." She half-swam, half-hopped toward the beach.

He followed her closely. As the water grew shallower, it became harder for her to move without putting any weight on her foot, and he reached out a hand to help support her by holding her arm. She turned a look on him that said she did not want his help, but at the same time could not refuse it. She struggled on for a few more feet and then stopped.

"Just give me a second." Her eyes were squeezed shut.

"Look, let me get you out of here." Unable to watch her discomfort, he picked her up in his arms and began to carry her to shore, trying not to think about her naked body pressed against his chest.

"Will, I can get there by myself."

"No need; you're here already." He walked out of the shallow water. Carefully setting her down on her good foot, he fetched her towel and spread it on the sand. She sank down on it thankfully and twisted her leg to see the sole of her foot.

He crouched down in the sand. "Here, let me do that. I can see it a lot better than you can." Reluctantly, she extended her leg to him, and he reached for the flashlight.

"Can you see them?" She craned to look as he shone the light on the sole of her foot.

"Yes, there are two of them right there." They were embedded deeply.

"If you can get a grip on them, pull them out gently." Her teeth were gritted. "You don't want to break the spines; then it's much worse getting them out."

"Can you hold still?" He grasped her foot with one hand.

"Just *do* it."

He had never been one to be flustered by an emergency, and he took his time looking at the spines to be sure he understood their angle before he caught one between his fingers and tugged gently. He heard her sharp indrawn breath as it came out in his hand. "That's one; you're doing great." He worked to get a hold on the other one. It was in deeper, and he had to try twice before he could get enough of a grip on it to pull it out. For a moment it resisted enough that he was afraid it might break, but then it came free.

He turned off the flashlight and looked up, still a bit light-blind in the darkness. As his eyes adjusted, he could see her relief.

"Thanks." She flexed the toes of the injured foot.

"I'm sorry it hurt." He looked into her eyes for reassurance that she was all right, his hand still resting on her ankle. He had been worried for her, but it was disturbing how much he enjoyed Elizabeth needing his help, even for such a simple physical matter as this. If she ever needed him for anything important, it would be like a drug, one he could become addicted to.

"It's much better now. It just stings a little."

She was looking at him with an expression he was not sure how to interpret, but now that the crisis was past, he was increasingly aware of how close her naked body was to his. With some embarrassment, he realized that she could be in no doubt as to just how much he wanted her. He remembered how it had felt to hold her against him as he carried her out of the water, and without coherent thought, he discovered his hand had moved to lightly stroke the calf of her leg.

He waited for her to make an objection, but when she did not, he made no effort to stop himself. It felt too good to touch her, too right, and as he began to understand what her look meant, all his carefully thought-out reasons seemed to vanish. All he wanted was to hold her in his arms and to make love to her until she was helpless with pleasure.

His hand crept up to her knee, and she gave him a saucy look. "Doing a little research of your own, Will?" Her voice was low and husky.

"It's being surrounded by all these scientists. I can't help myself. Do you want me to stop?"

In reply, she reached out and touched his lips lightly with her fingers. He felt the shock of the contact and ran his tongue along her fingertips.

"Who am I to stand in the way of science?" Her smile was all the permission he needed.

He leaned forward slowly, giving her plenty of time to draw back, until their lips met, first tentatively and then with increasing passion. God, the taste of her was sweet. It grew even sweeter as his hands caressed her body, discovering what she liked, exploring her breasts until she moaned.

Gently he lowered her down until she was lying on the towel. He lay beside her, and the shock as their bodies met skin to skin dissolved any reserve he had left. It no longer mattered that they were not in private, that Bingley and Jane were just a short distance away and could come upon them at any time, or that their bodies were sticky with salt from the bay. Everything else faded completely from his mind as his hands discovered her most intimate secrets and used that knowledge to steadily increase her arousal. As her body shook with pleasure under the provocation of his touch, he knew this was what he wanted, and he wanted it forever.

Had Calder really been so powerfully focused on her? It was consistent with his behavior, just not with her interpretation of it. Certainly he was a considerate lover, but she had assumed this was basic politeness on his part. But she had never thought him polite. That he would feel so involved in her response as to practically neglect his own came as a revelation.

At least his description of the action bore little physical resemblance to what had passed between them beyond the actual setting. He must have deliberately chosen to alter it.

There was no reason to do so for the story. She was fiercely glad he had kept that part of it private between them. That night had been too special—their coming together too magical—to share. It was a relief to finally admit it.

She realized how stiff she had become, hunched over the book as if it held the secrets of the universe. Her universe. It was already dark, and the lights over the pathway outside shone in her window. She got to her feet and shuffled into the hallway, down to the staff lounge. It was late enough that no one else was there. She poured herself a cup of leftover coffee and watered it down substantially with milk. No need to worry about caffeine tonight. She'd be up late. There was no way she'd be able to go to sleep before she finished reading the book.

She was in his room, and he was removing her clothes, and it was so incredibly, unquestionably right. This was how it should be; her mouth belonged underneath his, and her breasts belonged in his hands. When she looked up at him with that mischievous glint in her eyes, he knew he wanted to see that look directed at him every day of his life.

Her playfulness enchanted him, and her open, uninhibited response to his touch aroused him beyond his imagination. Her pleasure was like a gift to him, one he could not have enough of, as he sought to tell her with his hands and his body and his mouth all the feelings he could not express in words. And she seemed to enjoy *his* pleasure and *his* excitement equally, as if meeting and surpassing his needs was an entertaining challenge for her.

Finally, as satisfied desire and passion subsided into exhaustion, she fell asleep in his arms. As he listened to her light breathing, he felt as if he had been given a great gift, one beyond measure. Her spark had brought him to life again. It would be difficult, but they would make it work. If it came down to a choice between his family and Elizabeth, he had no doubt what his choice would be. He had spent enough of his life trying to be someone he was not. Now he intended to live for himself, and that meant being with Elizabeth.

He had never known this sense of connection before, this lightness of being that said he was no longer alone. There had been more than enough women over the years, but never before one who could give him such pleasure just by sleeping beside him. He stroked her hair tenderly, thinking of all the ways he would show her how much she meant to him. Yes, tonight had been for passion and the excitement of discovery; tomorrow would hold more of the same, but there would also be time for tenderness. A faint smile curved his lips as he drifted gently off to sleep.

Tightness gripped Cassie's throat. She knew what was coming next. After reading his eloquent description of happiness in her, how could she bear what was going to happen? And she had been so completely unaware of it, so wrapped up in her concern for the fragility of her own feelings that she had never stopped to think whether he might have any. If his writing expressed anything of what *he* had been feeling that night, then she had been unspeakably cruel to him.

Unshed tears blurred her vision. She had been so self-centered, yet how could she have known that someone like Calder Westing could possibly be interested in *her?* How could she have known the loneliness and emptiness he was feeling, or how hostile the world appeared to him? He never told her. From this account, he would have felt unable to say something like that, and now he was telling her the only way he could.

When he awoke in the morning, she was gone. For a confused moment, he wondered if it had all been a dream, but then he caught a hint of her scent on the pillow, and his body's memory reminded him of the reality of it. He stretched with a smile, thinking she must have awakened early and was waiting for him downstairs. Eager to see her and to hold her in his arms again, he put on a bathrobe and hurried down.

No one was there, not even Bingley. Puzzled and beginning to worry, he checked the deck and the porch before discovering a note lying on the kitchen counter.

Will,

I had to be at the lab early this morning and didn't want to disturb you. I helped myself to a bagel and OJ—hope that was okay.

Elizabeth

His first thought was relief to know where she was, followed closely by disappointment. He wanted to see her, to be with her. Well, he would go be with her, if she could not be with him. He showered quickly with the resolve to go immediately to the lab, and it was not until he was partway dressed that it occurred to him perhaps she would not want that.

He read her note again, and this time saw what was missing from it instead of what was there. There was no endearment, no sign of affection, no suggestion of seeing him or talking to him in the future. It was a note she could have left for a casual acquaintance. A sick feeling settled to the pit of his stomach. Could she possibly have regretted what happened between them? She seemed so pleased and content at the time, but was there more he didn't know? Could there be a man at home she had never mentioned?

A feeling akin to panic ran through him. He had to see her now, had to feel the reassurance of her presence; it was the only thing that would stop these racing doubts. But what if she did not want to be interrupted at work? Perhaps he was reading far too much into a simple note. Perhaps she was just uncomfortable expressing personal sentiments in writing, but he was now uncertain enough of himself not to want to risk upsetting her. No, he decided, he would wait, and she would no doubt call at some point. Maybe she needed some time alone to think through what happened. Certainly it was a profound change for both of them, and if she needed a little time, he would give it to her.

His calm resolve lasted only a few hours. There had

been no word from Elizabeth, and he could not bear it any longer. Perhaps *she* was waiting to hear from him. He went to the phone and found Bingley's list of numbers, leafing through it until he found the listing for "Jane @ lab." Quickly, he dialed it.

As soon as he heard Elizabeth's voice, something in him relaxed and was happy again. "Elizabeth, it's Will. I was wondering whether you'd like to have dinner tonight."

"Sorry, but I can't. I've got a lot of work here."

He wondered if she were perhaps feeling shy and needed some convincing. "How about if I bring dinner to you, then?"

"I'm afraid I'm going to have to work straight through. Thanks anyway." Was that coolness in her voice, or was he imagining it?

"Maybe tomorrow, then?"

He heard her sigh. "Look, Will, I appreciate what you're trying to do, but you don't owe me anything for last night. It was just something that happened."

Stung, he retorted, "I'm not trying to *pay* you for it. I thought it might be nice to spend a little time together."

"It's very nice of you, but it's unnecessary. Look, I need to go, okay?"

He felt unable to breathe. "If that's what you want, then."

"Yes. Thanks for asking, though, Will. Take care."

"You too," he said automatically, just before hearing her hang up.

For quite some time, he felt nothing but numbness.

He recognized her message. He had been the one to give it often enough in the past to women who were interested in more than he wanted to give. He had never spent a great deal of time thinking about how they felt, beyond trying to do it as gently as possible because he did not want to hurt anyone's feelings. Of course, he was sure Elizabeth had tried to avoid hurting his feelings as well. Unfortunately, that was impossible. She had stolen all his feelings away.

He had never been the one to be left behind before. For so many women, it was enough that he was rich and came from a famous family. That was all they wanted. But whatever it was Elizabeth wanted, he did not possess it.

The hurt did not begin until he went up to his room that night. She had only been there for a few hours, but the memory of her filled his room—her teasing smile, her laughter, her agile hands and warm body that seemed to accept him into it so gladly. But it was just a bit of fun for her, a release of tension, perhaps, nothing more. And he had been prepared to give up almost anything for her sake. He buried his face in his hands, feeling once again what it was to be unnecessary, unaccepted, and unloved. It was a position with which he was quite familiar.

Cassie could no longer control her tears. She couldn't separate out how much of her was hurting for the character of Darcy as Calder had created it and how much was hating herself for what she had done. If he had written this as a punishment to her, he couldn't have done a better job. But she knew better than that. From what little she did know of his character, cruelty wasn't part of it. No, this was raw, naked honesty, and it hurt.

If only she could stop reading. But she had to know what happened next, or rather, how much worse it would get. She already knew what was going to happen.

By the next morning, he was angry. He was angry that he had slept poorly, haunted by Elizabeth's ghost; he was angry with Bingley for coming downstairs whistling after Jane left for the day; and most of all he was angry at Elizabeth for leading him on and then giving him the brush-off. If she wanted nothing to do with him, why had she come into his arms and made love with him as if there were no one else in the world? Why had she given no indication that it meant nothing to her? Why could she not even be bothered to have dinner with him? Surely that was not too much to ask, that she let him down gently?

His resentment was fueled through the day by several strong drinks. By midafternoon, the combination of sleeplessness and alcohol overcame him, and he dozed off at his desk. Bingley woke him by pounding on the door at dinnertime. Darcy kept a grim silence during the meal, speaking only enough to keep his friend from becoming suspicious.

Afterwards he went out onto the porch, yet another drink in his hand, to watch the sunset and brood. He ran through in his head his brief telephone conversation with Elizabeth again and again, letting himself feel her abruptness and unwillingness even to talk. Then, in the midst of his anger, he realized what he had missed earlier.

Elizabeth's behavior during the call was out of character. Even when they had first met, when he had been unquestionably rude, she was unfailingly patient and pleasant with him. She never hesitated to take time to explain things to him, even when she was busy. She had never, never been abrupt or dismissive or unwilling to explain herself, not until that phone call.

He knew instinctively this was important, but his clouded mind could not see through the issue. He wanted to find Jane and demand she explain what Elizabeth was doing, but fortunately his good sense prevailed.

Elizabeth was upset, that much was clear. But why? Perhaps she was angry, either with herself or with him, for what happened; perhaps she was carried away by the moment and had gone further than she could be comfortable with, for some reason. Perhaps a commitment to someone else? No, that he could not believe. Or maybe it was a moral position; though she had obviously not been a virgin, it was equally obvious it had been some time since she had taken a lover. But she seemed so down to earth about it. That did not make sense either. Or . . . the realization suddenly hit him. He had made the mistake that any intelligent teenager knew to avoid. He had not thought about protection. It never even crossed his mind. Now *that* was something that would upset Elizabeth. She would have no tolerance, either for herself or anyone else, with that kind of carelessness.

He felt a huge sense of relief at having found an explanation. For a few minutes, all he could do was look blindly at the sunset and breathe deeply. Anger or anxiety: those were only stumbling blocks, not a brick wall. They could be worked through. He was impatient to fix things with her, but it would have to be tomorrow. He should talk to her in person; they had not done well on the telephone, and he should not be driving now. Not to mention the conclusions she would draw if he appeared unexpectedly at her cottage at night! No, it would have to wait until the morning, but now he *could* wait, now that it was no longer hopeless.

Despite his fatigue and the effects of alcohol, he awoke early and immediately readied himself to go to Elizabeth. Jane had said Elizabeth was often in the lab before anyone else, and he would prefer to talk to her when there were fewer people around. He walked down the Penzance Point road toward town, enjoying the early morning chill and solitude, filled with hope and energy. He *would* find a way to make it all right for her, and then they could be together.

Cassie braced herself for what was coming. He described his visit to her lab evocatively, his hopes as he arrived dashed by the coldness he met with from her. He had shown so little that day of what he was feeling, or had she simply not been looking?

Elizabeth rested her hand on her microscope. "I really don't have time for this kind of thing in my life right now; I have to focus on my work and getting tenure."

His heart sank. No time. That was the one reason he had

not expected to hear from her; he could not say *why* he had not expected it, as he had certainly heard it often enough in his life. Work always came first for the people he loved—it came ahead of family time, it came ahead of playtime, it came ahead of any desire to understand him. Unconsciously, he put back on the mask of formality he used to cover pain.

It was over. There was no point in arguing it. There was no reason to hope for sympathy just because he felt ripped apart. Still, there was one thing he still needed to say, and perhaps it might leave a door open. "All right, I can accept that. But if I can take another minute of your time," that precious time, he thought "I just want to say that I know I was irresponsible. I'm not used to doing that kind of thing on the spur of the moment either, and I wasn't prepared, or even thinking. But if there are any . . . consequences, I hope you'll tell me. I wouldn't want to be left out of it, no matter what decision you made."

She looked at him for a moment, and then realization dawned over her face. Unpleasant realization, it was obvious. "There's nothing to worry about."

It was as if the woman before him was a completely different person from the one he had thought he knew, and it left him feeling helpless. "I'm sorry. I really didn't mean to upset you."

She looked down at her papers on the bench. "I'm fine." It was a patent lie. "I'm just worried about my work."

"I guess I'll leave you to it, then. Good luck with your paper." He could not quite bring himself to say good-bye.

"Thank you." Her voice was firm, but when she

looked up at him, he saw a trace of the woman he loved in her eyes. "Good-bye, Will." She could have no idea how much it hurt him to see it. Without another word, he turned and left.

So much for that dream. It was nice while it lasted, the idea that a woman could value him for himself and not for his name or his money. But it was not realistic. There would be plenty of women who would be willing to put up with him for the material advantages he could offer, and he would have to settle for that.

His writing always had the power to move her, and this was agonizing. She had been so angry that day. She had done it again, put the worst possible interpretation on everything he said and treated him badly when he meant well. And she had failed completely to recognize how vulnerable he was.

She couldn't stop crying, and the worst was yet to come. This was going to be nothing compared to the Christmas party. And he had been so kind to her the day they met in Woods Hole, though she couldn't have deserved it less.

The book continued, telling the story of Darcy's return to New York and how he plunged himself into activities in an attempt to forget her. It turned to bitterness when Bingley reentered the picture.

Bingley was in New York for a meeting, and arranged to meet Darcy for lunch while he was there. They met at an elegant restaurant where Darcy was fairly certain they would be untroubled by celebrity-watchers. He was surprised at the difference in his friend's appearance since he had seen him last, just six weeks earlier. He looked a little thinner, but more than that, his mouth had a turn of discontent atypical of the usually cheerful Bingley.

Darcy knew he had only to wait for Bingley to raise the topic of whatever was bothering him. The appetizers had not even arrived when he was proven correct.

"I saw Jane last weekend," said Bingley.

Darcy buttered his roll. "How is she?" He did not particularly want to talk about Jane; the less they said about anything that reminded him of Elizabeth, the better, but it was the issue on Bingley's mind, and there was no avoiding it.

Bingley looked sad. "She was fine. She was working on a project and had to go in for part of the day on Saturday. I didn't realize how understanding Elizabeth was this summer. I wasn't even allowed in the Duke labs."

"So you didn't see as much of her as you'd have liked?"

"No." Bingley paused for a moment. "I hate this long-distance idiocy, first not seeing her for weeks, then an intense weekend together, then apart again. And I can't get away as much as I'd like, and she has barely any time off. She keeps saying it'll be better when she gets a new job, but that won't be till next fall at the earliest. I want her *with* me."

Elizabeth had told him straight out she had no time for a relationship. It was a painful thought, but it carried a little sweetness, too. Perhaps Elizabeth had considered the potential cost to him.

"Jane says she needs her job until she has a new one, but I don't know—academic jobs are in short supply, and what are the chances she'll get one in Boston? I can't do this forever. And I don't feel like I can ask her to quit her job for me. I care about her, but we were only together for a little over a month, and I don't want to make promises I might not be able to keep. She's worked a long time to get where she is today." He looked pleadingly at Darcy, as if he might have some sort of answer.

Darcy certainly had no words of wisdom on this subject. "It sounds like the question really is whether she'll have time for you in any academic job, not just this one. It's very demanding for a beginning professor. They have to work all kinds of hours, at least until they get tenure. Look at Elizabeth. She was hardly out of the lab all summer."

Bingley looked even more despondent. "I don't even want to think about that. I just can't do that. And I can't even blame her. I work long hours, too, and *I'm* not about to give up my job for her. God, I wish I'd thought of all this before we got involved!"

Darcy could sympathize with that feeling, at least to a certain extent. He would never be willing to give up the little bit of Elizabeth he had. The image of her face as she watched him playing Trivial Pursuit came to him, and he felt a sudden longing for her.

There it was, the one thing she had never been able to forgive him for—coming between Scott and Erin. Yet as he presented it, it was no more than the logical conclusion of the seemingly harmless white lie she told him when she said she didn't have time for a relationship. Erin had never changed her story about looking for an academic job.

It could have been so different if only they had talked about their feelings. It might not have worked out anyway, given their differences, but at least they would have had something. Or she would have had enough to really break her heart when it ended.

She continued reading Calder's description of the autumn, of how Darcy had grappled with feelings of loneliness and pointlessness by grimly dating, and occasionally bedding, a series of women. It wasn't a surprise, and she had no right to object to it, but it still bothered her.

She read Darcy's fantasies about Elizabeth with a different kind of embarrassment. If only his fantasies could have met hers, what a fine time they would have had. His memories of what he had seen as her tenderness saddened her. It took so little to mean so much to him.

Interposed with recollections of Elizabeth were bitter scenes with his family. He had devised relatives to fit the structure of *Pride and Prejudice* and put in alterations from his own background to disguise his family. Fitzwilliam Darcy came from a dynasty of powerful business moguls, not politicians. His parents were dead, leaving just him and his much younger sister. His aunt and uncle ran the family as if it were a business proposition and Darcy a failed enterprise. He was included at family events but hardly acknowledged, apart from his aunt's occasional attempts to mold him into a leader in high society. His uncle looked on Darcy's refusal to take a role in the family business as a personal insult and behaved accordingly toward him. It was hopeless, yet Darcy continued to hope that someday they would accept him.

No wonder he was so silent, if there was any truth to this portrait. Anything Darcy said within the family circle was used against him, so he learned to say nothing. His uncle seemed to be the worst of them. Cassie wondered which of Calder's relatives had inspired the portrait.

After a particularly virulent tongue-lashing from his uncle, Darcy abruptly left the family estate to spend Christmas with old friends of his parents. Cassie closed the book. It was late, and she would need her strength to read this scene. She tucked the book into her briefcase and headed back to her apartment. Each step of the journey seemed painful.

Once she was in the door, she dropped her briefcase on a chair and went straight to the sink to rinse her face with cold water. As she scrubbed away the last traces of tears, she paused to look at herself in the mirror. She wasn't sure she knew the woman in the reflection. How could she have misjudged Calder's feelings so badly?

She dried her face with unnecessary vigor. Then, drawn to the book like a magnet, she returned to her briefcase. As she reached for the book, she noticed the open letter from Ryan still sitting on the table where she had left it that morning. It seemed like a lifetime ago. She had meant to write back to him tonight, but the book had made her forget everything. It was a stark reminder that Calder's Elizabeth Bennet was a far cry from the real Cassie Boulton.

She smoothed the letter between her fingers. She'd write Ryan an extra-long letter tomorrow. For now, she needed to know what else Calder had to say. She folded the letter and then took the book to her favorite old tapestry armchair and opened it again.

He had vaguely dreaded the party, expecting to feel as hemmed in and overwhelmed as he usually did at such affairs, but it was better than he expected. There were several rooms he could move between when the crowd in one became too much for him, and the Carltons' friends were a more palatable group on the whole than the company he was accustomed to with his aunt and uncle. No one made a fuss over his presence, and none of the women he met developed that predatory glint in her eye. God, but he was sick of the women he knew! Sick of them, and done with them, at least for a while. They had done nothing to help him forget Elizabeth; if anything, they made it worse by contrast to what he had lost in her. He preferred to be alone with his memories than to be with other women who could never match up to her.

There were tastefully decorated Christmas trees in every room, twinkling with lights, and he allowed himself to imagine what Christmas would be like with Elizabeth. Would she delight in the traditions, or look on them with amusement, her eyes meeting his to share the joke? He could not imagine Christmas with her as the sterile affair it had been for him growing up, where all gifts were "appropriate" and to be received with calm and well-bred thanks. No, Elizabeth would enjoy making other people happy. But *he* would never be the one she would make happy. His moment with her was past.

And he had no one to blame for that but himself. As time passed, he saw more and more clearly the opportunity he had missed. Why had he given up immediately when she told him it wouldn't work? He never told her his feelings, or tried to talk to her about what her needs were in her work, to see if there was a way for him to fit into them. He would rather have a small part of Elizabeth than all of another woman. He never even asked her what she wanted. He just passively accepted her decision, never considering whether the outcome could have been different with Elizabeth than it had been with his parents. Had he the chance to do it over again, he would at least have *tried* to convince her.

But self-recrimination was useless. The past was over and done. With a sigh, he realized he had not been attending to the conversation for several minutes. It was a sign he needed to leave. He excused himself politely, planning to spend the rest of the evening in his room, but he was only halfway down the hall when he found himself face to face with the very woman who had been haunting him.

It took him a moment to recognize she was real and not just a particularly vivid fantasy. "Elizabeth," he said slowly.

The familiar glint of mischief appeared in her eyes. "Will." She matched his tone. "Why, fancy meeting you here."

He could not get over seeing her in the flesh—in the flesh and a low-cut, close-fitting dress of midnight blue that accentuated the body he remembered so well. "What are you doing here?"

She raised a mocking eyebrow. "I was invited, as it happens. I'm here with a friend. And you?"

His senses were robbing him of coherent thought. That look in her eyes—did it mean she was glad to see him? The sight of the curves her dress revealed made him think of running his hands over them, feeling her body against his, hearing her soft moans of pleasure as he touched her, losing himself in her. Her eyes bewitched him. He could not let her go again.

Something must have shown in his face, because she said, "Are you all right? You look pale."

The concern in her voice nearly undid him. "No, no, I'm fine. Just surprised to see you here. I was thinking about you earlier."

"Nothing too horrible, I hope!"

"No." He searched desperately for something to say when all he wanted was to see her smile at him. "You look very nice."

She laughed. "I think you mean you're surprised to find out I don't always look like I'm headed straight for the marsh."

"That's not what I meant." His eyes were already seeing what she would look like divested of the little she was wearing. He could not think clearly with her so near him. As if he could not help himself, he stepped closer yet to her. "It's good to see you again."

She gave him a hesitant smile as he reached for her, as if unsure what he was about. He touched her cheek first, marveling at the miracle of her soft skin under his fingers again and then tasted her lips gently. He meant it to be an innocent kiss, one that would not be unreasonable as a greeting to a former lover. But he had underestimated how intoxicating her lips would be, how overwhelmed he would be by the remembered scent and taste of her. Before he even knew what he was doing, his tongue was exploring her mouth and he was holding her, seeking to replicate those moments he had replayed in his memory so often. And, oh God, she had her arms around his neck and was responding to his kiss just as he had dreamed of.

The rest of the world faded away. He needed her with an intensity and an urgency that left room only for the thought that he had to get her to his bedroom before this raced completely out of control. But he could not stop kissing her either, for fear she would disappear like a phantom in his arms.

She was the one who finally pulled back. Her cheeks were flushed and her eyes held that look of desire he remembered so well, but perhaps a bit of doubt as well. "Merry Christmas to you, too," she said.

He reached for her again to bring her back into his arms where she belonged. At first he thought she was going to resist, but then she melted into his arms, making him shake with desire. His fingers could feel the heat of her body through the thin fabric of her dress, and he wanted to touch more and more. She arched against him when his hand slid gently up her spine until it rested on the exposed skin of her upper back. He felt her shiver and knew he was lost.

He stopped kissing her just long enough to whisper, "Let's go somewhere more private."

She seemed to freeze at his words. She stepped away from him and crossed her arms as if to protect herself from him. A chill went through him. Surely the universe could not be so cruel as to give her back to him just for those few minutes, only to yank her away again?

"So how is Charles?" she asked, as if she had not been pressing her body passionately against his a moment earlier.

"Charles?" he repeated blankly. "He's fine."

"Has he found a new plaything yet? Or does he save that for summertime?" Her voice had sharp edges.

He struggled to free his mind from the haze of desire. "Plaything? I don't know what you mean."

"Why, Jane, of course. He got tired of her, and I was just curious if he'd found a new model yet."

"He didn't get tired of her. He realized it wouldn't work. He wants a woman he can spend time with, and with Jane trying to finish her PhD and get a teaching job, it was going to be years before she had any time for him."

"Oh, I see." Her voice dripped with sarcasm. "How very *clever* of him. I'm glad he didn't waste any time worrying about how *she* would feel about it." She hesitated, and her expression suggested a confusion her words did not express. "Nice seeing you again, Will."

Before he knew what was happening, she turned and walked away, leaving him stunned. What had gone wrong? How could she have gone from kissing him like there was no tomorrow to being angry with him? He could not understand it. Or perhaps he could, he thought, running their conversation through his head again. God, yes. He had said about three sentences to her and then kissed her and suggested they go to bed. No wonder she backed off.

How could he have been so idiotically out of control as to scare her away the moment she appeared? He remembered his earlier regrets about not fighting harder for her. Through a great stroke of luck, he was being given a second chance, and he would not let her get away again, not without giving it his best try. Decisively, he strode after her.

She closed her eyes. She could feel the sharp pain to come, as if it were a physical injury. She forced herself to keep reading, hoping somehow it would turn out differently in the story. Unfortunately, the rest of the scene was practically word-for-word what she remembered. The words blurred on the page before her when she reached the part where she walked out, leaving him to believe she was glad to be rid of him.

He stood on the steps, watching the tail lights of her car disappear, feeling as if he had been kicked. He had not only failed his second chance; he had learned that he never had a chance in the first place. God, had she really hated him this whole time? Could it be true that all this time while he was dreaming of her kindness and tenderness, she was thinking he was arrogant and rude? Why had she ever gone to bed with him? Why had she kissed him like that? And why, *why* did he still care?

At least before he had the illusion she cared for him

in her own way, even if she put her career first. Now he knew better; he meant less than nothing to her. And God help him, he was still in love with her. That was the one thing he had learned for certain tonight. Any doubt about that had been laid to rest the minute he saw her.

To think earlier he had been fantasizing about spending Christmas with her. As if she would ever spend any time with him of her own accord! How could he have mistaken her veneer of politeness for love? It was nothing more than desperation on his part.

Despite everything, all he wanted was to see her smile, and to know she was happy. "Merry Christmas, Elizabeth," he whispered to the cold, empty night air.

He did not go back to the party; that would have been impossible. Instead he went to his room and hid there for hours until the last guests left. He alternated between pacing and sitting in the chair staring into space, unable to focus on reading and registering only pain as he listened to the laughter and music from downstairs. The physical weight of loss added to his sense of his own failure, that a woman like Elizabeth would have nothing but dislike for him. And why should she feel otherwise? What had he ever done to give her a good opinion of him? He had assumed that she, like all the women who pursued him, would want to be with him, and he had missed the basic truth. Those women had not wanted him, but only his money and his name. He was just what they had to tolerate to get what they wanted.

He chastised himself for sliding into self-pity, but with

the painful ache in his gut of knowing that the woman he loved wanted nothing to do with him, he could think of little reason why anyone *would* want to be with him. He liked to think of himself as concerned about other people's feelings, but as Elizabeth had so correctly pointed out, he never once considered how Jane might have felt. And then there were all the women he used while trying to forget Elizabeth—well, they had been using him too, but he had made no particular effort to make sure he did not hurt them the way Elizabeth hurt him that summer. No, she was right; he was selfish. At least she could not dislike him more than he disliked himself right now.

His head was starting to ache, making him wonder if the headache Elizabeth claimed to have was real or an excuse to get away from him. Probably the latter, given the way she left him so abruptly after he kissed her. He went to the medicine closet in the bathroom, took some painkiller, and went to lie down on the bed until his head felt better. If only there were something as simple he could take for the ache in his soul.

The next day at dinner, Eve Carlton asked him how he enjoyed the party. "I know you didn't know many of the people there."

"I met some interesting people, and I even ran into someone I already knew."

"Oh, who was that?"

"Elizabeth Bennet."

"Elizabeth?" She looked puzzled for a moment. "Oh, you must mean Lizzy, Doug Phillips's friend! Yes, she comes with him every year. A very nice girl. And you met her before?"

"Yes, last summer." So the friend she was visiting, whom she visited every year, was male. He felt as if there were a fist clenched inside him. Someone else had already discovered how to fit into her life.

"Do you remember Mrs. Phillips, Will?" Dan shook his head in amusement. "Remember how old-fashioned she is? It's quite the joke here; despite all the evidence to the contrary, she still insists on believing that some day Doug will settle down with Lizzy and get married. I guess there are certain facts of modern life she will never get used to, especially when they involve her darling boy."

"Apparently not." So at least part of it was true, that her job kept her from a full-time relationship, but how was he to bear that the small part of her that was available was reserved for another man?

It pounded at his head all day, that only a few miles away Elizabeth was laughing with Doug Phillips, playing with him, loving him. He had never known that emotions could cause the level of physical pain he felt through every inch of his body. He could see both Dan and Eve watching him with concern.

The following day Dan made a point of catching him when he was by himself. "Will, I don't know if you ever feel the need to be off by yourself, but we have a little cabin out in the middle of the woods not far from here. I go there when I need to be alone for a while. It's pretty primitive—wood-burning stove and all—but you can go snowshoeing or cross-country skiing. If you'd ever like to go out there for a while, just say the word and it's yours."

"Thanks, Dan." He understood that this offer was not coming out of the blue. He appreciated the kindness more than Dan knew; it meant something that someone cared enough to think of what he might need. "I might like to do that."

Dan took him out to the cabin the next day. It was not quite as primitive as he had suggested. Darcy was almost disappointed to discover it had electric lights and running water. He was in the mood for some true deprivation to take his mind off his current misery. Dan showed him how to work the wood stove and how to split wood before he went, and Darcy spent the next few hours becoming marginally competent with an axe and then splitting enough wood to last for days. By the time he was done, his hands were thoroughly blistered and his feet painfully cold. He restarted the fire, which had gone out while he was taking his anger and frustration out on helpless logs, and heated some canned soup on the wood stove. After eating, he found a way to make ice packs for his palms out of snow and dishtowels and sat with the lights out, watching the flames inside the stove and thinking despondently of Elizabeth.

It made the pattern for his days there. He woke up to the cold each morning and shivered until he had the stove going. Then he would go outside and spend the day exhausting himself, letting the ache of sore muscles and cold feet distract him from his unhappiness. Afterwards, he would spend his evenings consciously reliving every moment he ever spent with Elizabeth, the good and the bad, until the pain became too much to bear. Then he would imagine her in Doug's arms, content with his affection and her compartmentalized life. He forced himself to examine it closely, to think how she would react to another man's touch, and the pleasure she would offer him with nary a thought for Fitzwilliam Darcy.

No, that was not fair, he corrected himself. He had not imagined her response to him when he kissed her at the party, and she was not a woman who would take sexual pleasure from whatever man was nearest. She had clearly been upset with herself for being aroused by him, and it was understandable, if there was a man there to whom she owed her loyalty. No wonder she pushed him away with her anger; anger that he deserved for thinking she would fall into his arms just because he wanted her to. No, someone else had learned to be honest with her first and how to treat her the way she deserved. All he would have was memories and the knowledge that it could have been different, if only he had not tried so hard to protect himself behind a wall no one could breach.

He stayed there a week. Dan came by twice with fresh provisions, never inquiring into the source of Darcy's distress, but providing a brief break from his brutal introspections. Finally, he acknowledged to himself that it was pointless to continue to brood on the impossible and called Dan to tell him he was ready to leave. As he looked around the cabin for the last time, he realized that an era of his life had ended there.

Elizabeth Bennet was beyond his reach. He might never again meet a woman as engaging, with her combination of liveliness, wit, and passion for living and learning, but there had to be other people somewhere who could see him for the person he was rather than just a Darcy—if only he would let them, if only he *knew* who he really was.

He had always looked for understanding in the wrong places, among the people most likely to value the Darcy name and money above anything else, but no longer. Now he knew there were other people out there. That was Elizabeth's unknowing final gift to him. If he could never have Elizabeth, he would look for people like her and try to turn himself into the kind of person he would have wished to have been with her. It would be enough. It would have to be enough.

The End

Chapter 14

BE CAREFUL WHAT YOU *wish for. You just might get it.* Wasn't that what people always said? Cassie had never fully appreciated it before.

She dragged her mind back to the present. Some advisor she was. She couldn't even keep her mind from drifting when Chris was sitting right there in her office, waiting for her response. She tapped the paper listing doctoral programs in marine biology and oceanography. "If MIT/WHOI is what you want, Chris, it's worth taking a shot at it. It's tough to get into, but your grades are solid, and your MBL experience will help. They'll look at more than your test scores. Have you thought of other schools to apply to?"

"Brown's program at the MBL."

Yep, he was about as single-minded as she'd been at that age. Good thing there were two doctoral programs in Woods Hole these days. "Another great program, but hard to predict admissions because it's still so new. What else?"

"BU, University of Maryland, Duke, and of course UNC." Chris twisted a pencil in his hand.

"UNC's a safe bet, since Jim knows your work, and you could still spend summers in Woods Hole. What about Berkeley or Oregon?"

Chris's mouth set in a straight line. "I want to study the Atlantic. I want MIT/WHOI."

Just like she wanted Calder. And now it seemed he was within her reach. A few days ago, she would have said she'd be ecstatic to hear he cared about her. She *was* ecstatic. But facing the reality of it, she was also panicked. Reading his book, she'd realized how little they knew each other. What kind of basis for love was that? Was it really love at all? Maybe he'd get to know her and realize she wasn't who he thought she was. What about his family? They'd be horrified by her, and she wasn't so sure about them either. Fantasizing about Calder Westing was definitely easier than contemplating the reality of a relationship with him. And he'd be on her doorstep in two days.

"I know, and I'll do everything I can for you there. But you need to be realistic and have some backups. The other schools are very good," she said.

"They aren't in Woods Hole."

"I know. Believe me, I understand." Hadn't she schemed for years to be sure she could go back to the MBL? But the only reason she'd been able to go back this summer was because of Calder. It all came round to him again. "I'll talk to a couple of people I know at WHOI and see what I can find out for you." She gestured to the journal on his lap. "That won't hurt, either.

Not shabby, being third author on an article in *Annals of Marine Biology* as an undergrad."

Chris's expression lightened. "Yeah. Can't complain about that!"

"Wherever you end up, you can still work with me this summer, assuming my grant comes through." Not as safe an assumption as it used to be, but she intended to apply for more different types of funding this year. Better to be prepared.

Once Chris left, Cassie's mind immediately returned to Calder and the book she had finished late last night. She couldn't pretend she didn't know he was coming. He'd find out soon enough. She wasn't ready to talk to him by telephone, that was certain. But she wanted to see him. She wanted it so much it hurt. Finally she opened his last email and pressed reply. After several attempts, she decided to stick to the bare bones.

To: C. Westing
From: C. Boulton

So, what's a nice university boy like you doing applying for a job at an evil liberal arts college like this? Cassie

She clicked on Send and then shut down her computer. Otherwise she'd sit there all day checking her email obsessively. She lasted two nervous hours before she turned it on again and waited anxiously while new messages downloaded. Her heart began to race when she saw his name.

I should have known you would be a step ahead of me. How did you hear I was coming? Calder

She smiled with relief before pressing Reply.

I have friends in high places, or at least in the English department. CB

I take it you've guessed about Stephen West. SCW3

Scott spilled the beans when I saw him in July. Not his fault; he thought you'd already told me. And your new book was a little clue. CB

PS—No fair. You have more initials than I do.

The book? Sorry. I was going to look you up when I was there and tell you about that. SCW3

PS—You could use your middle initial. What's your middle name?

You still could, if you like. CB

PS—My middle name? That's a deep, dark secret.

I'd like that very much, whatever your middle name is. SCW3

Dinner that night? CB

You're on. Is there anything I should know about what you've told them about me? SCW3

They had some doubts as to why you would consider the position—you're overqualified, you know—and I told them I didn't know if you were serious about it or not, but I doubted the low salary was an issue for you. That's about it. Nobody asked what name I knew you by, so I didn't say.

Cassie

I'm very serious about it.

Calder

The message gave Cassie an odd feeling inside. She suspected he wasn't just speaking of his job prospects. She let that one sit overnight before responding.

Do you want me to tell the committee that?

Cassie

That's up to you, really. I'm trying not to make any assumptions.

Calder

It was amazing how much he could unsettle her with a few simple sentences.

***

Calder massaged the back of his neck with one hand as he reread Cassie's latest email, which took two sentences to say nothing at all. Except that she was still speaking to him after reading his book. That was something, at least.

It could have been worse. Once he decided to publish the story that had poured out of him compulsively after the ill-fated

Christmas party, he hoped it would explain to Cassie and to himself all the things he should have said a year ago. Even if he could never have her, he wanted her understanding, to be free of the constant ache of knowing she was angry at him. If he could believe she might have forgiven him, it would be easier to bear. She would read the book sooner or later and recognize he was the only one who could have written it. It didn't occur to him until it was too late that it might make her more angry.

Receiving her two short emails in the spring had meant an embarrassing amount to him. He'd been hard put not to betray himself by answering them immediately and in depth. Even knowing she had another man in her life, he couldn't help wanting more, but when he tried emailing her out of the blue in the summer, she didn't respond. He tried to pretend it didn't matter, but it left him feeling sick and rejected all over again, and it was weeks before he stopped watching for her name in his inbox. He hadn't hoped for anything beyond that until the end of the summer when he again visited the Crowleys. Unable to resist probing at his sorest spot, he asked them about Tim, Cassie's friend, and was regaled with a tale of his newest boyfriend.

Later that week he received her Trivial Pursuit email. When he saw a notice for the writer-in-residence position at Haverford, he knew it was fate. He would meet her on her own ground, he would give her time to get to know him, and when she did, he would tell her how he felt about her, without demands or questions.

Her email about meeting him at Haverford was an enormous relief, a sign he still had a chance. With each new message, he became cautiously more optimistic. Surely if she planned to reject him, she wouldn't go to this much trouble. Now he only had to keep the lines of communication open until he could see her. He thought for a moment and then began to type.

> I'm looking forward to seeing Haverford and meeting some of those students you're teaching how to think. Here's hoping they don't eat me alive—it's not as if I've ever taught anything in my life. Calder

> *It's easy. Just listen to them, and talk to them like they're adults. You'll do fine.*
> *Cassie*

> Talk?? Me? I hope they don't expect the seminar to last over five minutes!
> Calder

> *Now, now, I've heard you talk very nicely on occasion. Sometimes even four or five words at a stretch. We'll advertise you as laconic.*
> *Cassie*

He never thought he would feel so grateful for being teased. If she was willing to tease him, especially about his inability to express himself, then she wasn't just tolerating him because she had to.

He moved the mouse and clicked on a bookmarked site he had visited so often that his hand seemed to go there automatically. It was from a scientific conference two years earlier and contained small photos of the presenters. He gazed at Cassie's picture, wondering for the thousandth time what she had been thinking of when it was taken to give her that mischievous look he remembered so well. He closed his eyes and could see her before him again: toweling her hair dry at the beach, the look on her face when he touched her deep inside, her head on his shoulder as she lay asleep in his arms.

Once more he reread her emails, though he knew them from memory. Tomorrow he would know the truth.

***

Cassie's anxiety rose as Thursday approached. She began to remember some of Calder's annoying habits—his abruptness, his silences, and his sudden changes in mood. Even if she had a better understanding of him now, what would happen when he fell silent and she couldn't read him? How was she to judge what he really wanted from her when she was so ambivalent herself? What if he had already moved on from the feelings he had for her, or if his book was more fictional than she thought?

She was glad she had a lecture to give on Thursday morning. It would distract her from thoughts of what Calder was doing across the campus. But when she returned to her office after the class, she found a message from Dr. Yang requesting her attendance at a meeting that afternoon. Puzzled, she rearranged her schedule to allow her to go.

The entire English department was there. Cassie felt like a fish out of water.

"Well, any comments?" Dr. Yang asked.

"He seemed nice enough," said one person. "I couldn't see anything to object to, and as you said, we'd be hard put to turn down someone with his credentials, *if* he really wants the job."

"Yes, that's still the question, isn't it?" asked Dr. Gottschalk.

"For what it's worth," Cassie said, "he told me he's serious about it."

"Hmm. That's good news, I suppose," said Dr. Yang.

"He didn't really *sound* all that interested," said another doubtfully. "But then again, I found him pretty hard to read."

Dr. Yang raised an eyebrow in Cassie's direction.

"Don't look at me!" she said. "I could earn a second PhD in how to misread Ca . . . Stephen West."

"But you would favor hiring him?"

"I have no reason to think he shouldn't be hired," she said carefully.

Hal Bailey asked, "Did our beloved president have anything to say about him?"

"In fact, President Carroll said something quite curious on the subject," said Dr. Yang, watching Cassie closely. "He said, 'If you want my advice, hire him. I don't care if he can teach or write or even speak English, just hire him.'"

There were exclamations of surprise from around the room. President Carroll was notoriously hands-off in matters of hiring, preferring to respect the independence of each department in those matters. The comment was remarkably out of character.

Cassie hid a smile. If Calder was trying to pass unrecognized, apparently he hadn't been completely successful. Given that one of the major roles of any college president was fundraising, she had no doubt why President Carroll would want Calder Westing on the faculty. But it was a taste of things to come. If Calder took the job at Haverford, the secret of Stephen West's identity wasn't going to survive long.

"Dr. Boulton," said Dr. Yang pointedly. "Do you have anything to share on the subject?"

"Nothing in particular," she replied.

He removed his glasses and laid them on the table. "It is very difficult to chair a committee on hiring a candidate," he said acerbically, "when everyone around me appears to have important information that I lack."

Cassie said, "If you're suggesting I'm holding information back, you're quite correct. However, I'm *not* holding back any information relevant to whether he's qualified for this position." There was no point in trying to pretend at this point. If they hired Calder, they would learn soon enough that she had been keeping secrets. "As for President Carroll, I can *guess* why he said that, but if he's not saying, I don't think it's my place to do so."

Dr. Yang eyed her for a moment. "Your point is taken, Dr. Boulton. Nonetheless, this puts me in a difficult position."

Cassie endured his stare for a minute and then shrugged. She still needed tenure, and alienating a powerful faculty member wouldn't help her. She tore a sheet of paper out of her notebook and wrote on it:

He's rich as Croesus and very well connected. He's known in philanthropic circles, and President Carroll may have recognized him.

She folded the paper and handed it up the table to Dr. Yang.

He opened it and examined it, seeming to consider for a moment. Then he refolded it carefully and put it down. "You're right; this has no bearing on his candidacy," he said. "Does anyone else have any concerns I should be aware of before I have my exit interview with him?" He looked around the room. "If not, we'll meet again next week to make a decision."

Chapter 15

"THERE'S A STEPHEN WEST here to see you."

Cassie recognized the voice of Denise, the department secretary. "I'll be right out," she said and hung up the phone. Her heart was pounding.

She stood and paused nervously, looking around her office. Calder had seen her lab in Woods Hole, so he should be used to her piles of books and journals. She straightened her blouse and headed down the hall, assuming a confidence she didn't feel.

Calder was waiting outside the department office, dressed for an interview, with his coat slung over his arm. Otherwise, he looked just the same as she remembered—the planes of his face, his dark hair. The familiar look was in his eyes, the one that had always made her feel warm inside. Now, knowing what lay behind it, she could practically feel her legs trembling.

A couple of students lounged on a bench across the hall. Cassie held out her hand to Calder, conscious of the audience. "Welcome to Haverford, *Stephen*. How was your interview?"

"Very informative. Haverford is impressive, but you knew that already." He held her hand a little longer than necessary.

"I gather you were paying attention when I told you my opinion of a small-college education." She had to stop staring at him like an infatuated teenager. "Would you like the grand tour? We're very proud of our new building."

The corners of his mouth turned up. "Then I certainly must see it."

She gave him a sidelong glance as she led him down the hall to a large lab, still feeling the shock of their hands touching. That part of their connection hadn't changed. "This is where we have Bio 101 lab. Most afternoons it's full of pre-meds and one or two serious biologists. Quite a difference from my closet in Woods Hole."

He looked around, taking in the shiny new fixtures and the well-maintained equipment. "True, but that had its own charms."

She could feel his eyes on her as she pointed to the room across the hall. "The biochem and genetics students share this one. Down the hall, we have our main lecture hall. I'm not quite used to it yet. It makes me feel like I'm on the bridge of a spaceship. And this is my office. The most exciting part of moving to this building was getting an office with a window."

Calder studied the sign on her door listing her office hours and then followed her inside. "It's nice."

The small space made her even more aware of him physically. "Would you like to see my great accomplishment?" Nervously, she picked up a journal from her desk. "It came out last month. This is from the work I did the summer we met. It was a bit of a coup, getting it in *Annals of Marine Biology*." She opened it to the middle and handed it to him.

He didn't just glance through the dense scientific text as most non-biologists did but leaned back against her desk and read it. Cassie took the opportunity to study him unobtrusively. She remembered the lines of his face and the shape of his body so well, even after all this time. Her lips tingled as she recalled how his shoulders felt under her hands. It was disconcerting, this sense that her body knew his, even after all this time. Almost as disturbing as the sense that he was both a complete stranger and a close friend at the same time.

"The Great Sippewisset Salt Marsh. I never knew it had a name." Calder glanced up at her. He took a deep breath at the look on her face and then returned to the article.

She would have sworn the temperature in the room had gone up a couple of degrees. She gazed studiously out into the hallway, reminding herself it was just hormones and a primitive urge to procreate. She couldn't throw herself into his arms the minute he arrived. That hadn't solved anything for them before. They needed to talk this time.

Finally, he closed the journal and gave it back to her. "Very impressive. I won't claim to understand the statistics, but I'm glad you got your publishable results."

She remembered the time they had talked about her need for results, in his dark car on the way to the marsh, and what else had happened that night. "Thanks. I am, too."

He was silent for a moment. "I didn't think you'd hear about my interview." His expression took on a touch of teasing. "At Harvard, the science faculty don't even know that the English department exists, much less talk to them."

She gave an amused smile. "Things are different here." Her words took on a resonance she hadn't intended.

"I'm glad of that." He looked at her with that intent stare she remembered so well. "Are you still free for dinner?"

Free for the asking was more like it. She had to get control of herself. "Of course. I'm looking forward to it."

His eyes warmed. "When will you be done here?"

"I can leave now, if you want." She reached for her coat.

He took it from her and held it out. Cassie, unused to such treatment, awkwardly shrugged into it. As he brought the collar around her neck, his hands rested briefly on her shoulders. She could feel the after-effects of his touch all the way to her toes.

He put on his jacket. "Cassie," he said, sounding suddenly uncertain.

She looked up at him. The disquiet in his face was out of keeping with the aura of confidence he usually projected, but if his book was to be believed, the confidence was a false front. And he trusted her with his feelings, even after everything she'd done. It made her want to hold him and reassure him that everything would be all right. If only she could say that with confidence. There were still so many unknowns.

Instead she gave in to the temptation to touch him. She straightened his lapels, using the action as an excuse to let her hands linger on his chest for a moment. She was only inches away from him. "It's good to see you again."

"Thank you." Tension radiated from his body.

Of course he was holding back. She knew about his feelings from his book. He was still in the dark about hers. It was almost comic. "Oh, dear," she said, giving him an impish look.

His mouth tightened. "What's the matter?"

She pointed upward, and when his eyes followed her finger, she smiled mischievously. "No mistletoe. I guess I'll have to improvise."

She slid her hands up to his shoulders and linked them behind his neck. He seemed frozen in place. Standing on tiptoe, she brushed her lips lightly against his.

For one frightening moment, she thought he wouldn't respond, but then he reached for her. Her breath caught in her throat as she felt his arms slip around her. On pure instinct, she arched against him, and a surge of electricity seemed to pass through her as their lips met again.

She had forgotten how powerful her physical reaction was to him. Moving closer until she could feel the sensuous pressure of his body against hers, she sighed as his tongue teased her lips apart, fulfilling the aching desire that had been building in her since she read his book, since the last time she was in his arms.

She'd known that once he touched her she wouldn't be able to resist the temptation he offered, regardless of the difficulties between them. She had lost none of her dangerous susceptibility to him. She shivered at the pleasure of his touch.

She wanted more and knew it was insane, even thinking of how she wanted him to touch her. Her office was a far cry from a deserted beach late at night, and she couldn't allow herself the same loss of control she had then. It was crazy enough to kiss him here where anyone walking down the hall could see, even if the building was pretty much emptied out for the day. She gathered hold of herself, forcing back the feelings he was arousing and pulling away a little from his kiss.

He rested his forehead against hers, his breathing ragged. "So much for my plans to show some self-control."

Her hands were still on his shoulders, feeling the strength of him. "Don't apologize. I liked it."

"So did I." His mouth captured hers again.

One more kiss couldn't hurt, not when it felt so good. Not now, when she finally had the answer to her question about whether he still wanted her. But would he still feel that way in a month, when he knew her better? She couldn't let it go too far. Not yet. Touching her finger to his lips, she said, "We're a combustible combination. It doesn't take intent on either of our parts for our hindbrains to take over and try to get on with the business of perpetuating the species."

"Spoken like a true biologist," he said, but with a faint smile. "Maybe we should go to dinner before my hindbrain gets me into any more trouble."

She buttoned her coat. At least that way she kept her hands off him. "I thought we'd walk, if that's okay. There's a nice little restaurant just across from campus."

The sun was beginning to set, turning the autumn leaves into brighter hues of yellow and red, as they started down the tree-lined avenue that ran between the college and town. The crisp air was a blessing, cooling the heat on Cassie's cheeks. She pointed out several campus landmarks as they walked and then led him off the road to a split-rail fence with a small pond beyond it.

She rested her hands on the fence. "This is the duck pond. I come here a lot. It isn't the ocean, but it's the closest we have." Several mallards flocked toward her, quacking loudly. She took a small plastic bag of bread from her coat pocket. "They know I'm an easy touch." She handed Calder a piece of bread and began to shred the other, tossing the pieces to the ducks, who grabbed them eagerly.

She noticed Calder was still holding his bread, his eyes on her rather than the ducks. "You don't like feeding ducks?" she asked.

"I'm watching how you do it."

She paused, bread crumb in hand. "Don't tell me you've never fed ducks before."

"Okay, I won't tell you. Just remember how limited my education is."

"That overrated place up in Boston doesn't have ducks?" she teased. A large duck stuck his head through the fence, honking loudly. "Believe me, there's no wrong way to feed ducks."

He broke off some bread and tossed it to the duck that was farthest away. "In my family, there would have been a wrong way to feed ducks." He said it with light irony.

"Not these ducks. They'll be happy with anything you give them." Cassie dusted the last of the crumbs from her hands.

Calder bent down and held a piece of bread through the fence. A mallard promptly grabbed it from his hand. He smiled as he tore off another breadcrumb.

Cassie watched him as he carefully fed the quacking mob. When his bread was gone, he straightened and looked at her. His gaze left her awash with feelings.

He paused, as if weighing his options. "I owe you an apology. I planned to tell you about my book before it came out. I didn't want you taken by surprise."

On impulse, she put her hand over his where it rested on a fencepost, the warmth of it a sharp contrast to the cool autumn air. "Don't worry. It was a shock, but I'm used to discovering everything I know about you is wrong." She looked down at their hands. "I'm getting good at it."

"I knew the book itself would be a surprise, but I didn't realize anything in it would be." He sounded puzzled.

A smile touched her lips. "Calder, until recently I had no idea you ever gave me a second thought. I was stunned."

"You didn't *know?* How could you not know?"

She turned and looked out across the pond, wishing for some of his skill with words, at least written words. "Men like you don't look at women like me, much less want one. And besides, I thought you didn't particularly like me."

"You thought I . . ." He was dumbfounded. "But I kept looking for excuses to be with you. I asked you out. I came to your lab."

"I can be pretty oblivious sometimes. And you weren't talking much."

"I assumed you knew."

She finally looked at him again. "Neither of us ever said what we were feeling. You thought you didn't have to, and I was afraid to."

He turned his hand over and entwined his fingers with hers. "What were you afraid to tell me?"

This was it. He'd opened himself up to her in his book, and now it was her turn—if she dared. "That I was getting in too deep with you. That you were going away at the end of the summer and I was going to be hurt." It was strange. They'd been lovers, but she'd never held his hand before. It was intoxicating.

"Is that why you backed off?"

She nodded. The sound of laughter and footsteps came from behind them. She glanced toward the road and saw a group of students passing by. Reluctantly, she withdrew her hand from Calder's. "Sorry. I have to look professorial," she said in a stage whisper.

He stuffed his hands into his pockets. "When you said at Christmas that Scott hurt Erin, were you talking about yourself, too?"

"At some level, I suppose so." She felt oddly defensive in the face of his reaction.

He glanced at the road, clearly frustrated by the presence of observers. "I never meant to hurt you."

"I know. I never thought I *could* hurt you." She shivered as a chilly breeze whipped through her hair.

His gaze softened. "You're cold. We should get to the restaurant."

She didn't want any more misunderstandings. "Calder?"

"Yes?"

She held out her hand to him. "To hell with looking professorial."

His look of happiness was all the reward she needed.

***

Calder picked up his wineglass and watched the candlelight reflect in the red wine for a moment before taking a sip. "You never said what made you change your mind about me."

Cassie could hear the uncertainty behind his question. Hardly a surprise, after the things she'd said to him at Christmas. "A lot of things. You were so nice to me that day in Woods Hole. Then Scott let it slip that you were Stephen West, and I realized you couldn't possibly be the man I thought you were and have written those books."

"What do you mean?"

"I knew Stephen West was compassionate, insightful, and empathic. He wouldn't have disregarded my feelings. So I had to have made a mistake somewhere."

"Thank you, though I doubt it's deserved." He set his wineglass down.

She took a deep breath. "If I had any doubts, they would have gone away when I saw the MBL Annual Report."

"Oh. You weren't supposed to find out about that."

"Why not?"

He shrugged. "I thought you'd feel like I was trying to buy you, when I really only did it because I wanted to."

"See? Compassionate and empathic. Then I read your book, and suddenly it all started making sense. Including how I felt."

"And that is?"

Her breath seemed caught in her chest. "Among other things, we don't know each other that well yet. You have pretty high expectations of me. I don't know if I can live up to it."

"I want you to be yourself. That's all I need."

His comment left a silence she couldn't fill. "This talking part is hard," she complained light-heartedly, hoping to make a joke of it. "No wonder we never tried it before."

"No, we found other ways of breaking the ice." His gaze warmed. "Which gives me an idea for the house."

"The house?" She was finding looking into his eyes all too enjoyable.

"A hot tub," he replied.

Cassie wondered if she had missed some part of the discussion. "Don't you think you're skipping a few steps here?" she asked.

He gave her a perplexed look. "You don't think it's a good idea?"

Cassie laughed. "Calder, you're being incomprehensible again." With a mischievous smile, she took a pen and pad of paper from her bag and pushed them toward him. "Try writing it down. I seem to do better understanding what you're thinking then."

He laughed. Taking the pen, he looked thoughtful for a minute, and then began to write. She watched him in fascination as he wrote, then paused, and then wrote again. Finally he looked up and handed her the paper.

I imagine you know why I find the idea of you in the water to be sexy. When I move here, which I hope will be very soon, I think it would be nice to get a hot tub for our house here. I don't think we'd need one at Woods Hole. After all, in addition to all the other possibilities there, I have some longstanding fantasies about making love to you in your lab. Someday I'll explain all of them to you. And while I'm on the subject, let me mention that I wish we were alone right now, because I have a distinct interest in reacquainting myself with the softness of your skin and how sweetly you respond when I touch you.

Cassie turned scarlet. With an amused look, Calder said, "You told me to write what I was thinking about."

Her physical response to reading his note made it difficult to answer coherently. "Well, now I know where your mind is, but I still have some questions about this 'our house' scenario. *I* have an apartment. *You*, presumably, will have a one-semester nonrenewable appointment here. I don't see how you get 'our house' out of the equation."

He looked at her seriously. "I'm not coming here for the job. I'm coming because this is where you are. The job is a good way to learn about your world."

She couldn't believe he was saying these things. His eyes were more intoxicating than the wine. "Calder, I'm happy you're here. Very happy. But I'm not asking for forever. Being with you now is enough. I don't have a lot of faith in happily ever afters."

"I thought you liked your coffee with cream and your literature with optimism."

He'd remembered her words all this time? "I do. I just don't expect it in real life. Especially with someone like you, with all your advantages."

"What advantages? I'm rich and I have a famous name. I don't think you give a damn about my money, and being famous isn't all it's cracked up to be. All it gets you is tabloids digging into your privacy and publishing every embarrassing secret you've ever had. I wish nobody had ever heard of me."

A breath of fear washed over her. She hadn't thought about that aspect of being involved with him. "They wouldn't be that interested in me, would they?"

"Not right away, no. Once they work out that I'm serious, you'll get the full treatment. I'm sorry."

"Would they look into my past?"

"Of course. They're carrion." He took another sip of wine and then seemed to notice her distress. "What's wrong?"

She straightened the already impeccably placed silverware. "I'm very private about my past. I don't want people to know about it."

"Because your family isn't educated?"

"Shh!" She glanced from side to side but didn't see anyone she knew in the restaurant. "You're the only one who knows that."

He blinked in surprise. "But why? It's not a big deal."

"Not by itself, but then one question leads to another, and another, and another, and then it's a big deal." She twisted her napkin between her hands.

He hadn't come this far to give up over the tabloids. "Everybody has embarrassing secrets. I know. They've printed most of mine. It's not that bad, once you get used to it."

She took a slice of bread from the basket and placed it carefully on her plate, avoiding his eyes. "I'm not talking about being embarrassed. There are things about me no one knows, and they're dangerous. I could be looking at the end of my career, and if you take that away from me, there isn't much left."

"Whatever it is, it can't be that bad."

She broke the bread into several pieces and studied the remains. Finally looking up at him, she leaned forward and said in a voice just above a whisper, "I'm talking about possible prison time if this comes out."

He couldn't have heard her correctly. But her expression told him it was true.

"I'm sorry," she said. "I didn't want you to know. But you can see why I can't take the risk."

He took her hand again, desperate to feel the warmth of her skin. "What happened? You know I won't tell anyone."

"I've already told you more than I should, more than I've ever told anyone. Please don't ask me for anything else."

"But . . ." It was no longer about how to convince her to have a relationship with him. That could wait. Cassie was in trouble. He tried to imagine what she could possibly have done. Tax evasion? No, she was too honest and didn't have enough money in any case. Drunk driving? Hit-and-run? She was too responsible for that.

Accidental death? He had no idea. "There's got to be a statute of limitations."

Her mouth twisted. "Three and a half more years. Somehow I can't see you waiting around that long. And even then I'd be risking my career. The college frowns on its faculty members committing felonies, even if they can't be convicted."

He should have known it was too good to be true. "You're sure they'd find out about it?"

"I don't know. Only a couple of people know, and they wouldn't tell. But there's circumstantial evidence, and if they put two and two together . . ." Her voice trailed off.

The old hopeless feeling invaded him. It didn't really matter. Maybe the tabloids would never find it, whatever it was, but his father would be determined to separate them somehow, and he'd be hunting for something like this. He wouldn't be above using it to keep them apart, even if it meant Cassie going to jail. He'd take delight in ruining her life just to prove to Calder that he could.

No. He couldn't take that risk. Even if it meant never seeing her again, though God alone knew how he'd manage to stay away, now that he knew she cared. Maybe he'd go back to Ecuador. At least then he couldn't come to see her on impulse. Maybe she'd be willing to go with him. She'd be safe enough outside the country. But that was ridiculous. She wouldn't give up her career for him. It was grasping at straws, trying to keep the dream from slipping away between his fingers.

Her voice interrupted his thoughts. "Sorry you ever came here?"

"No. Just thinking."

"About what?" How did she manage to sound so calm when all his hopes were gone?

"Whether there are marine biologists in Ecuador."

"Ecuador? There's great marine biology there. They have the Galapagos. Why?" That was Cassie, all right. Always ready with facts.

He shook his head. "Just a random thought." A pipe dream, to be exact. He tasted defeat in the back of his mouth. "I'm sorry. I wish there were something I could do to help."

"The best thing you can do for me is to forget it completely."

He tightened his hand on hers. "I can try, but I don't forget things about you very easily." It was bittersweet, knowing she wanted him but that they could never be together. It wasn't a surprise, somehow. Just a different twist on not having time for him.

"You're not going to try to argue with me anymore?"

He shook his head. "As you say, there isn't any point. If there's something that could be used to hurt you, I can't expose you to that risk. Even if the press never found out, my father would, and he'd ruin you in a second if he had the chance. You're not the sort of woman he wants me to marry."

The word "marry" seemed to reverberate in the air between them. He shouldn't have let that slip.

Cassie recovered first. "What kind of woman does he want you to marry?"

"One who would be a political asset to the family."

"He's quite the romantic, I take it."

"The romance of power and money, yes. Don't believe the charming man you see on TV. He's ruthless."

"You sound very calm about it."

"He is what he is. It doesn't help to get upset about reality." He moved his thumb slightly, caressing her hand.

"Speaking of reality, as your unofficial consultant in marine biology, I feel obliged to point out that wounds from sea urchin spines are extremely painful, even once the spines are out. You have to soak them out, using vinegar."

"Caught in the act. Next time I'll ask you first."

She bit her lip. "You're doing that on purpose, aren't you?"

"What?"

"Saying things like 'next time.'"

He released her hand. "Not exactly. Just indulging myself in a little make-believe. I'll stop." If the only thing he could do for her was to pretend to want nothing more than companionship, he would do it. "So, how did you end up hearing about my interview?"

She accepted the new direction. With time, the conversation even became comfortable, reminding him how much he enjoyed her playful wit. It was just a new game of make-believe, pretending this wasn't unusual, that they could talk like this any time. Anything to avoid admitting to himself that in an hour he would be saying good-bye to her forever.

***

On the way to the restaurant, Cassie had walked as close to Calder's side as she could. Now she kept her distance. It was a far cry from the last time they walked together in the dark, that night at the salt marsh.

"Where's your car?" he asked when they reached the campus parking lot.

"At home. I walk to work. It's only a few minutes."

"At least let me give you a ride there. It's dark."

She wavered. Spending any more time together would just hurt more, but she didn't think she could argue with him without falling apart. She was having a hard enough time not crying as it was. "Okay."

It was the same car he had driven on the Cape. It shouldn't have surprised her. After all, why would he have changed cars? But it was one of those things she associated so strongly with that summer it shocked her to see it now. He opened the passenger door for her. As she got in, the familiar interior sent her senses spinning back to that night on the beach.

But there was no point in thinking of that now. Any future with Calder was even more hopeless now than it had been then.

Calder started the car, and Cassie directed him to a large old house set back from the road. "This is it. The owners made over the top floors into separate apartments. I live on the third floor."

He pulled into the driveway and turned off the car. "It looks nice."

"Thanks for dinner." What words were appropriate for saying good-bye under these circumstances? She would never see him again.

"It was my pleasure."

She swallowed hard. "I'm sorry about all the misunderstandings. I wish things could be different."

"I know. I'll tell the college I'm withdrawing my application." There was stark pain in his voice.

She wanted to tell him not to, but she kept her eyes on her hands. God help her, she was going to cry after all. Why did Calder have to be who he was? "I'm still glad I had the chance to see you."

He reached over and took her hand without a word.

Would she ever find another man who could make her feel the way Calder did? He could bring out more passion in her than she knew she had. Was her future to be always comparing other men to him and finding them lacking?

The temptation was haunting. Finally the words rushed out without control. "Do you want to come upstairs? I know we don't have a future together. But we still have today."

There was a moment of silence and then he leaned toward her and let his lips touch hers.

The kiss exploded with the force of months of longing. Suddenly his arms were around her and her hands were buried deep in his hair. A flood of desire seized her but it was different this time. This bittersweet desperation had been missing in their other encounters, the sense of grasping at a dream that was sliding through her fingers. She wanted to forget everything beyond the immediate reality of his body and hers.

His hands were underneath her shirt, tracing the curve of her back, lines of fire following where his fingers touched. It wasn't enough. She was already feeling the ache inside her, the need for his intimate touch. How had she gone without him for so long?

She gasped as his hand reached her breast. She nibbled at his lips, silently begging for him to move his fingers inward, knowing that once he touched her nipple she would be beyond the ability to stop. No—who did she think she was fooling? She had been beyond the point of stopping when he was still holding her hand. She had never been able to resist Calder Westing when he touched her. It was no different now.

"Cassie," he whispered, his breathing ragged. "I don't know how I'm going to get you out of the car, much less let you go afterwards."

She heard the uncertainty in his voice, and suddenly all she wanted was to make everything all right for him. She couldn't see his eyes clearly in the darkness, but she rested her palms on the sides of his face, wishing she could bring him happiness instead of loss.

"Make-believe," she said, kissing him between her words. "Pretend we have the rest of our lives ahead of us. Leave reality for tomorrow."

It was like watching a dam break. "Cassie." He pressed his lips against her face, her neck, her hair.

She pulled back, resting her fingers over the heat that was his hand on her breast. "Come with me." Somehow she managed to tear herself away from his touch long enough to escape from the car, but as soon as he was beside her, their hands joined as if unable to stay apart.

Calder followed her up to her apartment. When she turned on the lights, he said, "Very nice."

It was nothing more than a comfortably furnished room with too many bookcases. She knew he was accustomed to a far different standard. "Well, it's home."

He didn't look at all uncomfortable, sliding an arm around her waist and pulling her to him. "I've dreamed about this." His lips descended to meet hers.

"So have I." She shivered from the heady feeling of his body against hers. There was only sensation as she accepted the sweetness of his kisses. He reached again under her shirt, caressing her skin.

She thought she might melt from the heat he was creating in her. She unbuttoned his shirt until she could slide her hands up his bare chest. She had wanted this for so long; she ached for him with a need she couldn't suppress. He was no longer wealthy and famous Calder Westing, or even the talented writer she admired. He was only the man she had longed for and was so close to loving she could hardly tell the difference.

His hands skimmed her body under her clothes, sending burning jolts of desire through her. Without thought, she pressed her hips against him. He moaned in response, moving his hand to encompass the soft skin of her breast. His touch there felt electric and left her helplessly craving an even greater intimacy.

There was no more need for words then. It was just as she remembered it, the tide of arousal she couldn't resist. She moaned and moved against him as his fingers explored and tantalized. The ache and excitement continued to rise until she clung to him, shaking with tremors of fulfilled desire.

By the time they finally made their way to her bedroom, their discarded clothing lying in untidy heaps on the living room floor, she was making her own demands of him, encouraging him and pulling him closer until at last, at last she could feel him inside her. Where he belonged, more than any other man ever could.

Make-believe.

***

Her apartment was blindingly silent. Cassie had delayed coming home as long as she could, knowing this would be the hardest part, facing the emptiness that would never change. Only a few weeks ago she would have said she was satisfied with her life.

Now all she could feel was what she was missing. She didn't know how she would endure going to bed with only memories for companionship.

She dropped her briefcase by the door and kicked off her shoes, uncaring where they landed. Needing to quiet her thoughts and to forget all the years she would have to live without Calder, she went to the computer and entered her rarely-used games folder. Methodically she began to play game after game of solitaire, letting the addictiveness of it take hold of her, until she could no longer think. Finally she closed it down and went to the kitchen. She wasn't hungry, but she knew if she didn't eat anything she would wake up with a pounding headache.

She never made it to the refrigerator. Calder's book was sitting on the kitchen table, a sheet of paper tucked inside. It was a moment before she could bring herself to pick it up and read the careful handwriting. Whatever he said was going to hurt.

Cassie love,

Your last words this morning when you left were that you were sorry. Don't be. Neither of us planned to fall in love, but I wouldn't trade the memories of our brief times together for anything. No matter how much it hurts, I can't be sorry for loving you.

I don't want to do anything that will cause trouble for you, so I will stay away. I wish I understood better what frightens you so much, but it is your business and I respect your privacy. If you are ever willing to reconsider or even to talk it over, I'd be happy to hear from you, whether it is today, tomorrow, or in ten years. Whatever happens, remember that I love you.

Thank you for last night. It was an unexpected gift.

There is more I'd like to say, but instead I'm going to leave now, because if I don't I may not be able to.

All my love,

Calder

The words blurred before her and she let it fall to the table next to his book. The picture of the two couples on the cover seemed to mock her. Now she had two love letters from Calder: one in the form of a novel, and this new farewell. She had always hated unhappy endings.

She picked up the book to return it to the shelves. Just before she tucked it in next to Calder's other novels, she opened it to the dedication as she had so many times in the last two weeks. To her surprise, his handwriting appeared here as well. He had signed his name below it, and added a word so it now read 'To Cassie, who will *always* understand why."

Chapter 16

CASSIE TRUDGED HOMEWARD IN the cold, pulling her coat tightly around her. If she was going to make a habit of working late, she ought to start driving to the college. Even an affluent town like Haverford had crime, and she knew better than to walk deserted streets in the dark. Of course, she had told herself the same thing every day for weeks and set out each morning planning to return home at a reasonable hour. But when the time came, staying at work seemed more palatable than facing the emptiness in her apartment, especially on a Friday night with an interminable weekend ahead.

She couldn't stop thinking about Calder. It was strange that no one seemed able to discern the change in her, that part of her had been ripped away. The continual ache was so deep it ought to show in her face, but apparently it didn't, though a few people had commented that she had lost weight. It was easy to skip meals when she was working late.

Sometimes she wished for someone she could tell about her problems, just to be able to say, "I'm in love with a man and I can't have him." But that would only lead to questions she couldn't answer, so she kept the secret and the pain inside, hoping someday she would no longer feel as if half of her were missing.

Turning down the driveway to her house, she scuffed the dried leaves underfoot, stirring up the smoky scent of mold. She wished it would snow more often in Haverford. The whiteness of snow would relieve the endless dull brown that was wintertime.

She stopped abruptly when she noticed a man standing in the shadows by her door. He wore a long dark overcoat, his hands in his pockets. Adrenaline rushed through her as she took a cautious step backwards, almost losing her balance.

"Cassie, it's me."

She would have recognized his deep voice anywhere. It had been playing constantly in her dreams for the last three weeks. As if it were still a dream, she rushed up the steps and into his arms. The sheer physical relief of his embrace overwhelmed her.

He held her tightly, his cheek pressed against her hair. She didn't want him to let go, to break the spell, or do anything that might bring back the reality of their impossible position. She needed this too much.

But finally she knew something had to be said, and she loosened her grip on him. "How long have you been here? You must be freezing."

"Not long. I didn't call because I was afraid you'd tell me not to come. But no one knows I'm here, so you don't need to worry."

"I wasn't worried." She hadn't even thought about it. She was too grateful he was there. "Come upstairs and get warm."

Calder followed her up the two flights of stairs and waited as she unlocked the door and went in. She had barely closed the door behind them when his arms came around her again. It didn't matter to her why he was there as long as she could keep kissing him, drowning all the emptiness of the last weeks in the passion he could create in her. She didn't want to think of anything but his lips, his hands, and his body.

Finally he broke the kiss, leaning his forehead against hers. "I don't know what it is about you," he said, his breathing uneven. "No other woman makes me lose control this way."

"It must be the special biologist pheromones. That hindbrain at work again." She caressed the back of his neck with her hand.

"I thought you might be angry at me for coming."

She ought to be upset, but instead she felt something perilously close to joy. "I'm not."

He kissed her hard. She pressed herself against him as she felt him tugging her shirt out of her waistband. But when his hand encountered the flesh of her back, she involuntarily yelped and pulled away.

"Your hands are freezing." She took one of his hands between hers and chafed it.

"I'm sorry." His dark eyes were fixed on her.

She had to slow down, to ignore the tingling in her skin, the desire for his touch. Just because she longed to feel his body against hers didn't mean it was a good idea. She needed to know why he was there before she made herself any more vulnerable. "How about some hot chocolate? I could use a cup, and your hands need some warming up, at least if you're planning to put them on me any time soon."

The tense look on his face dissolved into a slight smile. "By all means, bring on the hot chocolate."

He followed her into the small kitchen. She could feel his eyes on her as she poured milk into mugs and placed them in the microwave. "You're making me nervous, watching me like that."

"I'm sorry. It's good to see you."

"It's good to see you, too. I've missed you." The words came out before she realized she was saying them. Embarrassed, she hunted for the cocoa mix in the crowded cupboard. When he made no reply, she set the canister down on the counter with unnecessary care. "I'm sorry if that was the wrong thing to say."

"It wasn't the wrong thing. I just don't have words for it."

She should have recognized he was in his monosyllabic mode, the one she used to think of as rudeness. If only she understood what it meant. "One of the most eloquent writers of our generation and you don't have words?"

His expression warmed at her teasing. "You have that effect on me."

Something inside her relaxed. "That could make for a very one-sided conversation. Would you pass me the cinnamon? It's on the shelf behind you."

Their hands touched as he gave her the spice bottle, their eyes holding until the microwave pinged. She took out the hot milk and began to stir in the cocoa, grateful for the distraction. She dusted the tops with cinnamon and handed one to him.

"Thanks."

Returning to the living room, she sat down on the couch with her feet curled under her. After a moment, Calder settled himself by her side and put his arm over her shoulders.

Cassie wrapped her hands around her mug, the mingled aroma of chocolate and cinnamon wafting past her. She felt oddly tentative with him. They'd never been together like this. It had always been either talking or sex, nothing in between. There had been no opportunity to develop little rituals. They weren't supposed to be together in the first place.

"How are you?" she asked, for lack of a better place to start.

"I've been better." He paused, as if searching for words. "I tried to stay away."

"Without complete success, I take it." It felt so right to be there with him. She took a quick sip of her hot chocolate. It burnt the back of her mouth.

He set down his mug abruptly. "Cassie, these three weeks have been hell. I miss you every minute of the day. Don't bother telling me I can't miss what I never had, because I've already told myself a hundred times."

She laid her head on his shoulder. She shouldn't be so happy to hear he had been struggling as well. "I know. I'm months ahead on my lecture prep because work is the only thing that distracts me."

He exhaled slowly, as if he were fighting to restrain himself. "I've thought about what you said. Maybe it's not reasonable, but I need to know what the trouble is, what happened that's keeping us apart. It's making me crazy."

Her pleasure faded into a vague nausea. "That's a lot to ask."

"I know. It's not fair to ask when you've already told me you don't want me to know. I'll try to understand if you still can't tell me. But I'm having a very hard time with not knowing." He hesitated as he spoke, as if expecting her to stop him.

Fear was the one thing that could overwhelm her need to touch him. She stood and walked to the fireplace, her breath tight in her throat. Crouching in front of it, she picked up an old newspaper from the pile and began to crumple it sheet by sheet. She took her time arranging the paper under the fireplace grate, then took a piece of wood into her hands, examining it as if the answer could be found somewhere in the splinters of wood and bark.

"Harboring a fugitive," she said. She placed the log carefully in the fireplace and set two more around it.

"Is that so serious?"

Her hand froze on the matches. "Since I don't have a criminal record, I'd probably get the minimum sentence under federal guidelines. Given that the offense was second-degree murder, that would be thirty-three months. You decide how serious almost three years in prison would be."

He crossed the room to kneel beside her. "I didn't mean to imply it wasn't important, just that it's not the same as . . . Never mind. I don't know what I'm talking about."

"That's right. You don't." She struck a match and touched it to the crumpled newspaper. She refused to look at him, her eyes on the small, yellow flame.

"Have you talked to a lawyer about this?"

"I don't need to talk to a lawyer. I'm perfectly capable of looking it up on my own." She blew on the flame, watching it shoot up in response.

"Not everything is in the statute books. Would you be willing to talk to one, or could I talk to one without using your name?"

She shook her head silently.

"What about Dave Crowley? He's a good lawyer, and you know him. Could I talk to him?"

"No!" She might only see the Crowleys once a year, but she didn't want to lose their good opinion.

Calder put his hand on her arm. "Cassie, how would you feel if I were in trouble and I wouldn't let you help?"

"There's nothing to help with. I did it, I knew what I was doing, and I need to make sure no one ever finds out."

"No matter what it costs."

She sat back on the floor, wrapping her arms around her knees. "I didn't foresee a situation like this at the time. It's too late now."

"What if it isn't too late? What if there's something we can do about it?"

She knew it was his concern and love—or what he called love—speaking. If only she could give him what he wanted, what they both wanted. He was so sure of himself, so insistent. She would have to tell him all of it. Perhaps then he would understand why he had to stay away.

"It goes beyond the legal problems. It's the dirt they could rake up on my family. If they were just poor and uneducated, I could live with it. But drug abuse, crime, gangs, some low-grade prostitution—it's all there. My sister would sell her life story—and her body—to the first person who offered her fifty dollars, and it would be ugly. I couldn't ever stand up in front of a class again."

"Maybe they'd be impressed with the obstacles you've overcome."

"Maybe, or maybe they would laugh behind their hands." Cassie stood, dusting off her knees, and returned to the sofa, avoiding Calder's eyes.

Calder followed her. When he put his arm around her this time, she found no comfort in it. "Cassie, it's you, not your family, that matters. Everyone has some embarrassments in the family somewhere."

She closed her eyes, not wanting to see his face. "I'm not squeaky clean myself. There's enough about me to give your parents heart failure just knowing you're in the same room with me."

"Like what?" Calder's voice was rough.

"Let's see—my first lover was black. That would be enough right there, wouldn't it?" She waited numbly to see if he would take his arm away. None of her friends would think twice about this piece of her history, but this was Senator Westing's son, a southern aristocrat. "He'd be happy to talk about me, too. He was proud of being the one who finally got me in bed, even if it was my idea. Not that I wanted to, but I needed him."

"You needed him?" Calder's voice was altogether too level.

She shook her head. "Not that way. For protection."

He reached out and put his hand over hers silently, but she could hear the question he was trying not to ask.

It didn't matter anymore. She already felt miles away from him. "Girls in my neighborhood who didn't have someone to protect them were fair game. I chose Jamal as a better option. I'd known him since we were kids and he'd always been good to me. And he liked me enough to be willing to use a condom, provided I bought it."

"Did he protect you?" Calder's tone was neutral. So the withdrawal had begun.

"He didn't have to. He was in a gang, so nobody was going to mess with his girlfriend."

"I'm so sorry you had to go through that."

She could feel Calder's tension and wondered whether he was sorry he came back. "I don't need pity. I did what I had to. I hung with the gang, did a little petty thievery for them. There are worse lives."

"The fugitive—was that Jamal?"

"Jamal? No, I haven't heard from him since I got on the bus to go to college." She paused, looking into the fire. "That was my brother."

"Your brother?"

"Ryan. He's in prison now. I don't want to talk about him." She picked up her hot chocolate again, but its warm sweetness couldn't soothe the pain inside her. "So you can see I'm not the kind of woman you can bring home to meet your parents."

"I don't care what my parents think. I'm even more impressed with you now than I was before."

She shook her head. "Thanks for the compliment, but that's not how the rest of the world would see it."

"I bet it never stopped Erin from thinking well of you."

"Erin doesn't know any of this. Nobody does." Her words seemed to echo in the air.

He wrapped his fingers around hers. "Thank you for trusting me with it."

The odd thing was that she was glad he knew, even if they never saw each other again. "I don't think you'll repeat it, and you don't intersect with the rest of my world anyway."

"I will if I take the job at Haverford."

The shock almost made her spill hot chocolate across her lap. "You said you were withdrawing your application."

He looked down, as if fascinated by something on the floor. "I know. I couldn't do it."

"What do you mean? All you have to do is write a letter."

"A letter that meant I was giving up my last hope with you."

"Calder, haven't you been listening to anything I've said? You can't be involved with a woman like me. Your family would disown you." It felt hypocritical to say when she wanted him to stay, but it was true.

"It wouldn't be the first time. That's why I went to Ecuador, but that's another story."

Her throat was tight. Needing distance, she stood and went over to her desk and then turned back to face him. "Then what about me? Even if I survived all these revelations, what happens to me in a year or two when you move on? I'm left with everyone knowing my humiliating past and nothing else."

"What makes you so sure I'll be moving on?"

"Because I'm a realist. You're Calder Westing, and I'm the girl from the slums." She rested her hand on a pile of scientific journals, feeling the slick paper beneath her fingers. This was her life, and she had to defend it against him. And against herself.

"I'm a man, and you're the woman I love."

"It's not that simple. You fell in love with a woman who doesn't exist. I made her up so no one would know the truth."

The desperation in her voice must have finally impacted him. "I fell in love with a woman who smiled when she saw me enjoying myself. A woman who was witty, intelligent, dedicated, and loyal. A woman who loved the salt marsh so much I could see it sparkling all over her, just like the bioluminescence. A woman who was excited by her work and what it meant. Now tell me what part of that doesn't exist."

Cassie turned away so he wouldn't see her tears. "I guess you can be articulate enough when you want to."

She heard his footsteps and felt his arms go around her. "Did you really think this would change how I felt?"

She nodded, hiding her face in his shoulder.

"If anyone should change their opinion, it's you," Calder said, his voice rough. "I'm being the selfish rich boy you thought I was, thinking only about what I want and not caring that you'd be the one paying the price."

She looked up at him then and touched her fingertip to his lips. "I know you care. You're just used to the idea you can have things if you want them badly enough. I've never been under that illusion."

"Isn't there any in-between ground? Some way we could see each other a little, without anyone finding out? If I took the job here, no one would think twice about it if I'm seen with you occasionally."

The urge to say yes was almost overpowering. "I want to be with you. I really do. But it would be dangerous."

He slipped his hand under her blouse again, letting it rest just above her hip. "We could cover it up. Maybe your friend, Tim, would be willing to pretend to be your official boyfriend for a while. You could go up to see him and I'd meet you there."

Cassie wondered if it was possible to hide an affair, even temporarily. For a while. That was what he had said. Could she do it—take the little bit he offered, knowing she would have to let him go eventually? The touch of his hand made her ache for him. Perhaps the ferocity of their desire would burn itself out if she gave it the opportunity, and then parting would be easier. Or perhaps it was an excuse because she couldn't find the strength to send him away. Slipping her arms around his neck, she pulled his head to hers and kissed him fiercely.

Calder followed her urgings, using his lips to explore her face, her neck, and finally her mouth. He suspected she was avoiding his question, which meant she was going to say no. The only thing left for him was to take whatever she was willing to give and hope it would be enough. As his hand moved upward to claim her breast, he stopped thinking altogether.

***

They ended up in front of the fireplace, in a nest of cushions and fleece throws. Cassie had turned out the lights, so the room was lit only by the flickering flames.

Now the fire was dying down. Calder woke himself from his half-hypnotized state to stir the logs and then found his place next to Cassie again.

He traced the line of her cheek with one finger. "How long can I stay?"

She caught his finger between her teeth and nibbled on it. "I don't have anything scheduled for this weekend."

"Will I be crowding you if I'm here?"

"No. I'd like that."

Relief flowed through him. It was only two days, but when they were together like this, he couldn't conceive of a life without her. He had the weekend to find a way to make it work.

Chapter 17

CALDER DRUMMED HIS FINGERS on the armrest of the chair as he spoke into the phone. "Dave, *honestly*, this is about a friend. I'm not in any trouble."

Cassie nervously straightened the journals on her desk. Poor Calder. It had taken him the better part of the morning to convince her to let him make this call, and now it sounded like he was getting a lecture from Dave.

"It's not about me. Really. I don't even know anyone wanted by the police." Calder glared at the telephone.

Cassie held out her hand for the receiver. Calder said, "Just a second, Dave." To Cassie, he added, "Are you sure you want to do this?"

She was far from sure, but she nodded anyway and took the handset. "Dave? This is Cassie Boulton. Tim Ryerson's friend. We've met at your Christmas parties."

"Of course. How are you?" Dave said.

"I'm fine. I'm the person Calder's talking about." She tried to cover her anxiety with a veneer of certainty.

"You are?"

"Yes, but you don't need to worry about it. It's not important. Calder . . . It's just bothering Calder. That was why he called."

"It's no imposition. But what's Calder's involvement here?"

"He's a friend." She waited through an interminable pause.

With an air of revelation, Dave said, "Ah. So you're Elizabeth, then."

"No, I'm Cassie." It took her a moment to realize what he meant. "Oh. That Elizabeth. Yes, I suppose I am."

"We've been wondering who that was. Well, now this makes more sense. So what is this situation he's worked up about? You harbored a fugitive, I take it?"

"Yes. But nobody knows."

"Cassie, are you talking to me as a friend or as your lawyer?"

She flushed. "As a friend."

"That's the wrong answer. The right answer is 'I'm talking to you as my lawyer, Dave, so you have to hold everything I say under lawyer-client privilege.' It doesn't mean you have to use me as a lawyer."

"Then I guess I'm talking to you as my lawyer."

"Good girl. Now you can tell me what happened."

"My brother was wanted for murder. He stayed with me for almost three months." Her hand gripped the receiver.

"When was this?" Dave didn't sound disturbed by her confession, but she supposed a lawyer wasn't supposed to sound disturbed.

"About a year and a half ago."

"Did you know he was wanted?"

It took her a moment to find her voice. "Yes."

"How did you know?"

"I called my mother. He wouldn't have appeared on my doorstep out of the blue without a reason. She told me the police were looking for him."

"Did she tell you why?"

"No. I knew better than to ask."

"When did you find out?"

"When the police finally called me, looking for him." She would never forget that moment. Ryan had been sitting across the room from her, and he knew immediately what the call was.

"What did you tell them?"

"That he had been there, but he'd left a few days before." She had told them Ryan was going to Baltimore. It was the first place that popped into her mind. They had asked who he knew in Baltimore, and she had said in her most authoritative voice, "I am a college professor. I have a reputation to uphold. Ryan is my brother, but we do not have friends in common."

After she had hung up, Ryan had hugged her and told her it was time for him to hit the road. She gave him all the cash she had and drove him to the train station.

"So he'd already left?"

"No. I lied." Watching Calder pace the room was making her even more nervous.

"Who knows you weren't telling the truth?" Dave asked.

"Only Ryan and me."

"Did anyone know your brother was staying with you?"

"Lots of people knew, but not why." Ryan had sat in on classes at the college, drinking in every word, reading the textbooks at night. Some of the professors, knowing he was Cassie's brother, had taken time to talk to him and tried to encourage him to enroll at Haverford. No one had any idea he had dropped out of high school years earlier.

"Anybody who knows he was still with you at that point?"

"He was at the college with me that day, but I don't think anyone would remember one day as opposed to another."

"So as far as anyone knows, you cooperated with the police when they called you."

"I suppose so."

"What happened to him?"

"He left then and was arrested a few days later on a disorderly conduct charge. They found out about the warrant in Chicago and shipped him back. He's in prison now." He had gone straight to Baltimore and made a general nuisance of himself until he was picked up. It was his way of making sure the police never questioned her story.

"Is there anyone who can testify that you knew he was wanted?"

"Just Ryan and my mother."

"Would Ryan testify against you?"

"No." She and Ryan had always shared a special bond.

"Your mother?"

"Not if she knew she shouldn't."

"Cassie, let me talk it over with one of my partners in criminal law, but this sounds manageable. If they can't prove you knew about the warrant, it isn't harboring. Also, they don't usually bother charging people with harboring unless it's an ongoing thing. The police have plenty of work as it is. If your brother's in prison, it's probably not worth their while to go after you."

Calder tapped her arm. "Can I ask him something?"

"Sure. Dave, I'm going to switch over to speakerphone. Calder has something to say."

"Just be aware that lawyer-client privilege can't apply if he can hear it."

It was a bit late for that. "That's all right." She pressed the button.

Calder said, "Dave, we're worried about what could happen if the tabloids found out about this."

"The tabloids? You mean because of her connection with you? Anything's possible, but it's not a very good story from their point of view. An otherwise law-abiding citizen trying to protect her brother isn't very scandalous. If he were a pedophile or something, they'd have a story."

"Isn't murder scandalous enough?" Cassie asked.

"Depends on the circumstances. Who did he allegedly kill?"

"Someone from a rival gang. It was in a gang fight."

"Now that's the story that would interest them—your brother being in a gang. Not the harboring. That's boring."

"Are you sure?" Calder asked.

"I'm never sure of anything, but I've known your mother all my life. I have a nodding acquaintance with the kind of thing that interests the scandal sheets."

Cassie left the bedroom soon after, giving Calder the chance to talk to Dave alone. She needed a few minutes to calm herself. It had been easier telling Dave about Ryan than it had been with Calder, but her nerves were still on edge. Eventually she went to look for him. He was still on the phone, but he held out his free arm to her. She went to him, linking her hands behind his waist and resting her head on his chest.

"All right. Thanks for the advice, Dave," he said. "I'll be in touch." He returned the receiver to its cradle and turned his attention to Cassie. "Are you okay?"

"I'm not sure. I need to think about it."

He kissed his way down her head to her ear, her neck, and then her face. She could tell he was pleased with the outcome. "I'll try to be patient. But I feel a lot better about risking scandal than prison."

She let him distract her with kisses. His happiness was infectious, as was his desire.

Without pausing between kisses, he picked her up and took her to the bed. As he lowered his body over hers, she teased, "Didn't we just do this?"

"That was hours ago." His hands busily worked their way inside her shirt, finding the places that tempted her most.

"Two hours, to be precise." She nibbled on his lip.

"That qualifies as hours ago."

She laughed. "I'm not sure why I bothered to get dressed."

"Good question. You don't ever need to get dressed on my account. I'm perfectly satisfied by you with your clothes off." He began wrestling with her pants.

"Satisfied already?" She insinuated her hand between their hips and stroked him through his jeans, an effective demonstration of his lack of satisfaction. To her surprise, he paused and put his hands beside her face.

"I've wanted to hear you laugh with me again so much. Since that night in Woods Hole, there hasn't been much opportunity for laughter. I love it when you laugh and tease me."

Looking into his eyes so close to her own was dangerous to

her peace of mind. "You'll just have to keep giving me things to laugh at, then."

He lowered himself between her legs. With a significant look, he said, "Let's see how long you can keep laughing."

***

Cassie spread her syllabus on the wooden table in preparation for class. Three weeks until Calder came back. Three long, lonely weeks. This plan of seeing each other occasionally to reduce the odds of discovery worked better in theory than practice. Next semester, when he'd be teaching there, they could see each other often without anyone being the wiser. It seemed like a long time away. If only her past didn't have to be such a secret, but wishing that was pointless. It was the price of keeping the respect of her colleagues and students.

This seminar, Topics in Marine Biology, was usually her favorite to teach, but today the subject matter only made her miss Calder even more. Good thing today's topic wasn't salt marshes.

It was a small class of a dozen or so biology majors. A couple of students trickled in a few minutes early. Chris was one of them, and he came directly over to Cassie, holding a stack of envelopes.

He looked nervous. "Dr. Boulton, I was wondering if you'd be willing to write a letter of recommendation for me."

"I'd be happy to." She'd been waiting for him to ask. Cassie took the pile of envelopes and flipped through them quickly, glancing at the addresses. All med schools. She turned to him in disbelief. "What happened to grad school in biology?"

Chris shuffled his feet. "There are so many unemployed

PhDs out there, and I have debts to pay off. This way I know I'll have a job when I'm done."

"But is it what you really want? No, scratch that, I know it isn't what you want."

"It'll be okay." He glanced around at the rapidly filling room with an embarrassed look. Everyone in the seminar knew he'd spent the summer working with Cassie, and it gave him a certain cachet among the serious biology students.

Cassie set the envelopes on the table. "Let's talk after class. I think you may be overestimating the difficulty of getting a job in biology."

"Rob told me he'd been looking for two years," Chris said.

Rob. Just what she didn't want to talk about. "Rob's looking for a very particular type of job. And you didn't hear him having any regrets about his choices, did you? If he knew you were thinking about this, he'd string you up by your thumbs."

"It's easy for you to say. You've got a job. You never had to worry about ending up broke and working at some dead-end job. But you were at the top of your class in grad school. Rob told me."

Never had to worry. That was a laugh. What else had Rob told Chris? But the other students were looking at the two of them with avid curiosity, and some were nodding. She sighed and pushed the syllabus to one side, turning to face the class. "How many of you are thinking like Chris is?"

There was dead silence, then one hand went up and another and another. All students she'd known for years. The seniors had started at Haverford with her—she as a new professor when they were freshmen. She had a sudden vision of talking to Calder in her lab, telling him she taught students how to think.

"Look, I'm not going to tell you that faculty positions are a dime a dozen. They're not. But it's like anything else in life. If it's what you really want, you'll find a way. If you settle for less, you're always going to wonder what you've missed." She wasn't reaching them. Their blank faces loomed before her. How could she make them listen? What kind of role model was she if they thought it had all come easily to her?

This was what hiding her past meant. She could teach her students how to think like scientists, but she couldn't teach them about life, because everything she said was a lie. They might not respect her if they knew the truth, but could she respect herself if she wasn't willing to take the risk of telling them? Chris was giving up his career aspirations because she was afraid of what they'd think of her.

She laid her palms on the table in front of her. Her mouth was dry. "Okay, let's talk about being broke. I'm an expert on it. I grew up in a slum like you can barely imagine. I'm the only one in my family who finished high school. Half the kids in my high school couldn't read. My brother's in prison, and my sister's never held a job." Not one she could mention in front of students, anyway. "But I knew what I wanted, and I never settled for anything less. If I was at the top of my class, it's because I worked harder than anybody else. So if you want to apply to med school, go ahead, but don't tell me it's because you don't have a choice."

The look on Chris's face was almost comical, a combination of surprise and shame. She shouldn't have spoken so harshly. It wasn't him she was upset with. It was herself, for telling a lie all these years. With an effort, she made her voice gentler. "You have talent and brains, Chris, and you'll do well at whatever you do, whether you're a biologist or a doctor. I'll give you an excellent recommendation for med school, and later on, if you decide to apply to some grad schools as well, I'll be happy to help with that, too."

"But we have work to do today." She straightened the pile of papers in front of her. "Sherry, is your presentation ready?"

At the end of class, the students filed out. Cassie opened her briefcase on the chair beside her and looked up to see Tony, a quiet boy who always turned in his work on time. "Dr. Boulton?" he said.

"Yes?"

"What you said about how we couldn't imagine where you grew up." Tony stuck his thumb in his belt loop and tilted his head to one side. "I can."

A smile tugged at the corners of her lips as she recognized his street stance. "Well. Congratulations, then."

"I *am* going to med school. I got a job waitin' for me, back home." He straightened his shoulders. "You go, girl," he said quietly and then sauntered out of the room.

Would her life have been different if she had been able to tell someone about her past when she was Tony's age? Another unanswered question to add to her endless list. But she hadn't been ready then. Too much adolescent shame and desire for acceptance. Wanting to pretend Chicago didn't exist. But after telling Calder the truth, pretending it didn't exist wasn't working anymore.

Calder. If only Calder were there with her, to talk to her and to hold her in the way only he could.

If it's what you really want to do, you'll find a way. If you settle for less, you're always going to wonder what you've missed. She walked slowly down the hall to her office, closed the door behind her, and sat down at her desk. She'd told her big secret. Half the department would know by tomorrow.

The phone was right there in front of her. All she had to do was to pick it up.

She reached into her briefcase for her wallet and found the dog-eared card inside it. Holding it carefully, she dialed the number on it and waited, her heart pounding, until Calder answered the phone.

"It's me," she said.

"Cassie? Are you all right?"

She drew a deep breath. "I love you, and I'd like it if you came back."

There was a long silence on the other end, and then Calder said, "Hold that thought. I'll be there tonight."

***

"You did what?" Calder stared at Cassie incredulously. Had he heard her correctly?

"I told them. No more secrets, except about the harboring. No more obstacles. You can stay as long as you want, and it doesn't matter who finds out." Her eyes were dancing.

It was hard to believe, after all these months of telling himself he could never have her. But he could see the truth of it in how she moved, in the energy that seemed to exude from her. He gathered her into his arms, holding her tight, making her laugh as he lifted her so her feet left the floor. "I don't deserve you."

She caught his face between her hands and kissed him. "Too bad. You're stuck with me now."

As the weekend progressed, Calder couldn't have been

happier. The way Cassie made free with his body—always touching his arm or taking his hand or sliding into his lap—charmed him completely, and he sought out her touch more and more. The intensity of their sexual connection didn't diminish with repetition. He found he was growing addicted to the heady delight of pleasuring her, to the point that she teased him by saying he seemed to enjoy her satisfaction more than his own. He denied this vigorously, but the fact remained. The more he had of her, the more he wanted.

The most mundane things could remind him how much he wanted her. After dinner on Sunday, as Cassie filled the sink with warm water to do the dishes, he said, "Maybe I should start looking for that house with a hot tub."

Cassie's hands, buried deep in soap suds, stilled on the dishes. "Isn't it a little early to be thinking about that kind of thing?"

"I'm sorry. I shouldn't make assumptions." Some of Calder's exuberance slipped away at the reminder that Cassie still might have reservations about their relationship, even without the complication of her past. "I understand if you don't want to live together right away, but I'd still rather have a place you'd be comfortable with in the long term."

"Calder, we've just decided to give this relationship a try. We're not ready to move in together. Besides, how can we live together if you can't mention me to your family?"

"I'm fine with telling my family about you. I'd just rather wait, say, 'til after our first child is born." He said it as if it were a joke, but he didn't want to let Cassie meet his parents before he was sure of her commitment to him. He couldn't take the chance of them scaring her off.

Cassie scrubbed fiercely at a stain on the pan. "That's okay. I don't want you to meet my sister, either. She isn't pleasant. And of course you won't be meeting Ryan. He won't be out for at least twelve years."

So she didn't expect him to be around in twelve years. "What about your parents?"

"I suppose you could meet them if you wanted. You wouldn't have anything to talk to them about, but she's okay."

"I could talk to them about you." He slid his arms around her, letting his hand creep under her sweater to lie against her skin.

She raised her eyebrow. "Why do I get the feeling your mind is not on the conversation?"

"No, it is. Sometimes I feel better when I touch you." It reduced his anxiety about losing her, but he wasn't about to say so.

"So I'm sort of a big teddy bear, am I?"

"A sexy teddy bear." He kissed her neck. "But I wasn't trying to distract you. And I bet your family is very nice."

"Calder, my mother is a cashier at K-Mart. My father works construction when he can get a job, and when he can't, he sits in front of the TV and drinks beer. My sister—well, you know what she does. The only person in my family you could have a real conversation with is Ryan."

"Ryan is different?"

She inspected the pan for invisible stains. "Ryan's a lot like me. He's smart and he wanted more from life than the South Side. I taught him to read when he was four, and he was stealing my books by the time he was in second grade. He dropped out of high school, but he's taught himself a lot."

"He's younger than you are?" For some reason, Calder had pictured a much older brother.

"Almost ten years. I left home when he was nine. I didn't go back much, so I never realized he was getting beaten up regularly by other boys because his grades were too good. So he learned to do badly at school. When he was fifteen, he wrote to me, asking if he could come to live with me. I was twenty-four, in my second year of grad school. I could have taken him. It wouldn't have been easy, but I could have done it. But I was finally doing what I had dreamed of after all those years of fighting to get there, and I didn't want a teenage brother to take care of." She rinsed the pan and handed it to Calder. "So I said no, and I never asked him why he wanted to leave. If I'd said yes, he'd be graduating from college instead of being in prison."

"You can't hold yourself responsible for that."

"I *raised* him, Calder. My mother worked two jobs to meet the mortgage, and we never knew when Dad would be working, so I took care of Ryan. Don't tell me what I can hold myself responsible for."

"But you were only ten."

"That's practically a grown-up where I come from." Her voice held forced cheerfulness as she changed the subject. "My mother named me after a soap opera character. That should tell you something about her."

He hated seeing the tension in her and the knowledge that some parts of her were still off limits. "She picked a character with a nice name."

"I was lucky. She almost named me after her second favorite, because she liked the name so much. Then I would have been Brandi—Brandi Boulton. I think I'd rather have died."

He pulled her back against him. "No, I can't see you as a Brandi. She was right to choose Cassandra instead."

"That's easy for you to say. You don't know what my middle name is."

"What's your middle name?"

She leaned her head back to kiss him. "That secret will go to the grave with me."

***

He woke up during the night with the sense something was wrong. At first he couldn't tell what it was; Cassie was in his arms and holding him tightly, but that certainly wasn't a problem as far as he was concerned. It took a moment before his thinking became clear enough to notice how tense her body was and the unevenness of her breathing. Concerned, he reached up to touch her face, only to discover that, as he suspected, she was crying silently. He kissed her forehead. "What's the matter?" he asked, afraid of what the answer might be.

She seemed to freeze. "Nothing," she said, her voice carefully steady.

"It's not nothing. I may be inarticulate, but I'm not stupid."

"No," she said into his chest. "You're not stupid."

"So tell me about it, then."

She was silent for a moment. "There's nothing really to tell. Just a lot of feelings, nothing sensible."

He held her close, stroking her hair. "If I've done something wrong, if I've pushed you too hard, please tell me. I don't want to frighten you away again."

"You didn't do anything," she said, her voice muffled. "I'm just scared, that's all."

"Scared of what?" He held his breath, waiting for her answer.

"That it will end badly—that you'll find out I'm not who you think I am, or that you'll get tired of living in my world, and I can't fit into yours."

"Surely you know I'm not that easy to get rid of by now." He could hardly stand the anxiety. It would be unbearable if she backed away from him again now. "What's this 'my world and your world' business?"

"We can do fine when our worlds intersect, but there's another part of your life. The charity balls, the high society, even the politics. I can carry off a fancy party every now and then, but I just couldn't breathe if I always had to worry about who knew what about whom. I'm not from that world, and it would show, and I'd embarrass you."

"Don't worry about that. I agree. I think you'd be unhappy in that world. But so am I, and I have been for years, and I'm not going back to it. I hate being in crowds of people, I hate having to say the right thing, I hate all the predatory behavior. The only reason I've put up with it is because I felt I had to uphold the family name, but I don't care about that anymore. If my family can't cope with the fact that I hate big parties, that's their problem."

"But what about your friends, like Scott? He'd expect you to do things like that, too."

"My friends know better than to ask that of me. Why is it so hard to believe me on this?"

"Because men leave. That's what they do."

Like her father had left her. He would have to be careful here. "I'm not going to leave."

"That's easy to say, but I'm still afraid of losing you."

He tipped up her face so she could see him. "Do you think *I'm* not frightened of losing *you?* I'm bloody terrified of it, I can tell you. You have nothing to worry about. After all, you're the one who wants to take this slowly, while I'm talking about marriage, a house here and probably one on the Cape, and if I knew whether you wanted them or not, I'd be talking about the kids, the station wagon, and the dog as well."

"You haven't been talking about marriage," she said in a small voice. "And please don't start. I'm scared enough as it is."

"I won't talk about it now, at least. But I have a confession to make."

"What's that?"

"I really *would* like to get a dog. I've always wanted one."

She laughed. "You can have a dog, that's fine. As long as it's not one of those tiny ones. I don't like dogs I can step on."

He pretended to be offended. "Of course not. I want a big dog, one that can go on walks along the beach with us. Don't be surprised if you come home from work some day to find a puppy. I've wanted a dog for a *really* long time."

She nibbled his shoulder affectionately. "I think I'm safe. My landlord doesn't allow dogs."

"See, I told you we needed a house," he said with a glint in his eye.

"You certainly like having your own way!"

"Yes," he said, rolling on top of her and neatly pinning her to the bed. "I like having my own way very, very much, and I especially like having my way with you." His lips came down on hers in a manner that left little doubt as to his meaning.

Chapter 18

THE NEXT DAY CASSIE asked, "Have you thought through the implications of taking this job at Haverford? Presumably the faculty can be trusted not to go around telling people who you are, but once students are involved, it's a different question. What if one of them recognizes you? Then everyone would know."

Calder found there was something reassuring about Cassie worrying over him. "It doesn't matter. I've decided to stop keeping it secret anyway. I may just tell the students flat out the first day, and let the chips fall where they may."

"But what about your family? Won't they be upset?"

"Probably." He wasn't displeased with the idea. Now that he'd made this much of a break, he was starting to enjoy it. "It's their problem, though, not mine."

"That's brave of you."

He shrugged. "I should have done it a long time ago. It's just a habit to do things their way."

"Whatever you think is best. But if you're going to do it

anyway, you might consider telling people sooner. That could be a disruptive way to start your first class."

When he had Cassie at his side, it was easy to believe his family was unimportant. Unfortunately, he knew that sooner or later he would pay for the illusion. It wasn't something he wanted to think about. "Tell you what. I'll announce it right away if you'll tell me what your middle name is."

Cassie laughed, as he had intended. "No deal."

***

Cassie gathered the dirty laundry into the hamper and put the bottle of detergent on top of it. Calder had done the laundry the last time, just to prove he knew how. The various household tasks that were a mystery to him were one of her favorite things to tease him about.

She picked up the basket to take it to the basement, but Calder came in the door carrying a newspaper before she had a chance. He didn't return the smile she gave him. Instead he threw the paper on the table in front of her. "It's started. My father's secretary called to point it out to me."

It was a tabloid, the kind she saw at the grocery store check-out. The teaser strip at the top of the front page read, "Calder's Love Nest?" next to a small photo of the two of them.

Cassie leaned over to take a closer look. "That's a fake, isn't it? I don't remember anyone taking pictures of us together."

"They don't bother themselves with facts. Wait 'til you see the story."

She flipped through the paper until she found the article. "Calder Westing in Love Nest with Sexy Scientist." A disbelieving laugh escaped her. According to it, she and Calder met for the first time at a party a few weeks earlier and had been inseparable since. It listed her as a professor at Haverford but said nothing about her background. That was something to be grateful for.

The remainder recounted what she hoped was a sensationalized version of Calder's past affairs and speculated whether this would last any longer than his previous flings. There was no reference to his writing or why he was at Haverford in the first place.

He rested his hands on the back of a chair. "How is the college going to react to one of its faculty members showing up in the tabloids?" he asked, as if the answer to his question was a foregone conclusion.

"I don't think it will be that much of a problem. It doesn't say anything bad about me. It might be embarrassing in my department, if anyone finds out about it. Maybe I should ignore it and hope nobody notices." She folded the paper and pushed it away.

"If you want, I could talk to them. After all, I'm the one the tabloids are after."

"Thanks, but no. What we need is to get them to see how ridiculous it is." She paused and then smiled wickedly. "I have an idea. Are you really ready to go public about Stephen West?"

***

It was 10:45, near the end of Biology 101, the largest class the department offered. Cassie took a deep breath, glancing down to make sure her PowerPoint was ready to go.

"Now, before we conclude today, I'd like to take a few minutes to review common errors in experiment design and write-ups. Not only do these occur in our lab," she clicked to display the cover of a lab notebook on the overhead screen "but also in some of our finer scientific journals." She replaced it with an image of the tabloid's front page.

The class was accustomed to her tongue-in-cheek humor, so it took a moment before any of them looked closely enough to recognize her picture. She spoke over the first gasps and whispered comments. "The scientific method requires following a particular series of steps. First, you make an observation, and then you formulate the hypothesis, a possible explanation for your observation."

She clicked to show the headline of the article, "Calder Westing in Love Nest with Sexy Scientist." "Your observation must be a neutral one that avoids bias. A good scientist will, of course, define any terms that might cause confusion." She used her laser pointer to circle the words "love nest" and "sexy." "And then there is the *most fundamental error,* which is to mistake the hypothesis for an explanation of a phenomenon, without performing experimental tests."

She had to raise her voice to be heard over the laughter. She flashed up the first paragraph of the story. "It simply will not do to formulate your hypothesis without a thorough review of literature. In this case, the *researcher* states that the two subjects under observation have just met, whereas a quick check of a book written by Calder Westing makes mention of their acquaintance well before this date." The acknowledgments page from *Pride & Presumption* appeared on the screen.

"Another common mistake is to ignore or rule out data that do not support the hypothesis. In this case, the writer implies that Mr. Westing's sole purpose for being in the area was the aforementioned scientist, ignoring the data showing that he had been interviewed for a job earlier that week at a small liberal arts college within a half mile of the so-called love nest." She put up an aerial photo of Haverford's campus, amused to hear excited whispers being passed back and forth.

"I hope this quick review means I will not see any of these common errors appearing in your lab reports, and if they do, I will urge you to drop out immediately and seek employment at the tabloid of your choice. Are there any questions?"

As soon as she finished, a dozen students had their hands in the air, well beyond the usual average. This was likely one of the more memorable lectures she had ever delivered.

***

They left the question of Christmas until almost the last minute. Calder wanted to be alone with Cassie, without all the distractions of her work, and suggested a variety of places they could be together—going to his apartment in Washington or visiting the Cape. He ruled out Virginia because he didn't feel ready to expose Cassie to his parents. Staying with her for Christmas meant he would have to spend New Year's with his parents, but it was a necessary price to pay to avoid the trouble his father could make for them.

In the end, the choice that could serve as a tradition for both of them was to accept an invitation from the Crowleys. Dave and Ann Crowley gave Cassie a warm welcome. They seemed delighted Calder had finally found someone who made him happy. If Dave was troubled by Cassie's past, he gave no sign of it. Dave teased them about having known both of them longer than they had known each other. "I should have had the sense to introduce you years ago," he said.

Cassie found it odd to be their house guest rather than just going to their Christmas Eve party. It was a more elegant household than she was accustomed to. The Crowleys wore their wealth lightly, but it was present nonetheless. Still, it was easier for her than it would be with Calder's family; Dave Crowley had earned his fortune in law from humble beginnings. The Crowleys still remembered the kind of world she lived in.

Calder slipped seamlessly into the Crowley home, his mood a startling contrast to the previous year. The longing, desire, and despair then had been the beginning of the blackest period of his life. But without it he wouldn't have Cassie by his side now, looking up at him with an impish smile. He didn't know how he had lived without her laughing eyes, the warmth of her touch, her gentle teasing. If she was still unsure of their future, he wasn't.

As they waited for the first party guests to arrive, Cassie asked him, "Do you remember kissing me here?"

"Vividly." He also remembered the agony that had followed.

"I *hated* it that you could make me feel that way so easily."

He touched her cheek. "You don't seem to hate it anymore."

"Nope," she said. "As a matter of fact, I've scouted out every piece of mistletoe in the house."

"How about we skip the mistletoe and go straight back to our room?" He eyed her body, encased in the same clinging midnight blue dress she had worn the previous year. It looked sexy as hell on her, and it represented to him how unattainable she had been. He was looking forward to getting her out of it. He wished he could rip it off her. That way no other man would ever see her in it again.

"You're just trying to get out of staying for the party," she said. "I hope you know I'm fine on my own if you decide you've had enough of the crowd."

If she thought he was going to leave her alone in that dress with other men and mistletoe hanging overhead, she was mistaken. "Thanks, but I want to be with you, just in case you run into some of that mistletoe."

This party was easier than most for Calder because he was so focused on her. Still, when midnight approached, he was ready to take her upstairs to their room. The door was hardly closed behind them when he set himself to removing her silky dress, working slowly and caressing each newly uncovered inch of her with his fingers and lips, until she stood before him wearing nothing and shivering with desire. He took her to bed then and devoted the next hour to making sure it was an experience she would never forget. When at the end she climaxed in his arms one last time, he held her close and whispered, "Merry Christmas, Cassie." This time she wouldn't drive away.

***

Cassie should have thought ahead to the New Year's Eve problem before Calder left. She didn't want to go to a party by herself and face questions of where he was, so she elected to stay home. She missed him more than she wanted to admit. It was embarrassing to feel so despondent over being apart for a few days. Watching the New Year's celebrations on TV only made her lonelier for him. Emails from Calder, no matter how regular, weren't the same thing as his presence.

Maybe he would call to wish her a happy New Year. She

wanted to hear his voice, and the mere idea he might call kept her staring at the silent telephone. Even going to bed alone was more appealing than sitting around missing Calder, but she couldn't sleep because she hoped the telephone would ring. Finally she turned off the telephone to stop herself from hoping for a call. She was disappointed, if unsurprised, to find no message from him in the morning.

Instead there was an email from Calder, saying he would be delayed for a couple of days. The disappointment was enough to make her want to cry. He didn't give any reason. It wasn't like him.

The next day an unexpected knock sent Cassie running to the door. Could it be Calder coming back early without warning? She opened the door, ready to throw herself into his arms.

Calder's father stood on the other side. He smiled winningly and said, "Hello, Cassie."

Cassie took a step backwards. She didn't like him appearing on her doorstep without the common courtesy of a call, and she wasn't fooled into thinking he remembered her from their brief meeting a year and a half earlier. "I'm sorry, Calder isn't here. Next time you might want to call ahead and save yourself a trip."

"I know Calder is away. I'm here to see you. May I come in?"

Cassie held the door open, wishing she had the courage to say no. She didn't trust Joe Westing when he was being charming. "What can I do for you, Senator?"

"It's Joe, please. May I sit down?"

"If you'd like."

"Thank you." He settled himself on her worn sofa. "I'm not your enemy, Cassie."

"I'm glad to hear that, but I doubt you came all the way from DC to tell me that." Cassie wanted to strike a balance between good manners and assertiveness. Whatever he had to say, she wasn't going to like it.

"I'm concerned about Calder."

"So I gather."

"He isn't in good shape, Cassie. If you had met him a few years ago, you would know that."

"He seems fine to me."

Joe shook his head. "He's flailing, trying to figure out who he is and what he wants, and rebelling against everything our family stands for. I understand. I went through a similar phase when I was young."

"I haven't seen any evidence of flailing."

"You haven't? No unexpected behavior or sudden withdrawals? Well, I suppose I'm glad of that, though you haven't been with him that long. Has he told you about Annette?"

"You're going to tell me about her anyway, so what does it matter?" Underneath Cassie's automatic retort lay the memory of Calder's sudden decision to stay in Virginia.

Did his father have something to do with that?

"Annette was everything I could have wanted for Calder. Attractive, intelligent, moved in the right circles, good family. Unfortunately, none of those things are a guarantee of good character, but it was quite a while before any of us realized that. All Calder meant to her was a guaranteed income. He refused to see it. Calder is very loyal, as I'm sure you're aware. It took flagrant infidelity on her part before he understood what was happening. It became quite ugly before he reached the point of breaking it off with her. Then he went into a tailspin, rejecting not only Annette but also all of their friends, his entire social circle, and even, to be quite honest, his mother and me. We had approved of Annette in the beginning, you see."

"Everybody makes mistakes."

He nodded gracefully in acknowledgment. "It's true. But the result is that he has been adrift for several years now. I take my own share of responsibility for that. I was caught up in his brother's campaign and I wasn't paying enough attention to Calder. I'm trying to make up for that now. When I saw what was happening with you, I decided we needed to talk."

He was good, very good, but she had to remember that Calder didn't trust him. "I'm listening."

"I appreciate it, especially as I'm going to say some things I don't expect you to like. I can see why Calder was attracted to you. You're strong at a time when he needs strength, and you're giving him a new world to live in. I hope you're also strong enough to realize what he's doing with you is playing house. He's living in a make-believe world because he still can't face his real world. It may make him happy for the moment, maybe even for a year or two. But in the end, it's not going to satisfy him. I can tell you that. As I said, I've been there. Sooner or later he's going to start wanting a family of his own, and then he's going to realize all he threw away, and that despite everything you give him, there are things you can't do."

"Such as?"

Senator Westing's look of concern would have been the envy of any actor. "Our family is privileged, but that has its costs. It's not easy to raise a child with the Westing name and heritage.

With no disrespect to you, you don't have the ability to move in that world and to help Westing children grow up. If your background were more like his, it might be different, but I'm a pragmatist, and I see what's coming. Without meaning to, Calder is using you, and sooner or later you're going to get hurt, and so is he."

"Or perhaps you underestimate me."

"How many of his friends has Calder introduced you to? How much do you know about the work he did before he came here? Have you been to his apartment in New York or his house in Virginia? Do you even know the addresses?" He leaned forward to emphasize his points.

This time his words hit home. It was true. Calder had never involved her in his world in any way. She had met Scott through Erin and the Crowleys because of Tim. It was suddenly hard to breathe. Was this why Calder didn't want her to meet his family?

"You don't have to answer, Cassie. He's not bringing you into his world; he's taking a vacation from it. Vacations end."

She wouldn't give him the satisfaction of seeing her doubts. "If you're so sure of this, why aren't you talking to Calder instead of to me?"

"Because Calder is very loyal, and it's hard for him to let go, even when it's obvious he needs to. I want to spare him that, and the only way I can do that is with your help."

"Calder isn't a child who needs protecting. He can make his own decisions." Or had he already made his decision? Maybe he knew what his father was doing and was taking the easy way out.

His expression turned to one of sympathy. "I realize I'm

asking a great deal of you. You clearly care about Calder, and I'm asking you to give up a man you love, a man any woman would be proud to have, one who can offer you every kind of security, all on my say-so that it's for his own good."

"Talk to Calder, not to me." If Calder wanted to leave her, he'd have to do his own dirty work, not have his father do it for him. Her only goal now was to get Joe Westing out of her apartment before she started to cry.

"I'm not unsympathetic to your position. I understand this has hurt you and cost you a great deal already, and while I can't take any of that pain away, I can make your life easier in other ways. I know money is an issue for you, and I'm prepared to see that you don't have to worry about that any more."

He couldn't have said anything worse. Cassie rose to her feet as anger pushed aside her doubts. "Sorry, I don't take bribes."

His hurt look didn't convince her. "I'm not trying to bribe you, Cassie. In my own clumsy way, I'm trying to make up for what you have to go through on account of my son. You need the money. You're barely managing to support your sister and her children. Don't you want your nieces to live in a safe neighborhood and go to a good school?"

How did he know about Maria? She had never told Calder about the money she gave her sister. He must have been investigating her. What else had he found out?

Cassie marched to the door. "The only thing I want is for you to get out of my apartment, and you don't have to pay a penny for that privilege." She shouldn't have let him in. She had faced dangerous situations often enough in Chicago. This was raising the same instincts, except this wasn't a thug with a knife;

this was a United States Senator with a concerned look on his face. She wished she weren't alone with him.

"Cassie, I'm obviously expressing myself poorly. I'm offering my help in exchange for yours. If you don't want money, let's talk about what you do want. What about getting your brother out of prison? Would that interest you?"

Cassie's breath caught in her throat. "Funny," she said bitingly. "And all this time I've been thinking you were a senator from Virginia, not the governor of Illinois."

"The governor of Illinois has bills he wants passed in Congress, just like everyone else, and I doubt he cares about the fate of one more prisoner. I can do it." He sounded as if he were discussing the weather. "How many more years until he's eligible for parole? Ten?"

"Twelve," she said automatically. He had trapped her so neatly. She would do almost anything to get Ryan out of that hellhole.

Her rational mind said he was toying with her. He probably couldn't make good on the promise, but if there was even a chance . . . Her fury fell away, leaving a dull helplessness in its wake.

Even if she broke up with Calder—if he was still interested in her, if he wasn't just playing house—what guarantee did she have his father would try to free Ryan? Once Joe had what he wanted from her, he would drop her. She had no control over his behavior, or over Calder's decision whether to come back to her.

"You're wasting your time, Senator. If you have a problem with our relationship, I suggest you take it up with Calder."

"He's worth more to you than your brother's freedom?"

Cassie couldn't remember the last time she had wanted so badly to hit someone. "Is getting your way more important to you than your son's happiness?"

"As it happens, I am working for his happiness. Since you seem determined to throw away this opportunity, I'll discuss it with Calder himself. He'll see the light. It'll hurt him more this way, but you're leaving me no choice." The earnest, concerned father act was turned off as if by a switch. He pulled an embossed business card out of his wallet and handed it to her. "If you change your mind, give me a call. I can be a good friend, or a very bad enemy. Did I mention I went to school with Charlie Altshuler?" He snapped his wallet closed.

It took her a moment to understand. Charles Altshuler was president of the Haverford Board of Trustees. Fear began to trickle down her body.

On the Chicago streets she had learned it was dangerous to let an enemy see your weaknesses. "How fortunate for me that there are some good opportunities for marine biologists in Ecuador. I've always wanted to work in the tropics. It is Ecuador Calder likes, isn't it?"

For a moment she could see his anger, and then the mask slipped back into place. "Think it over." He walked to the door. "I admire your spirit. There's no reason you and I can't work together."

She shut the door behind him without saying good-bye and then put up the chain and slipped the bolt. But it was going to take more than locks to protect her from Joe Westing.

Chapter 19

THE VIEW FROM THE big picture window of the Crowleys' house was bleak on these cold, gray days, almost as bleak as Calder's mood. Last year he had thought the pain couldn't be any worse. He had been wrong. Having to leave Cassie would be worse. This time he'd know what he was losing.

"So, what's this problem you need my advice about?" Dave Crowley asked.

"My father. He's trying to blackmail me into giving Cassie up." There, he had said it. He'd been walking around with a knife in his gut for the last two days.

Dave's mouth pursed in a silent whistle. "Up to his old tricks, is he? What's he holding over you?"

Calder rested his hand against the cold, damp pane of glass. "He's going to wreck her career if I don't leave her. Keep her from getting tenure, unless you can come up with some way to block it legally."

"Your father . . ." Dave began with a dark look on his face. "No, never mind, there's no point in me telling you my opinion of your father. What does Cassie have to say about this?"

"She doesn't know."

Dave looked at him sharply. "You're trying to figure this out on your own?"

"I'll talk to her after I know what my options are."

"What makes you think it's your choice to make? Seems to me the question is what's most important to her: her job or you. That's not something you can answer for her."

Calder stood and crossed the room. He knew what Cassie's answer would be—the same as it had always been. Her job came first. It was true, but he couldn't stand to hear her say it. "Do you have any idea how hard she's worked to get where she is? It's her life. How can I ask her to risk that for me?"

"What's it going to do to her if you walk out now? How long do you think it would be before she could bring herself to trust a man again?" Dave heaved himself to his feet and put a hand on Calder's shoulder. "I don't know what we can do legally, but there may be another way out. Maybe you shouldn't take your father's power as such a given."

"I don't know what you mean."

"I mean maybe you can use those brains of yours and come up with a double-cross. Something to keep your father from going after Cassie."

Calder shook his head. "It's a nice idea, Dave, but the truth is that he holds all the cards. He knows the right people, and he can persuade them to do what he wants."

"Oh, come on. There's got to be something. And I'd love to find a way to beat him at his own game. I owe him a few."

"Why? What did he ever do to you?" Calder had never heard Dave speak disparagingly of his father before.

"Well, if I were a better man I probably wouldn't tell you why I think your father is a sadistic old buzzard, but I'm not a better man, so I will. Your mother used to be the liveliest, most spirited girl. She fell in love with a local boy, one with no money, and he loved her. She fought her entire family until they finally agreed to let her marry him. Then your father came along. As near as I can tell, he decided to win your mother away from her fiancé just to prove he could. She was a challenge. Then he married her, and we all got to watch as he spent the next decade systematically breaking her spirit." He paused. "That's what I hold against your father."

Calder took this in silently. His mother, as long as he could remember, had been quiet, restrained, and implacably distant. She was the perfect political wife. In public she always said the right thing to the right person at the right time, but alone with her family, she would withdraw into herself. He had seen often enough how his father could make her stop short with just a glance.

"And that's why I'd like to see you fight back." Dave returned to his seat by the fire.

His mother had learned it was useless to fight back. "I don't really see how," Calder said.

"Surely there's some way to turn Cassie into an asset for him. You could go the publicity route, make everyone see this as the Cinderella story of the decade. Or you could play tit for tat. You're a writer. You could write an autobiography that would make him look like a monster. I doubt it would be much of a stretch. Tell him it'll go straight to the publishers if Cassie runs into any job trouble."

"Or go to the tabloids with the all the family's darkest secrets," Calder said.

"That's the spirit! Think outside the box. God, he'd take me to pieces if he knew I was encouraging you like this." Dave didn't sound at all displeased by this notion.

***

Cassie's imagination was her worst enemy. What would Joe Westing tell Calder? Could he convince his son to end their relationship? If he could, why would he bother with her instead of talking to Calder? Perhaps he didn't want Calder to blame him for the breakup.

Of course, she still had no explanation for Calder's absence. Maybe he'd lost interest already. He'd been in love with her when she was unattainable. Perhaps once he had her, he discovered she wasn't what he wanted. Or maybe he really had been playing house with her and was tired of the game. His father might have little trouble discouraging him.

She had always known this day would come. She'd hoped it wouldn't be this soon, but it had been a foregone conclusion that a romance between them couldn't survive long. Was it too much to wish for more than a few weeks together?

Perhaps she should have taken Joe up on his offer. If she was going to lose Calder anyway, why not take the chance he could do something for Ryan? A slight chance was better than none. But she couldn't bear to give up on Calder.

She couldn't sleep that night. Scenarios kept running through her head in which Joe Westing used his connections to destroy her career at Haverford. The trustees had no official say in the tenure process, but pressure could be brought to bear.

Major donors to the college were in extremely short supply. Assistant professors could be replaced easily. If he had a smear campaign in mind, he could ruin her reputation at Haverford to the point where it would be painful for her to stay. And if he ever talked to some of her colleagues about her family and they told him what they knew, he might put two and two together about what she had done. Even if she were found not guilty of harboring, it would never be the same.

By three in the morning she was ready to call Joe Westing and agree to whatever terms he wanted if only he would leave her alone. But eventually she cried herself to sleep, and in the daytime her panic receded a little and her pride reasserted itself. She wouldn't do anything until she talked to Calder. She needed his knowledge of his father. Even if he wasn't interested in her anymore, he wouldn't leave her in the lurch. He wasn't that kind of person. He would help her figure out what to do before he left.

Finally, tired of crying, she forced herself to take a shower and go to her office. She couldn't think well enough to make lesson plans, but preparing handouts didn't take much thought. She tried to catch up on her reading in professional journals, but she found herself flipping to the back to look at ads for openings for biologists at other colleges.

She didn't go home until late, reluctant to face her empty apartment where she had been so happy with Calder. At least she still had some sleeping pills from when the problems with Ryan were at their worst, and they would let her sleep through the night.

At home, she discovered a brief email from Calder, saying he would be arriving in Haverford the next afternoon. It began with his usual affectionate "Cassie love," and was signed "Looking forward to seeing you." She couldn't explain why it made her cry again.

***

Calder hurried up the stairs to the apartment, impatient to be with Cassie. The door to the apartment was locked. He frowned. He'd thought Cassie would be there to greet him. He checked his cell phone to see if he'd missed a call, but there was no message. Perhaps she didn't get his email, but that wasn't like her. Disappointed, he fished out his key and unlocked the door.

But she was there, sitting on the couch with her feet tucked under her, her face wan. She didn't make any move toward him, or even smile. What had happened while he was away? Had she changed her mind about him? Was that why there was no answer on New Year's Eve, when he finally broke down and tried to call her? He'd tried to convince himself she was probably with friends, but maybe he had been right to worry.

He should never have left her alone for so long. It must have given her a chance to remember all the reasons she shouldn't be involved with him.

If she was going to break up with him, he wanted to hold her one more time. He crossed the room and took her in his arms, afraid she would push him away. But she hugged him back, laying her head against his shoulder as if weary. He pressed soft kisses against her hair.

When she finally pulled back, her hands still clung to his. Cassie broke the silence first. "If you're planning to break up with me, I'd count it as a favor if you did it right away and didn't drag this out."

Where did she get these ideas? "I'm not planning to break up with you. Are you planning to break up with me?"

"No," she said. "Why would I want to do that?"

"No reason—every reason." The relief was shocking in its intensity. Then she was in his arms again, and he kissed her passionately as if their physical closeness could heal the distance between them. Then he tasted salt on her lips and realized she was crying. "What's the matter?"

She shook her head. "Nothing. I was sure you were coming to tell me it was over."

"No. Far from it. About as far from it as you can get."

"I didn't know why else you'd stay away so long."

He drew her over to the couch, finding an extraordinary relief when she leaned against him with a sigh. He slipped his hand inside her sweater for the comfort of touching her. "I ran into a problem. I found out my father's planning to create trouble for you at the college."

"I know."

"You know?"

"He paid me a visit the day before yesterday. He tried to bribe me to leave you."

"What? I suppose I shouldn't be surprised. He must have been afraid I wouldn't give in to his blackmail." Anger and fear smoldered in him at the idea of his father alone with Cassie. What had he done to make her so subdued?

"Blackmail?" Cassie blotted her eyes with a tissue. "What was he threatening to do to you?"

"Not to me. He knows he could threaten *me* forever and it wouldn't make me leave you, but hurting you was something else. He says you won't get tenure. That's why I needed time. I had to figure out what to do about it." He let himself feel the warmth of her flesh beneath his hand.

"You should have told me," she said fiercely.

"I know that now. That's one of the things I figured out."

"All right." She took a deep breath. "So what did you decide?"

"I came up with some different ideas. Mostly they were ways to blackmail him into backing down. It might still come down to that, but I don't like threatening people. I don't want to be like him." He took her hand and held it tightly, nervous about what was coming next.

"Fair enough. So that's the last resort. But what does that leave?"

This was it. Now he would find out the truth of what he meant to her. "It leaves getting married."

She pulled back abruptly and eyed him. Sounding more like herself, she said, "Isn't that a little excessive?"

"I have my reasons. But I didn't mean to tell you this way. I wanted to have a ring for you and the kind of proposal you deserve."

Cassie gestured with her hand, as if to say rings and proposals were nothing. "I can't see it stopping him. If he'd ruin my career to hurt you, he certainly wouldn't stop just because we were married."

"No, but we could stop him. The trustee he knows donates big bucks to the college. That's why he has power. If you're my wife, we can outbid him. Haverford's not going to want to lose you if you're a major donor."

"That would cost you a lot of money."

"I don't care about money. I care about you. Besides, the college is a good cause."

She looked away. "It's a bad investment on your part. I'd never earn it back in salary, not even close."

"It's not meant as an investment. If you don't want to work, I'd be happy to support you, but I know how important your career is to you. And it's in jeopardy because of me."

"No, it's because of your father." She twisted her hands together. "I've decided to put out some feelers for a new job anyway."

"Leave Haverford?" It was the last thing he expected to hear. "I'm wrecking your life, just like you said I would."

"It's not so bad. Remember, I'm resilient, like the marsh grass. I can tolerate a change of environment."

At least she hadn't said no. He reached out to tuck a strand of hair behind her ear, letting his fingers linger on the soft skin of her cheek. "Will you think about it?"

Cassie rested her head on his shoulder. "Later. Right now I just need you."

He didn't realize what kind of closeness she had in mind until he felt her hands inside his shirt. He was far from unwilling; it had been a struggle to restrain his desire for her. But he could tell it was comfort and intimacy she was seeking, not wild passion. He was determined to show her with every touch how much he loved her.

***

Afterwards Calder kissed her forehead. "I should have asked you to marry me about five minutes ago, when you were beyond refusing me anything."

She opened her eyes to look at him. "You're serious about this marriage business."

"Of course. It's the only way I'll ever find out your middle name."

She slapped his arm playfully. "Over my dead body. By the way, who is Annette?"

He gave her a puzzled look. "Annette? She was someone I dated for a while to please my parents."

"Were you in love with her?"

"Of course not. The only reason she was interested in me was because of my family. Why?"

"It was something your father said. I just wondered." Cassie had spent the intervening days trying not to think about Annette. She had been singularly unsuccessful. But she could tell by Calder's tone Annette meant nothing to him.

It was Joe Westing's fault. He had created enough misery in her life to last her for years and might well be preparing to do more. Was there any end to his ruthlessness? The hardest part was watching Calder suffer and being unable to protect him.

No. She would *not* be helpless this time. She could do nothing to fight the Illinois laws and prison system, but she *could* stand up to Senator Westing.

"Yes." She propped herself up on one elbow to see his reaction.

"Yes what?"

"If you really think it will stop your father, then let's get married. I don't want to wait to see what he's going to try next to break us up."

There was a moment of silence. "Do you mean it?"

She had been serious too long. She pounced on top of him, took his face between her hands and kissed him hard. "Yes, I mean it, you idiot."

A wide smile covered his face, and she could feel his body responding beneath hers. His hands slid down to cradle her hips. "I hope you don't think you're going anywhere."

***

To Cassie's relief, Dave and Ann Crowley took the news of their engagement well. It was the first time she had told anyone about it. Or more accurately, Calder told them. At the last minute, Cassie was too tongue-tied to get the words out.

After dinner, Dave Crowley sat across his elegant living room from them. "Are you sure you want to do this so quickly? It's a big gamble. Not that I don't have faith in the two of you, but sometimes unexpected things happen."

"I'm sure." Calder took a sip of wine.

Cassie wished she could be as certain. "It's happening too soon, but we don't have much choice. We can't announce the engagement because it might make Joe work faster, but we need to get married soon enough to counteract any smear campaign at Haverford. It's going to be tricky planning it in a month." She was still having trouble saying words like "engagement."

"You should talk to Ann about weddings. She's the expert, having married off all three of our girls. She loves wedding planning. But I'm the legal department, so I have to ask whether it's safe to wait a month."

"Not really," Calder said. "But I'm going to give my father a bigger fire to fight, and hopefully that will distract him until it's too late."

"A bigger fire?"

"You'll be reading about it in the newspapers. I'm raking up an old family scandal and feeding it to the media. Anonymously, of course."

"And by the time he's dealt with that, you'll be married. That's good," Dave said. "We should arrange for some good publicity for you."

***

Calder shifted uneasily on the couch. "Publicity? Do we have to?"

"No, but a preemptive strike would go a long way if your father intends to make trouble."

"What do you have in mind?" he asked, trying not to sound like he was going to his own execution.

"Something for one of the feel-good magazines. *People* or *Good Housekeeping* or something."

Now Cassie's expression changed to worry. "They wouldn't be interested in us, would they?"

Dave laughed. "For exclusive coverage of your engagement, you could get anything you asked for."

It was too much for Cassie. Contemplating marriage was hard enough, but when the equation began to include *People* and leaking stories to the press, it seemed impossible. It was easier to forget the differences between them when they were alone, but to hear them bandied about so easily with Dave made her intensely uncomfortable.

She couldn't sit still any longer. "I think I'll go see if Ann needs any help."

"Good idea," Dave said, but Cassie could feel Calder's eyes on her as she left the room.

Ann was in the kitchen putting away the last remnants of dinner. Cassie said, "Is there anything I can do to help?"

"You can dry the crystal, if you like." Anne handed her an embroidered dishtowel. "How are the legal affairs coming along?"

Cassie picked up a wineglasses and began to dry it carefully. "Dave and Calder are still talking."

"It gets a bit dull after a while, doesn't it?" Ann said in a conspiratorial manner.

"Confusing." Cassie felt suddenly lonely. She would have given anything for the kind of close relationship Calder had with Dave and Ann, but as usual she was the outsider. "I wish I knew whether we were doing the right thing."

Ann set down the bowl she was emptying and turned to Cassie. "What's this?"

"We're not ready to get married yet. We don't know each other well enough. The only reason we're doing it is because of Calder's father. What if Calder regrets it some day?" Cassie pretended to pay close attention to the glass she was drying, cleaning off imaginary spots.

Ann took the glasses that were already dry and put them away in a cupboard. "That's our wedding crystal. We've been careful with it, and it's lasted through raising three children and years of entertaining." She paused a moment, touching the rim of one of the glasses. "It would be nice if everyone was sure of what they were doing when they got married, but it's not always like that. When I married Dave, I knew he didn't love me. He was on the rebound from another woman. We even talked about it, and he told me he could never love me the way he loved her. I believed him; she was . . . something special, and I was just ordinary Ann Smith who had grown up down the block from him. But I'd loved him for years and he cared about me, and I decided that was enough."

"And was it?" Cassie could not imagine the scene Ann was portraying. Dave and Ann had an ideal marriage, as near as she could tell. But perhaps appearances were deceiving.

Ann smiled to herself. "Well, there were a few other important things I didn't take into account then, like mutual respect, being able to talk about problems, and the willingness to forgive mistakes. In some ways those are more important than love. Without them, I don't know if we would have made it. But we did, and the day Julie was born Dave told me he had been wrong, and he loved me more than he had ever loved the other woman. I told him I already knew that. He never stopped caring about her, but it was different after that. Dave has a lot of capacity for love. So does Calder, I think."

"Yes, he does." Cassie sometimes wondered if Calder had more capacity for love than she did. Certainly when he gave it, it was with his whole heart.

"Dave loves our three girls to death, and he would never say it, but I know he always wanted a son. Calder is special to him, and Dave wants him to be happy. Right now having you makes Calder happy."

"I want him to be happy, too." The issue was whether she could keep making Calder happy. "I should probably go see what they're up to."

"You do that. I'll be out shortly, and thanks for the help."

Calder shifted uneasily on the couch. "I appreciate your offer to draw up the prenup for us, Dave, but isn't it going to cause problems between you and my parents?"

"Nothing new. Your mother won't mind, and your father already knows what I think of him."

"If my father minds, my mother will, too. She believes anything he tells her." Calder knew his contempt was showing, but he couldn't help it.

Dave looked concerned. "That's not true. She disagrees with him about a lot of things. She keeps her opinion to herself."

"If she disagreed with him, why would she put up with the way he treats her? She'd leave."

Dave went to the bar to refill his wineglass. When he turned back, he said, "She did try to leave him once, you know."

"She did?"

"Yes, when you and Tommy were little."

"But she went back." Thinking of his mother leaving his father was like seeing a mirror shatter.

"She went back, yes, after Joe made it clear he was going to get custody of the two of you and she'd never see you again. He had the connections to make it stick, you know."

It made him sick, the idea that he was the reason his mother had gone back to his father. But it couldn't be that simple. "I can't see it. Maybe they had a fight then, but it's been what, fifteen years since Tom left home. If she wanted to, she could have left long ago."

Dave shrugged, as if to say he had done his best. "If I do the prenuptial, I'll need some information. What's your legal state of residence these days?"

Calder took Cassie's hand in his, calmed by her presence. "Still Virginia."

"Pennsylvania for you, Cassie?"

"That's right."

"What state will the wedding be in?"

Cassie looked up at Calder. "We're still working on that."

"And you're planning to get married in a month?" Dave raised his voice. "Ann!"

Ann came out of the kitchen, untying her apron. "Yes?"

"Would you please arrange their wedding?" he said plaintively. "These babes in the woods don't even know where they're having it yet. All I need is a state."

"Oh, my. We have a lot of work to do, then," Ann said. "What are your choices?"

"We want it to be small and quiet, and if we get married in Haverford, a lot of people will feel left out if they aren't invited." Cassie took a sip of her coffee, letting the heat run down her throat. "Cape Cod's a possibility, but it's off season there and most of the hotels are closed. That leaves Virginia or Chicago."

"It's not going to be in Virginia," Calder said. "My parents are not invited."

Ann exchanged a glance with Dave. After a brief silence, she said, "Chicago, then?"

"It would be hard. This isn't the sort of thing my mother could arrange, and I can't leave Haverford in the middle of the semester to set it up."

Ann looked excited. "If you can tell me what you want, I can help with the arrangements."

Dave laughed. "Here's the translation service. What Ann means is that she'll take over the entire event from start to finish. She loves planning weddings."

"I'm just trying to help," Ann protested, but with a guilty smile.

"I'm not sure these two wouldn't be just as happy if somebody took over the whole thing." Dave picked up a pen and pad of paper. "Meantime, I'll put down Illinois for location for now. We can always change it later if we need to. Cassie, what's your full name?"

"Cassandra D. Boulton." She spelled the last name for him.

"What does the D. stand for?"

She eyed Calder suspiciously. "You put him up to this, didn't you?"

Calder lifted his hands in a protestation of innocence. "Nothing doing."

"You really need this, Dave?"

"Not absolutely, but it would be better. What's the problem?" Dave asked with amused curiosity.

"Nothing," Cassie said firmly. "Just Cassandra D. Boulton."

Calder failed to smother a smile. Cassie glared at him and said under her breath, "Over my dead body."

***

Calder looked restless after they retired for the night, picking up a book, then pacing to look out the window into the darkness, then sitting on the bed to watch Cassie brushing her hair.

She paused, putting down the brush. "Is something the matter?"

"Do you ever think about having kids?" he asked abruptly.

She wasn't fooled by the apparent casualness of the question. She came over and sat next to him on the bed. "I think about it, of course. Why? Do you want to have kids?"

"That's really up to you. I'm fine with whatever you decide."

"That wasn't what I asked, you know—I asked if you *wanted* them."

He looked uncomfortable. "I don't know. It depends on what you want."

She took his hands in hers. "Sometimes I wonder whether you defer all these decisions to me because you don't like making decisions or because you're afraid I'll be angry if you make the wrong choice."

"Probably some of both. Mostly I don't want to scare you off by asking you to do something you don't want to do."

She eyed him for a moment and then abruptly pounced on him, pushing him back on the bed. He gave a startled laugh and pulled her close to him. She said, "In case you haven't noticed, I'm planning to marry you, so you don't need to worry about scaring me off. But I don't like not knowing what you want. I'm afraid you'll wake up one day and realize you're unhappy with everything we've done."

He drew her face to his and kissed her deeply. "I won't be unhappy."

"I still want you to trust me enough to tell me what you want. I'm not your father; I'm not going to be mad if I disagree."

"I *do* tell you what I want. I want *you*, and all the rest is details."

"So, do you want children?" she asked challengingly.

"Only if you do."

She rolled her eyes. "I didn't ask you if we should have them; I asked you if you *wanted* them, regardless of my opinion."

"Yes, I think I do, but I'm okay with it if you don't," he said finally.

"Thank you," she said firmly. "It's funny, you know—when I first met you, I thought you were used to demanding whatever you wanted, but you're really quite the opposite. You're very good at giving, but you don't know how to take."

"I think I'm pretty good at taking." He slid his hands down her back to cup her hips suggestively.

"No, you're not. But you're going to learn."

He laughed at her determined air. "And how do you plan to teach me?"

She caught his hands and moved them to his sides. "You are just going to lie there and let *me* give to *you* for once. No touching me, no nothing, got it?"

"Not fair. I love giving you pleasure—you know that."

Her face softened. "I know. But I want you to see that the world won't fall apart if you put your own pleasure first for once. Now, are you going to let me have my wicked way with you, or not?"

"How can I refuse an offer like that? Besides, I'll get my revenge."

"Oh, no, you won't." She began to unbutton the front of his shirt, trailing her fingers lightly down his chest as she went. "This is *my* turn." When she was finished with the buttons, she took her time tantalizing him, first with her fingers, then with the delicate touch of her mouth. She could feel his tension rising as she approached his belt buckle, and she raised her head to give him a mischievous smile while she disposed of the obstacle. "Are you enjoying yourself yet?" she asked archly, letting her hands pause in their exploration for a moment.

"*You* are trying to torment me."

"That's right." She felt his hand at her breast, caressing her nipple through her blouse. Despite the burst of pleasure it sent through her, she pushed his hand away. "Behave yourself. You can look, but don't touch." With a devilish smile, she began to remove her own clothes slowly as he watched hungrily.

Once she was done, she found her place atop him again, giving a low laugh when his hips thrust up involuntarily. "Hmm, I guess you *are* enjoying yourself after all." She wasn't ready to give him what he wanted, though, sliding away to allow her hands scope for ever more intimate explorations of him.

He groaned, and she said softly, "Tell me what you want."

"I want to touch you," he ground out.

"No. Tell me what you want *me* to do to *you*."

"Cassie." His voice was full of deep frustration.

"Or do I have to guess?" She shifted so that her mouth was poised just above him. "Could this be it?" She waited for an answer.

"You little torturer," he gasped. "You know it is."

She gave him a satisfied look as she began to give him what he wanted, making him moan with pleasure. He reached out for her, but she determinedly pushed his hands away, taking him closer and closer to the edge of pleasure.

"For God's sake, let me touch you," he pleaded.

She decided to take mercy on him and released him. Poising herself over him, she slid herself home, answered by a convulsive thrust. "There," she said mischievously, as he struggled to control himself. "You're touching me. *Now* what do you want?"

He caught at her hips, his eyes nearly wild, pulling her to him again. Then, apparently needing more, he surprised her by flipping them over so that he lay on top of her. It took only a few fierce, uncontrolled thrusts before he climaxed hard and slumped upon her.

He lay still for a minute as she stroked his back gently and then said, "God, Cassie, I'm sorry."

"What are you apologizing for?" she asked with amusement.

"Losing control," he said, clearly uncomfortable. "Not taking time for you."

"Excuse me. I was *trying* to make you lose control. You try to make *me* lose control all the time. You make me lose control so much I don't have the stamina to try to make *you* lose control most of the time."

"That's different."

"No, it isn't. You clearly liked it, and there's nothing wrong with wanting me to do things to you—I'm not going to get mad at you or anything."

"You're taking advantage of me. I'm in no condition to argue."

"I have to take advantage when I can," she said with mock dignity. "But I *am* serious—I want you to be able to tell me what you want, whether it's about having children or where we live or what you like in bed. I won't always agree, but I'd like to know."

He rolled off her and propped himself up on his elbow. "Cassie, my favorite fantasies about you mostly involve making love to you when I know that I've pleasured you again and again. It turns me on, okay?"

"You're hopeless," she said with amusement.

He leaned over and took her nipple in his mouth, teasing it with his tongue before suckling it gently for a minute. When she gasped with pleasure, he released her. "I don't notice you complaining most of the time." He returned to her nipple again, this time while sliding his hand between her legs. As she pressed hungrily against his fingers, he said, "But I suppose I can survive if occasionally you want to have your wicked way with me *before* I try to drive you out of your mind."

***

The story Calder planted about his missing uncle broke a few days later in the *New York Times*. "First page, but below the fold. Not bad," Calder said philosophically as he began to scan it.

Cassie read over his shoulder. It had a surprising number of details, including reports from his commanding officer in Korea and one of his early caretakers. Calder's grandfather was deeply implicated, but the investigators also found financial documents linking his father and other uncle.

"Now life will get exciting," Calder said. "I'm glad we're running away to get married soon."

The article provoked a furor in Washington. Fortunately, since Calder was seen only as a bit player in the story, it had little impact at Haverford. Several reporters called with questions, despite his continuing refusal to comment. When Cassie was caught once by a journalist, she cheerfully denied knowing anything beyond what she had read in the papers. She neatly sidestepped the trap when asked if she agreed with Senator Westing's actions toward his brother. "Do I agree with him?" she said. "I'm a Democrat and a scientist. I don't agree with Senator Westing on *anything*, including the basic facts of nature."

Chapter 20

A FEW DAYS LATER they finally left for Chicago, the wedding plans still a tightly kept secret. Their ostensible reason for leaving midweek was to avoid the media splash at Haverford when the article in *People* came out. Cassie was more nervous about introducing Calder to her parents than about the magazine.

They went to her parents' tiny ranch house for dinner that night. Both the house and the yard, always neat, were immaculately tidy. Her mother was already at the door when they walked up.

Cassie hugged her tightly, tears pricking at her eyes. When had her mother become so small? Swallowing the lump in her throat, she said, "Mom, this is Calder. And this is my father." As she kissed her father's cheek, she saw Calder taking her mother's hand in both of his own.

"It's a pleasure to meet you, Mrs. Boulton. Cassie's told me a great deal about you. Thanks for inviting us."

"I'm so glad you came." Her mother sounded choked up.

"I wouldn't miss this for the world, the chance to meet Cassie's family and see where she grew up."

Sometimes it was useful that his parents forced all those social skills down his throat, but Cassie could tell it didn't come naturally. "The house looks great, Mom." But it, like her mother, had grown even smaller while she was away.

Her mother had clearly worked hard over the hors d'oeuvres and explained that Cassie's sister Maria and her children would be arriving later, along with the Crowleys. Cassie had mentioned to her at one point that Calder was often quiet in large groups, but she hadn't expected her mother to adjust plans to accommodate for it. She was touched by how much effort her mother had put into making this evening a success.

Cassie didn't know what to talk about at first, but plans for the wedding made a subject they all had in common. Her mother filled her in on the last-minute details, seeming anxious for her approval, and took Cassie back to the bedroom to show her the mother-of-the-bride dress she had chosen.

To her relief, it was quite tasteful, although she suspected she had Ann Crowley to thank for that. She fingered the fine fabric. Her mother had probably never owned anything like it. None of them had. "Have you seen Ryan recently, Mom?" Cassie wasn't sure if she wanted to hear the answer, but she couldn't help asking.

Her mother's smile disappeared and her eyes became suspiciously misty. "I go down every month."

"How is he? His letters don't say much."

"He gets by. He's helping some of the other men with their cases, and they protect him in return. But he's too thin."

Ryan had written her about working in the law library at the prison. Cassie was pleased he was developing an interest in something, not realizing he had another motive for doing it. "He says I shouldn't visit him."

"He doesn't want you to see him like that. He's always wanted you to be proud of him."

Cassie bit her lip hard. She wanted to ask more, but it would make her cry. Instead, worried about leaving Calder for long with her father, she steered her mother back to the men, only to discover them engaged in a lively discussion on the White Sox's chances for next year. She blinked in astonishment, never having heard Calder so much as mention sports before. They seemed happy enough, though, so she left them to it, but when an opportunity arose later, she whispered to him, "So, when did you develop such an interest in the White Sox?"

"I'm from a family of politicians. The first thing to do when going to a new city is to learn about the sports teams so you have something to talk about."

She gave him an amused look. "It certainly seems to have worked."

Dinner went relatively well; although the fare was simple, Cassie's mother had gone to an effort to fix her childhood favorite dishes. Ann Crowley kept the conversation going with no apparent effort, for which Cassie was eternally grateful. Calder, while quiet, seemed in good spirits.

Cassie's mother had just served coffee when Calder's cell phone rang. With a look of annoyance, he flipped it open and glanced down at the caller ID. A shadow crossed his face for a moment. "Excuse me, please. It's my parents. I'd better talk to them." He walked into the living room before answering it. He had wondered how long it would take for his father to respond to the news in *People*. Apparently just a few hours.

"Hello?" Calder could hear the conversation in the dining room continuing in the background.

"Calder," came his mother's voice, and he relaxed slightly. His mother would say whatever his father told her to, but at least she wouldn't set traps for him. "Your father told me the news, and I just wanted to tell you how delighted I am. She sounds like a lovely young lady."

"Thank you," he managed to say. "I'm very happy about it."

"I hope I have the chance to meet her soon. Your father and I were thinking we'd like to have an engagement party for the two of you. All our friends will be anxious to meet her and to offer their congratulations in person."

Damage control. He'd been expecting something like this. His father knew how badly it would reflect on him if he didn't approve of the marriage, so he was switching positions. For the moment, anyway. It would only last until he thought they were vulnerable again. Apparently there was to be no mention of his failure to tell his parents directly about his engagement.

"I'll have to talk to Cassie about that," he said.

"Is she there? I'd love to say hello to her," she said with an appearance of warmth.

"Yes. We're having dinner at her parents' house."

"You are? Oh, how very nice. Please do give them my best regards, and tell them I look forward to meeting them."

"It's been very nice to meet them face to face, since I've only spoken to them on the phone before," said Calder. "Cassie's mom made us a wonderful dinner. I may not need to eat for a week." He wondered if his mother would notice he had more contact with Cassie's parents than with his own.

"Just a second." He was uncomfortable handing her over to Cassie, but not willing to make an issue of it. Returning o the dining room, he spoke in Cassie's ear. "My mother is asking to talk to you. They want to have an engagement party for us."

Cassie took the phone with a curious look and followed him back out of the room. "Hello?" She leaned back against Calder as he slipped his arms around her.

Calder couldn't quite hear his mother's voice. Cassie's side of the conversation consisted mostly of pleasantries. After a minute Cassie put her hand over the phone and whispered, "She's asking whether we've set a date. What should I say?"

He reached for the phone, and she said brightly, "Just a second. Calder wants to say something."

"Hello again," he said.

"Oh, Calder, she sounds charming. I was asking her if you'd set a date yet."

He knew with a fierce anger that his father was behind the question, wanting to know how much time he had to put a spoke in the works. "Yes," he said deliberately.

"How exciting! When will it be?"

His first instinct was to prevaricate, but he was finished with that part of his life. He took Cassie's hand in his. "Saturday."

His mother laughed graciously. "You'll have to give me a few more hints than that. There are a lot of Saturdays, after all."

"Day after tomorrow. Four o'clock."

He could guess at the hurried conversation between his parents in the ensuing silence. At last his mother said, "Are you *quite* serious, dear?"

"Yes."

She sounded injured. "You weren't planning to invite us to your wedding?"

"After Dad insulted Cassie, slandered her, threatened her, and harassed her, you think I should invite him to my wedding?" he said in an icy voice. It was probably more words than he had said to her in any one sentence in years.

"Why, Calder . . . I just don't know what to say."

"Probably best not to say anything, then." He knew it was her strategy for survival as much as it had been his. "Tell him you can both come if you like, but there's no need. *I* won't have any problem explaining why he isn't there."

"Well . . ." her voice sounded a little shaky. "Maybe you'd better tell me where it's going to be."

He felt a certain guilt over putting his mother in the middle. After all, she still had to live with his father, and he hadn't forgotten what Dave Crowley told him about her. A little more gently, he told her the address.

"I'll talk to your father," she said. "We'll call you back."

Calder hung up and dropped the phone back in his pocket. Cassie slipped her arms around him and laid her head on his shoulder. He let himself breathe in the light scent of her hair until he began to relax.

***

Half an hour later his phone rang again. It was his mother. "If your invitation still stands, dear, we'd like very much to come," she said.

"It still stands. I'll add you to the list. There's a dinner to follow the service."

"Your father has arranged for us to fly out first thing tomorrow morning. We'll be there by eleven o'clock."

He was fairly certain his father would behave in public. In private was a different question, one he didn't plan to explore.

"Cassie and I are tied up tomorrow with the rehearsal and the rehearsal dinner."

"Speaking of the rehearsal dinner, I understand you must have made arrangements for that already, but I hope you will let us take the usual responsibility as groom's parents," she said delicately.

He smiled sardonically. "Thanks, but that's not necessary. It's all been taken care of."

"Oh, but this is important to us. Please do let us reimburse you."

"I'm not the one taking care of it. Dave and Ann Crowley are hosting it," he said with a certain grim satisfaction.

He could hear the shocked silence. Finally his mother said tentatively, "Dave Crowley?"

"Yes. He and Ann have helped us enormously. They've known Cassie for years."

There was a rustling at the other end, and his father came on the line. "Calder? I don't know what you said to upset your mother, but I'll thank you to stop it. She's quite hurt enough by hearing about your engagement from the media."

"I was just telling her the Crowleys have known Cassie for

years." Calder didn't for a moment think his father was truly concerned for his mother's welfare, but he was surprised she had been so upset by what he said.

"Nevertheless, you could make an effort to be kind to her. We'll call you later when we've made arrangements."

When he returned to the others and announced his parents would be coming after all, there was a moment of silence, and then Cassie's mother said brightly, "Oh, that's nice. I'm glad they can make it."

Apparently his family wasn't the only one that could ignore unpleasant realities.

***

It had been at least five years since Cassie last set foot in the church where she had once attended Sunday school. It hadn't changed at all. The cushions on the pews were perhaps a little more worn, and the stained-glass windows were just as grimy as when she had spent many bored hours studying instead of listening to the sermon. But she did not regret coming back for her wedding, although once the thought would have horrified her.

Still, she must have been out of her mind to agree to a formal wedding, however small. At the time it made sense. Now she wondered if they would all survive the rehearsal. In the vestry, Scott made a labored attempt at conversation with Cassie's parents, glancing occasionally at Erin, while Erin, never moving from Cassie's side, pretended Scott didn't exist. Calder was silent and radiated stress, whether from all the people around him or the thought of seeing his parents at the rehearsal dinner she couldn't tell.

Cassie hoped desperately that Ann would finish her arrangements with the minister so they could start the rehearsal. At least then no one would have to talk to each other.

There was a stir as the doors opened to admit an older woman dressed with casual elegance, followed by Senator Westing. Just what they needed to make the occasion perfect. Cassie turned to Calder to say something sharp about not warning her that his parents would be attending the rehearsal, but recognized the grim set of his jaw. This must be another case of his father turning up uninvited.

"Calder," his mother said calmly, leaning in to kiss his cheek before turning to Cassie with a warm smile. "And you must be Cassandra. I'm delighted to meet you."

"It's my pleasure, Mrs. Westing," said Cassie. Calder had talked about his mother much less than he did about his father, almost as if she had been an invisible part of his past.

"Please call me Caro."

"Thank you." Cassie noticed Mrs. Westing didn't make a move to kiss her or shake her hand. Something about her stance suggested perhaps she didn't like to be touched.

"You know my father, of course," Calder said.

"Indeed." Cassie was damned if she would say she was pleased to see him. "Good afternoon, Senator."

He flashed his politician's smile. "Joe, please."

"I think I'll stick with Senator, actually." She didn't bother to hide a slight bite in her voice. "It'll keep me from getting above myself."

She had reason to be thankful for Calder's excellent public

manners as he stepped in to make the rest of the introductions. If Cassie's mother had seemed stiff before, she looked rigid now.

Finally the minister called them to the altar and began running through the order of the service. Cassie wondered if he had ever married a couple whose attendants conspicuously ignored each other before.

They made it through the first part of the rehearsal without any difficulties, but when the minister instructed Scott to give Calder the ring, there was no response. Sneaking a peek over Calder's shoulder, Cassie saw Scott was staring at Erin.

Calder touched his arm. "Scott, the ring!"

"Oh. Sorry." Scott rummaged in his pocket and produced the ring. Erin raised her eyes from the floor just long enough to hand the other ring to Cassie.

Cassie wished the minister would hurry so she could put Erin and Scott on separate sides of the room again. Then again, given the number of people at this rehearsal she'd like to keep apart, she doubted any room could have enough sides.

"Cassie, Calder, now you turn together and face the congregation, then proceed down the aisle. Good. Mr. Dunstan, you offer your arm to Miss McKinley. No, turn the other way. The *other* way. That's right."

Cassie and Calder had almost reached the doors when Cassie heard a sound. It was Erin, still at the altar, her hands over her face, while Scott stood by looking helpless.

Dropping Calder's arm, Cassie hurried back and put her arm around Erin, directing a glare at Scott. "Oh, sweetie. I'm so sorry." She should have followed her instincts and chosen a different maid-of-honor, but that would have hurt Erin's feelings, too. She was acutely conscious of the number of eyes on them.

The minister cleared his throat. "Perhaps Miss McKinley would be more comfortable in my office."

Cassie steered Erin toward the side of the altar and into the office where she and Calder had met earlier with the minister. Scott trailed after them, despite her glares. Cassie placed the tissue box from the minister's desk in Erin's hand. Cassie made a point of standing between Erin and Scott, who hovered just outside the door. She was tempted to close the door in his face.

When the minister joined them a few minutes later, Erin looked up just long enough to choke out a few words. "I'm sorry."

"Weddings are very emotional occasions, Miss McKinley." He seated himself across from her.

Cassie turned to Scott. "I think we can handle this from here."

"I'll stay." Scott wove past Cassie to stand next to Erin's chair, placing his hand on her arm. "I'm sorry, Erin. I shouldn't have said anything. I didn't know it would upset you."

Erin dabbed at her face with a tissue, which made little difference since tears continued to run down her face. "You didn't know? What do you think I am?"

The minister pointed to a chair. "Mr. Dunstan, perhaps you should have a seat as well."

Scott looked guilty. "I'm sorry. She's upset because of something I said."

"I heard what you said." The minister spoke in a calming voice. "But I'm not the one you need to explain it to."

Scott squirmed, as if trying to find a place to hide in the

chair, but he didn't let go of Erin's arm. "I couldn't stand it, Erin. Listening to them going through their wedding vows. We couldn't even get them to admit they breathed the same air, much less that they liked each other. Remember? You and I had everything going for us, but now you'll barely speak to me. I'm not blaming you, I just can't help thinking that it should be the other way around. This should have been *our* wedding."

Cassie fumed as she watched Erin cover her eyes with the tissue. She couldn't believe Scott would do this.

Finally Erin choked out a few words. "I don't want to talk about it."

The minister spoke in a kind voice. "The ability to communicate is God's gift to us. Where would we be if we never spoke to each other? That's how wars and hatred start. Charity and forgiveness begin with understanding, and for that we have to talk. Even when we don't want to." He rose stiffly to his feet and laid his hand on the doorknob. "Cassie, I'm sure they're waiting for you at the restaurant. We'll manage here."

Cassie found herself shuffled out of the office and facing a closed door. Her first instinct was to charge back in, but what could she do there anyway? Erin was a big girl and could take care of herself. She made her way back into the church. It was empty except for Calder, sitting in the back pew.

He stood and took her hand. "Is Erin okay?"

"She's upset. Is Scott religious?"

"Not particularly. Why?"

Cassie couldn't help but see the humor in the situation. "Neither is Erin, and I have the feeling they're both about to get a lecture from the minister. I wish I could watch."

"Maybe he can do some good where we couldn't. I wouldn't mind that."

"Me either." But she thought it unlikely. "Where is everybody?"

Calder released her. "At the restaurant. Ann herded everyone out. My parents took Alicia and Teresa with them."

"Oh, no." The idea of Calder's parents with her nieces was a more dangerous proposition than the minister with Scott and Erin. "We'd better get over there before somebody's killed."

Astonishingly enough, everyone seemed to be conversing amicably when they arrived at the dimly lit Italian restaurant Ann had chosen. Cassie had to hide a laugh when she heard Joe Westing ask her father whether he thought the Sox could take the pennant this year.

Alicia ran between the tables and skidded to a halt in front of them. "Cassie, look what Uncle Joe gave me!" She pointed to a gold locket around her neck. "It's to wear at the wedding, and it's got a *diamond*. Teresa has one, too. Wait till Mom sees us!"

"*Uncle Joe?* I hope you thanked the Senator nicely." Cassie wondered how he had managed that. Calder's father couldn't have known who was in the wedding party. Perhaps he came with his pocket full of potential bribes and improvised. Cassie wouldn't put it past him.

"We did, and we got to ride in their limo. It has a *refrigerator* in it, and he gave us pop."

Joe Westing turned to look their way. Cassie wondered if it were possible to be any more mortified. She couldn't imagine what Calder was thinking, especially when Joe started to amble in their direction.

Alicia lit up even more at his approach. "It has a TV in it, too, don't it, Uncle Joe?"

Yes, it was possible to be more mortified. "Thank you for giving the girls a ride, Senator, and for the lovely necklaces as well."

"My pleasure, and I told them to call me Uncle Joe. I suppose it should be Great-uncle Joe, but that's such a mouthful." He radiated sincerity, as if he always told multiracial slum children to call him uncle.

"How kind of you," Cassie said with a tinge of sharpness. "Calder, perhaps we should find our seats."

"Good idea," Joe said, as if it had been an act of ingenuity on her part.

Once they were seated, Cassie could avoid looking at the impossible combinations of people around them. Gradually the others came to their places at the long table, Cassie's parents and the girls at one end while the Crowleys sat with Joe and Caro at the other. Erin and Scott's seats remained glaringly empty. It was an uncomfortable fifteen minutes before Ann told the waiters to go ahead with serving the meal anyway.

Erin and Scott had still not arrived by the time dessert was served. Caro left her seat and approached Cassie. "We're hoping you and Calder will come back to our hotel for a drink afterwards. We'd like a chance to get to know you."

Cassie didn't need to look at Calder; she could feel his tension. "Thank you, but I'm afraid we can't. After a busy day like this, Calder and I do best if we have some quiet time." She watched his mother for a reaction, wondering if she knew that her son would be feeling overwhelmed by the crowd at the rehearsal and dinner, no matter how pretty his manners were. She didn't see anything, though; she had the feeling her future mother-in-law was going to prove very difficult to read. "Perhaps we could manage something tomorrow morning."

"That would be lovely, dear. Tom and Fiona won't be arriving until after lunch, I'm afraid. They're cutting it a little close, but it's hard for him to get away. Would lunch work, or would breakfast be better for you?"

Calder said, "Lunch will be fine."

Cassie winced as Alicia and Teresa spotted their opportunity and swooped down on Joe. Perhaps she could say it was their bedtime and take them back to the house.

***

Cassie went straight to the telephone when they arrived back at their hotel and dialed Erin's extension. The phone rang several times, long enough to worry her, but finally Erin answered.

"Erin, it's Cassie. Are you okay?"

"I'm fine. I'm sorry about missing the rehearsal dinner. I hope it wasn't a problem." Her voice seemed oddly stiff.

"Don't worry about that." Cassie could understand why she might want to avoid it after the episode at the church. "But I felt bad about deserting you with the minister." Not to mention Scott.

"It's fine. He was very nice."

If Erin was determined not to tell her what had happened, there was little Cassie could do about it. She wondered what kind of shape Scott was in, if Erin was refusing to talk. "Are you sure you're okay?"

"Everything's fine. Don't . . ."

Cassie heard a rustling, then Scott's amused voice. "She'll talk to you tomorrow, Cassie. We're busy. Good night."

There was a click at the other end. Cassie stared at the phone and laughed.

Chapter 21

CALDER BUTTONED HIS CUFFS carefully. His mother would be certain to notice it was the same shirt he had worn the night before. He could picture the little frown on her face. But it was the only dress shirt he'd brought along, apart from his tux. "I can't believe I'm wasting part of my wedding day having lunch with my parents."

"It could be worse. Your father and I will probably fight enough he won't have energy for you. I can't tell what your mother is thinking, though." Cassie slipped on her black shoes.

"Neither can I—never could. Until Dave told me how she used to be, I assumed she was happy being my father's shadow. Now I don't know what to make of her."

Cassie put her hand on his arm. "It took me forever to learn to read you, and that was with a lot of help from your book. I wish your mother came with a book."

His parents' hotel suite was just what he expected—large and at the most exclusive hotel in the city. There was a linen-covered table for four in the sitting area, with a small buffet off to the side. He had hoped they would be eating in the restaurant. There was less to worry about in public.

His mother evidently decided she should show more interest in her future daughter-in-law. "Is everything ready for the wedding?" she asked Cassie.

"I certainly hope so. But I don't know much about it. Ann Crowley made all the arrangements."

Caro handed Cassie a white plate. "I hope you're not too disappointed you didn't have the chance to plan it yourself."

"Not at all." Cassie helped herself to shrimp salad. "It's hard to put a wedding together on short notice. I'm grateful Ann did it for me, and I'm sure she did a better job than I would have."

"You should have told us about it sooner," said Senator Westing in a manner that suggested no one would question his opinions. "We all need to stand together right now."

"Right now?" Calder asked dryly. So his father was going to ignore the last-minute nature of the wedding.

"Yes, this is a bad business with my brother Stephen," Joe said. "No question it's going to be damaging, but we have to try to contain it. That article in *People* was a good idea, Calder—helped give people something else to think about. But warn me next time."

"I'm glad you approve," Calder said. As if his father's approval mattered. "Did you ever find out how the story got out?"

Senator Westing scowled. "Not yet. We've learned which editor at the *Times* assigned the story to the reporters, but my sources haven't been able to find out how he knew there was something to look for in the first place. We will, though, and then there'll be hell to pay."

"So, I'm dying to meet your other son and his wife," Cassie

said as she carried her plate to the table. Calder automatically held her chair for her. "Calder has told me lots about Tom, but I haven't heard much about Fiona."

"Fiona is harmless," said Senator Westing dismissively. "She's a good hostess, but she lacks ambition. Tom needs someone who will push him more."

"House of Representatives by, what, age thirty? Doesn't sound like a lack of ambition to me," Cassie said. Calder was glad she was doing the talking. It took the burden off him.

"He could have been there sooner. He needs to make a bigger name for himself, so we can keep the seat in the family when I retire."

"And all this time I've been thinking it was an elective office, not a hereditary fief," she said.

Joe burst out laughing. "Oh, the innocence of youth. It's time for you to start thinking like a Westing."

"I hope you don't think that marrying Calder is going to convince me to vote Republican."

"Oh, *that* doesn't matter," he said.

"Can I quote you on that?"

"Don't quote me on anything." Joe took his place at the head of the table. "It's probably better for me this way. I have to work with the damn Democrats all the time, and it'll win me some points if I can complain to them about my daughter-in-law, the Democrat. That's more useful than one more Republican vote in Pennsylvania."

"In that case, maybe I'll have to take another look at the Republican candidates." The corners of Cassie's mouth twitched.

"No, just move to Virginia, and we'll run you as a Democrat

against Tom, and we'll win either way." He was clearly enjoying himself.

Calder watched the conversation with a certain cynicism. He had no doubt his father was against his marriage, yet at the same time, he seemed delighted with Cassie. Perhaps he recognized her as possessing the audacity his sons lacked, but which he himself had in such ample quantities. He felt a little sick every time Cassie laughed at one of his father's jokes, praying she wouldn't be taken in by him.

His mother gave the appearance of someone who was attending closely to the conversation while being peculiarly absent at the same time. Calder tried to see any evidence of the lively, daring girl Dave had described, but it was impossible. Had she ever been like that? When he was very young she had played with him, and he distantly remembered games of hide-and-seek around the house. Then that all stopped, and she became the drill sergeant of proper manners and behavior, until he was more frightened of disappointing her than he was of the social occasions she was trying to groom him for.

He remembered, too, a time when he failed, when he was six. His parents trotted him out during a party in his uncle's honor, most likely when he won the vice-presidency. There were a host of political cronies and powerful men in attendance, and he blurted out the wrong thing to the wrong person. His father laughed at the time and sent him up to bed with his nanny. But late that night, he appeared in Calder's room, woke him up, and delivered a tongue-lashing as brutal as the unexpected beating that followed it. It was the only time he remembered his father hitting him, but it was memorable. He cried for his mother, but she didn't come, not until the next day after his father left the house. She brought him something for the pain, and rubbed some liniment gently onto his bruised back, and then quietly but firmly began the lessons that would dominate mealtimes with her for years. He hated it, the endless repetitions of "If someone says such-and-such to you, what should you say?" until the answers were so automatic he could give them even when terrified. He knew from books that other parents read their children stories at bedtime; he had bedtime lessons in public deportment.

Now, as he watched her, he couldn't fault *her* deportment, but he wondered what lay behind it. Did she ever think of those years and wish she had read him stories instead of teaching him how to behave? He doubted it. He wondered how much of a disappointment he was to her. After all her training, he was choosing a life where his ability to perform in public didn't matter.

***

The discussion over lunch was illuminating to Cassie. Once Senator Westing managed to stop subtly maligning the members of his family, she discovered he could be a stimulating conversationalist. It was clear where Calder came by his sharp intellect and quick thinking. She could see his father's success in politics lay not only in his ability to charm, but also in his talent for infusing energy into even the dullest subject. It reminded her of Calder's writing ability, the way he engaged a reader's feelings. How easy it would be to be caught up in his father's self-assurance, if it weren't for how he treated her before. She would never trust him, but she understood his famed charisma better now.

Finally it was over. Back in the car with Calder, she let out a deep sigh. "I hope we don't have to do that very often. I'm exhausted." When Calder didn't reply, she looked over at him with concern. "Are you all right?"

He shrugged. "Just thinking."

"What about?"

"You had a good time talking to my father."

"*Someone* had to keep the conversation going. Your father is smart, funny, and quick on his feet, and I'd rather be in a room with a poisonous snake."

"Really?" He gave her a sidelong glance. "It looked like you were getting along pretty well."

"Calder, I do my best to get along with *everyone*. Do you think I don't notice those little cuts he makes? The only reason I'm civil to him is because he's your father."

He was quiet for a minute, but she could see his shoulders relax. So he had been unsure of her loyalty to him, just hours before their wedding. This was happening too fast.

Cassie stepped out of the car in front of the church that afternoon to face a barrage of flashes. Startled, she froze for a moment but regained her composure when Dave Crowley materialized, taking her arm and leading her into the church. "Don't worry," he whispered. "We've got security here, and the press know that anyone who tries to ask questions or intrudes will be thrown out."

"How did they find out? I thought no one knew," Cassie said in dismay.

"Who do you think wants full publicity for the fact that he's here and smiling?" Dave said, a note of distaste in his voice. "Never mind. The only photographer inside the church is the one Ann hired. She runs a tight ship."

“And I’m grateful for it,” said Cassie. If her picture was to be splashed all over the papers, she was glad she let Ann talk her into an elegant gown.

Her father was right behind them, looking uncomfortable in a suit and tie, and no doubt even more ill at ease about the cameras. When they paused in the vestibule and Dave slipped away into the church, Cassie wondered how her father felt about giving his eldest daughter away not only to another man, but also to a different world he could barely imagine and would never be comfortable sharing. But she had moved out of his world when she signed up for her first library card at age twelve, and there was no going back. She felt a moment of sadness, realizing how little common ground they ever had beyond living in the same house. She wished she had tried harder to find some interest to share with him. Calder had shown how easy it could be with his sports talk. She had just never made the effort. Her thoughts were interrupted as the doors opened in front of her and her father held out his arm for her. She smiled at him and gave his arm a squeeze as she took it.

***

The actual service passed in a blur, more like a movie than her own life. Cassie remembered looking into Calder’s eyes while saying their vows and seeing both his affection for her and his discomfort at being the center of attention. It didn’t begin to feel real until they exchanged rings and she could see the solid proof of their marriage on her own hand. She had a hazy recollection of receiving people’s congratulations and passing by a gauntlet of news photographers, no doubt tipped off by Joe Westing.

The reception, in the private room of an elegant restaurant, had few trappings of a traditional reception beyond a wedding cake and place cards, a last-minute addition to limit the Westing family's exposure to the other guests. Cassie paid little attention to the food, though everyone else seemed to be enjoying it—everyone except Scott and Erin, who were too busy looking into each other's eyes to notice anything.

When she and Calder started to circulate through the room, their first stop was a duty visit to his family's table, where Calder introduced her to his brother. Tom was a pleasant young man with some of his father's polish but lacking his sharp edges. Cassie chatted with him and his wife briefly and found it hard to imagine Tom and Calder as brothers. Life seemed to have touched Tom Westing only lightly, but she reminded herself how much she had misread Calder at first. Perhaps Tom had hidden depths as well. If so, they were well disguised beneath the veneer of the promising young politician.

Cassie said quietly to Calder, "I want to talk to Jim for a minute. He and Rose have to leave early to catch their flight."

Calder looked across the room to where his father worked the room as if votes from Pennsylvania mattered to him. On an impulse, he said, "Go ahead. I'm going to stay here for a bit." He caught Cassie's eye as he sat down next to his mother, and she nodded slightly.

Deciding to talk with his mother was easier than doing it. She said all the correct things about how lovely the wedding was and how beautiful Cassie looked, the meaningless but proper conversation he detested.

"Your Cassandra is a very nice young woman, Calder. You've

chosen well." Caro Westing's hands were neatly folded in her lap.

Calder kept his shoulders straight, the way she had always insisted upon. "There's no reason to pretend, Mother. I know perfectly well that as soon as my back is turned he's going to be out there trying to break us up."

She arched a perfectly curved eyebrow. "I don't believe so, Calder. He's come to the conclusion she will be good for you."

"Without money and the right connections? I doubt it."

"She has something he values more. She's ambitious. He knows where she started and how far she has come. He thinks she'll make something of you." She might have been speaking of the weather for all the emotion in her voice.

"Of course, I should have known," he said icily. "Whatever makes you happy and keeps him off my back is fine with me."

"No, that's not what makes me happy." She turned to look full at him for the first time in the conversation. "I'm happy because she'll keep you safe. Excuse me, Calder." She rose and walked gracefully in the direction of the restrooms. He watched her for a moment, his eyes narrowed, wondering what she really meant.

***

Cassie hugged Jim, trying to remember the last time she had seen him in a suit. "I'm glad you could come on such short notice."

"Wouldn't miss it for the world. You've been leading an exciting life. Not that I'm unhappy about the results, mind you. I always did think he was interested in you, no matter what you said."

"Yes, you can say you told me so. I bet you'll never let me forget it." Thinking about Calder was comforting.

"No, I won't. Especially since Rose got curious when we found out he was a writer and decided to read one of his books."

Cassie blushed fiercely. "Oh, God. I was counting on you scientist types never picking up a book without footnotes. Now I'm embarrassed." A thought suddenly struck her. "I hope Rob hasn't read it."

"Everybody read it. It has a marine biologist as the heroine, it's set at the MBL, and you're listed in the acknowledgments."

So everyone from her old lab knew the intimate story. And this was just the beginning. Her entire life would be fair game.

It must have shown in her face, because Jim said, "Nobody knows it's about you and Calder except Rose and me, and probably Rob. Even I wasn't sure it was supposed to be the two of you until I read that scene where we played Trivial Pursuit. I don't think I've ever been a character in a book before. It was kind of fun. But speaking of Rob, he asked me to give you this." He pulled an envelope out of his pocket and handed it to her.

Cassie accepted it reluctantly. Rob wouldn't have sent it with Jim if it were bad. After a moment's hesitation, she ripped it open.

It was a traditional wedding card with a picture of bells and a flowery verse. At the end Rob had written, 'I hope you find all the happiness you deserve. Love, Rob.'

She blinked back the hot tears that filled her eyes. "How is he doing?"

Jim laid his hand on her arm. "Don't worry, he'll be fine. I think he'd been hoping things wouldn't work out with Calder and that maybe later . . . Well, it's good you're married. That'll help him move on. So, how do you get any work done these days, with all this excitement?" he teased.

Cassie frowned. "Time is the least of my worries. It looks like I may have to leave Haverford."

Jim's face registered astonishment. "No! Why?"

"It's a long story, and this would be a particularly bad time to go into it," she said, her eyes flickering in the direction of Calder's family. "I'm probably going to go on the market in the fall."

"There are places that would be glad to have you. When you get home, send me an email about what you're looking for, and I'll do some nosing around for positions that might be open."

Cassie was grateful, both for his faith in her and his help. Networking was more likely to come up with a job for her than watching the ads. "There's an opening I'm looking at for this fall, but I can't decide whether to take it seriously or not. It's a step down the academic ladder, but it's at the MBL."

"What is it?"

"It's with Boston University's Marine Program at MBL, teaching undergrads concentrating in marine science. I'd have the chance to do some research of my own with the Center for Ecosystem Studies if I can get a grant."

"What's the catch?"

"It's part-time, and it's not tenure-track." She was embarrassed to tell him she would even consider such a thing. "They say there may be an opportunity for a tenure-track position someday, but realistically, I'll never have the high-powered research credentials they would want. And those jobs only open up once every blue moon, anyway."

Jim looked at her in silence for a moment. "I'd think with

marrying Calder Westing you wouldn't have to worry about things like tenure and salary anymore. So where's the problem?"

"I don't want to be dependent on Calder. If anything goes wrong, I'll still need my career, and you know how hard it would be to get another tenure-track position after giving one up."

"Rather pessimistic thoughts for a newlywed. Are you really worried about Calder leaving you destitute, or is it just hard to give up the prestige of the tenure-track?" When Cassie flushed guiltily, he added, "Don't give me credit for mind-reading. Rose faced the same thing when we got married. Our specialties were too close; we'd never been able to find tenure-track jobs together. So now she manages the lab, because she had the guts to quit the track and I didn't."

"I don't think it's a matter of guts."

"Oh, yes, it is. You should ask her. You see, Rose isn't afraid of being just Rose, whereas if you took away 'Professor of Biology at the University of North Carolina' and my list of publications from me, I don't know what would be left. No, there isn't any question I didn't have the guts to leave the track. I couldn't even take time to be a father. Instead I raise grad students and send them off into the world to make all the same mistakes I did. There's a *reason* I've been telling you to get a life all these years, you know."

Tears sprang to her eyes again at his obviously heartfelt words. She had thought Jim would be the last person in the world to suggest she give up her academic career. He was one of the few people who really understood her drive to succeed.

Seeing her stricken look, he put his arm around her. "Now you stop that," he scolded. "I don't need six-foot-plus of your new husband getting mad at me for making you cry."

She managed a watery smile. “You’re just trying to stay on his good side because you want him on your team for Trivial Pursuit.”

“Damn straight. I know which side my bread is buttered on.” He paused. “I hope you do, too.”

Suddenly lonely for Calder despite all the people around her, she began to make her way to his side again. She passed by Dave Crowley in earnest conversation with Calder’s mother.

“He’s a fine boy,” Dave said. “You should be proud of him, Caro.” Cassie was unable to make out Mrs. Westing’s murmured reply, but she heard Dave say in a quietly intense voice, “Damn it, Caro, you don’t have to thank me. In a different world, he’d have been mine. You know that.”

Disturbed, she hurried away before they noticed her. She found Calder with Scott and Erin and slipped her hand into his. “I’m ready to leave now,” she said.

“Me too. But first I have something to tell my father.”

“Should I come with you?”

“No. This is something I need to do alone.”

Joe Westing was now seated again with Tom and Fiona. Calder rehearsed his lines in his head as he approached the table. For once he was glad of a crowd of people around him. There was safety in numbers.

“Cassie and I are leaving,” he said to his father. “Since I won’t be seeing you again for a while, I wanted to tell you something.”

“What’s that?” Joe still had his jovial manner on.

Calder felt dizzy, but he didn’t want to sit down. He needed the advantage height gave him. “You were wondering earlier how the press found out about Uncle Stephen.”

The set of his father's mouth would have made him want to run when he was younger. Joe said, "What about it?"

"I told them."

"Calder, this isn't a joking matter." There was a definite threat in his father's voice now.

Calder felt a paradoxical relief now that his father was openly angry. "I'm not joking. I called the editor at the *Times*. And I'll do worse if you ever go after Cassie again."

"You what?" Joe put his hands on the table and half-rose.

"That's all I have to say." Calder turned to his brother. "Tom, I'm sorry if the story has made trouble for you."

Tom grabbed Joe's arm. "Sit down, Dad. There's a photographer here."

Joe hadn't taken his eyes off Calder. "Don't think you're getting away with this, young man."

Calder wondered why he'd never done this before. "I'm not trying to get away with anything. I'm just getting away." He turned and on impulse went to the corner where his mother stood with Dave Crowley.

He kissed his mother's cheek. "I'm going now. Stay away from the old man for a while. He's furious."

Caro's expression didn't change, but she nodded almost imperceptibly. "My best wishes to both you and Cassie. I hope I'll see you again soon."

Calder turned to Dave. "Thanks for everything, Dave."

Cassie was waiting for him near the door. He took her hand, hurrying her out before anyone could notice they were leaving.

They were met by a barrage of flashes. In the heat of the confrontation with his father, Calder had forgotten about the press. From habit, he dropped his head. Cassie squeezed his hand, and he felt strength flowing from her.

Deliberately, he turned toward the cameras and waved, smiling his public smile, and then began to walk again. He could feel Cassie's surprised eyes on him.

"How about kissing the bride, Mr. Westing?" a male voice called out.

It was just pictures, and the press would find a way to get them one way or another. "Oh, why not," he said in a voice so low only Cassie could hear it. He pulled her into his arms and kissed her. The warmth of her lips was almost enough to compensate for the flashes surrounding them.

But enough was enough, and the car was at the curb. Calder turned on the ignition and pulled out of the parking lot, checking the rearview mirror to make sure they weren't followed.

"So, who are you and what have you done with my publicity-shy husband?" Cassie asked with amusement.

He spared her a smile. "Your husband. I think I like that."

***

Cassie and Calder had tickets for an early flight out of Chicago, so she was still half-asleep when they got to O'Hare Airport. She was not so tired, however, as to fail to notice at check-in that Calder told the attendant they were flying to Boston.

"Philadelphia, you mean," she corrected.

Calder looked embarrassed. "Actually, it *is* Boston. I have a surprise for you there."

Cassie raised an eyebrow. "You've been plotting!"

"Well, you said I should tell you what I wanted."

"What's in Boston?"

"The Old North Church, Harvard Square, the Charles River, swan boats, the New England Aquarium, all sorts of things."

"That's not what I meant!"

"Yes, but that's all I'm going to tell you." He looked inordinately pleased with himself.

Although desperately curious, Cassie refused to give him the satisfaction of pestering him with questions until after they arrived in Boston. As he drove the rental car south, she said, "We're going to the Cape, aren't we?"

"That's right." He glanced at her with a brief smile. "I need to pick something up."

"Pick something up? Have you ever considered using the postal service? Or FedEx?"

"Patience, patience," he teased. "You'll see soon enough."

She bided her time as he drove, apart from the occasional teasing threat. He laughed, but as they crossed the bridge onto the Cape, he began to seem inexplicably nervous. He turned off the main road north of Woods Hole.

It was a route Cassie knew well. "Are we going to the salt marsh? It's not the most welcoming of places in March."

Calder only smiled as he followed the road to Chapoquoit rather than toward the marsh. He turned off on a private dirt road, then another. Cassie recognized where they were. It was the narrow spit of land extending along the beach at the north end of the marsh, with half a dozen houses scattered along the length. There was an expansive view of Buzzard's Bay to the right and the salt marsh to the left. Calder drove slowly, as if looking for something, and finally pulled up in front of a grey-shingled Colonial.

"This is where you have to pick something up?" she asked dubiously.

"That's right. Want to come with me?"

As if she could resist getting out of the car into the sea air! Her eyes were drawn immediately to the water, so she almost missed it when Calder plucked an envelope off the deck and opened it. He handed her the key that was inside. "It's your wedding present. It was a little too big to ship, so we had to come here instead. I hope it was worth the detour."

She looked from him to the key, then to the house and back to him again. "You bought me a *house* as a wedding present?"

He flushed slightly. "Well, I was working with a realtor here to keep an eye out for promising properties, and when this one came on the market, I didn't want to lose the chance on it. I thought you'd like to live by the salt marsh."

"Of course I would. I'd just never thought I'd do it. Are you sure it's ours?"

He laughed at the look on her face. "Maybe you don't want to look around inside, but I do. If you don't like it, we don't have to keep it."

She glared at him balefully. "I *like* it."

"Without even looking inside?" he asked mildly.

She unlocked the door and held it open to him with a flourish. "After you."

"You can't get away with that!" He swept her into his arms and carried her over the threshold. She laughed merrily and pulled his face down to hers for a kiss. "Now put me down and let me see my house!"

Cassie moved through the house, checking out each room. The

kitchen was old-fashioned, but she was pleased by the overall dimensions, the original fireplace in the living room, and the expansive views of the bay. Finally she opened the large glass doors off the living room and stepped onto the wide deck overlooking the salt marsh. She paused, leaning her hands against the railing, shivering a little in the March breeze. Tender green grasses appeared between the dead stalks of last year's growth, early signs of spring.

She felt Calder slip his arms around her from behind. "Thank you," she said. "It's just perfect."

"Really?"

She leaned her head back against his shoulder. "I've always envied the people who lived in these houses. It's the perfect spot."

He kissed her hair. "I can tell you like it. You haven't said a word about it costing too much."

"Nope." She turned in his arms and wound her arms around his neck. "For this house, I'll consent to being a kept woman."

He raised his eyebrows. "I wish I'd known that a year ago."

"I wish *I'd* realized a long time ago that your surface is as deceptive as the plainness of the marsh. I might have had the sense to look past the surface," she said with unusual seriousness. She rested in his arms until a particularly strong wind blew past, driving them back inside.

She gazed around the interior again with pleasure. "I wish we could just stay here forever."

He touched her cheek. "It'll be here waiting for us every summer."

She looked out the window at the salt marsh. "Or I could give up the apartment in Haverford, and we could live here."

He looked at her as if unsure how seriously to take her comment. "What about your job?"

"I could quit it and take the job in Woods Hole." She studied his reaction, suspecting he would have trouble telling her if he objected to the idea.

"But you said you couldn't do that because it isn't tenure-track," he said, his face impassive.

She shrugged lightly. "What's the point of worrying about tenure if I'm going to be a kept woman? But the question is where *you* want to live."

"I suppose I'll be in trouble if I say I'm fine anywhere as long as I'm with you."

"That's right," she said. "You're learning."

"I like it here. With you. I was planning to give up my apartment in DC anyway."

"Won't that upset your family?"

"I don't care. I'm probably going to be disinherited again, anyway."

"Will that be a problem?"

"Didn't you pay any attention to that prenuptial you signed?" he asked. When she shook her head, he added, "I have a trust fund from my grandfather, and the interest is enough for us to live comfortably on. We don't need anything from my father unless you have a yen to go in for major philanthropy."

"I don't think so, thanks," said Cassie cheerfully. "Besides, I don't think he'll disinherit you. In fact, I expect you're probably going to get along better with him now."

He looked dubious. "Why would you think that?"

"Your father spends an enormous amount of energy trying to

make people submit to his authority, but you know something? I don't think he likes it when they do. I think he likes the battle. I'd go so far as to venture a guess that, even though he'd have stopped you from marrying me if he could, he actually likes me, in his own disturbed way. And I think he likes it that you fought back. He'll keep trying to make us submit, but I bet it won't break his heart when we don't."

"I don't know. But in the meantime, can I take you to dinner?"

She smiled at him mischievously. "Do I get apple pie out of it?"

"Deal," he said, taking her hand. He had a sudden image of the last time they were at the Dock of the Bay Café, a year earlier, when she had been in tears in the street, thinking she would not be able to return to the MBL. When her future at Haverford was threatened, she was angry, but philosophical about it. "Can I just say one more thing, though? I think you ought to take the job here. I think Woods Hole is more important to you than Haverford."

She looked at him in surprise. "You could be right. Despite that overrated university education."

"It happens occasionally."

Chapter 22

"WHAT IS THAT?" CASSIE stared in disbelief at the black-and-white bundle of fur skittering across the living room floor.

Calder looked embarrassed. "It's a puppy. I hope you don't mind."

"You got a puppy without talking to me first?"

He picked up the puppy and cradled it in his arms. "I didn't mean to. The department secretary brought him in today. Her neighbor's dog had puppies, and nobody wanted this one. They were going to take him to the pound, so Margaret said she'd try to find a home for him."

"We can't do this now. We're not allowed to have dogs here."

"I talked to your landlord, and he agreed."

"I don't believe you. He'd never agree to pets."

"Well, there was the little matter of a very large security deposit." He came closer, and Cassie laughed at the sight of two pairs of dark eyes looking at her beseechingly. "He's a really sweet puppy."

She ruffled the fur on the back of the puppy's neck. "I don't suppose you thought about getting dog food?"

***

Cassie went out to the car with a long list of pet supplies in hand. Crate, dog dishes, dog food, leash, collar. All the things a new puppy would need.

She didn't notice the vans with satellite dishes on top on the street at first, but she couldn't miss the bright lights that were turned on her. The media again. This celebrity business was getting old. Was getting a new puppy really newsworthy? At least they were staying off private property.

She dropped the list on the front seat of the car and strode toward the reporters. She didn't want to leave them for Calder to deal with on top of the puppy.

It seemed like a lot of reporters for a human interest story. It must be a slow news day. As soon as she reached the end of the driveway, several huge microphones were thrust in her face. The camera lights made it hard to see.

She held her hands up in front of her. "Have some pity, guys. He just left his mother this morning. Let him settle in a bit, and I promise we'll come out for pictures tomorrow."

"You know where his mother is?" A tall man demanded.

"Yes, of course."

"Where is she?"

She certainly didn't want them pestering the department secretary. "I don't know exactly, but Calder does."

"Did you know about this in advance?"

"No, it was a surprise to me."

A woman with a face familiar from the TV news stepped forward. "Did she offer any explanation for her actions?"

"Explanation? Why would we need an explanation?" Cassie was baffled, and all the bright lights in her eyes weren't helping. "Are we talking about the same thing?"

The correspondent looked taken aback. "I'm talking about Caro Westing."

How did Caro get into this? "I'm sorry. I thought you wanted to know about our new puppy. No, I have no idea where Caro is. We haven't talked to her in weeks."

"Then you don't know she's left her husband?"

"Caro?" Cassie asked disbelievingly. "Now I *know* we're not talking about the same thing."

The reporters jostled one another to get closer to her. One said, "Senator Westing was served with divorce papers this morning. Do you have any comment?"

The only thought in Cassie's stunned mind was that she was grateful Calder was safely inside. "This is news to me. We've been busy with our puppy."

"You haven't heard from either of your husband's parents?"

Her temper snapped. "You're obviously better informed than I am, so there's no point in talking. Excuse me." She hurried back to the house and raced up the stairs.

***

The puppy explored the apartment on his stubby legs. Calder trailed after him, watching for the tell-tale sniffing of the floor that would be his signal to take him outside. He was utterly fascinated with the ball of fluff that was Nobska. Trust Cassie to think up a Woods Hole name for the puppy, after the lighthouse overlooking the shoals of Vineyard Sound. He hoped it wouldn't be too confusing when they moved there.

Nobska cautiously poked his head into the kitchen, as if suspecting there might be monsters there. He looked up at Calder with pleading puppy eyes. "Okay, I'll come with you."

Cassie slammed the front door, breathing heavily. Nobska skittered back to Calder's feet. Calder gave into temptation and picked him up. "He's doing just great."

"That's nice." Cassie headed to her computer and booted it up.

"Is something wrong?" He ran his fingers over the soft fur. "Why are you back so soon?"

"Give me a second here." She tapped on the keyboard.

He recognized the *Washington Post* website from across the room. It wasn't where Cassie usually got her news. He felt sharp teeth on his fingers and looked down at Nobska, chewing happily on him. "No, pup, no biting."

Cassie sank down in her desk chair. "You'd better come look at this."

Her ominous tone worried him. "What is it?"

"It's your parents. Your father was served divorce papers citing . . ." She stopped for a moment and looked up at him. "mental cruelty and adultery. It must have been leaked to the press. They've got pictures of the papers being delivered. No reaction from your father. Nobody knows where your mother is."

He strode across the room. There must be some mistake. But there were the pictures. "When?" he asked. As if that mattered.

Cassie scanned the screen. "This afternoon. Let me check

CNN and see if they have anything more up to date." She typed for a moment and then read again. "Not much. Your father's staff isn't talking to the press. Tom made a statement that it's a personal family matter and he won't comment on it."

He sat on the couch in shock. Nobska immediately climbed away, ready to explore. "I don't believe it. Why would she leave him?"

Cassie came to sit beside him. "I can think of any number of reasons someone might leave your father. I wouldn't stay with him for a minute."

"You're not my mother. She likes things to be his way. She's the perfect political wife."

"She accused him of adultery. Has your father had affairs?"

"I have no idea. Probably, I suppose. It would be surprising if he hadn't, but I can't imagine it's anything new." His mind was refusing to work.

"Maybe it *is* something new. Maybe he was planning to leave her for another woman."

Calder snorted. "Not likely. That could cost him votes. Compared to votes, love is completely unimportant."

"What do *you* think, then?"

"I don't know," he said with uncharacteristic irritation. "Are you sure there isn't anything else about it there?"

Cassie returned to the computer. "No, that's it, apart from speculation on how this could affect next year's elections."

"Maybe it's some kind of ploy." He watched Nobska jump off the couch and put his nose to the rug.

"Damn!" Cassie snatched up the puppy. "I'll take him out."

"No, I can." He wanted to stay with Nobska.

"Sorry, you're not going out that door for a while. You're the one the reporters want." She didn't give him time to answer before she disappeared, the puppy under her arm.

***

"Success," Cassie announced when she brought Nobska back in. "It took him a while to figure it out, but he managed."

Calder hadn't moved from the couch. "Good."

She set the puppy on the floor. He made a beeline for Calder and settled at his feet, gnawing on the tip of his shoe. Cassie hurried to the kitchen and found an empty plastic bottle. "Here, you can chew on this until we get you some toys."

Nobska showed no interest. Cassie wished she knew more about puppies, but her experience was limited to occasional contact with friends' dogs. "Any clever ideas?" she asked Calder.

"None."

She noticed his eyes then. They held a sort of distance she had never seen in them before. Forgetting about the puppy, she sat and put her arms around him. "What happened while I was out there? Did someone call?"

He shook his head. "No." He didn't look at her.

So he was back in his monosyllabic mode. What a time to have to play twenty questions. "What happened?"

"I remembered something," he said in a conversational voice.

"What's that?"

"Something that happened a long time ago, when I was maybe five or six."

"Is this something you never remembered before?"

"No, I've always remembered it; I just never paid any *attention* to it."

"Do you want to tell me about it?"

He glanced at her for a second only. "It's bad." He sounded as if he were discussing the weather.

"That's okay. I can take it." She reached down to pry Nobska off Calder's shoe. There were tiny teeth marks in the leather.

"I was trying to think if I'd ever seen him with another woman." He closed his eyes. "Then I remembered this. One night my parents got into a fight. I don't know what it was about, but I remember my mother yelling at him. I was already in bed, but I could hear her. It was scary, because I didn't remember ever hearing her raise her voice to him before. Tommy was scared, too, and climbed in bed with me. He must have been two or three."

Maybe puppy love could help. She put Nobska on Calder's lap. "And?"

"Then it got quiet, but I was too nervous to sleep. So I went downstairs for a glass of water." His hands closed over the puppy, and he was silent for a minute. "My father was putting on his coat. He said that he was going somewhere he'd be welcome in a warm bed." He stopped. "I thought he meant he was going to my uncle's house."

"But he wasn't?"

"I don't think so. He didn't come back for a few days, which wasn't unusual when Congress was in session, but my mother cried almost all the time. I never thought about why until today, just that she was upset because of the fight. But it must have been because she knew where he was going. He was punishing her for fighting with him," he said, his voice hollow.

"That's sick. That's truly sick." She didn't know what else to say.

"But you know what's worse? I spent all these years thinking that she didn't care enough to stand up for me when he was attacking me, never once thinking about what would happen to her if she did." Nobska curled up in a ball on his lap, Calder's fingers between his teeth. Calder seemed disinclined to stop him.

"It's not your fault. You didn't know what was going on."

"I should have guessed." He laughed bitterly. "Mental cruelty. I suppose that's one way to put it."

"I'm *glad* she's left him," said Cassie fiercely, wishing she could somehow protect Calder from this. "I hope it ruins his reputation for good."

He looked at her, his eyes filled with pain. "Don't go anywhere, please."

She gazed at him in concern and hugged him. Despite everything his father had done, it must be a shock to Calder to lose what sense of family he had. "I'm not going anywhere. This is where I belong."

Calder remained subdued the rest of the day. There was no further news of his parents. Between stress and the new puppy, neither of them slept well that night. Cassie decided to stay home the following day, reluctant to leave him alone for long.

That afternoon the phone rang. Cassie answered it and then held her hand over the receiver for a moment. "It's Dave Crowley. Do you want to talk to him?"

Calder held out his hand for the phone. "Hi, Dave," he said, sounding dispirited.

"How are you doing there? I've been worrying about you."

"We're making do."

"I have a message for you, from your mother. She asked me to tell you that she's safe and just fine, but she's not going to be in touch with you directly for a while because she doesn't want you caught in the middle."

"Caught in the middle? I don't think I'm likely to have *that* problem. I wish she'd left him a long time ago. *I'd* have been happier, at least."

There was a pause. "She hasn't said as much, but I think she left now because he's weak. You've got away from him, and the bad press about his brother leaves everyone ready to believe the worst of him."

"I suppose."

"Is there anything you'd like me to tell her?"

Calder thought for a moment. "Tell her . . ." He wanted to ask him to give her his love, but found he couldn't quite say the words. "Tell her she's always welcome here," he said finally.

"I'll do that," Dave said. "Ann wants to talk to Cassie now."

Calder wished he could say something light before he turned the phone over to Cassie, but his mind seemed frozen, so he just said good-bye.

"Ann! How are you?" Cassie said cheerfully.

"Just fine, thanks. How about you?"

"We're a little stressed, as you might imagine, but otherwise everything's going well," Cassie said.

"I wanted to ask a favor of you, dear."

"Of course. Anything."

Ann coughed delicately. "I've been spending a good deal of time with Caro. She needs to talk about what happened during her marriage, and I've been hearing a lot of it."

"Ah," said Cassie uncertainly.

"I know Calder has some issues with her, but could you

help him understand she needs to be treated very gently right now? She's been through a great deal. Frankly, I try not to think about it too much. Some of her stories are pretty horrific. There was a lot that happened behind closed doors he doesn't know about."

"I imagine there must have been." It didn't take much imagination to recognize how badly Joe Westing could have hurt the woman who had to share his bed. "I'll do what I can, of course, but I don't think you need to worry. I think his sympathies are in the right place."

She could hear Ann's sigh of relief. "I'm glad to hear that, dear. I don't think he knows how much he means to her."

"I expect you're right in that. I'd say he has no idea whatsoever." It was news to Cassie as well.

"That's what I was afraid of. I'll do what I can from this end, and if you can help him understand, maybe we'll get somewhere."

"Thanks for telling me, Ann."

"No need for thanks, dear." She lowered her voice to a confidential level. "I like to consider myself a non-violent person, but I'm beginning to think I could make an exception for Joseph Westing. I couldn't trust Dave with some of what Caro's told me."

"I understand," Cassie said slowly. Worried about Calder, she ended the call quickly.

Calder was kneeling on the floor, scrubbing at a wet spot on the rug. "Sorry. He made a mess. I didn't catch him in time."

"That's okay. It's going to happen." Cassie found a roll of paper towels and tore some off. "So your mother's with Dave and Ann, I take it?"

"I'd guessed that already."

"You had?" Cassie wondered why he hadn't said anything about it before.

"Yes. This whole thing, the press knowing when the divorce papers were going to be delivered, her disappearance. It all smacked of Dave Crowley. I did some checking on the web. Mental cruelty isn't even grounds for a divorce in Virginia. It has to be physical cruelty. But it's great PR to make sure everyone knows mental cruelty existed." He pressed down on the paper towels to blot up the remaining liquid.

"Is it Dave you're angry at, or your mother?"

He sat back on his heels, his eyes remaining on the wet spot. "Neither. I wouldn't wish my father on anyone, even my mother."

Cassie winced. "Sounds like you're pretty upset with her, too."

"I feel sorry for her, but the truth is that she wasn't much better than my father. Maybe it was because she was unhappy. I don't know. But she was the one, even more than my father, who tried to make me into something I wasn't. She was the one constantly pushing me into social events, always harassing me about my manners. My behavior was the only thing about me that mattered to her."

Cassie thought about what Ann had said about Calder's issues with his mother. "You said before that he punished her for fighting with him. Is it possible he punished her if you didn't perform socially the way he expected?"

"I suppose. Though that's . . ." He trailed off into silence.

"Though that's what?"

"No, I was the one he punished for it," he said grimly. "She was trying to protect *me* by making sure I never made those mistakes again."

"Oh, love." She reached down to put her arms around him. "I'm sorry."

"There was one time . . . I'll tell you about it some day, but not now. But she was right to worry."

Chapter 23

THE LAB WAS FILLED with the freshness of salt air. Cassie leaned over Calder's shoulder to check the computer screen. So far, so good. Calder was better at entering data into the lab computer than he was at handling scientific glassware. Good thing he didn't have to earn his living as a lab assistant. But this way he could be with her, which was what he said he wanted. Now that the distraction of the move to the Cape was over, he seemed distinctly out of sorts. In truth, he hadn't been himself since the news of his parents' separation.

Rob stuck his head in the open lab door. "Anybody home?"

"Rob!" Cassie hadn't known he was in Woods Hole. "Come on in."

"Thanks. How are you?" Rob looked happy, more his old self than the last time she had seen him.

"Fine." Cassie was suddenly conscious of Calder's presence behind her. "You remember Chris, of course, and this is Calder. My husband."

Rob's smile slipped a fraction, but he still shook Calder's hand. "Cassie's told me about you."

Yes, the temperature in the room was clearly dropping. "Rob is one of Jim's post-docs." This wouldn't be a good time to start telling Calder about Rob's role in her life.

"Not anymore. I have a new job."

"Really? Where?" The kind of academic research position Rob wanted was hard to find.

Rob grinned. "MIT/WHOI. Tenure track."

"Rob! That's fabulous!" Cassie gave him a quick hug. "I'm going to have to call *you* the golden boy."

"Thanks." He was visibly proud of his accomplishment.

Chris looked at least as excited as Rob. "Congratulations. That's great news."

Cassie recognized her assistant's hungry look. "You'll be hearing from Chris next year. He has his heart set on MIT/WHOI for his PhD."

"Give me a call when you're ready to apply. I'll be happy to do what I can."

"Thanks. I will." Chris looked barely able to contain himself.

Cassie suddenly remembered Calder's presence. He had that look of being hidden behind his eyes again. "MIT/WHOI is a joint graduate school in oceanography. Very prestigious. It's the brass ring."

"Congratulations, then." Calder definitely had his pretty manners on. Not a good sign.

Rob rubbed his hands together. "So, Chris, how's that research of yours coming?"

Chris practically glowed. "Pretty good. I tried your method of collecting data this year and got a great spread. Want to see it?"

"Love to, but I have to be at WHOI in fifteen minutes. Want to walk with me and tell me about it? If Cassie can spare you, that is."

Cassie suspected the WHOI appointment was an excuse to get away, but she could understand that. "Sure, go ahead."

Chris began talking and gesturing to Rob before they were even out in the hallway. Cassie heard their voices fade away. That was the future. Chris would be in the Boston University program with her for a year, and after that he'd be going for his PhD, likely with Rob at MIT/WHOI. It wouldn't be surprising if he chose Rob as his advisor, given their interests. Rob would be there to see Chris do his best work, to mold him into a professional scientist as Jim had molded both of them. Cassie would be left behind with Chris's undergraduate years. Chris's first publication would have Rob's name on it, not hers. She'd given that up when she chose to work with undergrads instead of shooting for a research position like Rob had. She had been the star of the lab in grad school, and now he was surpassing her. What had Jim said about it being hard to give up the prestige of the tenure track?

But it was what she had wanted. Chris would succeed in grad school because Cassie had done her job well, teaching him to think like a researcher and passing along her love of the field. That was where the real scientists were made, at the beginning, not when they wrote their dissertations. But it also meant saying good-bye to them and sending them off into the world.

She shook off the moment of melancholy, realizing that Calder had been silent since Rob and Chris left. He appeared to be focused on the computer screen, but Cassie could feel the tension exuding from him. She stood behind him and massaged his shoulders gently. "What's the matter, love?"

"Nothing." He turned over the data sheet and started to enter the new data.

"If you don't want to tell me, that's okay, but don't pretend nothing is wrong."

He leaned his head back against her midriff, his eyes closed. "Who is he?"

"Rob? An old boyfriend. We were in grad school together."

"Chris seems to know him pretty well."

"Rob was around a lot last summer. We tried dating again for a while, but it didn't work out. Obviously." She watched his face carefully.

"You were seeing somebody last summer, and you never mentioned it to me." He didn't look at her.

"I didn't feel like talking about it. I treated Rob pretty badly."

Calder typed in a string of data and then let his hands rest on the keyboard. "What else don't I know about?"

"Plenty of things, I imagine. Do you really think I'm keeping things from you deliberately?"

"I don't know what to believe anymore. I thought my mother didn't give a damn about me, as long as I didn't embarrass her. I thought she was happy with my father. I knew my father would always try to control everything I did, but I didn't think he . . ."

"You didn't think he would what?"

He gave a tired sigh. "I didn't think he'd deliberately hurt her." He lapsed into silence again. "He isn't always awful, you know. He was really great sometimes when I was a kid. He'd take me places, show me things—maybe because it was good for people to see he was a family man, but I loved it. I even liked it when he'd take me to work with him. He'd make a big fuss when I brought home a good report card. It didn't get bad until I was old enough to think for myself."

At least he was finally talking. Cassie was relieved about that. "There aren't any easy answers, are there? For all the terrible things your father did, he was still better than his own father."

Calder shook his head. "You're too generous. My grandfather had his problems, but he was a saint compared my father."

"Your grandfather told *his* eldest son he'd rather have him dead than be an embarrassment. That's ruthless. I can't imagine what it would be like to grow up knowing that if you mess up, you're going to be locked away forever like your big brother. *Your* father just expected you to keep quiet."

He was silent for a minute. "I suppose so. I never thought about how that affected him, only how he could have condoned it. It still doesn't excuse what he did to my mother."

"No, of course not. I just like to put things in context. I always have to know the entire ecosystem, not just an isolated bit." She dug her fingers into the tight muscles of his shoulders, kneading until the knots began to loosen.

He dropped his chin to his chest. "I'm sorry. It seems like all I give you is trouble."

"Calder." Her hands stopped. "Don't you know what my life was like before you came along? I enjoyed my friends, and I'd do fun things from time to time, but I lived for my work and I didn't let anyone close enough to see my feelings. I was running away from myself, and you made me stop and look at what I was doing and ask myself if that was all I wanted in life. You gave me a *reason* to want to have more. Don't you know that?"

"No. It seemed like you already had everything you wanted."

"Except someone to share it with. I needed you to give me the courage to do that." No, she didn't regret giving up the glory of the tenure track. What she had now was more important.

***

Calder was starting to understand the peace Cassie found in the salt marsh. Often, during the daytime when Cassie was at the lab, he took long walks with Nobska along the beach and into the marsh. Cassie made an effort to come home in time for dinner instead of working late. Erin and Scott were on the Cape most weekends and often spent time with them, but business concerns kept Scott from staying in Woods Hole full-time as he had in the past.

Calder was happy to simply spend time with Cassie after all the stresses of the last semester. Nobska, grown large and gangly, sat at their feet whenever he could. By the end of the first month, Calder could name most of the flora and fauna of the salt marsh and the intertidal zone.

But despite the distraction of dealing with renovations and housebreaking the dog, the silence from his mother was a constant irritant. It made no sense, since he had gone for months without taking to her in the past. This was different. He didn't even know how to contact her. The brief emails his father sent made no mention of her or the divorce.

But enough was enough. Calder sought out Cassie in the spare bedroom serving as her study. She was perched on a chair, organizing the books on the top shelf. She flashed him a smile.

The bronze sculpture of a fiddler crab he had given her for Christmas stood in a place of honor on her desk. He switched on the desk lamp standing over it, studying the sheen of the bronze. "I'm wondering if I should try to get in touch with my mother."

She paused and stepped down to the floor. "If you want to. Do you suppose Dave knows how to reach her?"

"I thought I'd ask him to pass along a message. That way she can be in control."

Dave proved very willing to give her the message, although he didn't offer Caro's telephone number. He seemed pleased Calder wanted to talk to her. But there was no point in sitting around waiting for something to happen. It might be days, or even weeks, before his mother called. He was surprised when only an hour later the phone rang and he heard his mother's voice greeting him on the other end.

"How are you?" He realized with discomfort he wasn't sure what to call her. She hadn't been Mom since he was a teenager, but Mother seemed too distancing. "Thanks for calling."

"I'm doing well, thank you," she said in her evenly modulated tones. "And you?"

"I'm fine." Acutely uncomfortable, he tapped Cassie on the arm, giving her an eloquent look and pointing to the extension. "Hang on, I think Cassie's getting on as well. She wants to say hello to you."

"Oh, good. I'm hoping to hear how you're settling into your new home."

He had forgotten; even if he had no idea what to say, his mother never missed a beat in any conversation. "Umm, it's going well. We like it a lot here."

"I absolutely love it," Cassie cut in. "It's in the perfect spot, right by the salt marsh. I still can't believe Calder found this house. We get the most beautiful sunsets over the water. I hope you'll come down and see it soon."

"That's very kind of you, dear," his mother said non-committally. "It sounds lovely."

Cassie filled what could have become an uncomfortable silence by telling her about the renovations they had done on the house in the spring. Calder listened silently, wondering how long they were going to pretend nothing had changed.

Before the conversation ended, she tentatively told them her new telephone number and address. "But I'd rather Joe didn't know where I am."

As if Calder would ever tell his father anything he didn't have to. "I won't tell him. I hope you'll stay in touch. And think about what Cassie said. We'd love to have you visit when you feel up to traveling." He hoped he wasn't saying the wrong thing. His mother thanked him, though, sounding genuinely grateful for the invitation this time, and said she would talk to them again soon.

***

Calder exchanged a few cautious emails with Tom, with convoluted references to "the situation in Virginia." Tom was in close contact with their father. Calder supposed it would be difficult not to be when they might run into each other at the Capitol any time. Neither mentioned their mother, and when she eventually agreed a few weeks later to a brief visit to the Cape, Calder elected not to put Tom in a difficult position by telling him about it. He was anxious enough about it without any extra complications.

What if they had nothing to say to each other when they met? They hadn't had more than the most superficial of conversations for years. He wondered if she would disapprove of his lifestyle. If it weren't for its location, their house would be no different from many other nice houses on the Cape; certainly there was nothing in it to suggest the wealth he was born to. Apart from Scott and Erin, they socialized only with Cassie's friends from the lab. It was a far cry from the society his mother moved in.

He couldn't be certain, either, that she bore him no anger for having been so distant and for never having helped her. Certainly he blamed himself for it and saw no reason why she wouldn't, despite Cassie's reassurances.

The day of her arrival approached more quickly than he might have wished. They drove to Hyannis's small airport to meet her flight. Her plane was slightly delayed, and they waited outside security until a group of passengers came through. Calder ran his eyes over them but didn't see her, and was surprised when Cassie stood up and waved to someone. "Who is it?" he asked.

She shot him an odd look. "Your mother, of course."

He looked again and did a double take. Cassie was right. It *was* his mother coming toward them, but he wouldn't have recognized her if they'd passed on the street. Instead of the sleek chignon she always wore, her hair was cut into short, feathery layers close to her head. Even more surprisingly, she was dressed in an Oxford shirt and jeans—his mother wearing *jeans!* He couldn't recall her wearing anything but dresses. She still looked stylish, but now it was as if she had stepped out of an L.L. Bean catalog. No wonder the news media hadn't found her. They didn't know what to look for.

He greeted her more stiffly than he wanted to. He was grateful for Cassie's presence; she took much of the conversational burden off him, giving a running commentary on the Cape as they drove back to the house. His mother was as poised as ever. If it weren't for her changed appearance, he wouldn't have known anything was different.

When they reached the house, Nobska took an immediate shine to Caro. Although she didn't say anything, it was clear she was uncomfortable with fifty pounds of rambunctious dog enthusiastically greeting her.

"Just tell him to sit," Calder advised her.

"Sit, Nobska," she said tentatively. The dog wagged his tail.

Calder grabbed Nobska's collar before he could jump up on his new friend. "You have to sound like you mean it," he said. "Try it again."

"So speaks the man who nearly failed puppy obedience classes!" Cassie said with a laugh. "But he's right. Nobska likes people to be in charge, so you have to sound like you are."

His mother took a deep breath. "Nobska, sit!" she said firmly. Her look of well-bred surprise when he actually sat wasn't lost on Calder.

"Now you have to tell him he's a good dog," Cassie said.

"Good dog," her mother-in-law repeated obediently. With a look of playing dice with the devil, she reached out to pet him.

"He's really a very nice dog," said Calder. "But if he bothers you, we can put him in his crate."

"I bet Caro's going to be better at keeping Nobska in line than you are," Cassie said with an affectionate smile. "Calder spoils him whenever my back is turned."

***

"So this is the famous salt marsh," Caro said when Cassie took her out on the deck. "It's just as I pictured it from Calder's book."

"Did you read his book?" Cassie wondered with embarrassment how much his mother had understood about the story.

"Of course. I read all his books." Her mother-in-law looked out over the marsh. "I didn't know there was a real Elizabeth. But I recognized Will Darcy right away, not to mention his aunt and uncle."

Cassie winced, recalling the portrayal of his aunt as a cold, ambitious woman. "I hope you know none of the characters were true to life. It had to make a good story."

"There's a lot about my son I don't know, but I know when he's telling the truth. It's all right. It was something I needed to know."

No wonder his mother hadn't expected Calder's support or understanding! "For what it's worth, I don't think he had any idea what *you* were going through until quite recently," Cassie said. "It hit him hard."

His mother seemed to withdraw into herself. "I didn't mean to upset him."

"I wouldn't worry." Cassie was struck by how little it took to frighten the confident-looking woman before her. "I think I'd categorize it as something *he* needed to know. It's helped him understand a lot of things."

"I never wanted him to know about it. He had enough problems of his own."

"He has a lot of strengths, too, and I don't think they appeared by magic. But it's hard for people to think of their parents as real people with feelings and failings. I've just started to value what my parents gave me and to stop blaming them for not being what I wanted them to be."

"Yes, but you invited your parents to your wedding. Calder wasn't even going to tell me he was getting married."

This was dangerous ground. "But it wasn't you he was trying to exclude; it was his father. Joe was doing everything he could to split us up. Calder couldn't very well invite you and not his father." She knew, even as she said it, that it wasn't completely true. Though Calder hadn't objected to his mother coming to their wedding, he had felt no desire for her presence either.

When there was no reply, Cassie looked over at the older woman and was dismayed to see tears running down her cheeks. That was the only outward sign of her distress; Cassie had never seen anyone be so quiet and still while crying. It was frightening to see, all the more so if she thought about why her mother-in-law would have learned such control. Awkwardly, she reached over and stroked her arm. Ann Crowley had been right about Caro's fragility.

"I'm sorry," the older woman said. "I cry rather easily these days. For a long time I never did."

"You know, Calder told me you used to protect him as much as you could, sometimes at your own expense. I imagine you gave him all you could manage, and I'm going to be totally unfair and ask you to give him one more thing."

"What's that?" Caro asked steadily.

"Time. He thought he understood what was going on between you and his father, and now that's all been turned on its head. He needs time to take it in, and he has to get to know you all over again."

There was silence for a moment, leaving Cassie wondering if she had overstepped her bounds. Finally, though, her mother-in-law said in a subdued voice, "Thank you. That's good advice."

Cassie strove to lighten the moment. "You know, I was shocked when Calder's friend Scott told me that Calder was Stephen West. I'd read his books and admired them, and now Scott was telling me that the most inarticulate man I knew had written these eloquent, sensitive books. I'd have been more likely to believe the sun would rise in the west."

His mother's eyes brightened a little. "I wasn't surprised a bit," she said quietly.

***

"I like your new look," said Calder as they finished dinner, "but it takes some getting used to."

His mother laughed lightly. "If you think *this* is hard to get used to, you should see what I looked like just after I left! I was *so* tired of having to dress to Joe's orders that the first place I stopped was a Goodwill store right by the train station. I bought a couple of rather appalling outfits, and changed into one of them and left my old clothes behind. I cut my hair with a pair of scissors in the restroom at the station. I looked *horrible*, and I loved every minute of it. Your father would have died on the spot if he had seen me."

Cassie couldn't help laughing, both at her mother-in-law's evident delight in her misbehavior and Calder's failed attempt to hide his shock. "I can just imagine it," she said. "Did you have that all planned out, or was it an impulse?"

"Oh, I had every detail worked out. I'd been planning it since the story about Stephen came out."

"Joe's brother?" Cassie could feel the tension emanating from Calder. "It sounds like that upset him a lot."

"Anything about Stephen upsets him. It always has," said Caro. "When we were first married, he was miserable for days every time he came back from seeing Stephen, and he'd talk about how things would be different when his father died. But by that time he was already running for the Senate, and Matthew was lieutenant governor and beginning to make a national name within the party. They were both too vulnerable to scandal. So nothing ever changed for Stephen, except that Joe stopped being upset after seeing him and started to be angry instead."

"I hadn't realized he cared about Stephen," Cassie said.

"Oh, never doubt it, Joe loved Stephen. He idolized him as a boy, and it was a huge shock for him when his hero came home from Korea barely able to talk. Then, when his father refused to acknowledge Stephen, Joe had to become one of his jailers, and he hated himself for it. Stephen was his weak spot. Joe never cried when his parents died, but he cried when he heard Stephen was dead."

"And came home angry at me," said Calder bitterly.

"Yes," his mother said. "But that's Joseph all over. He can't tolerate feeling pain. He has to take it out on someone else." She looked as if she wanted to say more, but stopped.

Cassie nudged Nobska, asleep under the table, with her foot until he got up and stretched. "Calder, I think Nobska's getting restless. Would you take him out so he can run for a bit?"

He gave her a grateful look. "Sure. Come on, pup."

"I'm sorry," Caro said once the door had closed behind him. "I suppose I shouldn't have said that. I really don't want to drive any more of a wedge between Calder and Joe than there already is."

"I don't think you need to worry about that," Cassie said, feeling awkward. "It's just his uncle Stephen is a sore point. Calder identifies with him. And it's hard for him to hear what you went through."

"It wasn't bad before the boys were born, just the occasional cutting comment. He didn't like having to share my attention with them. That's when he started trying to control everything I said and did." She paused, and for the first time bitterness entered her voice. "You have no idea, my dear, how much easier it is to tolerate abuse yourself than to watch your children being abused and be helpless to stop it. Joe knew it, and he used it against me."

Cassie was at a loss for what to say. She had never heard of Calder before they met, but *everyone* knew who Caro Westing was. She was American royalty, along with Jackie Onassis, Princess Grace, and Caroline Kennedy. And here she was at Cassie's dining room table, talking about her troubled marriage. "I'm sorry."

"Thank you, but I'm not looking for sympathy. Overall, it's been much better in the last few years, at least until just recently. I'm trying—rather clumsily, I'm afraid—to tell you something about Calder. I imagine he's told you what Joe could be like, but he never saw the whole picture. Sometimes Joe would attack him for something he did, but more often it was for no reason at all, because when Joe was angry at me, he'd take it out on

Calder. He knew that hurt me worse than anything he could say to me. But poor Calder—what he learned was that nothing he did would ever be good enough. No matter how hard he tried to please his father, he never could for long, and he always blamed himself. And Joe—he never understood it was making Calder hate him, because what he was doing to Calder seemed so mild to him compared to the kind of discipline he had as a child."

Cassie had been curious about this piece for some time. "Calder seems to have liked his grandfather. I take it he was harder as a father than a grandfather."

"Lord, yes. Joe has scars. His father didn't believe in sparing the rod. When Calder was born, Joe said he was never going to raise a hand to a child of his, and he never did, except one time when he lost control. *That* was a nightmare. But he never realized how much damage he could do with words."

"What I don't understand," said Cassie with great care, "is why you're trying to defend him."

"Defend Joseph? Hardly. I'll *never* forgive him for what he did to my children. But I don't want Calder to believe his own father hated him when it isn't true."

Cassie studied her. She remembered what Ann Crowley said, that Calder didn't realize what he meant to his mother. "So you're still trying to protect Calder."

"If you will. He didn't deserve what happened to him. He was a very sweet child, you know."

Cassie smiled. "I can imagine. He's still very sweet, once you get to know him."

Chapter 24

CALDER AND CASSIE SPENT the next morning showing Caro the local sights, touring her past Nobska Light, located on the point of land that had given their dog his name, and visiting some of the historic captains' houses of Falmouth. After lunch, when the tide turned, they strolled along the beach by their house and showed her the pleasures of swimming in the bay.

By late afternoon, they retreated indoors, tired by the sun. Calder was showing some signs of strain, and Cassie wanted to make sure he had some quiet time. She suspected his mother might benefit from it as well.

When the phone rang, Cassie reached for it. She recognized Joe Westing's voice, as apparently she was expected to, since he didn't bother to identify himself. After perfunctorily asking her how she was, he said, "I understand Carolyn is there."

Cassie considered denying it, but decided it would be pointless. "Very efficient spy system you have."

"I want to talk to her." His tone was designed to brook no argument.

"I'm sure you do. Let me check with her." She clicked mute and looked over at Caro. "It's Joe. He's asking for you."

Caro blanched. Cassie asked, "Do you want to talk to him? You don't have to if you don't want to."

Her mother-in-law silently shook her head. Nobska, apparently sensing something was wrong, wandered over and sat down beside Caro, pressing his head into her lap.

"Sorry, she isn't feeling chatty," Cassie said brightly into the telephone. "Anything else I can do for you?"

"You can put Calder on the phone."

She didn't need to ask Calder if he wanted to speak to his father. "I don't think he's feeling talkative either. We've had a long day. I'll be happy to take a message."

There was a pause. "Tell him he can't get away with this forever." His voice was angry.

Her eyes narrowed. "I'll pass that along. I'm sure it's very nice of you to call. It's dull for me, sitting around with two such untalkative people, and I'd hate to get so desperate for conversation that I'd have to go chat with some of the reporters hanging around town."

She heard the click of the receiver being hung up on the other end. Switching off the phone, she said to the room at large, "It is beyond me how a purportedly intelligent man can have failed to work out by now that I don't like being told what to do."

"What did he say?" Calder asked.

"Nothing much, just chucking his weight around."

"Excuse me," his mother said softly, and disappeared upstairs to her room, leaving a worried-looking dog behind.

***

Chris answered the lab phone with his usual "Yo." A pause. "Yeah, she's here. Can I tell her who's calling?"

Cassie looked up from her data analysis with annoyance. Once her thought process was interrupted, she had to go back to the beginning and think it through again. She should have told Chris to say she was out.

Chris's lanky body stiffened from his usual slouch. "Just a minute, please." He held out the phone to Cassie and whispered, "It's your *father-in-law.*"

Great. Just what she needed. More of Joe Westing's idea of fun and games. She slammed shut the reference book and took the phone. "Yes, Joe?" She tried to sound as businesslike as possible.

"Cassie. How are you?" It was his cordial voice. That meant trouble.

Cassie stared up at the ceiling. "Busy. And you?"

"Very well, thank you. Since it's so dull for you with all the untalkative people around, I thought you might like a little conversation."

What was he up to? She drummed her fingers on the desk. Maybe he wanted to use her as a conduit for information to Calder. That would explain why he called her at work. "How very thoughtful of you."

"It's always a pleasure to chat with you. What have you been doing since we talked last?"

If he was hoping to pump her for information on Caro, he could think again. "I've been performing a multivariate analysis of covariance for the levels of littoral nitrogen to determine the parameters for my next protocol." That would teach him to ask nosy questions.

"How intriguing. I've been learning about prisons."

Tension slid down Cassie's spine. "Really?"

"They need to keep discipline there, you know. If they suspect an inmate is up to no good, they can make his life difficult. Very difficult."

"So I've heard." She was aware of Chris watching her.

"But that's just for problem inmates. Of course, problems are in the eyes of the beholder."

The silky threat raised goosebumps on her skin. "What do you want from me, Joe?"

"You started this, and you're going to stop it. You're going to convince my wife she's better off coming home, and you're going to keep Calder in line."

"I don't know where you get the idea I have that kind of influence on either of them. Certainly not on Caro." Her chest felt tight.

"Perhaps you'd better think about how to get that kind of influence, unless you don't mind your little brother sitting in solitary confinement for the next twelve years. That's always assuming he gets paroled, which I wouldn't bet on."

Cassie tasted bile in the back of her throat. "You bastard."

"Don't call me names, Cassie. I don't like it."

No doubt Calder or Caro could come back with a smooth response, but it was beyond her abilities. "*Good-bye*, Joe." She slammed down the receiver.

She leaned her elbows on her desk and rested her face on her hands, fear racing through her. She couldn't let him hurt Ryan. Solitary confinement would kill him. Painfully, minute by minute, day by day, year by endless year.

Maybe she could convince Calder to play along. If he knew what was at stake, he'd be willing to go through the motions. He'd done it in the past. But that wouldn't work with Caro. She'd never go back, and Ryan would pay.

"Dr. Boulton, are you all right?" Chris sounded hesitant.

"No, I'm not all right!" she snapped. "Don't you have some work you should be doing?"

"Sorry." Chris slunk to the back of the lab and turned on the faucet to wash the glassware.

What was wrong with her? She'd never spoken to a student like that in her entire career. One conversation with Joe, and she was acting just like him. Poor Chris looked terrified.

"Chris, I'm sorry. I was upset by the phone call." How could she tell him Joe was arranging to torture her brother? How would she tell Calder? He'd blame himself.

"That's okay, Dr. Boulton." Chris sounded subdued. Cassie hoped he would never know what it meant to be as frightened as she was.

Chapter 25

CASSIE SPENT THE DAY trying to think up, and then dismissing, ways to keep Ryan safe. Playing along with Joe wouldn't last. Contacting someone from Ryan's old gang—they all stood up for each other, and they had power in the prisons—was too risky. Calling a reporter wouldn't help because there wasn't anything she could do to prove Ryan wasn't making trouble, and drawing attention to him would make his life more difficult. There had to be an answer, but she didn't want to go home until she'd found it. It was too scary to think there was nothing she could do.

She stayed at the lab into the evening, even after Chris went home. The silence and darkness suited her.

A shadow fell across the desk. She looked up to see Rob's figure silhouetted in the doorway.

"You're here late," he said.

"Look who's talking. And I actually work here. Don't you belong down the street at WHOI?"

He tipped his head toward the window. "I was walking to my car, and I saw your light was still on. I know you go home early these days, so I came up to check if everything was okay here."

So he was still looking after her. "Thanks, but I'm just working late. It happens, even now."

"Did you have a fight with him?"

"Who do you mean?"

A ghost of a smile flickered across his face. "Your husband, of course."

"Everything's fine with Calder, not that it's any of your business. I have a lot to do before tomorrow." And she didn't want to go home until Calder and Caro were asleep. She'd called to say she wouldn't be home till the middle of the night. She couldn't face them yet. She wouldn't be able to pretend nothing was wrong.

Rob raked his eyes around the lab. "No experiment set up, and you're reading a journal. Doesn't look too critical to me." He took a step closer. "And Chris stopped by to see me and said you were really upset."

"The little traitor. I should have known."

"He's worried about you. He cares about you."

"And he'd love to see me ditch Calder for you. Sorry, no deal."

Rob pulled up a lab stool. "Well, I can't blame the boy for having good taste. So, what's wrong that you won't go home?"

"Look, I won't deny that I'm worried about something, but I can't talk about it, to you or to Calder, and you'll only make things worse if you try to help. So please, leave it alone."

He shook his head. "Sending me away won't help because it'll just be Jim down here next trying to pry it out of you."

"With friends like you, who needs enemies?" She'd meant it

as a joke, but it only reminded her that she did have a real enemy. A dangerous one.

"Yeah, well, if you ever start letting your friends know when something's wrong, we'll stop hassling you all the time."

He was going to make her cry if he kept this up, and she didn't want to cry. Not without Calder there to hold her. Calder. Suddenly she realized that was what she needed. Even if he couldn't do anything to help, she needed to be with him. She'd always faced her problems by herself, but she couldn't do it anymore.

She grabbed her keys from the desk. "I've got to go." She stopped with her hand on the door and looked back at him. "Thanks for being concerned," she said with a catch in her voice.

He smiled wryly, as if finally accepting his dismissal. "Any time."

***

She had to tell herself to slow down on the drive home. The road was empty, but it had too many twists and turns to go over the speed limit in the dark. But she bumped over the potholes of the dirt road to their house with unusual disregard for the car's struts.

She tried to be quiet going into the house. Calder would probably be asleep already. She wouldn't wake him. It would be enough to sit by the bed and watch him sleep. She didn't know what to tell him, anyway.

Clattering sounds in the kitchen drew her attention. She peeked over the breakfast bar. A rumpled Calder, wearing his bathrobe, was slicing bread, with Nobska at his feet, hoping for any crumb that might fall. A half-empty glass stood on the counter.

Cassie felt oddly shy, as if she had been away for months and not just for the evening, and tears pricked at the corners of her eyes. Sometimes she still couldn't believe that, of all the women in the world, he had chosen her. She spoke his name quietly.

He stiffened and then turned toward her, a slow smile warming his face. "You're back. I didn't expect you until later."

The sound of his voice was all it took. She ran to him, her force making him take a step back as his arms closed tightly around her. She buried her face in his shoulder and let the tears she'd been fighting flow.

He tightened his grip on her. "It's all right, love. Everything's all right."

She shook her head without looking up. "Where's your mother?"

"She's upstairs in bed. What's wrong?" His hand stroked her back soothingly.

She sniffed. "I can't tell you." Her words were muffled by his robe. For a minute she thought he would accept it as he took her by the hand and led her to the couch. She took a tissue and mopped her eyes.

He stroked her hand, and she could feel his concerned gaze on her, even though she wouldn't look up. "Now tell me what happened."

"Just hold me. That's all I need."

He gathered her to him, gently smoothing her hair back. "I'll always do that. But you still have to tell me what's upsetting you. Did my father do something?"

"How did you know?"

His jaw tightened. "Anytime somebody's this upset, it's usually because he's done something. What's his dirty trick this time?"

She didn't want to tell him any more than she had to. "He

wants me to get your mother to go back to him. I don't know why he thinks I can."

Calder frowned. "I don't know either, but that isn't enough to put you in a tailspin. No more stalling. Out with it."

There wasn't any way around it. "He says he'll make Ryan's life miserable if I don't. Solitary confinement. No parole." The picture of Ryan alone in an empty cell came back to her. She put her head in her hands and started to cry again.

"Damn him. But just because he says it doesn't mean it's going to happen."

"How can I stop him? There's nothing I can do."

"Maybe so, but I have a few ideas stored away." His fingers massaged the back of her neck.

Caro's elegant voice floated across the room. "There are a few things I can do, as well."

Cassie stopped in mid-sob and turned to see her mother-in-law standing at the bottom of the stairs. Calder, sounding unsurprised, asked, "How much of that did you hear?"

"Enough. If you'll excuse me, I need to make a call." She crossed the room and picked up the telephone, dialing a number from memory. For a moment she looked uncertain, but then she squared her shoulders and put the receiver to her ear. "Joseph?" she said in a firm voice. "This is Carolyn." She paused. "Yes, I know what time it is."

"I'm very well, and you?" Caro sounded completely poised, her voice evenly modulated.

She was silent for a moment. "I'm glad to hear it. Now, I want you to stop this nonsense with Cassie's brother. It's beneath you."

Another pause. "I don't believe you for a second. You're

nothing but a big baby, Joseph, having a tantrum because you can't have what you want. Well, that's exactly why I left you, and I'll tell you one thing: the only way I'll *ever* think about coming back is if you show me you've changed."

Cassie couldn't believe it was Caro talking this way, tapping her foot as she listened to his response.

"I'll put it another way, then. It's either a no-holds-barred interview on television, and I've had plenty of invitations for those, or a cordial joint appearance with you at a campaign event next fall. Your choice, Joseph. I am *not* going to stand by while you act in this ridiculous manner."

"Well, you think it over, and I'm sure you know how to reach me, whether I like it or not. If I hear that Cassie's brother has so much as a bad day, I'll know what to do.

"Yes, I'm sure people do have bad days in prison. I guess you should make certain he doesn't. Good-bye, Joseph." She hung up and set the phone down, suddenly looking weary. But she looked straight at Calder as she said, "I've bought you some time there. But it won't last forever."

Calder nodded, leaving Cassie with the feeling they were somehow communicating silently.

Cassie blotted her eyes. "Thank you," she said shakily.

"Don't mention it, dear. He knows the power of hurting someone you care for, but I don't intend to watch him do it any longer." Although she was speaking to Cassie, Caro's eyes rested on her son. "But it's very late. I'll see you in the morning." She headed slowly up the stairs.

Cassie waited until the footsteps had stopped and she heard the bedroom door closing. "That was a surprise."

"You're telling me. I can't believe she called him a big baby." Calder sounded admiring.

"Well, he is a big baby, just one with way too much clout." The sick feeling returned to her stomach.

"Ryan will be okay. I'll make sure of it."

Cassie's throat was tight. "Maybe."

Calder frowned. "Something happens to you whenever Ryan's name comes up. You get tense and panicky. Why?"

"Because I abandoned him when he needed me, and I didn't help him when he asked." Her heart was pounding in her ears. "I was selfish, and Ryan's paying the price."

"You weren't selfish. You were young."

Cassie squeezed her eyes shut. "You don't understand. I was twenty-four and in love for the first time. What happened in high school turned me off men for a long time. I was so happy with Rob, and I knew he wouldn't like having a teenager around. Plus he'd find out all the things I'd hidden from him, and he wouldn't want me anymore. I was terrified of losing him."

"So you chose Rob over Ryan."

"Yes." She sank her teeth into her lower lip until she tasted blood.

Calder was silent. "You don't have to choose between Ryan and me."

"Not now, maybe, but sooner or later I will. Your father knows my weak spot now. I can't spend my life waiting for the axe to fall."

"Cassie, love." His voice was as quiet and tender as his hands. "Relax. Take a deep breath. We can beat this."

"How can you be so sure?" Tears of despair leaked out despite her best efforts to contain them.

"You'll see. Trust me. I've dealt with him all my life, and I've never given in on something truly important to me. Not going into politics. Writing my books and publishing them. Marrying you. I'm not going to let him chase you away."

She hadn't realized how badly she needed the reassurance that Joe could be beaten. "I can't even trust myself."

"When Ryan wrote to you, when you were twenty-four, what did he say?"

She remembered it clearly, because she had been surprised and pleased to get a letter from him, at least until she read it. "That he wanted to get out of Chicago."

"If he'd told you he was on the verge of joining a gang, using drugs, getting beaten up, and dropping out, would it have changed your mind?"

Cassie sniffled. Calder's shirt was getting damp. "Of course it would."

"You would have risked losing Rob?"

"Yes, but I didn't think. I should have realized there was trouble. I'd convinced myself by then it was just a poor neighborhood with a lousy school because I didn't want to remember what it was really like. If I'd thought, I would have known." The confession broke down her last reserves, and she held onto him as if he were her only surety.

"You can't take responsibility for the entire universe, love. Does Ryan blame you?"

"I don't know. I didn't ask. But it doesn't matter." Suddenly she remembered his words. *At least one of us got out.* He didn't want her to feel trapped. "Do you really think you can stop your father?"

"I have some pretty good cards up my sleeve. I can convince him it isn't worth the price."

"How?" She wanted to believe him.

"Give me a few days to see what I can do. But right now it's time to get some sleep."

She nestled in against him. It went against the grain to turn her problems over to him, but it was such a relief to share the burden. "I'm surprised you were still up."

Calder flushed. "I was asleep, but I woke up."

That wasn't like him. Calder was a sound sleeper. "Something the matter?"

"I got a phone call."

"Who'd call at this hour?" She could tell he was avoiding the question.

"If you must know, it was Rob."

"Rob called you?" That was the last thing she expected of him. "Was he worried I wouldn't make it home safely?"

Calder rubbed his hand over his mouth. "Not exactly. He wanted to talk to me."

"Oh, God. What did he say?"

"That you were really upset about something, and weren't planning to tell me what it was, and if I wanted to know why I was going to have to push hard, because you had all your walls up."

Cassie's jaw dropped. "And you did it, too. You kept pushing until I gave in, didn't you? Because Rob said so?"

He shrugged. "Well, I never had much luck before when you were determined to keep me out. I thought I might as well try his method. And Jim told me I should listen to him."

Cassie put her hands on her hips. "Jim was in on this, too?"

"He's the one who gave Rob my number."

She laughed sardonically. "Well, if I have to be awake half the night, I'm glad to know I'm not alone. You, Rob, Jim, your mother, your father, not to mention all the king's horses and all the king's men."

"But did we manage to put Humpty Dumpty back together again?"

She shook her head. "Humpty's not going to be in great shape until I'm sure Ryan's safe. At least from your father." She paused. "I'm scared. What if you can't stop him?"

"He taught me everything he knew. I can beat him at his own game. There *are* some ways I'm like him. I'm not going to let him hurt you."

"You're *nothing* like your father."

Calder held her close, letting himself relax in her love. But if she thought he wasn't like his father, she might be in for a surprise.

Chapter 26

ON THE LAST DAY of Caro's visit, she seemed content just staying at the house. She didn't mention her phone call to her husband the previous night. Instead, to the surprise of all, she spent the morning on dog training, first observing Cassie putting Nobska through his sit and stay drills, and then hesitantly volunteering to take over for her.

She had infinite patience for it, as did Nobska, who couldn't imagine anything finer than performing for treats and praise. Cassie watched from a distance, and when a surprised-looking Calder came by, she said to him, "Frankly, I think it's doing her a world of good to order someone around and have him listen. He loves it, too." She didn't add her thoughts on why Caro, normally so restrained, was lavishing the dog with uncharacteristic affection.

Later, Caro volunteered to take the dog for a walk and surprised Calder by saying she would rather go alone. "It'll be a nice change," she said. "It's not safe for me to be out by myself in Pennsylvania, with Joe's detectives looking for me. But he already knows I'm here, and Nobska will take care of me."

Although dubious Nobska would do any harm to a potential assailant apart from jumping up on him enthusiastically, Cassie said nothing. Once Caro had left with the dog, though, she turned to Calder with a look of amusement. "Do you think I should give her your secretary's phone number so she can get in on the next batch of puppies?" she asked. "If she comes back for another visit, I'm not sure if she'll be coming to see us or the dog."

"I'd go with a breeder," said Calder. "I think *she'll* definitely need a purebred."

***

Cassie was leaving for work when Calder stopped her for one last hug. "Can I take you out tonight?" he asked.

Even after two days, Cassie could hardly bear to leave him, even for the lab. Ryan's situation never left her mind for long. "If you'd like. Where should we go?"

"It's a surprise. Dressy. Sorry about that."

Cassie touched his cheek. "I think I can manage not to embarrass you."

He smiled. "Who knows? Maybe I'll embarrass you."

She didn't give the remark a second thought until that evening when they arrived at a large resort. A hotel restaurant didn't seem like Calder's idea of a night out, but there wasn't anything nearby. "Why are we stopping here?"

Calder opened her car door for her. "It's a fundraiser for Gina Obermayer. Dinner, a few speeches."

Was he joking? "A fundraiser? For *who?*"

"Gina Obermayer. She's running for re-election to the State Senate."

"I know *who* she is. I contributed to her campaign. But she's a *Democrat*. And you *hate* this kind of thing."

"That's true."

"Calder, if this gets back to your father, he'll be livid."

"Livid enough to make a deal to keep me from doing it again?"

Cassie's lips formed a silent O. "This is what you've been working on?"

Calder looked proud of himself. "Right in one. But we should go in. Dinner's starting soon."

He led the way into a banquet room packed with elegantly clad men and women. As Cassie followed, she wondered how he did it. She was nervous herself, out of her depth among the women who looked as if they had groomed themselves all day for the event. She was probably the only woman in the room without a manicure. But Calder never faltered, even though the crowd must have made him edgy. He went straight to the candidate's side and introduced Cassie to her. She must have known they were coming; the state senator showed no surprise at the appearance of one of the enemy.

A waiter showed them to the front of the room. "The *VIP section?*" Cassie asked under her breath.

"The whole point is to be noticed." Calder touched her arm lightly, as if to reassure her.

She supposed it would be good practice for dealing with his family, but it was intimidating to find herself among the political and financial elite. Calder seemed to have no problems, chatting with their tablemates as dinner was served. Cassie was relieved when the speeches started and she didn't have to socialize. She let her mind drift as the first guest of honor, a current congressman, spoke.

Then it was the candidate's turn. Senator Obermayer spoke to enthusiastic applause. Cassie wondered how much longer this would go on. It had been a long day, and she wanted to go home. She was disappointed when the senator announced there would be an additional speaker.

"I have a surprise guest tonight who would like to say a few words. And I mean surprise. It certainly astonished me when I received a phone call from him saying he wanted to support my re-election campaign. So you might want to put down your coffee cups before I welcome our next speaker. Ladies and gentlemen, Calder Westing, son of Senator Joseph Westing."

Stunned, Cassie turned to Calder, expecting to see a look of horror, but instead he rose gracefully to his feet and approached the podium amid dead silence. Finally there was polite applause, led by the candidate and her staffers. To all appearances, it didn't bother Calder, who addressed the crowd with an engaging smile.

"Thank you, Senator. I can't blame the rest of you for doubting me. After all, my name spells 'die-hard Republican.' And what could I tell you about Senator Obermayer that you don't already know? Not a thing. But she wanted me to speak anyway. Not about her, and not about this campaign. She asked me to tell you why I'll be voting Democratic on November fourth."

Cassie's mouth dropped open as a flurry of whispers ran around the room. Joe was going to kill him. Maybe she'd better start thinking about those job opportunities in Ecuador. One starting tomorrow, preferably.

"The easy answer is that my wife is an environmentalist, and I want her to be speaking to me on November fifth." There was a light scattering of laughter. "But that's not the real reason."

Calder rested one hand on the podium, his voice taking on a more intimate tone. "I'm Joe Westing's son. You know what that means. I grew up on deals being cut over the dining room table. I knew what *quid pro quo* meant before I could read. I heard my father make promises, and I knew which ones he intended to break.

"I knew all about the damn Democrats, too. Yes, the damn Democrats. I was in fourth grade, studying American history before I realized 'damn' wasn't part of the party name. I'd always assumed that when people referred to Democrats, they were using an abbreviation, like calling Republicans the GOP." This time the laughter was more genuine.

Cassie felt disoriented. This was worse than when she learned he was Stephen West. The last thing she expected was that Calder could be an eloquent public speaker. He looked completely at ease, his intonation rising and falling rhythmically, gesturing fluidly, drawing the crowd in. It was like watching an actor on TV.

"The Republican approach made sense to me. You had to provide incentives to make people want to work hard and get ahead. I lived in a protected environment where no one challenged those ideas, at least not to my face. After all, I'm Joe Westing's son.

"My wake-up call came when I spent a year in Ecuador. That was the first time I'd seen poverty face-to-face, and I saw it every day. I saw people die from treatable illnesses. I saw people go hungry when the crops were bad. Not me, though. I never went hungry, even in Ecuador. Because I'm Joe Westing's son." This time he said it with distaste.

No, Cassie decided, he wasn't a public speaker. He was a demagogue. From his self-mocking tone to the cadenced repetitions, it was a speech calculated to evoke a reaction. It was a speech Joe Westing could have written.

"I couldn't believe people had to live that way. Then my friends enlightened me about people in the United States who are no better off. We have people here dying from treatable illnesses, not because the nation doesn't have the money to treat them, but because they don't have health insurance. There are children in the United States going hungry while we have food sitting in warehouses. I was stunned. The more I thought about it, the more I realized that the measure of a country isn't in how its richest citizens fare, but in how its poorest citizens live." That brought real applause.

"That would be a nice ending to the story. A boy grows up and starts to think for himself. It happens every day. But I'm Joe Westing's son, so it wasn't that simple. I came back from Ecuador, and I had the good sense to keep my new thoughts to myself. But now I listened to those conversations over the dinner table with a more critical ear. I heard about corruption, about greed, about playing into the pockets of special interests. I heard about intimidation, voting discrepancies, and abuse of power. I heard things that shocked me."

A man in the audience called out, "Tell us more!"

Calder acknowledged the interruption with a nod. "Next time, maybe. But to get back to my story, I was disgusted by politics. I decided to stay away from the whole thing, and to focus my time and energy where I thought I could do the most good. I wouldn't have gone as far as to call myself a liberal—after all, I'm Joe Westing's son—but I thought the government had a responsibility to provide a basic safety net. Then I met a woman." He looked over at Cassie.

"She could have been a poster child for the Republican ideals of my childhood. She grew up in a poor, uneducated family and decided she wanted something better. She worked hard and made sacrifices. By the time I met her, she was a successful professional. I started thinking again. Behind all the corruption, maybe there was something to the Republican carrot-and-stick idea. But there was a problem with my theory. She wasn't a Republican. She was a damn Democrat, and it didn't take me long to find out why.

"There are other people like her where she came from, ambitious people who are willing to work hard, but they didn't have what she had, a scholarship. They aren't professionals now. They're working dead-end jobs if they can find them, or they're in prison or selling drugs or on the streets. Smart, hard-working people, who could have had a chance if someone had offered them a helping hand." He held out his hand to the audience and then abruptly clenched it into a fist.

"So I have some ambitious ideas here. A safety net so nobody goes hungry or lacks for medical care. Programs so people with the drive and ability can get ahead. Most armchair politicians would stop there and declare it their position. But I was raised on the Republican catechism according to Joe Westing." His voice lowered into a passable imitation of his father's southern accent. "Those damn Democrats are full of ideas, but they don't know how to pay for them. They're fiscally irresponsible. They'll drive this country to ruin." He dropped the accent. "So when I thought about my wish list of programs, I had to think about where the money would come from, because I'm not a damn Democrat. Everybody knows that." There were chuckles from around the room.

Cassie didn't know whether to hide under the table from embarrassment or to be infuriated at being called a Republican poster child. But Calder's intent was obvious. He was deliberately fanning the flames. This wasn't a speech about why he was a Democrat. It was designed in every particular to infuriate Joe Westing.

"Now, some people like to think about how they'd coach the Red Sox if they had a chance. I'm Joe Westing's son, so I make up government budgets in my head for fun. My father used to give me figures from the Senate Budget Committee to practice my math on. Now I had another math problem to solve. What programs was I going to cut to find the billions of dollars I'd need to fund my projects?

"Repairing the infrastructure and building the information highway? No, can't cut there, not if we want to move forward. Protection of the environment? Can't cut there, either, or there'll be no future to move forward to. Business incentives, so our economy can grow? Well, I'd better not answer that one here. I was raised Republican and I'm not letting go of everything." More laughter. "So I had to look harder. How about pork barrel projects? Cut." He slapped his hand on the podium to emphasize his point. "Tax breaks for people like me, who already have more money than they know what to do with? Cut. Wars nobody wants that will never accomplish anything? Cut." The applause was loud and sustained.

Calder managed a look of embarrassed pride. "There were only two problems with my budget. One was that it was hypothetical. The other is that I'm Joe Westing's son, and this was the budget of a damn Democrat." His voice rose on the last words to demonstrate his shock and dismay and was greeted by laughter.

He placed both hands on the podium and leaned forward, making eye contact around the room. "You know where I come from. Son of Senator Joseph Westing, Republican of Virginia. Grandson of Governor Stephen Calder Westing, Republican of Virginia. Nephew of Vice-President Matthew Westing, Republican of Virginia. Brother of Congressman Tom Westing, Republican of Virginia. And you should know who I am, because I've told you often enough tonight that I'm Joe Westing's son." He paused dramatically. "But you can call me Calder Westing, Democrat of Massachusetts." Applause. "I'll see you at the polls—and the victory party."

Calder left the podium to loud applause, waving his hand to the audience as if he did this every day. Cassie watched in utter bewilderment as he appeared to bask in the public eye.

Calder slid into the seat beside her and whispered in her ear, "I feel sick." Then he took a deep breath and turned to the couple beside them, accepting their congratulations on his speech with a gracious smile.

So this was what his mother had taught him. She had done it well. Cassie would never have seen through Calder's veneer. It didn't break for a second as well-wishers stopped by the table to shake his hand.

A reporter from the *Boston Globe* was one of the first. "That was quite a speech, Mr. Westing. Are you considering entering into the political arena yourself?"

"I'm a writer, not a politician."

"Writers can become politicians, can't they?"

Calder rested his elbow on the table, looking completely comfortable. "Well, let's just say I have no *immediate* plans to run for office."

The reporter's eyes brightened with the prospect of a scoop. "But you wouldn't rule it out for the future?"

"Would you believe me if I said yes?"

The reporter scribbled something down. "So that isn't a denial, Mr. Westing?"

Cassie couldn't believe it. Calder hinting at running for office as a Democrat? Joe was going to go berserk. Ecuador might not be far enough away. Maybe Mars. She hoped Calder knew what he was doing. He certainly looked as if he did.

The congressman who made the first speech drew up a chair next to Calder. "Does your father know about this speech?"

Calder laughed. "No. Would you like to tell him? Be my guest."

"No, thanks. I want to make sure I'm several states away when he finds out."

Calder clapped him on the shoulder. "Good plan. The Westing family Thanksgiving dinner is going to be exciting this year. I expect I'll be carved up in place of the turkey."

"You sound like him, you know. You have his ability to hold an audience, more than your brother does."

"Thank you. That's quite a compliment. I may disagree with my father, but I admire his skill as a politician."

The representative eyed him. "We should talk more another time."

"I'd be delighted." Calder handed him a business card. "This is my private number."

Cassie didn't recognize the smooth operator inhabiting her husband's body, but she wanted the old Calder back. He was going to have some explaining to do later.

***

Cassie gave him a sidelong glance as she guided the car out of the hotel parking lot. "You're good at that." It sounded more accusing than she meant it to.

Calder leaned his head back against the headrest and closed his eyes. "Of course I'm good at it. I spent the first twenty years of my life learning how to do it."

It was a relief to hear him sounding like himself again. "It's not a side of you I've seen before."

"But it's still there, whether I like it or not. And that's the important thing."

"What's your father going to do when he hears about it?"

"He's going to have a fit to end all fits. Then, when he tells me never to do it again, I'll agree, as long as he leaves Ryan alone. If he doesn't, I'll fight him at his own game. I'll be at every Democratic event I can find. I'll stick so close to the next Democratic presidential nominee, he'll think I've used superglue. That speech will be refined by the best speechwriters in the country, and he knows I can deliver a killer speech. He taught me how. He won't risk it."

Cassie found herself near tears, and she had to force herself to concentrate on the road. "But you'd hate that."

"Compared to losing you, it would be easy. Don't you know that?"

She didn't answer. How could she admit she'd never have dreamed he would do something like that for her? It made her feel warm inside, warmer than she'd been for a long time.

***

Cassie expected the answering machine to be in flames when they arrived home, but it was ominously empty. Other friends called on the weekend, and Calder's answering service was full of requests for interviews, but only silence from Virginia. "Maybe he hasn't heard yet," she said.

Calder shook his head. "He knows."

Chapter 27

CASSIE WISHED SHE DIDN'T have to go to work on Monday. She remembered how Joe had appeared at her apartment in Haverford, and she was afraid he might try the same trick with Calder while she was at the lab. Of course, the Cape was farther from Washington than Haverford was, so perhaps that would keep him away. But the worry stayed with her. Sooner or later the explosion was bound to come.

At least work was a distraction. She was examining microscopic specimens when she heard a voice that was too familiar greeting her.

She should have remembered he would do the unexpected. "Joe, what a *pleasant* surprise. I hadn't realized you were in town."

Joe's presence dominated the lab. "I'm full of surprises. Just like Calder."

"Yes, he's been surprising me lately, too." She switched off the microscope lamp and stood. At least the lab door was still open. If Joe really went after her, Chris would go for help. She hoped.

"When I said you'd make something of him, this wasn't what I had in mind." He paced around the lab, inspecting her desk.

Cassie realized Chris was trying to make his six-foot form disappear in the corner. This wasn't the place for one of her fights with Joe. That was probably why he chose to come here. He knew she'd have to play by the rules, and he wouldn't. She made an effort to remove the barbs from her voice. "Can I show you around the lab, Joe? Or is there something else I can do for you?"

He picked up a gel frame and examined it. "You can tell me what Calder's planning."

Her palms were damp. "That depends on you. I imagine he'd be perfectly happy to stay home and write."

"Or is his ambition finally showing itself? Is this just an excuse to throw his hat into the ring?" He peered into the microscope.

"To go into politics? I'd be surprised." Cassie reached over to switch the lamp on for him and lowered the magnification. "If you're interested, those are microscopic organisms from salt marsh peat. High anaerobe content—bacteria that can survive without the presence of oxygen."

Joe adjusted the focus. So he knew his way around a microscope, creationist or not. Or maybe the creationism was just a public stance. "It's an intriguing strategy. He could go farther as a Democrat running against the family heritage than he could as a Republican."

Cassie couldn't help herself. She burst out laughing. "I don't think that crossed his mind."

Joe looked up from the microscope, his hands resting on the edge of the lab bench. "You don't know him as well as you think, then. I guarantee he's thought of it."

She couldn't understand his reaction. Joe had never hesitated to show his anger in the past, but he seemed untroubled by Calder's foray into Democratic politics. Was it an act? An attempt to lure her into giving him information?

Suddenly it hit her. They had completely misgauged his response. Joe was *pleased.* Apparently the positions he espoused with such passion meant less to him than the idea of another Westing in politics. She didn't know whether to laugh or cry.

She had to say something. "Perhaps you're right. He hasn't filled me in on his plans."

Joe wandered to the bench where Chris was working on Petri dishes. "What's this?" he asked.

Cassie squeezed past him to stand protectively by her assistant. "That's Chris's research project. He's looking into bacterial contamination in shellfish beds."

"No multivariate analysis of covariance?"

Was Joe *teasing* her? It reminded her of the night she gave Calder the tour of the lab. If there were marinara cooking on the Bunsen burner, the scene would be complete. She wondered how Joe would deal with squid. "Not until his data is collected. First things first."

There was a knock at the door. It was Ella Connors from the administrative office and someone Cassie vaguely recognized from public relations. "Cassie? Are we early?" Ella asked.

"Early?" Cassie had no idea what she was talking about.

Joe strode forward. "You must be here to give me the tour. I'm Joe Westing." He held out his hand.

"Ella Connors, and this is Michael Houtman. Welcome to the MBL, Senator."

Cassie narrowed her eyes. "I didn't realize this was an official visit, Joe," she said in her sweetest voice.

A smile touched his lips. "That's why I'm here. The Senate Budget Committee is interested in how the National Science Foundation funds are being used."

"Joe," she said warningly. "Don't even start."

"Start what?" He sounded as if he couldn't imagine what she was talking about.

The director of the MBL appeared in the doorway. Ella performed the introductions.

Next it would be dancing girls. Cassie propelled herself forward. "Joe, I hope you enjoy your tour. Make sure they show you the display on the *evolution* of whales. It's particularly interesting."

He raised an eyebrow. "I'm sure it is."

The director frowned at her. "Won't you come this way, Senator?"

"Thank you." Joe started to follow him out the door. "I'll see you later, Cassie."

She watched as they disappeared and their footsteps echoed down the hall. She could feel Chris's eyes on her back. Shaking her head, she said, "I miss having a dull life."

***

Calder paced back and forth in the small space between the lab benches. "Maybe he isn't coming back here after the tour."

Cassie eyed him sympathetically, even though it was the third time he'd said the same thing in the last half hour. "Maybe not, but why don't we give him another few minutes anyway?"

As if on cue, the stairway door banged as someone let it fall closed. All the researchers knew to close it gently. A sudden noise could ruin careful experiments.

Joe strolled in and closed the door behind him, looking as if he owned the lab. He flashed a smile at Calder. "I wondered whether you'd make your way over here."

"Cassie said you were here." Calder's face gave no indication of his feelings.

"So, you think you can do better running against me than with me."

"That's right." Calder sounded as if he were discussing the weather rather than stepping on an unexploded bomb.

Joe nodded at Cassie. "See, I told you so."

Cassie smiled with an excess of sweetness. "I don't know politics. I just know what I like."

"It's clever," Joe continued, as if Cassie had said nothing. "It has possibilities."

Calder crossed his arms. "You think so?"

"Gets a lot more attention this way, no question. Reporters coming after you much?"

"I don't talk to them. I'm a writer, not a politician."

"So *that's* what you're playing." Joe nodded sagely as if he had solved a mystery. "You're going for the big game, aren't you? Well, good. Make them drag you in kicking and screaming. Voters will eat it up." He checked his watch. "That should be long enough. Let's go out." He held open the door and gestured to Cassie to go through.

She studied his face for a minute before deciding to comply with the implied order. She didn't trust this new, mellow Joe Westing. "Are we going anywhere in particular?"

He gave a secretive smile. "Just out."

She passed him cautiously, waiting in the hall for Calder to join her. Joe whistled a tune as he led the way to the stairs. When they reached the first floor, Cassie saw a crowd on the steps outside. Lots of cameras. There wasn't much press in Woods Hole that could be called out on an hour's notice. Someone must have tipped them off that Joe was coming.

Joe stopped just short of the door and turned to Calder. "Are you ready?"

Calder's eyes flickered toward Cassie. "As ready as I'll ever be."

"Good." Joe pushed open the door and then paused on the steps as flashbulbs went off. He put his hand on Calder's shoulder. "No fun for you today, boys," he said to the reporters. "Calder's coming back to the family and the Republican fold."

Calder looked stunned, and then he stepped forward into a barrage of flashes. "That isn't true. I'll always be a Westing, but that doesn't mean that I can't hold my own political views. And act on them."

Joe turned to him with a frown and said in a low but threatening voice, "There's never been a damn Democrat in the Westing family, and there never will be."

"I'm sorry you don't like it. I respect you and what you've done with your career. But my life is my own, not hostage to some idea of the Westing family heritage."

"You're really going to do it." Joe stepped back as if in disbelief. "You're going to turn traitor to your own family. I suppose your *wife* put you up to this. I told you she'd be no good for you."

Cassie opened her mouth to respond, but Calder's hand descended on her arm, gripping it tightly. She supposed he must know what he was doing. Heaven help them, the reporters were getting every word of this. She didn't want to think about what tonight's news would say.

"I'll thank you to leave Cassie out of this," Calder said calmly. "She's the best thing that ever happened to me."

"You don't care that you're hurting your brother's career. Breaking your mother's heart. You don't care about any of us." Joe's voice was getting louder and full of outrage.

"I trust that they love me enough to accept me for who I am."

"For who you are? You're a disgrace. A traitor. A liar." Joe stabbed a finger at Calder and spoke slowly and deliberately. "You are not my son."

Calder flinched. Cassie moved closer to him. How dare Joe do this to him, and in public, too?

Calder made a visible effort to calm himself. His voice seemed quiet after his father's ranting. "That's for you to decide. But you'll always be my father, no matter what."

Joe snorted and turned and strode into the crowd of reporters, ignoring their shouted questions. Calder took Cassie's hand, and together they watched as Joe disappeared into his chauffeur-driven car.

The reporters turned on their new prey. "Mr. Westing, does this mean you plan to run for office?"

He shook his head. "I'm a writer, not a politician."

Cassie had the feeling she was going to be hearing that statement a lot.

Another reporter called out, "Does he mean it? Will he disown you?"

Calder's face closed. "You'd have to ask him." He took Cassie's hand and headed back into the building.

When they reached the lab, Cassie put her arms around him, wishing she could take away all the pain his father caused. "I'm so sorry, love. I shouldn't have believed him. I should have realized it was a trick to get at you."

She felt his chest shaking beneath her cheek. Calder never cried. She was going to kill Joe Westing for this. Slowly, and with a dull knife. Then she realized the sound she was hearing was quiet laughter.

"No, you were right," Calder said. "He isn't upset with me. That was his idea of a present."

He had gone out of his mind. That was the only explanation. "Calder, that was verbal abuse, not a present."

He tipped up her chin and kissed her. "You're not thinking like my father. If I were really running for office as a Democrat, that scene would have won me thousands of votes. The devoted son, disowned for his beliefs. And he laid himself wide open to make me look good."

"That was an *act?*" She couldn't believe even Joe could fake that level of fury.

"Of course. You know my father. If he were angry with me, he'd be off somewhere concocting a scheme to get me in line, not yelling at me in public. But . . ." His voice trailed off.

"But what?" Cassie stepped back so she could see him better, but held tightly to his hands.

He wore a look she'd never seen before, an almost pained disbelief. "He knew I'd see through him and play along, even without warning. He may have just disowned me, but it's the first time he's ever treated me like his son."

"Calder, what are you talking about? That isn't how fathers treat sons."

"Maybe not in other families. But that was a vote of confidence in me. He was treating me as his political equal, and that's as big a compliment as he'll ever give."

"Compliments like that I can live without."

He laughed. "I know the feeling. Say, is there a back way out of this place, or are we stuck here until the reporters give up?"

***

Cassie had disappeared when they got home, but a few minutes later, Calder found her standing by the fireplace mantel, holding a framed picture. "What's that?" he asked.

Cassie jumped, apparently startled by his voice. "I just brought this down." She handed it to him.

He studied the faded photograph in the inlaid wood frame. He'd never seen two of the people in the picture, but he knew who they must be. The background was a crowded school gymnasium. A much younger Cassie was wearing a cap and gown, clutching a scroll. On the other side, an attractive adolescent girl with too much makeup looked bored. Between the two of them, holding their hands, was a towheaded boy with a bright smile that revealed missing front teeth. "Ryan and Maria?"

Cassie nodded. "That was my high school graduation. We didn't take pictures much because they were so expensive, but Mom was really proud of me. She couldn't understand why I wanted to go to college, but she knew the high school diploma was worth something. And Ryan . . ." She paused, her eyes far away. "Right after they handed me the diploma, Ryan came racing down the aisle and threw his arms around me. He was so excited, and he wanted to sit with me and the rest of the graduates. So he spent the rest of the time on my lap, wearing my mortarboard. Poor Mom was mortified."

"Do you have other pictures?"

"Just this one. There are a few more in Chicago."

Calder set it on the mantelpiece. "And now it belongs here."

"Yes. It does." She shook her head slightly, as if clearing it of memories. "I got a letter from Ryan yesterday. He says it's nice that the prison commissary keeps making mistakes in his favor, but he hopes I'm not going to get myself in trouble. It's something, I guess."

Nobska whined and scratched at the door, as if he knew the moment needed lightening. Cassie smiled ruefully and said, "I'll take him out." The dog darted through the door as soon as she opened it.

"Okay. I'd better call my mother and warn her what's going to be on the evening news."

"Say hello for me," Cassie said as she disappeared out the door.

***

Cassie stood on the beach in front of the house, her arms wrapped around herself. Finally some peace and quiet. A cool breeze blew in over Buzzard's Bay, whipping up whitecaps that broke on the shore, coming closer and closer to her feet as the tide came in. Around her lay the flotsam of the last high tide; strands of seaweed, broken shells, and here and there an empty shark egg case. Mermaids' purses—that was what children called the egg cases when they discovered them on the beach. A used-up, dead shell that once protected a baby dogfish or skate, and now it would be a child's treasure.

Nobska barked as he ran back and forth, trying to catch an elusive seagull. But Cassie could feel the sea's peace creeping into her, a little more with each wave that spilled up the beach before retreating into the vastness of the bay. It couldn't wash away the pain of the last two weeks. She couldn't pretend any more that she was just a clean-cut, dedicated marine biologist. She didn't want to. She was the girl from the slums, and part of her was trapped in a prison on the plains of southern Illinois. She was Calder's wife, with all the privileges that came with it, like the house standing behind her. And she would fight to protect the people she loved.

She heard the crunching sound of footsteps in the sand and then Calder's arms stole around her waist from behind. She leaned back, letting the comforting warmth of him flow into her, knowing he didn't want her to be anybody but who she was.

"What'll we do if Nobska ever catches one of those gulls?" Calder's warm breath tickled her ear.

"Beats me. I'm not sure he wants to, anyway. It's the game he likes." She watched Nobska charging through the waves.

"Maybe so."

"What's your father going to do when he finds out you're not going into politics?" Cassie raised her voice. "Nobska, no! Come!" Nobska veered off at the last second to avoid the bank of poison ivy between the beach and the marsh.

"That won't happen for a while. I'll give a few speeches, drop some more hints, and that'll keep him guessing." Calder threw a stick into the water. Nobska plunged in after it.

"But you can't stand that kind of thing."

"It doesn't bother me as much as it used to. Having you helps. Who knows, maybe I'll surprise us all and run for office someday."

She looked at him in shock. "You wouldn't!"

He laughed. "No, probably not. I'd much rather write."

Cassie picked up a round stone, smoothed by the sea, and rubbed it between her fingers. She'd had enough changes in the last few weeks to last a lifetime. "I hope your father stays away for a while."

"Me too. But we'll make do if he doesn't." He tucked a strand of her hair behind her ear, just like he had the first time they made love, not a quarter mile down the beach from where they stood. "Remember what you told me about the marsh grass? It's resilient."

"And it can tolerate a change in environment."

"That's us. We're the marsh grass in the midst of the complex ecosystem." Calder swept his arm to include the bay and the salt marsh.

"You're starting to sound like me." Cassie leaned her head against him affectionately.

"Promise me one thing." Calder's voice turned serious. "No more secrets."

"No secrets. Unless they involve birthday presents." She'd already decided on that. "There's one thing I'd better tell you, then."

"What's that?"

"My middle name. Don't you dare laugh. It's Desiree."

He didn't laugh, but he did smile. "I have a secret to tell you, too. I already knew."

"You already knew?" She couldn't believe he'd never said anything.

He scuffed his foot in the sand. "My father had you investigated last fall. He gave me a copy of the report at New Year's. I threw it away without reading it, but I couldn't miss your name, since it was right there."

"Why didn't you say something, instead of letting me tease you about it all this time?"

"You didn't want me to know, and I didn't want my father to take away one more thing from you. Besides, I like it, even if it isn't your style. The desired one." He fell silent, but there was a faraway look in his eyes. "That was the original title for *Pride & Presumption*, you know—*Desire*. But it sounded too much like a corny romance. Which it wasn't, at least not then."

She put her arms around his neck. "You just ended it too soon. Maybe *Pride & Presumption* needs a sequel."

"I suppose I shouldn't leave poor Will Darcy sitting there all alone forever."

Her lips curved in a smile. "Certainly not. Maybe I can even give you some inspiration later on. The water's still warm, and there's no moon tonight. Just us and the biolumes."

A light kindled behind his eyes. "I think I could be convinced. Purely in the pursuit of art, of course."

"Don't forget science."

"How could I possibly forget science?" Calder traced the edge of Cassie's lips with his fingertip.

Cassie felt his touch through her whole body. Then Nobska bounded up the beach and shook himself vigorously, spraying them with salt water. Calder ducked, but not before his clothes were soaked.

Cassie laughed as she grabbed Nobska's collar. "No, pup, we're going swimming *later*. It's back to the house for now."

Acknowledgments

THIS BOOK WOULD NEVER have reached this stage without the encouragement and help of many people. Maria, Nabby, HeatherLynn, Joy, Sarah, Eli, Marsha, Wanda, Beth, Dorothy, and Sylvie offered excellent feedback and support throughout the writing process. Carol, Susan, and Kathleen gave important advice on the final draft. If it were not for Ellen taking mercy on my technical incompetence, this book would still be languishing on my hard drive. Last, but never least, the readers at Austen Interlude and Hyacinth Gardens for providing inspiration, companionship, and enthusiasm.

My deepest thanks to all of you.

About the Author

Abigail Reynolds is a lifelong Jane Austen enthusiast and a physician. In addition to writing, she has a part-time private practice and enjoys spending time with her family. Originally from upstate New York, she studied Russian, theater, and marine biology before deciding to attend medical school. She began writing *From Lambton to Longbourn* in 2001 to spend more time with her favorite characters from *Pride & Prejudice*. Encouragement from fellow Austen fans convinced her to continue asking "What if . . . ?" which led to four other Pemberley Variations and her modern novel, *Pemberley by the Sea*. She is currently at work on another Pemberley Variation and a sequel to *Pemberley by the Sea*. She lives in Wisconsin with her husband, two teenaged children, and a menagerie of pets.